Antonia Swinson grew up in Hertfordshire and has lived in Rome, Edinburgh and London. She is a popular newspaper columnist and now lives in a converted 1920's department store overlooking the Firth and Forth with her husband and two children.

THE LOVE CHILD

Harriet is married to Richard, a very handsome art dealer, who has lived life to the full — expecting a large inheritance from his mother. Things start to go downhill when his mother dies and Richard discovers that she had already spent all of her money! She did, however, bequeath a painting to Harriet of a beautiful violet-eyed woman in a Scottish castle. But when Harriet goes to Scotland to research the background to the portrait, she meets Murdo, a handsome young Scot — and the story becomes increasingly involved . . .

ANTONIA SWINSON

THE
LOVE
CHILD

Complete and Unabridged

ULVERSCROFT
Leicester

First published in Great Britain in 2000 by
Hodder and Stoughton
London

First Large Print Edition
published 2001
by arrangement with
Hodder and Stoughton Limited
a division of the
Hodder Headline Group
London

The moral right of the author has been asserted

All characters in this publication are fictitious and
any resemblance to real persons, living or dead,
is purely coincidental.

British Library CIP Data

Swinson, Antonia
The love child.—Large print ed.—
Ulverscroft large print series: general fiction
1. Middle class—Scotland—Fiction
2. Large type books
I. Title
823.9'14 [F]

ISBN 0–7089–4437–X

Published by
F. A. Thorpe (Publishing)
Anstey, Leicestershire

Set by Words & Graphics Ltd.
Anstey, Leicestershire
Printed and bound in Great Britain by
T. J. International Ltd., Padstow, Cornwall

This book is printed on acid-free paper

To my daughter Ella

All original lyrics supplied by Alan Reid.
With grateful thanks from the author

Safe in your Arms
Made to Measure
Don't Turn Your Back On Me This Way
That's What Life's About
Going Back To Arizona
Rena
*I've Been Happier Almost Any Time
  Than Now*

1

London 1995

It was one of those funerals when it didn't take long before the Guinness was flowing faster than the tears. One of the old men had already hit the piano, rocking back in his chair and lifting his head with the abandon of a practised bar Romeo. '*Oh, Dublin Mary, Mar-ee* . . .' The thick smoke of the high-tar cigarettes made Harriet want to heave, but she continued smiling dutifully at the guests. Feet were tapping; at any moment, given just half a glass more, they would break into a jig. She could see across the room that her husband Richard was fighting to keep both feet firmly planted on the ground for under that immaculate Savile Row suit, his wild Irishness was never allowed to show. Unless, of course, he happened to be making love.

'*Mary with her brown, darling hair!*' The fact that Mary Ellen's hair had been bright red and out of a bottle as a matter of principle clearly did not occur to the old man at the keyboard, though Harriet could see it did to Richard, who was wearing his

1

boy-stood-on-the-burning-deck fixed grin. *'Dublin Mary's my girl!'* The last line was spun out, milking the applause. The room was thick with history and reminiscence. Harriet could already hear the fiddles tuning up the hall and then saw that Richard had decided enough was enough and that bringing out the Bollinger was the only thing to do.

The moment he'd heard of his mother's death he had hit Fitzroy Square like a small boy just let out of school. Harriet could just picture the scene: the roaring car sheering past some downtrodden meter maid and into a space. How charmingly he would have sweet-talked the housekeeper into letting him into the flat, and when her back was turned would straight away have tried to find the bank books. He was only human and he had waited an awfully long time for this. Then the careful conversations with the accountant and the lawyer who were all going to tiptoe about and hum and haw about the granting of probate just to make him suffer. Before he would finally know how much was left, for God's sake! For this was the end of a long love-hate-hate relationship and Richard would soon have a nice large seven-figure trust fund to break open. A super-rich yummy Easter egg of a trust. And, best of all, he was now freed from a parent who for years had only dished out large lectures and very small cheques.

Even after the furore of the last few days Richard still had the desperate fortitude of someone who couldn't quite believe that this day had finally arrived. Boo-hoo-bloody-ray! Now he was bending over dishing out the bubbly to all the old ladies; at this angle she could see that his thick curly hair was slightly thinning on top. He was putting on his professional art dealer's charm to all his parents' friends whom he hadn't seen for years. Harriet knew he would probably try it on, suggesting *en passant* that he cast an eye over their picture collections — for insurance purposes, you understand. Never a boy to let a chance of money pass him by, however it had been earned. She couldn't help smiling. Richard the life enhancer! There he was, trying not to cough at the smoke from fags hanging out of the women's mouths. He must have thought they had all keeled over years ago and yet here they were, miracles of modern medicine, in their high heels, furs and bright red lipstick, holding out their glasses for more champagne and more Longbridge magic; it was only a matter of time before the Bolly kicked in and then they'd be flashing lacy knickers at him in the reels and asking for a kiss.

Kanga Tryon had once said that Richard Longbridge on a good night could make Alan Clarke seem like a white line on a white wall. And even now Harriet knew her husband inside out, with all his infuriating contradictions, she still admired those rare male qualities he had in trolleyloads: glamour and charisma. You couldn't just pick them up at Sainsbury's on the Cromwell Road, however rich you were.

She had a sudden vivid recollection of Bob Geldof's hoarse Dublin voice during Live Aid. 'Giveus de money! Giveus de money!' It had become an unofficial slogan in the eighties, a brief impulse of rebellion when everyone else had been getting into shoulder pads and big business. Even though Richard's accent was thoroughly modulated and as English as his name, it was as if today he was silently shouting the same hoarse cry: 'Giveus de money!' in an agony of impatience even as he was dispensing charm with the bubbles.

Pop went another champagne cork. Now he was laughing at one old dear who was tugging at his tie; he might as well have had a large bubble coming out his head with the appeal written in large black letters. No more bloody trust funds and begging letters. Freedom! 'Gimme de money, the dosh, the moolah!' He was throwing back his head to roar with laughter at some feeble joke. It looked as if he was about to crash through the ceiling from sheer high spirits. Why did he still make her go weak at the knees when he was in this mood? When Irish eyes are smiling, you know you're in trouble!

Certainly Mary Ellen's funeral had made a splash. Sitting in the front limousine earlier that morning on the way to the crematorium, Harriet had been sure North Soho had never seen anything like this. First had come a man in a top hat carrying a stick, his white face slashed with a pencil moustache. The horses drawing the coffin wore black plumes and highly polished harnesses glinting in the weak late-April sun. The coffin was piled high with flowers. MARY, spelt in white carnations against a bed of red roses, could be seen at the back. (Richard had drawn the line at MUM.)

Behind them had followed the Rollers and Daimlers, flowers on the door handles and great cushions of them on the roof. OUR GIRL, MA LONGBRIDGE, OUR MATE all spelt out in purple and red, costing hundreds, proclaiming universal devotion to one small woman with a big ego who had made her mark on the world and on the people who had got in her way.

Up through Great Titchfield Street the cortège had snaked, towards the traffic light and the Park. Executives from the local publishing companies and data processing businesses, the people in the rag trade and all the TV types sitting out at tables nursing cappuccinos in the early-spring sunshine, just gawped at the East End villains up west for the day, thick gold Rolexes resting on the open windows. These people really knew where the bodies were buried. It was a side of Mary Ellen's life Harriet had always felt it wisest to ignore.

'Your ma-in-law was a marvellous woman.' 'What a woman — bloody wonderful!' Now, back in Mary Ellen's huge mansion flat, Harriet moved from room to room. Voices rang out around her, keeping the old woman alive. As if she would come through the door at any moment, bawling out the maid for using the 'bloody Minton' and kicking off her Emma Hope shoes right along the hall. For Mary Ellen Longbridge had never given in gracefully to old age.

Harriet's marriage to Richard had caught his mother on the hop; it had been one of the few decisions Richard had made that she had not been able either to disapprove of or control. She and the young wife had circled each other warily at first, but they were both good businesswomen who knew how to handle Richard and make magic with a fiver and, slowly, Harriet had even become fond of the old woman, in spite of her lashing tongue.

Born one of ten children in a damp tenement, by twelve Mary Ellen had become an assistant to her midwife ma, yanking out a thousand scrawny babies on to Dublin kitchen tables; then there was laundry work with the city's unmarried mothers, and later bar work mixing cocktails which eventually bought her ticket to London. Mary Ellen had always had a generous nature and the first Screwdriver she had made for George Longbridge, one June day in the Strand in 1937, had reportedly had him on his knees and at her feet in five minutes flat. By marrying they joined the cheek of the devil with the luck of the Irish. With notable results as even the *FT* respectfully acknowledged.

'He's going it a bit, isn't he?' Katya, Richard's daughter, appeared by Harriet's side. Tall, skinny, dressed as usual from head to toe in black, with a stud in her tongue, her nose, and probably her brain. Harriet could see her taking it all in as she slouched against the wall, a thin streak of Generation X insouciance. Today she had dark purple nail varnish to match her lipstick. It brought out the flecked blue of her eyes. 'Irish eyes put in

7

wit' a smutty finger,' Mary Ellen had always said. 'And God knows her conception was smutty enough. A love child! Richard never could keep his pecker to himself!' Harriet remembered this sentence being repeated constantly as Mary Ellen visibly aged in the last few months. How often Harriet had arrived in Fitzroy Square to find the old lady nursing her wrath with Father Patrick. Yet in spite of the shame Mary Ellen had felt about Katya's illegitimacy and her impatience with her only son, she had loved the girl with a passion in the few years she had known her. They were equally bloody-minded, and Katya was her only granddaughter after all, as Mary Ellen had observed every time they had met. Certainly Harriet didn't seem to be in any hurry to produce any more — as if babies could just be ordered up like a Fortnum's hamper.

'Katya, have a heart, this is a difficult day for him.'

'Poor bastard.' Katya, twenty-three, ex-Queen's Gate, ex-art school, ex-cessive, breathed a long stream of smoke into the room, making Harriet feel a hundred and ten years of age instead of thirty-seven. But there you go, that was the generation gap for you. Yet surely there had to be some vocabulary of feeling inside that cold little head? In the last five

8

years Harriet had only managed to discover one element which turned Katya on: money. Just like her father.

Katya. The very name had a sharp and painful edge to it, a fierce thorn in the side of Harriet and Richard's marriage. In their stylish coverage of his expensively misspent youth, the glossies had omitted the small detail of Miss Katya Holland. Though Harriet might have known, of course, with his track record. More fool her. Of course you do get married in the touching belief that you know most of someone's life, that they will have told you the Hey events, both good and bad, just to fill you in. To be polite. Not Richard. Forgetting to tell his new wife about a stray love child had been no big deal to him. As if the passing years had absolved him of all responsibility.

Harriet still remembered in technicolour the day the girl had simply turned up on the doorstep while Richard had been away in Prague buying new work. The shock of it still twisted like a knife in Harriet's gut. Katya had announced herself and then marched into their home and started looking around at all the pictures, as if taking an inventory. It had been left to Harriet, just back from honeymoon, to find a teapot, boil a kettle and glue the shattered pieces of this new marriage

9

back together, constructing a different reality which feverishy sought excuses for this curious memory slip of Richard's; to find a way to get through to this cold girl. Thankfully since then they had rarely met for Katya's very presence, her casually proprietorial attitude towards her father, was uncomfortable for Harriet, proof of dishonesty in yet another husband she had loved.

Harriet now thought the phrase 'happily ever after' pretty pathetic. It was what her friends had said on her ending years of lonely widowhood. Very droll. No, real life meant hard work and forgiveness, and her marriage to Richard had needed plenty of both to survive. Cinderella herself would have discovered this the day after the fairytale wedding, when Prince Charming's housekeeper briefed her on Palace politics. She would soon have learned just what the Prince had really been up to with Dandini all those years, and how many nice girls picking up sticks in the woods he had seduced. Soon she would have been powdering over the grime in her life just like everyone else. Harriet knew her reaction to the girl wasn't logical — Katya hadn't asked to be born after all — she always forced herself to be pleasant to her, but with that black make-up and sour scowl she hovered perpetually just offstage, as angry and unpredictable as a bad fairy.

Pop! Richard had opened another bottle. Now the wake was warming up in earnest. Three couples were reeling in the dining room where the furniture had been pushed back, while in the large sitting room small groups of guests chatted animatedly. Jamie, Richard's fifteen-year-old son, was having his hair ruffled by an old man with a diamond ring on his little finger. The boy blushed and tried to pull his head away while Billy, her own son, also fifteen, looked on, as if trying to understand some foreign language. Harriet smiled across the room at them both, lovely boys, her allies in battle.

The drawing room was dominated by a large portrait of a beautiful woman in evening dress hanging over the fireplace which made Harriet jump every time she saw it. But it was in the framed photographs and newspaper cuttings displayed on the piano that everyone could see how George and Mary Ellen had really lived. In the forties it had been scrap metal and surplus stocks; in the fifties boxing promotion and bomb-damaged land reclamation; and in the sixties property development on the back of George's casino profits which had brought the Longbridges huge wealth and status.

For when the 1961 Gaming Act came along George had opened the Garden Club in Mayfair and it had proved his gateway to the stars. He and his wife had known everyone. There was a photograph of George and Mary Ellen with the Kray twins, Lady Docker, Diana Dors, Richard Harris, Frankie Vaughan, the Everley Brothers, Sophie Tucker. Even Judy Garland with her arms round Mary Ellen, both of them looking tiny in spite of large red mouths open in surprised 'O's. Mary Ellen in bunny furs and diamonds, her red hair in a lacquered beehive.

George Longbridge had been born in Hackney, the son of a stevedore with Italian and Romany blood. A tall dark flashy man in a trilby hat and a camel coat who spent fistfuls of fivers on Richard and sent him off to public school only to see him come back ashamed by his parents' pink Roller and gold taps in the loo. George had keeled over one day in Sloane Square from a heart attack, but thanks to modern medicine Mary Ellen had outlived him for years with her hairy little dogs, her housekeepers and hangers-on. What *schadenfreude* she had enjoyed, watching her son lose his Cork Street gallery in the early-nineties recession along with his Belgravia house. His efforts to start dealing for private clients from a small house in North Kensington she had derided, saying it was an occupation fit only for rich bankers' wives. There was enough truth in this observation to make Richard grow an extra foot with fury.

Then suddenly at seventy years of age her heart just stopped. It was like waking up one day to find that a troublesome wart had disappeared, as warts magically do sometimes, leaving you shocked and staring into the mirror, feeling curiously bereft. Harriet was perceptive enough to realise that Mary Ellen had been a vital ingredient in the alchemy of her relationship with Richard. His mother's invective had made Harriet feel loving and protective, even when she had wanted to kill him.

A familiar hand passed over her shoulders, tweaking the clasp of her pearls. 'You're a bit gorgeous, Mrs Longbridge. Anyone ever tell you that?' Richard was standing looking down at her, smiling. Then he glanced into the hall where coats were now being presented to reluctantly departing guests. 'God, I need a drink!'

Katya was the last to leave. She had waited for her mother to come, but it had been obvious to Harriet that Amanda, Chelsea's sixties hellcat, would not. Why should she after all this time? Finally Katya stretched and unwound herself from an armchair and said she had to get home. Like a stray cat, disowned by everyone, she slunk past Harriet and Richard, airbrushing a farewell with purple lips and nodding vaguely to the boys. Then she was gone, just her heels tick-tick-tocking away down the stairs to the lobby.

The caterers were hovering, waiting for a tip, and a draught came up from the hallway as boxes of glasses were carried out. Suddenly exhausted, Harriet kicked off her shoes and began to wander about the dead woman's flat, feeling like a trespasser yet struck by the notion that all this furniture, all these pictures and the memorabilia, would soon be dispersed, sold or thrown away. What a lot women take on with a second marriage! Pantechnicons full of family alliances, grudges and ancient history.

'Do we have to go back to school tonight, Mum?' Billy lay slumped on the settee. It had clearly been a strain, acting like part of the family when you were really only there by marriage. Like Harriet, he had pale red hair and green eyes, and the sort of transparent skin which goes white and wan with tiredness. Jamie was almost asleep too. As Mary Ellen's only grandson, he had been the centre of attention, particularly when it was discovered he was running a lucrative black

14

market in cigarettes and other desirables at boarding school. Chip off the old block! How lucky they had been best friends at school before they became step-brothers. It had made it easier for Harriet to communicate with him through Billy. Easier to be a stepmother at one remove.

'Don't worry, it's too late to get the train. I'll ring your housemaster and you can go down tomorrow. Let's go home. Jamie, are you OK? You did really well.'

Both boys smiled sleepily back at her and she fetched their coats and started switching off the lights. Richard came in from the hall having paid the caterers. 'Isn't it incredible what they expect for serving a bit of cold chicken? Anyway, according to old Prosser, we're to gather tomorrow to hear the will. Very Agatha Christie. Still, then we'll know how much. No doubt it will contain a lecture about my shortcomings but even she has to let go some time. Come on, boys, let's go. I'll pick up a take-away. I'm starving. Let's hope the traffic on the Westway isn't bad.'

* * *

Trust Richard to want to make love after his mother's funeral. And not just the usual two-minute fumble before the lights went out, but a full, swinging-from-the-chandeliers performance: the hot kisses, the kneading her as if she were a pound of the most expensive and desirable pastry, the declarations of love which he obviously did mean at the time, and then the climax. Just why did he insist on rolling his eyeballs up to the ceiling at that moment of ecstasy? Harriet found herself thinking quite dispassionately. Then the rolling over and best of all the cuddle which, in spite of all disenchantment and exasperation, persuaded her that, Katya or no Katya, they were still two musketeers against the world. And, as the society glossies continued to insist, that he was still one of the most gorgeous men in London.

Two hours later she was still awake. In the distance she could hear a police siren chasing down Ladbroke Grove, or perhaps Holland Park Avenue. One of the sounds you hear so often in London, but it is only when sleep doesn't come that you start imagining the drama behind the sound. Richard was now breathing heavily, stretched out as usual diagonally across the bed. She had once joked they could have a huge eight-feet wide Führer-sized bed and he would still sleep the same way: right across it. He had laughed and said that any bed would feel empty without her in it beside him.

Her thoughts tugged her back to the day's events like a persistent child. She hated funerals. That stomach-jolting first sight of the actual coffin. She knew instinctively that this funeral had rearranged the landscape of her life though as yet she had no clear understanding of the details. Mary Ellen was gone. All passion spent. All blood under the bridge. Or so Harriet hoped.

2

Richard Longbridge was hard to ignore. Like a giant cat wearing New & Lingwood, continually on the prowl and on the scent. Restless eyes taking in the pictures on your wall at a hundred yards, summing up their quality, totting up the price. Charming, fascinating, challenging, never boring or predictable. Marriage to such a man could be an endless *affaire*, if you were lucky. All cream and no cake.

Harriet would always remember that hot summer they had first met: 1990, endless humid, sticky months when London seemed to be melting as fast as the economy. Richard tearing down Cork Street after her in yellow silk socks in his anxiety not to lose her, not bothering with shoes in the searing heat. How weary and poor she had felt that day, bills mounting up, courage failing at the price of living in London. She remembered the city grit scratching her eyes and prickling at her hairline. And there he'd been, standing smiling down at her, offering her tea, almost pleading with her to come in. He wasn't a man, she had thought that day, he was a

18

natural phenomenon, like a typhoon or a volcano, impossible to ignore. And yet, scared and unsure, she had turned him down, too timorous and distrustful of men to accept a date with one like Richard. Silly little Harriet Gosse, celibate for years since her famous husband's death, reduced to wondering whether, as they said, making love really was like riding a bike. And too frightened to find out.

Fast forward to the street party, another memory from that hot harsh summer of 1990 which had stayed with her always. The little poky Hammersmith street with its brightly coloured terraced houses, Alimony Villas where husbands on second marriages came to lick their wounds. Trestle tables laid out with sandwiches and cake, children dancing in bare feet on the tarmac to the neighbourhood band playing *Jailhouse Rock*. Shabby London chic with the aeroplanes roaring overhead every forty seconds en route for Heathrow; the street occupants mingling and barriers breaking down. Then erupting into all this fun an animal roar coming down the road and Richard's Aston Martin plunging into the party, shattering the peace and banishing forever the illusion that anyone there was in any way well off or successful. Bond Street calling. Once again Harriet had been struck by his energy as he had leapt out, his smile infectious, sunlight glinting off his white teeth while his eyes exuded a concentrated charm which reduced even the men to fans and the women to jelly. That was what had finally enthralled her; that infectious *joie de vivre*, the boyishness beneath the gloss. Richard Longbridge actually believed that life really was a party.

Nevertheless Harriet had put up a fight for a long time. She had ignored him, or tried to, and had frozen him out like a Snow Queen. But in the end she had succumbed. It was only after their marriage that she had discovered just how many had succumbed before her, and she never knew whether to be proud or irritated that it was she who had actually proposed to him. She had soon learned that making love to Richard was nothing like riding a bike.

Of course, not being stupid, she knew that Society, whatever that was, considered she had really hit the big time when they married. He was a London social hero with a Belgravia house and a mantelpiece six deep in invitations while she was just a single working mother. Her first marriage to Tom Gosse, bad boy of the BBC's top soap, was considered more a reason for commiseration than congratulation. Only an actor. Her own

20

successful small company teaching foreign languages to business people over the phone was written off as a source of enormous fun and double entendres — the English of a certain milieu always secretly believing that if the natives didn't understand the first time, one should simply shout louder. Then there was her home before the marriage, a terraced house in darkest Hammersmith. Well, Brackenbury Village if you *insisted* on being grand — which Harriet, probably wrongly with people like that, did not. Though of course she had inherited the whole of Marcus Whitehead's picture collection. Important stuff; it made a difference. But even so, all in all, Harriet's marriage to Richard was thought to be a very lucky break indeed for her. At first their new life together was a ball. The parties Richard threw at his Europa Gallery in Cork Street were legendary; Hollywood stars working for fourpence-halfpenny in West End theatre (trying to prove they could actually act) would join City traders and diplomats in fighting to get tickets. Richard had such a track record! In the early-eighties, when everyone else had been joining the Japanese scrum to grab Impressionists, he had made the market in new names and undiscovered post-war talents, winkling them out of Spain and

Germany and France, and blazing the trail even further afield as the Cold War thawed. Even when recession hit in the early-nineties and Cork Street galleries were being boarded up like a mouthful of rotten teeth, Richard and his army of admirers continued to have faith that big bucks were just around the corner. Harriet too continued to believe in spite of all her business instincts. But then she believed that, unlike herself, he had the means to weather bad patches.

When Richard had first started in the art business, old George Longbridge had been around to bail him out. After his father's death he had prevailed on Mary Ellen several times until his luck and her patience ran out. Yet even when his cashflow was spiralling rapidly in the wrong direction, Richard always remained full of confidence, a master of personal PR. There was a joyousness about him which transformed every roomful of people into an instant party, and won him ready forgiveness for his excesses. Richard's elegant hand could summon a waiter at fifty paces, and doormen scurried to open doors for him. But it couldn't last. The remorseless economic cycle caught him up and ground him down until the crash of 1993. The Belgravia house went, the gallery went, a Lamborghini went. Harriet kept her own money and a cool head and nursed him through the financial pain, buying a new home, paid for by selling some of the pictures she had inherited, a smart stuccoed house in Notting Hill near Julie's Bar, which had given him another backdrop almost as smart as the one he had lost. She took on all Richard's past — his son, his love child, the poisonous ex-wife — and with hard work and affection had made a success of this second marriage. Now she felt she could breathe more easily; the art market was picking up, the stock market was booming. Really, if it had not been for Richard working from home and bounding around like Tigger, life would be practically perfect she had thought the week before Mary Ellen died. Tempting fate, as it turned out.

'Son, what a dance we've led each other over the last years. What a source of fine words and sorry actions you have been for your poor mother. Well, I'm sorry but this time you'll have to stand on your own two feet. You can do it — you're a big strong man, with a clever wife. You might even surprise yourself.'

Henry Prosser was reading the letter aloud in a well-bred monotone. He never looked up, keeping his eyes on the typed sheet in case he missed a comma or a word, yet Mary Ellen's Irish phrasing kept creeping through. Richard shifted his long legs and folded his arms across his chest. He cleared his throat and looked down at his knees, as if he was almost asleep. Harriet wanted to nudge him awake. But she could not. Katya sat between them, wedge-shaped in grey, looking disdainfully at a Monet print behind the lawyer's head. She might have been waiting for the dentist. Jamie, sitting on Richard's right, was stroking the old-style radiator, over and over, as if a genie might appear and whisk him away from all this embarrassment. Outside, the traffic clawed its way past Barker's while taxis decanted journalists back from lunch into Associated Newspapers. Not a flicker of emotion appeared on the lawyer's face. He had done this too often before.

The old Yiddish saying was Mary Ellen to the life: 'When you have money, you are clever, you are wise, and you sing well too.' Everyone knew she had money and so of course she was considered a real *grande dame*. One of life's enhancers. A little bit on the sharp side, never could suffer fools gladly, but she certainly knew how to live. With enough rings on her fingers and bells on her toes to be everyone's favourite fairy god-mother. As any financial adviser will tell you, the difference between an old woman and an old lady is a really good pension, and if Mary Ellen had never been a lady exactly, then she had at least always had money and swank enough to break the rules successfully.

'I am past being surprised, of course, because by the time you read this I'll have popped my clogs and gone to the Almighty, God rest my soul. Anyway, please read on, and remember that money isn't as important as people. Try and bear this in mind before you damn and blast me to high heaven . . . '

Harriet could tell from the flatness of the lawyer's delivery that the day was going irrevocably downhill.

Fitzroy Square

When you are used to money constantly in the background, its sudden loss is like an amputation. The pain is enough to make you howl.

Harriet certainly wanted to. Another bit of Richard's past had come back at her like a

25

metaphorical demolition ball. She could hear an all too real power drill forcing up floorboards on the other side of the hallway in Mary Ellen's flat. 'Damn!' There was a ripping sound. 'My bloody suit's torn. It *must* be here somewhere. It can't just be all gone! Swine . . . bastard . . . come up!' A sound of splintering wood. Her husband was on the rampage.

'Richard, please stop! It's no good. Stop doing this. The lawyers will sue! This isn't even your property!' Please stop, thought Harriet. She could hardly think straight for the pity she felt for him, and for Jamie. What a prize bitch Mary Ellen had turned out to be.

'Bugger!'

Another ripping sound, a whine of the power drill, and another board was ripped up. Richard was unstoppable. It was no good warning him about lawyers and probate and actions for trespass. His blood — every drop of it, English, Romany, Italian and Irish — was up. God help anyone who got in his way.

The shock of Mary Ellen's will had driven him, this Saturday morning when he would normally have been lingering in his Jacuzzi with the *FT*, to invade Fitzroy Square like a Turk. Armed with a power saw and a savage

26

scowl, he had hurtled into battle with the floorboards to see where that mad old cow had really left her dosh.

He had also instructed his solicitor by fax to start proceedings against his mother's lawyer, accountants, IFA, the executors of his trust fund and assorted grey suits — which had made him feel better until Harriet had gently pointed out that he could not afford to sue the postman for a stamp.

What a bloody mess! George Longbridge had left Mary Ellen extremely well provided for when he'd died of his heart attack in 1985. There had been investments and property and assets of all shapes and sizes as well as many favours to call in, and Mary Ellen had enjoyed her widowhood hugely, a regular at every health farm south of Birmingham as well as on the *QE2* — a large signed photograph of herself hugging Big Daddy at the Captain's table took pride of place on her bedside table. The stock market highs in the eighties and the subsequent property boom had been very advantageous and she had prospered in spite of her propensity for giving away money to doe-eyed younger men, always undiscovered musical geniuses, whom she would pick up and put down on holiday in Florida and the Seychelles.

However, from what they could gather from her letter and the lawyer's guarded summary, round about the early-nineties, at the time when she was refusing to help her son out with his failing gallery — assuming such high moral ground, Richard spat, that he was amazed she hadn't suffered from oxygen deficiency — Mary Ellen had in fact been more in hock than he was, for one significant reason: Lloyds. Many a minor public school boy has since regretted falling in with the dinner party set who lured him on to the financial rocks. But Mary Ellen, who had so prided herself on being shrewd, had also been seduced, managing to pick every dodgy syndicate in the market. Not that she'd known they were dodgy at the time, she'd explained in her posthumous letter to her son. It was just that each year the demands for money came rolling in, bigger and bigger, like an Irish curse.

But she knew very well that perception was all. So while other distressed Names were, in their eyes, throwing their small children to the lions of the State education system and parading on the streets of the City with placards saying 'Give Generously', she had continued to present an elegant and prosperous front to the world with her chauffeur and her maid and her housekeeper. Without a word to her son she had sold her London mansion flat to a finance company in return for a monthly pension — payable until her death.

And still the syndicates carried on doing their worst with the widest possible exposure to all manner of American floods and hurricanes with odd-sounding names as well as Far Eastern forest fires. Asbestos claims rained down. Then the recession bit and her share portfolio was on the floor, and so off to the finance company went the apartments in New Jersey and Malaga and various fetlocks of assorted Lambourn race horses. Mary Ellen had never been the sentimental sort.

This would have been enough to see her through, but Mary Ellen had always loved a flutter. 'Better than sex,' she would say with conviction. And so to cheer herself up after the Lloyds letters she had begun to bet a little more and a little more, 'little' being hundreds, sometimes thousands, several times a day. And when her bookie had become just a mite heavy, Mary Ellen began that dance known in the legal trade as the 'trust fund drip'. As long as she could prove need, Richard's trust fund — worth around £10m in 1988 — could be opened up and its funds dispersed to her. The executors, old friends of George's, never could say no to her and neither of them had much time for Richard who lacked, in every sense, his father's killer instinct. And so money from the liquidated investments trickled out. The taxman scented blood in 1994 and by the time Mary Ellen had had a pacemaker fitted, spent several weeks in the most expensive of nursing homes and given large gifts to friends, retainers and hangers on, the trickle had quite quickly turned into a tidal wave.

'Ten thousand, four hundred and fifty pounds, thirteen bloody pence!'

It was a banshee howl, a sort of desperate chant, which Harriet now knew as accurately as her pin number at her bank, her son's birthday and the dates of the battles of Hastings, Britain and Waterloo. Her husband was not now to be multi-millionaire art dealer, just an art dealer with impatient creditors who, on learning the truth about the paltry sum his mother had left him, would start queuing up. Now the power saw was off again, this time in the corner of Mary Ellen's study. Wood splintered and then broke. Richard was forcing up yet another floor-board.

'Richard, this is *not* our property. It belongs to the finance company now. They will sue! We only have permission to clear it. Stop it, Richard, STOP!'

Silence.

'We need to think! We need to keep calm and think, Richard! Please, darling, please stop it!' Silence. 'Look, at least no one can say any more that I married you for your money. It's *only* money! Please stop this!'

Derderderdereder went the drill into the expensive American oak flooring. Harriet sighed and decided she would make some coffee.

Apart from the money — £10K still seemed quite a lot to Harriet, she could have lived on that for a year quite happily before marrying Richard — there were a few assorted goodies left. These Mary Ellen had bequeathed to Katya, Jamie, and to Harriet's surprise, to Billy and herself.

Jamie, who had wanted to be a fashion photographer since he'd been ten and a half, had been left money for photographic equipment, as well as the very snug little trust fund for his education and future life which had been set up at his birth and was worth at the day's prices around £25K. There was also much sage advice on photography, which would probably have been extremely useful at the time when The Shrimp ruled London. Billy was given £500 which, as he had always been terrified of the old lady, was a pleasant surprise.

Mary Ellen had left Katya her pearls. Six rows, the size of small bird's eggs. 'How much are they worth then?' she had asked the lawyer. Just for a second the cold insouciance disappeared and she had been a little girl inspecting the contents of her first Christmas cracker

'A lot,' Richard had said, scowling. 'I'll get them valued.'

Katya had not bothered to answer him, just fished the necklace off the table and stuck it in her bumbag. 'She might have left me some money.' The solicitor had cleared his throat and looked at the floor, unable to look her in the eye.

Harriet's own bequest now stared down at her from the wall. It was the only object in Mary Ellen's flat which had ever given her pleasure. She had always called it The Picture, for though there were numerous glorified fairground works with small dewy-eyed children holding kittens displayed on every wall, this portrait was the only work of art. The only reason in fact, she'd been able to stay so long listening to Mary Ellen droning on and on about long-dead people and half-forgotten times, was because of the distraction it had provided. And now it was hers. What a thrill. Harriet stood looking up at the picture, fingers stroking the rough paint, eyes hardly able to take in the subtlety of colour and effect. Just for a moment, pleasure flooded her, drowning out the splintering sounds along the hall, the loud curses and the self-pity.

The portrait was of a woman, slim and young, dressed in a long lilac late-Victorian formal dress, sitting at a window with rich brocade curtains. Behind her in the distance was a wide river, a pier and a large yacht riding at anchor. The woman's face seemed to be in the act of turning, as if at any second she would be looking out of the window and shouting out to some beau who was running down to the water, or perhaps up from the shore towards her. The artist had captured her just as she was about to move. There was an enormous animal vitality about her. Harriet was sure this woman must have been able to run fast in spite of her crinolines and petticoats.

It was the eyes which really held the viewer. Improbable eyes, with thick black lashes. Real violet. Even Elizabeth Taylor's famous violet eyes were more blue with attitude, but these were truly the colour of violets, so vivid that they verged on purple. The woman had a high forehead and upswept black hair. She wore diamonds at her ears and throat and had been painted half smiling as if she knew a really good joke and at any minute would share it with the room.

There was beauty here, and youth, but most powerful of all was the allure the woman held in her eyes, the knowledge that she was the sexiest, most desirable woman on the planet. The contrast between the frilly, fussy dress and this womanly power appealed to Harriet, who had never been entirely sure of her own allure. The fire and determination in this face were like a challenge, a beautiful gauntlet thrown down across a century to all her exhausted, overworked, liberated sisters; as if to say that any woman who could not persuade her man to vote in the way she wanted, was a disgrace.

One of Mary Ellen's sayings suddenly came to mind: 'Without women the world would be bread without the soda.' Well, this painted lady was a four-course meal at the Savoy.

The picture badly needed cleaning but, looking closely, Harriet could see how cleverly the artist had blended the skin into the hairline; how its tones reflected the light from the window. The initials 'F.H.' were visible in the corner, small and neat and seemingly added more as a tribute to the beauty of the subject than a triumphant statement of ownership. She must look him up, Harriet decided, and wondered why, automatically, she'd thought F.H. was a he? She suddenly realised that the woman was having far too good a time teasing the painter to be sitting for a female artist. 'A portrait is a painting with something wrong with the mouth,' Harriet remembered the famous Singer Sargent quote. Nothing wrong with that mouth! It looked as if it could swallow up a man whole and still tackle a glass of champagne for afters.

Derde-derder. Richard was off again. Rip. Another curse. Then a shout. 'Harriet, have you got some plasters? I cut my bloody finger, dammit!'

Feeling a deep sigh coming on, she went to get her handbag. How the hell was she to hide her pity from him?

Richard had done a fine demolition job. Harriet could only stare mutely at the devastation. The study floor was almost entirely taken apart, with the empty spaces between the joists now black and exposed. Box files were strewn over the large mahogany desk, and papers and files had been thrown about. Blood from Richard's thumb was dripping on to the only patch of unstripped floorboards.

'Darling, this is madness,' she began. 'Look, here's your plaster. Just nail this lot back and stop it. Take my advice, for God's sake!'

'So, Mastermind, where do *you* think she put it?'

Her husband's voice was almost a snarl and his face a white mask of fury. Dust was sticking to the sweat on his forehead; his thinning hair was covered in shavings. Harriet could barely look at him. Now she had to fight to keep not just pity from her voice but disgust.

'Richard, you don't keep millions of pounds under the floorboards! Your mother wouldn't have anyway. Get used to it. It will all have gone on the three o'clock at Wincanton or Doncaster. It's obvious from the letter that she went through the lot. I'm sorry but it's gone. Move on!'

'Stop sounding like a bloody barking New York psychotherapist! How *can* the money have gone? Who was she to spend it? It was *my* inheritance from *my* father! Mine!'

Give me my ball back. Billy's voice from long ago, yelling in a playground. *Give me back that ball — it's mine.* Richard sat down on the desk, the power drill across his knee like a brigand's rifle. He was still breathing heavily after the exertion of ripping up six-feet-long floorboards, tiredness and bitterness carved into his face. He would not even

36

look at her, just kept repeating 'Where is it?' As if she could reply, 'Well, dear, behind the breadbin on a spike with the gas bills'.

His old mother had really done it this time! She must have known that the financial services people would give him oh so much rope to hang himself with. And that Richard, secure in the knowledge of his birthright, would duly coil it around himself Houdini fashion, certain he would escape their clutches when the time came. In Harriet's mind the rope of Richard's financial commitments seemed to wind, like the chains round Marley's ghost, all the way down the stairs and into the square below, cash boxes dangling from it like a lethal charm bracelet.

'I always thought I'd be able to buy back the lease on the Cork Street gallery, open up again, get another house in SW1 — you know.' He looked up and smiled wryly. 'That everything would be all right on the night. That Dad would see me through OK. So, why this? And never a hint to me. Bitch!'

The loss of his millions seemed of far greater significance than the loss of his mother. Difficult to understand for Harriet who had lost her own mother at the age of five, now a barely remembered angel smelling of Yardley's lavender water. But then, Mary Ellen had been no angel.

'Look, let's leave this. Now. I'll get a joiner to come in and sort it out. We can take advice and come back on Monday. We might be able to get some compensation. Please come now, Richard. We'll get through this. You're a fighter.'

His face was set in a grimace, as if the wind had changed and it had become stuck halfway between laughter and a howl like a maddened gargoyle's. Harriet took his hand and pulled him to his feet and he allowed himself to be led out, unprotesting. A pile of box files suddenly slipped off the desk and crashed down between the joists into the void beneath. They walked out of the flat, and the heavy mahogany door closed behind them.

'Still, there's that bloody great oil she's left you. Matt Mercer's been on at her for years to sell it to him — should be good for a few grand. I'll get Gander & White to take it round as soon as the paperwork's sorted out.' Richard's voice was suddenly back to being normal, pleasant, upbeat. Richard the salesman had now stuck back his mask for the benefit of the Saturday morning traffic. A Willie Loman in Lobb, out there on a smile and a shoeshine.

'Richard! You're not going to sell that picture. It's mine! I love it. You mustn't say that. Darling, we can sort it all out, there'll be some way we can get some redress from her advisers, but selling a picture I really love isn't going to make things better. It was the only thing in her horrible flat I ever liked.'

'Oh, yes. Very amusing. As if you haven't got enough bloody pictures!'

They were walking out into the grey street. Still fighting disgust and disillusionment, Harriet was determined not to get into a row. He would have to simmer down. He didn't really mean that about her pictures, surely? Oh, God, was she in for a great weekend! She took his hand in hers and smiled sweetly through gritted teeth. It would be all right. She would work to make it all right. He would be a winner again somehow. But he was not going to sell her painting, wherever his money had gone. Over her dead body.

Hackney

London's East End specialises in its very own brand of wind. Quite different from the genteel zephyrs of Holland Park, or even the south of the river squalls. No, East End wind blows directly in your face, redolent of an exotic mixture of spices and dust and rotting fruit and stale tobacco and grit and kosher meat. As if you might not have got the message that you are in a glorious, historic, suffering stew of a place, it whips up the white tunics of the men hurrying to the mosque, and the flapping skirts round the halal meat counters piling on to the street, and the veils of the Asian women, bowed down with their bulging plastic bags. The packed buses cut through the wind, but leave in their wake splattered vegetables and junk food cartoons scudding across the street. The East End wind particularly dislikes children; it whirls up all the muck and grit most carefully at buggy level, mixing the stench with the exhaust fumes of the cars piling down Kingsland Road. The wind snatches their baby cries and makes off fast down the road.

Katya loved that wind. She loved its power, venom and caprice. It made her feel alive, and in touch with everyone else in the street. It was invisible and yet making its mark. She had always felt invisible too, but hoped one day to make her own mark.

She got off the bus and headed to the cash dispenser outside her bank. She punched in her pin number and waited while the screen told her all about the new cut-price holiday insurance on offer. Holidays. Some hope! The wait seemed to take ages. Feet shuffled behind her and she spun round. You never knew round here. But it was just an old lady, her beehive of brightly dyed red hair swaying dangerously in the wind, and behind her a beautiful Somali woman, carrying a baby, standing in the bitter wind with the air of resignation as if she had been told she would have to walk a hundred miles for water. Katya loved her stillness. Beep! Would you like to display your balance, get a mini statement or withdraw cash? Beep! The old woman's heels clicked behind her, and Katya could almost taste the whiff of chemicals from some cheap hairdresser's and the even cheaper perfume.

Unkind people had dismissed Katya's first post-college artistic efforts as those of a Hoxton princess. For the ten thousand or so artists living around Hackney and Hoxton and Bethnal Green — Europe's largest concentration of artistic talent — enjoyed their own cliques and clubs, and bugbears and bitchery and pecking orders, and were not particular interested in yet another twenty-three-year-old ex-Queen's Gate posh bitch dressed in black with a fag hanging out of her mouth. You couldn't blame them. They didn't get to know this solitary girl for Katya never wore her heart on her sleeve. Indeed she would have been hard pressed to have told you where her heart was. She was not

41

gregarious, and lacked the emotional vocabulary to network. Instead she would edge around any crowd, like a cold cat prowling, trying to find a life.

But she had a grim determination to get on. Torn between conventional painting and more conceptual pieces, she constantly switched styles, trying to find a niche in which she could make a living. And so in the last year she had managed an exhibition of her paintings in the very publicly funded Chalkwell Gallery and had also been commissioned by the National Bank, with five other artists under twenty-five, to create an installation to illustrate the meaning of money. This would mean a fee of £2,000 and coverage in the art press. Like all her generation Katya was nothing if not horribly realistic. She could see the installation already in her mind's eye. It would be the most talked about event in the show. That wouldn't be difficult. So much in the world of corporate art was suffocatingly safe, dead boring.

Beep! Her mini statement slid out of the hole in the wall. £1,898 overdrawn. Oh, God! That was the real meaning of money. There was never enough. Only £102 before she reached her overdraft limit. Then what? She withdrew £20. Her bar work tomorrow would see her through. Deciding that she could after all afford some ciggies, Katya stuffed the money into her bumbag and wandered off to the newsagent's. She thought of the pearls now resting in her drawer with assorted knickers. So quaint and Miss Marple they were almost post-modern retro irony. She could always flog them up Hatton Garden if the going got really bad. The old cow might have left her some dosh, though. She'd said she'd look after her granddaughter. Ha bloody ha.

Until Mary Ellen had called her a love child, Katya had never heard the term before. It was a weird old sort of word, like snuff box or periwig, which had little meaning in real life, particularly when love was in fairly short supply. Katya had grown up knowing that she was an inconvenience, a hindrance to her mother's freewheeling life. So she had never been anything as exciting or precious as a love child. She had not contradicted her grandmother, however, for she hadn't known her that long. And now Mary Ellen was dead and no one would call Katya a love child again. It wasn't an accurate term anyhow. Bonk child would have been more precise. She suddenly wished her grandmother had lived longer.

★ ★ ★

It was still light outside and the sun had finally decided to shine, bouncing off the still, slimy water of the Grand Union Canal which slid past the back of the building. The studio, one of fifty in a converted veneer factory, was Katya's pride and joy, ten by twenty feet of personal space for £140 a month. She could not envisage life without it. It had a large north-facing window over the canal and the Kingsland basin, and a skylight which meant the light was never affected by shadows.

Plans for her new commission were spread all over the floor. She had had many ideas for the installation in the Whitechapel Gallery. The real meaning of money . . . She had liked the idea of a path representing a time line. First she thought people would come through a doorway with junk mail flapping in their faces as well as blown up on a screen, all offering different rates of interest and huge discounts. Then they would have to walk in a circle, meeting piles of empty boxes of toasters and TVs and computers, all pegged up on a washing line to represent consumer spending. Then bank statements would be projected against a wall. When you touched a button, a recorded voice would read out a nasty letter from a bank, threatening repossession through the County Court. A row of clocks would tick-tock in a line, and a lesson in compound interest would be projected on to another screen at the back. When the public punched in one of three numbers, a computer programme would calculate the interest payable on various amounts over twenty-five years. She had thought a friend might design the programme. But most of these ideas had had to be junked. Too expensive. The Reality Of Money would have been a better title. Blissfully unaware that her sponsors would prefer to emphasise the positive benefits of saving (even if you had to get into debt each month to do it) Katya was off in a fantasy and so did not hear the banging at the door for several minutes.

'Katch — Katch! Open the door. Are you there?'

Becca, whose studio next door was almost as perfect although it didn't have the skylight, yelled through the lock. Katya stood up and opened the door.

'Hi, you coming to the club then?'

'Nah, I'm working tonight.'

'At the Beehive? Are you still there?'

'Yes. And tomorrow. Pay day then, I might be able to eat.'

'Felix said he would be there. Yes, he did! He's ditched Tamara, so you might be in there.'

'Hardly!'

'Go on, give it a whirl, girl. He likes skinny women. You lucky bugger! Did you hear he's gone and sold another piece? Some snotty bank or other wanted their hall made human. That'll make him even more bigheaded. Look, here's a copy of that Central England Water crapola. It's not long before the entry date, but it might be worth going straight for it and sloshing some oil on canvas. Keep you in Es for a bit! See you.'

Becca disappeared along the corridor. She had obviously been working with red paint as bloody footprints stamped themselves down the hall.

Katya went back inside and looked at her studio, now a mass of paper and cardboard boxes and old bits of metal. The Real Meaning of Money. Felix Rosen, the most gorgeous man on the planet and toast of St Martin's, had once screwed her after a party when he was drunk. Just a shag for him, but for Katya, well, it had been heaven on floorboards. After that, nothing. No phone call. In this post-modern world it was hardly cool to have the hots for one man, let alone such unrequited hots you hadn't had sex for three months. Sad or what? But then Felix, being from Hampstead Garden Suburb, only liked women with money. Not least to keep him in recreational white powder. He had only been interested in her in the first place because someone had told him she had been to Queen's Gate, normally something she kept very quiet about. Then he had found out she didn't have fourpence and didn't really do drugs either. Couldn't see the point of them, it made people so boring. All of which had cancelled her out big time in his eyes. Sighing, Katya picked up her bag and her key and slammed the studio door shut.

It took half an hour to get to her flat. The bus had gone so there was nothing for it but to walk. Emma Lane, the street she lived in, was named after the mother of a professional twenties tea dancer who had had an accident and lost his legs. He now spent his time sitting by the roadside telling passers-by about his beautiful, larger than life mother and how special she'd been. Katya hoped he would have gone in for his tea by the time she got back. He could be a pain sometimes if she wasn't in the mood. She would never tell the world about her mother, if she lost both hands as well. Didn't need to.

As she crossed through Dalston, making her way towards London Fields, she found she was still carrying the leaflet Becca had given her. Portrait competition. Portraits? God no. Too difficult. Faces were dangerous. She remembered the first time she had met

Harriet. She had been nice to begin with, but when Katya had introduced herself she had just stood there, as if adding up a long sum, her face frozen. Katya supposed most people would be shocked to find their husband had a child they didn't know about. She had answered all the questions and then suddenly two and two had made five thousand and Harriet had invited her in, taking her by the arm very gently and leading her through to the drawing room, as if she was a piece of Meissen on wheels which might chip going through the doorway.

Katya remembered the house. What a place! Dead grand, not far from Harvey Nichols, oozing money. They'd moved not long after. Money worries, her mother had said with satisfaction. Richard's probably, not Harriet's, for all over the walls hung pictures. Hers. And so many! Harriet had seemed pleased at Katya's interest and told her she had inherited them all from a friend, a rich old gallery owner who had exhibited her father's work. A treasure trove of Lucien Freuds, Conroys, Auerbachs, Matthew Smiths, even a large Hockney; the canvases had spilled out into the hall and up the stairs.

Katya remembered she had been almost happy for a few moments, or perhaps really happy, it was so hard to tell the real thing from the counterfeit. Then suddenly she'd recognised her own mother, legs sprawled wide open and head thrown back, apparently smiling up at the artist, the light catching her forehead and the fag in her extended fingers. Amanda Holland, artist's model and Soho slag *extraordinaire*. Then Katya had felt incredibly sick and Harriet had offered her tea and told her to sit down. Richard was away on a buying trip in Prague, apparently, but his wife would speak to him about Katya. There was no edge to this woman Harriet's voice. She had apparently been pleased to hear that Katya was at art college and they had spent time looking at each painting, until Amanda's body came spread-eagled into view. Not that Katya had told Harriet that the paintings hanging over a collection of framed photographs of her precious son featured one of her new husband's more careless former lovers. She had learned the hard way the value of revealing facts only on a need-to-know basis.

Stopping to cross the road, Katya looked again at the leaflet. The Central England Water Plc Young Portrait Artist of the Year Award. Annual PR crap to atone for doing bugger all about the rivers. Anyway she wasn't a portrait painter, that was for establishment wankers. But the zeros on the £25,000 first prize suddenly danced before her in the cold wind. Followed by the other zeros of the runners up prizes of £5,000. Could she do it? It would make Felix 'sit up. But definitely no moronic women in hats. The green man whined on the other side of the road, telling her to cross. Then she caught sight of an advertisement for mobile phones on a hoarding on the side of a house. A man in a suit was running towards a girl. He was expensively dressed, incongruous in this low-ticket street unless you knew that the middle classes came down here on the buses to Liverpool Street.

Her father's face came into her mind's eye. More clearly than usual because she had just seen him. How she wished he would look at her like that man was looking at the girl with the mobile phone. Bastard! Except, of course, that *she* was the bastard. And she wasn't pretty like the girl. Just young and thin and not ugly. No love child. She felt the sharp familiar pain which dug into her shoulders like a heavy rucksack. The wind pushed and prodded her along the pavement. Sod it, why not have a go? Slosh some oils. On Richard. Win £25,000, the price of a can of Felix. Risking the swirling grit, Katya began to laugh.

3

Largs

'It's just as well you're big, son.'

Murdo Wilson was tall, six feet four inches high, which was just as well as half the boxes in the shop were stacked on shelves, high up over the fishing tackle and the old books.

The old woman quickly rifled through a box of magazines. There were faded copies of *Vogue*, *My Weekly*, *Woman* and *Woman's Own*. The covers showed cheery girls in headbands and scrubbed clean faces, with the black eyeliner and pale lipstick of the sixties.

Murdo was pleased when the old dear took a fiver's worth of the magazines and a small china bell for £2.50. Finally, she wrapped her plastic rainhood over her head and grabbed her dog, who was trying to pee against the umbrella stand. 'Cheery bye the now.' He opened the door for her and stood watching as she marched smartly down the square towards the bus stop. She was off to a meeting of the Guild, the local Church of Scotland's sizzling grannies' Mafia which pretty much sorted out Largs and its business, over tea and biscuits. He could imagine the conversation. 'That grandson of yours, dear, see what a big boy he is now. And him not married yet!' He knew Mad Izzy would nod then and say something about Rena and those girls in catering college having far too good a time cooking in class to look after a man. And then they would settle down to a critical analysis of Murdo's every imperfection which would probably continue over a bar lunch, for Scotswomen of every age always took their fun hunting as a pack. He had long ago discovered that, as a tall, reasonable-looking unmarried male, he was very easy meat to swallow.

The old woman had reached the bus stop where her friends were waiting. Sure enough they were soon deep in conversation. Beyond them, the ferry to Millport was about to leave. The horn sounded, and as if in reply the wheeling seagulls mewled back. Murdo liked the drama and expectation of leaving, even if it was just the Millport ferry over the bit of water to Great Cumbrae. Anything could happen. Except he had never left.

With a practised eye he counted the tourists now hanging over the side of the boat. They always hung over, taking in every last view of the green hills of the island and the sweep of the bay, as if they would be rationed in a future life. The locals, of course, were safely tucked inside away from the drizzle. They had seen it all before and rarely took in any of the scenery except to complain about the West Coast Scottish climate and how it brought on their rheumatism.

Just eight tourists. Brill. Domestic tourism was 10% down this year, it said in the paper. What was keeping those soft southerners away? If one more person told him the season was hotting up, he'd jam a haggis down their throat. He couldn't wait for *Braveheart* and *Rob Roy* to be released. That would get bums on seats in the coach parties. With luck. What Largs needed now was a nice wee TV drama. Preferably about a vet or a policeman or both. Sighing, Murdo shut the door and went back to pricing the goods he'd picked up in Sunday's car boot sale.

This box was OK. No price tags, which meant the dealers had not already tried to flog it elsewhere. Nice untouched goods from people's houses. Jumble sales were good if you turned up really early, and the kirk sales. It was like panning for gold. He'd once found a lustreware pot that had sold for £1,200 at Christie's up in Glasgow. Rena and he had had a week in Lanzagrotty on the back of it. Rifling through the box he found the usual collection of junk, but a brass toddy warmer was lurking at the bottom, might get £5, and a pair of grape scissors, pretty and blunt, but good to impress the neighbours with: £17 quid he'd ask. Never know. He moved the box of old golf balls from the window and placed the scissors next to the perfume bottles. Some woman would bite.

Tourists always came to The KOOC. Short for 'knocked off old crap'. The shop was in the Gallowgate Square, where the hangings had once taken place. It was nice and handy for the ferry and the high street and the station. The KOOC's owner was worth looking at too. In fact, tourists would come back again and again to enquire about the price of the golfing memorabilia for Uncle Peter's birthday. Murdo would either throw back his head and laugh and sparkle, or be brooding and melancholy. Both equally satisfactory sales techniques.

Tourists with every modern gizmo back home in Milwaukee or Potters Bar would be seduced into paying £10 for a mercury jar, £4 apiece for WWII ration books. Old biscuit tins, made when the contents were transported thousands of miles away to our boys manning the Empire, had somehow managed to end up in Murdo's shop, priced £2–£4. Carrs of Carlisle tins were the best. Underneath them, old knitting patterns were a pull for the locals. Scotswomen are champion knitters. Wool shops thrived in the high street and if you wanted the 1940s look, and enough still did, then The KOOC was the place to come.

The centre of the shop was taken up with thousands of books in low bookcases. Tourists would go for old Walter Scotts and Robert Louis Stevensons, even if the size of the type was so small, and the paper so thin, they would be sure to give up after chapter one and head off to a bookshop for a classic paperback. Murdo liked to prop his feet on the paraffin heater and feel the heat under his legs while he read the stock. It paid the rent and gave him a home. Anyway he liked the past, it was so much more exciting than the present, it gave him something to kick against. He could close his eyes and imagine he was William Wallace or the world's first guerrilla fighter, the Duke of Montrose, fighting for Scotland's pride and freedom. Though of course the landowners and aristocrats were carving things up then good style, while the peasants just suffered and tugged the forelock. Just as they did now from their executive cars. Scotland's trouble was it had never had a revolution. The French had had theirs, so had the English — except it had come too early. But the Scots had never got around to it. Too bloody busy fighting the cold and each other. There was going to have to be Independence. Only way to wake the people up and sweep away the vested interests. That was the other good thing about owning a junk shop, it gave you time for plotting. Sometimes, he thought the SNP weren't radical enough and Alex Salmond looked like a couch potato.

Murdo picked up a copy of *My Weekly*, 13 July 1968, price 6d. '*Make it a Swingin' Summer by wearing this up-to-the-minute dress. Its absolute femininity is sure to appeal to every fashion-conscious young lady.*' This was a pattern offer for a blue cotton shift. The material was the floral design you see in the sticky back plastic on the back of recipe books in fifties kitchens. Just 2/3d post free!

Those were the days! If he called Rena a 'fashion-conscious young lady' she'd brain him with her mobile phone. He flipped the page. '*With only ten pounds between us and two months of summer ahead, my husband and I set out on the most wonderful holiday of our lives . . .* ' Ten pounds. Lucky cow! Now rent and rates ate thousands, God help him.

The doorbell tinkled and Wee Shug came in, his arms full of leaflets and posters. 'You've got to get out more, pal. Reading women's magazines will make your brain soft. Do us a favour. Now, are you canvassing the night or what?'

'I said I would, Shug. Stop hassling me, man.'

'I'll see you at five. Prompt. And don't be late. We've got to do fifty houses tonight and tomorrow.'

'OK, Shug, OK. Quit nagging me.'

'Well, we want to give those smug Labour and Tory bastards a bloody nose, don't we? Try a read of these leaflets of our great and good party, instead of that sixties crap.'

What a nag. He's worse than Mad Izzy, Murdo thought. The morning rain had stopped and the sun had picked up just enough strength to reach inside the shop. The ferry was making its way back from Millport to the jetty. Summer. About bloody time. Murdo picked up his accordion and a chair and went outside the shop. He shoved the magazine back in the pile, then suddenly realised that his mum would have looked just like that eager young girl in the blue dress in the pattern. All smiles and hope with the big bouffant hair and the pale lipstick. Poor Mum. Now Dad had popped his clogs, somehow the lines down the side of her mouth went as far as Australia; she had also raised 'nursing her wrath' to a new art form, giving him grief if he didn't stop by every day. Sometimes he felt like bloody Tam O'Shanter, forever having to apologise for stopping off with the boys for a pint.

Back in the sixties, too, Mad Izzy would have been a swinging fifty or sixty something. He tried to imagine this but failed. So instead he sat outside in the weak sun and played *Donald, Where's Your Troosers?* This usually pulled the punters straight in off the boat. Either that or *My Love Is Like A Red Red Rose*. He might even smile for the rootless rich Americans on the hunt for their wastrel ancestors. It was a living.

What had he ever spent his energy on before discovering sex and the Scottish National Party? They seemed to take up all his spare time and money these days. Candidates for girlfriends had to have long legs and cheeky smiles and not give away the punch lines to his jokes or yawn during his gigs at the folk clubs. They also had to be able to travel; he was being rung up from clubs all over these days, Gretna to Gairloch. And they had to be good cooks and not mind spending Saturday mornings getting stuck into jumble sales and being mauled by wee wifies with sharp teeth and umbrellas. Thankfully, in his Arran sweater, black jeans and leather jacket, and with a smile that could light up Glasgow on a wet Monday night, Murdo had never found it a problem finding willing candidates.

In his political life, too, candidates he worked for had to be hot as mustard. Murdo had no time for losers. At present, with just five days to go before the Council Elections, his world as a humble canvasser was divided into four groups of people: Fors, Probables, Doubtfuls and Againsts. He wanted Fors, lots of them.

The trick as a canvasser was to be as pessimistic as possible in spite of the natural urge to feel victory coming on. And so the 'I've voted for you before' was only a Probable, while 'I'm listening to your arguments' was a Doubtful. 'Yes, I'm looking forward to voting for you' could be a For, but then again it might be a bluff by a member of an opposing party trying to lure you into a false sense of well-being. 'Bugger aff, I'll set the dog on you' on the other hand was a nice clear Against. Fellow canvassers for the opposition would always offer to discuss policy to waste your time. The Labour lot would offer tea, while the vanishing Tories, poor sods, offered sherry and possibly a biscuit, as long as you removed your shoes before stepping on their 'guid carpet'.

Shug and Murdo had been given two apparently endless streets to complete. Their job was not to convert them to the true faith of Scottish Nationalism, but rather to mark off F, P, D or A on the local voter rolls. It was not so bad in the spring or summer. Largs people spent hours in their gardens tending immaculate lawns and huge rose bushes and so were easy to catch. But in the winter it was impossible to get them to answer the door. Old ladies would be convinced you wanted to murder them in their beds, and when they finally did poke their nose through the chained up door, the smell of lentil and haugh broth made you want to give up and go home.

Now it was spring, more or less, and so hope sprang eternal, in the shape of the local candidate standing for the Largs Central ward of North Ayrshire Council. A real flesh and blood contender, rather than a paper candidate, someone's wife or granny put up on condition they wouldn't actually win. Some paper chase in Mad Izzy's case. She had once been a paper candidate, then three days before polling the Labour man had keeled over and she had romped home with a landslide and her picture in the *Sunday Post*. For four or five years she had made everyone's lives on the Council such hell, the *Largs & Millport Weekly News* had christened her Terrierwoman.

Now Largs was changing from a small tourist spot which had seen better days into a commuter town with incomers who drove to the new high technology plants at IBM or Compaq. There were also the financial services types who commuted up to Glasgow by train each day with shiny briefcases and wanted the town spruced up into a little suburbia. The different worlds existed uneasily side by side, sometimes meeting at clubs or church.

Murdo preferred Largs' high Victorian past when Glasgow was the second city of the Empire, when hard-working meritocrats could triumph and the City's rich and powerful would come 'doon the watter' in the steamers for the summer. He would often let his imagination wander further back in time, to 1263 when the Vikings had brought a huge fleet into the Bay to force the Scottish Crown to recognise Norse authority over the Scottish western seaboard. Thousands of men praying to Thor had taken on the waiting Scottish army of hot, new Christians who, with God on their side, had poured down the hills from Kilbirnie. The Battle of Largs . . . did they know it would come to be called that afterwards? Largs was the last point of the highlands, so the men would have been tall and swarthy like himself. Sometimes, when the wind howled, Murdo could see men with horned helmets rushing through the cold grey water on to the shore, shields in hand, while the Scots in kilts roared vengeance down the hill. How the clashing and the shouting must have resounded round this small village, then more trees than cottages. This battle perhaps had given Largsmen their sense of being continually under siege, whether from Vikings, tourists or the bloody English — it didn't much matter whom.

By seven o'clock, Shug and Murdo had reached halfway up Milton Drive, a road which seemed to be made up of B & Bs with immaculate crazy paving and fancy strip lighting over the doorways. 'Vacancies' the neon lit boards outside announced rather desperately. These people rarely voted for the Nats, they were far too busy trying to keep what they thought they had got under the Tories and sharing their lives with dozens of strangers for months just to cling on to their bricks and mortar.

'Good evening, madam, we're representing the Scottish National Party, can we expect your support at next week's council elections?' Shug was putting on his best Morningside accent for the woman, who had such a rigid pink-tinged perm, it looked as if it was made of the guests' morning crispy bacon. 'You may not, young man. Good evening.'

Murdo knew the woman. She had once come into the shop trying to flog some books of her son's. He had buggered off to Uni and never come back. Could you blame him? He'd offered three quid for the box, a fair price for all those useless bluffers' guides, but she had given him a lecture about those who lacked a University education not knowing really good books when they saw them and trying to get away with paying paltry prices. Murdo had just smiled at her until, infuriated, she had stormed out. He had tried University. He'd gone up to Glasgow and had stuck out Scottish History 1, before realising that it was a waste of time. Scotland's entire history was just one glorious feudal maypole and failure for everyone else, unless you emigrated or went to the right school. And the past was no different from the present. Nothing had changed. Whereas once the landowners would have cleared the land, now they flogged it off to developers for executive housing none of the locals could afford, which sent the local schools bursting at the seams, while they pocketed the money and sent their own kids to posh public schools down south. It all stank. And the lawyers and all the other professionals spent their lives with their noses up the landowners' arses in one great greasy pole of feudal privilege. Why spend your life brown nosing the professors and learning about Scotland's mega-low glass ceiling, when you could spend your time working on songs and reading? Achieving 'freedom which no honest man gives up but with life itself.' The people who wrote that Declaration of Arbroath had the right idea.

Murdo had been brought up by Mad Izzy on stories of Bannockburn and Culloden, but for him, as for thousands of Scots, it was the Poll Tax that had been the final straw. Until then the Scot Nats were seen as just a load of nutters whining on about betrayal in the '79 referendum. And then Maggie Thatcher and the rioting crowds in Trafalgar Square had somehow touched a nerve. Murdo and his friends suddenly realised how tired they were of tourists' belief that they would be interested in the Test score at Headingly; that for the English, Scotland was just a bit of England tacked on to the top of Carlisle for themselves and the Royals to holiday in. That all decisions were being taken by a bossy Englishwoman with blonde hair, who never came near if she could help it. They also realised they had learned more about the Tudors at school than their own history.

Murdo helped set up a junior SNP branch

in the school and soon was going to conferences. The first time Shug and he heard Winnie Ewing speak, they had come back thinking that Scotland need not be an also-ran after all. They learned that in 1910, when Largs was still welcoming guests down from Glasgow for the summer, Scotland had the highest GNP in the world. It could be independent and successful again, an educated new Norway which could keep its oil and its wealth for itself, with all the EC wadges thrown in like the Irish enjoyed. All those Westminster wankers could piss off and govern the home counties. And land reform would get the bastard landowners taking notice of the people's wishes. These arguments were irresistible to Murdo and forced him out on many a windswept night to deliver leaflets when he could have been tucked up in his bed.

By eight o'clock they had finished. Milton Drive had 12 Fors, 16 Probables, 4 Doubtfuls and 17 Againsts. Strathearn Street seemed more fertile territory, more incomer families in cheaper housing, who were open minded: 27 Fors, 8 Probables, 3 Doubtfuls and 13 Againsts. Shug compared the electoral rolls against the last canvassing returns. The Fors were mounting slowly. It was uphill, given that North Ayrshire Council had been sewn up by Labour for years, but it was a start. With the new boundary changes, this ward was now turning, Probables were converting into Fors. Satisfying. This was the slow foot-slogging, door-knocking reality of politics.

These evenings always made Murdo think about what possessions were really worth. All the identical ornaments and figurines these upright citizens had on their window sills, all bought for hundreds from ads at the back of colour supplements and actually only worth about fourpence. God knows he had enough of them in the shop.

'Is that us then, Shug? I'd kill for a carry out.'

'I think so, Murdo, aye. Are you going down the club later, singing or what?'

'I might, but I'm knackered. Though I've got a new number. A sort of post-modern *Flower of Scotland* for the wee fearties who won't vote SNP. Let no one say I don't know my angst-ridden middle classes.'

'You're just something else, Murdo Wilson, so you are. I see you sookin' in wi' them down the shop. Ever thought of marrying one of they wee wifies? Some of them must be worth a bob or two. You could bump her off with a recipe for Guild broth. A bit of arsenic, and Rena and you could live in luxury in

Brisbane Road for the rest of your natural.'

'Shut it, Shug. I'm off.' It was useful Shug had a good head of hair to ruffle; Murdo knew it really drove his friend stir crazy that he was a foot taller. Still smiling, Murdo headed off back to the town centre.

Twickenham

'So that's what she left you, was it, the pearls? No money? Shares? Typical. What are they worth, do you know? We'll get them valued ostensibly for insurance purposes, might be worth selling. I'll ask Monty, he'll know.'

'OK.'

'So, what was Rich left? How delicious after all these years trailing after Mummy.'

'Ten grand.'

'What fun! I wish I had been there to see his face. What a turn up. She never liked me — only met her twice but I could see she thought I was trouble. Not a titled girl, so not good enough for her little boy. What a joke! Particularly as I was after a title too. More fool us. Now pass me that scarf. On the bed. Carefully! I've just ironed it.'

Katya was standing behind her mother. The dressing table was now a sticky muddle of small pots and brushes and dirty paper handkerchiefs. The woman staring intently at her reflection was a carefully made up invention of late forties' normality. It still amazed Katya how much her mother had changed in just a few years. She felt cheated to think that she had had a very different parent right throughout her childhood, only to find it was all an act and this respectable lady had been underneath all the time.

'Now, are you going to work tonight? There's £50 in it for you, but you'd have to keep your mouth shut. I can't imagine why you did that. Studs are so terribly dangerous.'

To wind you up, you stupid cow, thought Katya. 'I suppose I could come,' she said. She had only managed to be mutinous, never out and out confrontational with her mother. She was just not strong enough, even now.

'Well, don't come crawling to me for money, Katya, you're old enough to earn your own. It's an opportunity for you to meet nice business people rather than all those artists.'

'Well, *you* had enough artists.'

'Exactly. They're all children. Mind you, as I said to Phillipa yesterday, if you could manage Francis Bacon in a bad mood, you can easily manage a bloody-minded egomaniac director who hates his wife. All men are stupid bastards. Talking of whom, did your father ask after me?'

'Harriet did.'

'Oh, did she? How sweet. That woman sounds nauseating.'

'He said to say he sent his regards.'

'Oh, very useful for paying the gas bill, regards.'

Her mother had a habit of carrying on thinking about the subject under discussion long after she had spoken and now her mouth moved as she muttered silently to herself. It was just one of her many irritating habits.

Katya had spent all her life knowing that her mother was beautiful and she was not. It was one of those unchanging truths, along with the sun always following you to school and cream always floating to the top of the milk bottle. Most of her early childhood had been passed in dark corners of artists' studios, silently playing with old cartons and tins while her mother modelled, usually in the nude. By the time she'd started nursery school, Katya thought every mother took her clothes off and was shocked to find her friends' mothers even locked the door when they went to the loo.

While others' childhood smelt of coloured dough and baby lotion, hers had smelled of piled ashtrays and the sour stench of empty bottles, green glass usually, sometimes square clear bottles, shoved inside the bin for the

dustmen. There were always different dustmen because they were always moving, with
different au pairs coming in, usually lasting
about a week, possibly a month, before her
mother would scream at them. One or two
Katya had even grown to love before,
inevitably, they left. There had been lovers,
too, men who stuck around long enough to
turn into uncles, and then even a husband, a
photographer, who had lasted five years.
Home then had been a tiny little house in
Chelsea and Katya had been happy there.
Then the rows had started and the drinking
and they had finally moved out, this time to a
poky little flat in Lavender Hill behind
Clapham Junction. Her mother house-sat and
baby-sat and still modelled though now she
was less in demand, as the weight had piled
on together with the wrinkles.

Life was often frightening for Katya, inured
though she was to constant instability; her
days were an unending commute to school
from one end of London to the other with a
key in her pocket to get in, never knowing
what there would be to eat. One day she had
asked her mother about her father and she
had spat out his name like a dry crust and
had said that no, Katya bloody well could not
go and see him. As long as he kept paying the
school fees that was all that mattered. And

pride. More fool her for taking Old George's money and running. Katya had wondered who Old George was.

Eventually, when she was thirteen, she had found her father's name on her birth certificate, snooping around when Amanda was out at work. Then by chance she saw the same name and his picture in a magazine and found out that he owned the Europa Gallery in Cork Street. One day after school she had gone on the tube to Green Park and walked up Cork Street, planning to rush into his gallery and surprise him. But the double doors seemed enormous, and the gallery so large and spacious and grand, she had just stood there watching. Her heart was thumping so loudly it made her ears tingle. Then she saw a tall man wearing a suit and stripy shirt talking to a smartly dressed lady; he was bending over her and smiling, and quite suddenly Katya began to cry. Just as she was wiping her nose on her sleeve, a young woman came out of the gallery and asked her what she wanted. Her tone was snooty and unfriendly and Katya had run off down the road, feeling a coward.

From then on she had put all her feelings into her painting. She began to realise that in the hours she had spent watching her mother pose, in total silence, on pain of a beating and no supper, she had been learning, through some curious osmosis, from some of the greatest artists of the century. She had also learned young the power of silent watchfulness and now worked as they had, her painting soon becoming the most successful pain killer.

The following year she and a school friend had gone back to the gallery. They had gone in and she had announced that she was Richard's daughter. Katya had expected her mother's brand of fireworks, but he had seemed pleased and had taken them out to the Ritz for tea and asked pleasantly after her mother. She wanted to ask him why he had never wanted to see her, why he never sent her Christmas cards and birthday cards. But she had not had the courage in those opulent surroundings, and anyway she thought it would make her cry. 'He's terribly handsome,' her friend had said when they left. 'He's profiled in Mummy's *Tatler* this month. Lucky you!' Lucky Katya.

She wrote to Richard and he would reply but she always had to initiate contact. He made no attempt to come and see her in their horrid little flat and she assumed that was what had been agreed years before. None of her business, her mother had once said. 'You've no idea how bloody hard it was to be a single mother. No bloody state handouts and council flats then.' But Katya had written and asked him who Old George was, and was he still alive, and could Richard give her his address and telephone number? He had written back to say that his father was dead, but his mother was still very much alive. So one day Katya had simply rung her up. She was eighteen then and expected little from anyone, but the old woman had invited her for tea. Katya had found Mary Ellen surrounded by smelly little dogs and a huge housekeeper called Mrs Ross who bossed her about. It appeared that the old lady too had known all about Katya but had never made the effort to get in touch. More evidence, as if she had needed it, that she was not worth bothering with.

They had got on surprisingly well; she had laughed more with Mary Ellen than anyone. They'd picked horses on the telly to bet on and old Mary Ellen would ring through the bets to her bookie. It was at the end of one really fun visit, when she had won £150 at 8 – 1, that the housekeeper had said to Katya, while showing her out into the lift: 'Like antiques, do you? And money and jewellery? Back again soon, I expect. Think we don't know your game? Think she doesn't?' Her piggy little eyes had glinted with pure venom.

It had taken a minute for the significance of what she'd said to sink in. After which Katya rarely visited, in spite of the old lady's increasing pleas and letters. Make her wait. It had all been spoilt.

She spent every minute working for her exams and painting, just living for the day when she could afford to leave home permanently. Then one day, a month before the start of her second year at college, her mother had come home from the supermarket, not scowling as usual as she banged all the bags on to the kitchen table but announcing that she had met an old school friend who ran a corporate hospitality business and had offered her work. And so it seemed that the moment Katya had moved into digs, her mother had cleaned up her act. The drinking went and so did two stone. Amanda began to dress better and, after starting off as a waitress, soon progressed to hosting parties and managing events. She became eligible for a mortgage, and a small legacy helped her buy a terraced house in Twickenham. She was finally free and happy. Unencumbered.

Nowadays she drove around in a smart red car and her small house had been extended tastefully up into the loft and out into the garden. She gave off the aura of a successful businesswoman; her earlier career now providing an added allure, even immortality as her younger body hung in the Tate, the celebrated subject of works now valued at seven figures.

Katya watched her mother briskly brush her shoulders and pick up her coat and gloves. Old Mary Ellen was dead. She hadn't said goodbye to Katya, but the pearls had showed she hadn't been forgotten. It was all so stupid. Now the grand old flat would be emptied. The bitch housekeeper hadn't even shown up at the funeral.

'So, coming? Wakey, wakey, Katya!'

'Yes. I'll change when we get there.'

'Well, you'll have to be quick — and make sure your nails are clean. And don't forget to smile! We don't want any of that moody street cred while you're serving the canapés. Now, I'll check I've got everything then I'll start the car.'

Katya followed her mother down the stairs wondering why Amanda always made her feel invisible. As if she didn't have a separate identity and was just her mother's shadow. Still the overdraft was anything but shadowy so she would earn £50 being nice to those tense, wrinkly businessmen. She was good at silently doing what she was told. Good at watching faces too. And she would be painting her father's picture for the competition. He'd agreed rather formally in writing. The knowledge that hearing of this would turn her mother into a screaming banshee was a prospect Katya rather enjoyed. Both of them were going to have to stop ignoring her very soon.

4

The thick black curly hair was thinning and there was just a hint of a paunch above the immaculately tailored Huntsman suit, but only just. If Richard breathed in very hard, pulled himself up straight, it disappeared. Until he ran out of oxygen. He had become very practised at pulling in his stomach muscles in front of mirrors. He couldn't remember when it had first become necessary. When did a washboard stomach disappear? Thirty? Thirty-five? Anyway it was rotten. For at least half a minute he mourned the passing of his youthful body and then decided, because he had to, that he looked pretty good for a man of forty-six. Didn't he? The greying at the temples looked rather distinguished, surely?

Harriet had told him it did. As this was a seeing clients day, he could have done with her repeating it this morning. Particularly with the client he would be seeing today. But she had left at 7 a.m. to fetch the boys home from school for the weekend. Soon the house would be full of teenage testosterone and thumping music cracking the ceiling plaster and long legs sticking out from prostrate bodies in front of the television eating crisps. Happy days.

Richard looked closely at himself in the mirror. Lord protect him from nasal hair. When did a Mr Yummy turn into a Mr Yucky? 'When you were disinherited, old son,' he said to his reflection. His expression swiftly turned into a sort of Cagney scowl which, when he realised it gave him at least five more lines down his face than usual, he quickly turned into the pleasant, charming, devil-may-care 'I'm about to make a sale' smile he always used.

Trouble was, now the shock had worn off, for the first time in his life he was feeling poor. Really poor. It was an unpleasant sensation and made him feel vulnerable. This was not the 'strapped for cash while waiting for my millions' sort of poor he had felt for years, perfectly acceptable to every hostess in London and no handicap to the eligible bachelor tag he had long enjoyed. No, this sort of poor was the cash-strapped, mortgage-victim poor, a Poor Bastard sort of poor, which gave him, he knew, a hunted look about the eyes, and stretched his smile too tightly over his teeth. He recognised this because he had always despised other people who looked like that. They had a different smell about them, too. For if the rich are different, it is because they breathe a purer brand of oxygen, their aura crackles with a special brand of electricity. And they buy pictures, not sell them.

Suddenly panicking, Richard grabbed a bottle of aftershave and splashed it on. Some of it dripped on to his shirt. Bugger! his reflection said back to him. Richard didn't know which of the two men in the Huntsman suit reeked more strongly of disappointment.

As any Londoner will tell you, the normal rules about managing money don't apply to life in the capital. London eats money, like a caterpillar eats leaves. It crunches up thousands, without any effort on your part. So that even if you are a walking piggy bank, shining with financial integrity, still the creeping caterpillar slides in and munches up the lot. The trick in London is not to handle money, but to handle debt. Now debt is another animal altogether, a sort of leech which sucks your blood out slowly some months and others slurps you dry, afterwards ballooning massively. No one ever finds the courage to whack on a ton of salt and get rid of it, for that would be too uncomfortable. It would mean redefining your life and moving down the property ladder. Or, shock horror, moving out of London altogether. To the

North or somewhere ghastly. Richard had always considered life north of the Euston Road as belonging to another planet.

Handling debt, he had long ago discovered, was all a matter of exuding confidence. He would have to do the business today, however poor he was feeling. Please God, Matt Mercer would buy the Barcelona canvasses this morning.

A memory suddenly surfaced, of how his first wife Anne Osborn had once described him. They had only been on a second date, at the American Bar in the Savoy appropriately enough, and she had been smoking low-tar cigarettes, coolly exhaling over the other drinkers in those halcyon days when you could still smoke with your alcohol and enjoy it. 'You're the sort of guy with the big personality which guarantees him the best tables in restaurants — even if the maître d' thinks your cheques will bounce.' This was said with all the confidence of an Osborn of Osborn Fidelity, the oldest investment house in Manhattan. That night he had fallen in love with her preppy East Coast American vowels, her thinness and sophistication. He had thought she would love him for himself, whatever the state of his bank balance, naively not realising until much later that she'd had him checked out. Who had married whom for their money? Then Jamie had come along like another small cost centre in the middle of their relationship, and within three years they were divorced and living on opposite sides of the Pond.

Of course, the joke was that *her* cheques had bounced. The family were bought out by the Japanese, but Anne had not been on the side to receive the yen. And so the brownstone propping up her Upper East Side gallery had been thrown to the banks in the early-nineties recession. Just as his own Belgravia house had been.

After her departure in the mid-eighties, the big C had arrived in London in a white blizzard. Whoever had said that cocaine was God's way of saying you were making too much money was well off the mark. It was everywhere. People always knew where to get it. Being a fool, Richard had tried it. It was hard to avoid with the sort of people he met in London. You soon got to know the ones who scored because they would arrive late at dinner parties, wearing dark glasses to hide their huge pupils, and then would dribble on for hours, boring for Britain, while under the impression they were happy and having a wonderful time. He had once been at a party and seen a girl encouraged to snort all ten lines on a glass mirror. She had got up and danced naked on the dining-room table. He had only stopped laughing the next day when he had looked at himself in the mirror, and realised he had frittered away £5K. It hadn't seemed like a lot of money at the time. Sell a picture or two to cover it. No problem. Then one of the group had snorted a stash which was spiked. With Vim, the coroner had said. Something you use to clean the lavatory. It was the squalor of that which did for Richard. Got him into the nearest Narcotics Anonymous meeting. He couldn't afford to lose control. Not even oblivion can make you happy.

Then Harriet had come into his life, together with her penchant for squeezing toothpaste tubes till they squeaked, cutting out coupons and turning off lights as if she was still living in World War II. Her Puritanism appealed to him. It made him laugh and feel secure. Her body and that face had enthralled him. How infuriated he had been when she had turned down his offer of a date. Unheard of! But Harriet had made saying no to him into an art form. She seemed to have been able to do without sex, drugs, and even alcohol for years. If his charm left her cold, then had she been impressed with his home, his interior design, his tasteful Philippe Starck accessories? Had she hell!

In the end, he had become so desperate to have her he had enrolled in her tele-language school, impersonating a friend who ran a PR consultancy. He'd never been a morning person so those 6 a.m. Italian lessons with her had nearly killed him. She had taught him to roll his 'R's and learn the Italian subjunctive. *'Se io avessi mille sterline, comprerei due biglietti a New York,'* Richard announced to his impressed reflection. 'If I had two thousand, I would buy two tickets to New York.' Good God, he could still remember it! When she had discovered who her early-morning pupil really was, she had gone potty. In a fit of remorse, wanting to win her back, he'd gone minimalist like her, chucking out all his furniture, every stick. He had thrown most of his possessions into black refuse bags and simply left them out for the bin men. The moment she had asked him to marry her had been like a small nuclear explosion going off in his head. Pow! Better than sex. Well, almost. Then married life had come along instead, reinventing his social life, keeping him on the straight and narrow. And Harriet still squeezed the toothpaste tube till it squeaked.

Now it was a matter of survival. Somehow, he just had to smile and do the business today. Mercer would be good for ten grand perhaps, even fifteen if Richard could persuade him to buy two of the small Catalan mixed media. So he smiled at his reflection in the mirror and told himself he really was a great-looking guy who could still fetch the women (even Harriet on a good day), throw fun parties and generally kick ass. 'You're cool, Longbridge.' His reflection politely nodded agreement. It was usually easier to agree.

Read the *Sunday Times* Rich List and you would find Matt Mercer was worth £500m. This Richard suspected was an underestimate — scruffy financial journalists not usually being permitted near the books. In the City his name was Midas Mercer, for he was the ultimate English pirate. A recent profile in the *Financial Times* had lauded his ability to create something out of nothing, persuading other people to slave for him until he sold out at the top of the economic cycle or else buying undervalued assets during times of recession when the tide had gone out, leaving the over-geared naked selling to survive. He had found the alchemist's stone for he always made the top three tiers of management rich with him. The poor sods beneath toiled for fourpence, of course, working long hours and never seeing their children. As he had once been quoted as saying, in an off-guard moment, 'Poor sods will always be poor sods, whatever crusts you throw at them.' A staff family picnic with champagne had apparently drowned out his usual cautious approach to PR.

Why couldn't I have worked this out when I was twenty-two? Richard asked himself, drowning in a cocktail of self loathing and admiration for the other man. Each time Mercer had sold up, he had got straight into bed with some big new institution who had given him another slice of money to manage so that, with another built-in stake, he went on to make yet another fortune. Truly the Midas touch.

Richard's talent was selling pictures. He loved it, enjoyed seeing people's eyes light up across a room when they took in a canvas, and that greedy 'I have to have it' smile, which was as good as money in the bank. Possessing a beautiful painting was like possessing a beautiful woman, except they rarely aged as fast and did not make demands or argue back. It appealed to the same hunter's chemistry in the male brain. Even now he no longer had a gallery, he could still divine what would sell. It was a gift, like attracting women was a gift. They were probably about the only two gifts he had left.

Alas for Richard, this particular morning

Matt 'Midas' Mercer was not quite as lovely as he had painted him in his mind, though he was trim enough from working out, with an expensive even tan and a full head of hair. He was relaxed, too, while Richard, now tense underneath his smile, was wondering when he could afford his next holiday. But the Barcelona canvases lacked depth, Mercer told Richard, and of course the Catalans were fun but too small for what he had in mind. He accepted coffee and then wandered through the Longbridges' drawing room drinking it, taking in instead Harriet's cache of pictures. Richard knew they were good for business — you couldn't be seen as too down on your luck if you had Tate quality twentieth-century paintings adorning your walls and a beautiful wife who knew almost as much about art as you did. Trouble was, as an artist's daughter, Harriet had never been able to see her collection from a dealer's point of view, simply as products to be bought and sold on, like baked beans or cars. Their first serious row had been over the European *droit de suite* which gave commission on resales to the artist.

And in the last few days all these pictures had begun to get on Richard's nerves. As if the egos of the artists who'd created them were sucking all the oxygen out of the house.

Now he was broke, they struck him in the harsh morning sunlight as untapped assets. Harriet could be pig stubborn when she wanted to be; she didn't mind lending them to galleries but the rest just hung there, transfixing every visitor. He'd lost count of the offers he had had. It was embarrassing saying to good customers that they were not for sale. It put up barriers when everyone knew he would flog anything given half a chance.

Matt Mercer, however, put down his cup without remark. He smiled pleasantly and looked at his watch. And then he saw it. The runt of the litter, Richard called it. That bloody chocolate box painting his mother had left Harriet. It badly needed cleaning and re-framing but Harriet was so stuck on it — she refused to let it out of her sight. Who had ever heard of Forbes whatisname outside some sad people sitting in the Glasgow branch of Christie's, valuing pictures for toothless old crones who would be queuing up to get on *Antiques Roadshow* before you could say 'insurance purposes'. Matt Mercer just stood before the portrait looking at it. He exuded such concentration that Richard knew not to talk. He recognised that look, of course. The man couldn't take his eyes off the portrait. The hunter was stirring.

'I asked Mary Ellen to sell me that so often.'

'Yes, I remember her saying.'

'Of course Lindsey, my wife, knew her better. She was quite a lady. I was sorry to hear the news, Richard.'

Which news? he thought. That she'd keeled over, or that she'd bloody well spent all my dosh?

'Thank you, Matt.'

'I wonder if you would sell it to me now? I would give you twenty thousand for it.'

What! Every man has his price, and Richard knew his own was rapidly falling these days, but the words 'twenty thousand' ricocheted round and round the room like a rubber ball. The man was nuts. It couldn't be worth more than two, three at the most.

'Well, I don't know . . . '

'I realise Mary Ellen left it to you. But, you see, I want it.'

The inference being that what Matt Mercer wanted, Matt Mercer got. The confidence that wealth bestowed made the loss of Richard's father's money, and the status and power that accompanied it, so bitter that he nearly gagged. The woman in the painting was smiling at them both. Any advance on £20K? she seemed to say. Then the words 'twenty thousand' stopped bouncing round and seemed transformed into a large rugby ball which crashed through the window to terrorise all the well-heeled Holland Park ladies who were walking up the road to Julie's Bar for coffee.

'That's a very generous offer, Matt, but . . .'

'What do you mean 'but', man? Come on, you know it's not worth a tenth of that.'

Richard felt he was suffocating. He could see through the window that the chauffeur had got out of Mercer's Rolls-Royce and was looking up at the house, noting the cracked stucco underneath the parapet with a sneer.

'You see,' Richard's voice seemed to go up an octave of its own volition, like a twelve-year-old boy's, 'Mary Ellen left it to my wife Harriet. It's not mine to sell. I shall have to consult her. May I ask why you want it so particularly?'

'Personal reasons. Mary Ellen wouldn't sell, she was so stubborn! But you're a reasonable man, and I'm sure your wife's reasonable too. I've met her, haven't I?'

'I believe so.'

'Well, look at the painting, Richard. What would *you* pay for a woman like that? What lives she must have wrecked — you just know that to look at her. I'll wait to hear from you. Good luck.'

Why pay so much for some stupid woman grinning at him? It didn't make sense. It would be cheaper to get someone to copy it. Even as Richard was thinking this, Matt Mercer was shaking hands and clapping him on the shoulder. Then, with his cheque book unused and tucked inside his extremely expensive suit, the fifth richest man in Britain strode down the hall and out into the street.

As he closed the door, Richard could feel his own smile cracking. The muscles in his face ached with disappointment. He walked slowly back inside the drawing room and caught the eye of the woman in the portrait who was still smiling at him. 'Who's a big laddie then?' he could just imagine her saying.

'Bitch!'

Half an hour later the second post had brought his bank statement, now crumpled on the kitchen table, and he was on his third cup of black coffee. He skimmed the morning paper and saw on the front page of the business section that a boy he was at school with, a little nerd called Wilmot, had just floated his mobile telephone company on the markets and was now worth £80m. Other school friends regularly turned up in the press, in nice, cushy, bonus-filled, share-optioned jobs in arbitrage and derivatives and shorting bonds and God knew what. The biggest dick brain in his House had even floated a pasta joint called Lasagna Line on the Alternative Investment Market for £38m. Yet who had been voted Businessman of the Year in the sixth form for his investment tips? Who had been expected to double his father's money? And who was now just a jobbing picture dealer with a near Fergie-level overdraft?

Richard found that his hands were shaking, but he managed not to spill his coffee down his shirt. He couldn't even ask Harriet for money; their finances had a brick wall between them. Upstairs in the office the phone began to ring at the same time as the doorbell. Richard did not move. Go away! He buried his head in his hands. He didn't expect sympathy, he'd played the naughty boy at Annabel's and assorted blackjack tables for far too many years for that. But could someone please tell him, as a favour, just what he was supposed to do next?

* * *

Of course, being a hell day, the doorbell didn't let up. Wearily, Richard straightened his face into some semblance of normality and went upstairs to answer it. He then remembered he had kicked off his shoes under the kitchen table and would now encounter God-squadders or the traffic warden in his yellow silk socks. Though it just might be Mercer coming back with second thoughts about the Barcelona stuff. Miracles did happen.

Richard swung open the door. But no, Nemesis in the form of his next-door neighbour from hell, Georgiana Gaskell, stood on the step. She was wearing knee-length navy blue shorts and, as she dashed back to her car, he could see they did not disguise the knobbles and varicose veins meandering like the Danube down each leg.

'Jolly good, Richard! Thought I might catch you. You're usually in these days, aren't you? Robert and I were just saying the other day, you *must* come to dinner. It would be *such* fun! And here's the quince jelly I was telling Harriet about. Left it in the car. Such a *Noddy*. Is she here . . . no? Never mind. Let's fix a date for dinner. Why not come over to us on Sunday evening? Nothing fancy. We'd love to see you, and we do so *love* all your friends. We were over at the Van Stadens' only last week. By-ee!'

She then rushed down the step leaving him standing shoeless on the mat, holding out the jelly like an unsatisfactory urine sample.

He looked at his watch. Only eleven-thirty. Too early for a drink, but he needed one. Medicinal purposes. He watched as Georgiana zoomed off in her new bright red Porsche. She was nothing if not predictable. One had to admire the Gaskells' ability to move like very fast crabs sideways into other people's social circles. In Georgiana's case, this sideways Zorba's dance had extended from the house next door to Harriet's in Hammersmith, round Shepherd's Bush roundabout and up Holland Park Avenue, turning left up Portland Road towards Clarendon Cross. The house next door had come on to the market the day after their former neighbour Robert's chartered surveying company had been bought up by the Americans. Before you could say 'topping out', Georgiana (large crab) and Robert (small, well-padded hermit crab), had installed themselves, winkling their ghastly children into Kensington schools and gobbling up all the Longbridges' friends. They had obviously considered Harriet's marriage frightfully useful for judicious social climbing, and their ambitions had been achieved with breathtaking success. Now they met the Longbridges' friends for dinner without the Longbridges on a regular basis, where no doubt they all speculated about 'poor Richard' and his fall from grace.

Back in the kitchen he threw the jar into

the swingbin and, firmly folding up the newspaper, made himself some more coffee. The doorbell went again. He ignored it. But it rang and rang, setting off Georgiana's horrible bloody dog next door, yap yap yap, and so he stormed upstairs again.

Katya was waiting on the doorstep blinking nervously up at him. In the harsh sunlight her black eyeshadow looked more panda-like than usual. Her spiky hair was sticking up as if glued there. Richard couldn't even try to look pleased. What a day! A conspiracy to put him six feet under. He must have been really wicked in a previous life.

'You said it would be all right. It's taken hours to get over here from Hackney. Is this OK?'

He could only stand and stare. Why was she here? How was he supposed to behave? Then he was surprised to see that his daughter seemed nervous, in spite of her dangling crucifix earrings and set jaw.

'It's fine,' he lied. 'Come in, I'll make some coffee.'

It was only when she had dumped down her bag that he remembered the portrait. She'd come to choose what he would wear. Damn! Harriet was supposed to be here. What could you say to a girl who, for whatever valid reasons, you had only seen a few times, had never bonded with, and couldn't even now quite find the conviction to think of as your daughter? It was far too late to play happy families. So why had he said yes to the portrait? Vanity, that's why. Face it, Longbridge, he told himself.

In theory, Richard had always thought himself a real family man. It was all that hot blood coursing though his veins: the Irish, the Italian and the Romany. He had read all the books when Jamie was a baby, instructing all Anne's expensive nannies over the years. When she had left him for an installation artist from the Hamptons, he had been upset, of course, but even more out of his depth when she had proposed that he should have custody of their son. What sort of mother was she? She had proved to be even more of a parenting theorist than he had. Determinedly hands off. Jamie, by then a squawling, mewling four-year-old horror, had stayed this side of the Pond and had gone through a succession of Norland nannies before the blessed day when Richard had taken him to the Holland Park sandpit. Small girls had wailed to their Filipino nannies about the killer child who was blinding them with his sandgun, but that was the day they had returned to find Mrs Thing, sent from the agency, a lady with a flourishing moustache and unpronounceable name who knew no theory whatsoever. She had ruled the household with a rod of stainless steel until Jamie had reached the advanced age of seven and could go to boarding school.

Now his parenting of Jamie was almost exclusively confined to tetchy conversations, usually ending in 'whatever you want, I can't afford it', with Harriet acting as referee. Richard by now realised he was not cut out for fatherhood. Didn't have the vocabulary or the nerve. So how was he supposed to form a relationship with an adult child? Why had he been flattered into agreeing to let her do his portrait? To remind everyone that he was still alive, perhaps? He had never felt so vulnerable in his life.

'Look, er . . . I've been thinking. It's a great honour to be asked but I'm not sure I have the time nor, frankly, the inclination. Is this really a good idea?' He stopped. Now Katya was standing looking at that blessed portrait.

'Isn't it wonderful? I always looked at it when I was at your mum's. It looks great in this light. What a cool picture!'

'Do you think so?'

'Yes. Anyway, let's talk about yours. Can we go and look at your clothes? What you're gonna wear. I've brought some of my work. You know, to show you. I'm not expecting

96

you to represent me or anything.' The girl said this defensively with her chin stuck out like a mountain goat's.

Richard felt more comfortable handling artwork than emotions. He spread it out on the table and was surprised to see how good it was. There was drama and movement in the figures, which were well drawn though a bit weak on composition. She just stood there, looking at him with her hands in her pockets until he put the drawings back into a pile and handed them to her.

'Tell me what you had in mind.'

'It's for the Central England Water Competition, so it's got to be in oils or acrylics. Set size and a portrait of a single person.' She might have been reading out the spec for a shed. This appealed to Richard; he couldn't bear the usual artist's bullshit.

'Do I get a cut if you win?'

'Hardly! I'm skint. Can't eat and make the rent half the time. But you can keep it after. Actually I thought your mum might have left me a bit of dosh.'

'Didn't we all?'

As she almost smiled at him, almost, he took her up to the bedroom and Katya sat on the bed while he took out various suits. What could he say to this gawky girl sitting watching him with her pebbly eyes? Women sitting on his bed did not usually look so unimpressed. But he didn't know her. She had been just a direct debit sorted out each year by his accountant. He had rather hoped at first that Harriet would provide him with a new start, with a pretty little red-haired moppet with blue eyes who would clamber on to his ageing arthritic knees and flatter the life out of him. But no such sugar and spice little creature had arrived. Just as well. He couldn't even afford a Farley's rusk now.

'The fact is, you need to wear something which is 'you' without looking too smooth. And I need you to come to Hackney, to my studio for the sittings. There's a great light off the canal, and I feel OK there. This — ' Katya glanced at the Linwood desk and the Giacometti anorexic standing in front of the window — 'just isn't me.'

Richard noticed that her blue fingernails were bitten. The girl had not even washed her jeans, they had some sort of glue down the front. She had his long legs, not her mother's curves, and the skin around the jutting cheek bones was chalk white.

'Well, it's a long way . . . I don't really have the time. And I'm not sure, frankly, that I really want a portrait now. I know I said yes in my letter, but it's a bad time for me, I've just lost my mother.'

'Yes, so the mask isn't quite in place. Good. Come on, take a risk! What have you got to lose? Give me two sittings — three at most. Visit your City mates on the way back. Anyway, don't you think you might need a different way of looking at art? At yourself? Don't you think you might learn something?' Her voice was challenging, like a VAT inspector who has finally found an entry in the books which doesn't add up.

'Look, I'm perfectly aware Hackney is achingly cool and trendy and I might find some good work there, but portraits are very personal things. I don't — well, know you. For a start.'

Silence. He could feel her trying various answers on for size.

'Are you a coward?' She was looking at him mockingly and he suddenly realised that, though there was still something childish about her, he didn't really know what she had been like as a child. Amanda had never sent photographs; he'd never asked for any. He'd never been curious enough. It wasn't as if she was a boy. What a stupid question. Of course he was a coward! Shit scared. She wasn't exactly Little Bo Peep.

Katya was now looking at the ties he had laid out on the bed. They were his armour, his trademark, commented on for years in the style pages. He had them designed in Italy, and would not have divulged the name of the designer under torture. One had to have a few secrets. This girl's existence had been a biggie. He had never told Anne. It would have been another stick to beat him with. It had all been in the past, he had felt, and didn't concern her. He would not have told Harriet, except the girl had come marching into the frame in her Doc Marten's. Other men he knew had successfully maintained separate families for years on the quiet. It was only at funerals that people discovered the simultaneous life stories. He had once been at a conference where the main topic of conversation, once the women delegates had gone to bed, had been love children: how to keep them and pay the school fees without the wife finding out. Those men had seemed exhausted, perpetually eating two meals and living lies, like double agents. They must have needed the danger. No, the trick was to pay up, not to keep the mother on, not to love the child, and as much as you could, to forget about them. It made life so much easier.

The girl was looking at him.

'What?'

'Are you a coward? You don't think *she* was afraid, do you?'

'Who's she? The cat's mother.' Richard

thought of Amanda, who had sprawled on her back for every artist in Soho at one time or another.

'No, not Mother! Do me a favour. The woman. Downstairs! In the painting! It's stunning because she was taking the guy on. Daring him to find her out. It must have been like a mugging, not a sitting! That's what I want. Look at it. She's bloody well bursting out of the canvas. OK so you don't have a 36DD bust, but don't make it too easy for me.'

'Oh, God, do *not* mention that bloody painting. It's been left to Harriet. I've just been offered twenty grand for it — *twenty grand*! And I know what she's going to say before I tell her. OK, you win. I'll do it. As long as it only takes a couple of sittings and you take some mugshots to work from *and* make it bloody flattering. Agreed? And, remember, I'm doing it because you are a promising young artist, not because of our connection, OK? I don't mix work and family, and I don't want any hassle from your mother. Let's be professional about it. Yes?'

'Yes.' She looked at him properly and he suddenly saw the tense little girl he had taken to the Ritz, who had been concentrating so hard on his face that she had spilled the tea into her saucer.

'Good. Now what about this?' Ground rules established, Richard picked out a pale green linen suit from the wardrobe. Italian, built to show his muscles and not his small spare tyre, it made him feel like Mr Charisma.

'Cool! Good colour against your skin. Makes you look tall. Wear that. With the purple tie. Strong colours.'

'You know, if you're going to do portraiture, you have to work on reducing your palette, not expanding it. Rembrandt only used six colours.'

'You know all about portraits, too, I suppose?'

'I've sold enough, though in my experience they're always trouble. Said he, walking into this with his eyes open! Don't ever call me a coward again. Where's my diary? I can see you next Wednesday, OK?' He wasn't exactly snowed under. He smiled at her, but there was no answering smile, just a shrug of agreement. Women usually dropped their eyes when he smiled at them. Not this one. She picked up her bag

'Are you going?'

'Yeah, I'm off to see the Argent show in the All Saints Road. I'll find my way out. See you Wednesday then, with the green gear and the tie. It'll be great. See you, Rich.'

He heard her clonk down the stairs and slam the front door. Then he realised he had never actually called her by her name. Hadn't called her anything at all, in fact. What had she called him then? Rich. Like Amanda, her mother. School nickname. Sick joke.

London W6

Some habits die hard. Some refuse to die at all. Charity shops and Harriet were a habit that defied all financial sense. The fact that she had more money than she'd ever had in her life before did not stop her needing her fix.

London was booming, again. Traffic, which had been mercifully light during the recession, was now back at a perpetual crawl. And as even grotty little terraces behind Hammersmith flyover were fetching a quarter of a million, so the local charity shops were charging high prices for chain-store goods. They also were taking a commercial walk on the wild side, bringing in new goods in competition with ordinary shops while not paying the same rates. Professional managers now ran them, armed to the teeth with the latest marketing techniques, so successfully that the commercial property sector saw them as desirable institutional tenants. You no longer got that throat-catching, second-hand smell which used to hit you as you came through the door. Now it was all scented candles and point-of-sale presentation.

Harriet had long ago discovered that you could rate an area not by property prices but by its charity shops. Now, browsing through her old home patch in W6, it was clear from the designer labels that big spenders with media careers to tend, who had been priced out of Kensington in the eighties, were blanking out the noise and pollution and moving in here. Twenty-four pounds fifty for a Ralph Lauren jacket! OK, if you didn't look at the snagging on the front, but what a price compared to just a couple of years ago, when anything over a fiver was an exception. Trouble was it didn't feel so much fun to hand over nearly £25 for clothes which had someone else's life imprint on them. Charity shops people raising money for the third world never understood that you didn't shop there to *do* good, but to *feel* good. That the feeling of conquest when you found a designer bargain was every bit as driven and piratical as that felt by the colonising empire builders who had established the Third World diamond and gold mines in the first place. All hunters seek tasty, undervalued assets which make them feel rich, well-fed and successful. Just ask an estate agent.

Harriet had sold her business on a generous multiple to Europe's biggest tele-language company. Now there were plenty of empty mornings to fill and she liked the feeling of earned security. She still found her leisure a source of guilt, as if she should not be shopping in the middle of the morning, but how could she resist the charity shops of W6, all clustered together in one road, so that she could go from one to the next, a bargain basement bumble bee? Outside the traffic crawled past the Lyric Theatre; a young black couple jaywalked in the middle of the road, holding hands and laughing. The sun picked out their wide smiles, and their youth.

She turned back to look at a circular book stand. Another example of how charity shops keep your feet on the ground. All the authors hyped and fêted in the sixties and seventies and even the eighties were there, price 50p. Familiar titles made her smile. Georgette Heyer she remembered reading under the covers at boarding school, drooling over the heroes who always had lips which twitched when they were amused. Dennis Wheatley had regularly frightened her to death while Agatha Christie was so familiar she could, even now, see the words without opening the books at all. Lesser known bodice rippers and whodunnits were also jammed into the rail.

At the bottom of the stand she could see old albums and larger how-to books. Bending down, she saw *The Essential Sampson House 1986*. It must have been waiting for her. On the cover the cast smiled for the camera, their clothes curiously dated even now. And in the middle was husband number one, Tom Gosse. Voted *SoapMag*'s Sexiest Soap Star of 1984, a lifetime ago. Young, handsome and mischievous, just like Billy was now, there he stood with his arms round two of the cast, smiling that familiar lopsided smile, life and soul of the party. She could feel tears at the back of her eyes. Opening the book, she saw all the people she had shared her other life with for years. Interviews, top tips, Secrets You Didn't Know. (Oh, yeah?) Characters from another time and place and world. There is nothing so dead as an axed soap opera.

In retrospect, Tom's timing was perfect. He had got out just at the right time. Typical that he had had to die to do it. Laura Marchant was also there — a younger Laura, without the oofle dust of big money and fame. 'Laura as in *Wow*! Not Laura as in *bore*. Haven't you ever heard of Petrarch's muse, darling?' Ex-lodger. Ex-best friend. Ex-Billy's favourite unofficial aunt. Part of their lives, long amputated. She was standing with her arm round Tom, grinning from ear to ear, the cat who had got her best friend's cream. What an idiot not to have guessed! What a convenient *affaire* to have had during all those long lonely years when Tom had been away filming and she had been bringing up Billy and building up her business. More fool Harriet. Was it pity or love which had finally driven Laura to confess? And, boy, did she choose her moment! Ever the actress.

It was the night after Harriet had finally decided she loved Richard and couldn't live without him. The rain had crashed down in a summer storm. How grateful she had felt to Laura for finally releasing her from her grieving widowhood. Harriet looked out of the window, seeing the traffic streaming over the Hammersmith flyover in the distance, remembering. The next morning, after no sleep at all, she had jumped into her car and driven like a madwoman over to Belgravia to find Richard standing in the hall throwing out all his possessions for the bin men, in a bid to be less materialistic and more like her. She had punched him in the stomach in fury and fallen over a bin bag. It was only then she had noticed he was wearing nothing but a PVC apron. And just what a wonderfully tight muscular body he had! Completely bloody irresistible. She was only human. Clinch on the doorstep and Gosse was a goner. Tom and Laura would have both thought it great television. At the wedding, Laura had been maid of honour and the press had gone wild. It was only after her marriage that the real poison had seeped into the bloodstream, when Laura's company reminded Harriet that her marriage to Tom had been just a farce, with herself the 'feed' to two class-act comedians. Some months later, Harriet drew up the drawbridge and now saw no one from that former life.

The album was priced at £2, far too much for the painful memories, so she put it back on the rail. With Richard, she now had a real soap opera to live in. You couldn't make him up.

An old woman had come into the shop and was bending over a cardigan examining the button holes. Clearly dissatisfied, she shoved it back on to the hanger and went on to the next. She had lines which ran north and south of her mouth like a tube map and her eyes were narrowed in concentration. This was obviously business. The volunteer who sat behind the counter was reading Proust. He was a young man, who spoke like Derek Nimmo and obviously dressed head to foot in the stock.

Harriet suddenly realised, that like the assistant and the old woman, she now needed the charity shops just as much as they needed her. Because of Richard, she needed to remember the past, to remember what a lot of money £5 really was, and what it meant to go without. In the long wait for his parents' money, it had ceased to be quite real for her husband, more of a resource magicked up through smoke and mirrors and lunches with bank managers. His lack of control was more frightening than poverty, a high-wire act to which she was the terrified and fascinated audience. But as she grew older she needed more than ever to know it was all real, every penny of it. Marriage to Richard was increasingly like living with Toad of Toad Hall. Parp-parp!

She whisked the coat hangers faster round the rails and might almost have missed the dress. But it hit her between the eyes in a blaze of bright pink. Jean Muir, with that wonderful restraint of detail. How amazing that it should turn up again in a charity shop fourth hand this time — it had been second hand when she had first bought it and now it was back again. She took it to the changing room. Just holding it against her brought back that Speech Day. The heat, the mud, the peacocks and Richard. Billy singing in the choir, so proud to see his mum in the front row. A ten-year-old Billy with a high-pitched voice who did not have spots and rounded shoulders and a million causes of embarrassment.

Harriet was standing admiring her reflection when the young man suddenly spoke up. 'Ladies, we're expecting a visit in five minutes' time from our Member of Parliament. He's coming to see the shop. Would you like to be in the photograph for the local paper?'

God, no! She knew him. Harriet jumped out of the changing room as if scalded and, tossing a ten-pound note to the man, grabbed her bags and ran out of the shop. How odd. She was now too embarrassed to be found in a charity shop. What an establishment animal she had become. Richard would be proud.

Largs

'Safe in your arms,
You are the heart of me,
The part of me
That sets my spirit free.
You keep me warm and secure
Forever in my life,

110

A shining light
That's showing me the way.'

If you want a roomful of moist women, sing to them. Murdo Wilson had learned that at fifteen. Tonight the room was full of wee wifies down from Glasgow. Though none would see fifty again, their eyes were all lit up and they stared at him flirtatiously. It worked well, this number. *Safe in Your Arms* always wowed them, whether they came from Cincinnati or Welwyn Garden City.

'Time was a drag for me
Now it is my friend.
Life was a loser's game,
But now I'm on the mend.

Safe in your arms.'

Murdo was trying not to cough in the thick cigarette smoke. His voice was good tonight and seemed to be getting deeper. There was nothing like playing your own music; other people's stuff just felt like karaoke, no matter how much it pleased the crowds. No, there was nothing better than having an audience in the palm of your hand. The female half of it anyway. He could tell that the men were itching to head off to the bar for another pint, but the women sat rapt, their eyes fixed on him. Their attention touched him. It was like when he was a wee boy, making up to his ma or his granny for butterscotch pieces.

It was hot in the *ceilidh* boat. Luckily the sea was calm, but earlier there had been wind enough to make them shut the doors and windows. The light was too bright so the punters looked pale as death under the strips. The Formica top tables were already running with drink, but still everyone seemed happy enough. They had paid their money and he was earning his.

> '*I was lost and now I find,*
> *One true love that isn't blind.*
> *To the key that says I can,*
> *Lose the weakness and the sham,*
> *Now I know that I can bring,*
> *To the world a song to sing.*
> *And share forever in my life*
> *A love that's strengthened by your might.*
>
> *Safe in your arms,*
> *You are the heart of me,*
> *The part of me*
> *That sets my spirit free . . . '*

Final chorus, slow down a bit. Milk it, Murdo old son.

He enjoyed *ceilidh* nights. Trying out new ideas, evolving a fusion of soft rock, country, folk and pop, which achieved his own sound, his own voice. It made a change from the folk club circuit with the same old faces, using the same old chords, singing the same old lines about bastard bosses and the swine English.

Politics and music, rocking the boat, rocking the rhythm. Enter Murdo boy, agent provocateur. They'd done it last week at the elections! Busted up the Tories good style and put the Scot Nats on the Council for Largs for the first time. Yes! 928 bloody votes. It had been a great party afterwards. How many new numbers had he sung that night? He'd been hoarse for two days afterwards.

Tourists were almost as good value as voters. New faces to try out his songs on, gauging reactions; which phrases worked, which bombed. There were always requests for the same old favourites, of course: *The Bonnie, Bonnie Banks of Loch Lomond; My Love is Like a Red Red Rose*. Good old tartan tourism. It was a living. With his pay tonight he could do the car boot sales up in Glasgow, get some new stock in.

The Mhairi, which had probably never

seen better days, departed from Largs bay every Friday and Saturday night from April until September, weather permitting, and chugged up the water and down again. At first it would be all jolly with plenty of dancing, then the men would start getting blootered together up at the bar and the women would weep behind their husbands' huddled backs, before getting drunk themselves and standing riotously on the tables showing off to their girlfriends. Wee Shug, who had done his degree in psychology up in Paisley, said it was 'cathartic'.

Murdo ended the song with a flourish. There were several female shouts of 'More!' 'Get 'em off!' came from a frisky wee pensioner with her girlfriends in the corner.

'Cheeky!' laughed Murdo. 'You know the rules, girls. No sex before we're married . . . or nearly married.'

He paused again for the punchline. Deadpan. Never failed.

'I've been nearly married hundreds of times.'

The old dear's teeth nearly dropped out. Or in. He couldn't see which, but she almost choked. Laughter ricocheted round the boat's scabby white ceiling. And right into song number two. You're doing good, Murdo boy, he thought.

'My dear Ma, she said to me . . .'

Hurray! went the crowd. Shug was now on the banjo. What a combination.

'Son, I'm done looking after thee.
It's time you left this house of mine.
To look for a wife that's sweet as wine.'

The audience started to stamp and clap. Go it, son! Murdo personally hated this song but it was a real crowd pleaser. He'd only written it to prove a point. 'Why can't I write songs?' Shug had once complained, and Murdo had said it was easy. Just hang it on a phrase, wee man. He'd taken Shug's jacket, bought off the 'barras'. Made To Measure, it said on the label. That was all it took. Made to Measure. A phrase. Any pile of shite, and there you had it. A song.

'But love can never be made to mea-
    sure
Any old fool won't find this treasure.
Love needs a-huntin' and trackin'
    down.
No good woman's just hangin' around.'

The women were now standing up and jigging about. Charm bracelets clinking, hair swaying dangerously, challenging the lacquer. The smoke was almost making him heave. Last verse.

> '*Now my boy's reachin' four and*
> *twenty,*
> *Eyein' the girls who are mighty flirty*
> *Lookin' out for the precious one,*
> *Who's gonna be his bride and give him*
> *a son.*

> *But love can never be made to*
> *measure . . .* '

Repeat of the chorus, loud foot stomping. Milk it, milk it. Finish. Bloody great! The applause rang out. Fierce and long. Shug, who was now calling the dances, yelled over his shoulder: 'Are we the stripping the willow now, Murdo, or what?'

'Och, no, give the poor buggers an eightsome reel. Something to get their teeth into.'

'Their teeth'll drop out.' Shug, always on the look-out for female talent, was not enthusiastic about the pensioners' groups in from Glasgow and Wolverhampton.

A group of Americans from Wisconsin were whooping it up in the corner. They'd obviously enjoyed the country touch. Murdo loved their energy and their all-inclusive bonhomie. History did not seem to have touched them, even though the clearances had chased their ancestors off the land and into the New World. Suffering had long since stopped clogging up their genetic memory. Murdo's past, on the other hand, lay in bin bags in his brain, with the tales of high times and lost fortunes stuffed into him by Mad Izzy. They weighed as heavy as the real black bin bags of yesteryear crap he held as stock for the shop. Largs' grand 'doon the watter' past bulged out of these bags. He was bored by it. A rut. Made to measure.

Two of his friends had escaped to London, one had even stayed there, but somehow he'd never made the break. His mother had tried to break away and make it in London, and look what had happened to her. Whingeing, chain smoking, an insecure, frigging pain always on the receiving end of Mad Izzy's tongue. She had been so pretty once. Full of big ideas of marrying a doctor or some big-shot businessman. She must have been a conservative wee soul underneath her Lulu pudding basin cut. She'd have been better going off to San Francisco with flowers in her hair, or the Isle of Wight anyway, for all the good her escape did her. Still, her old vinyls had started him off, scratching out tunes on a second-hand guitar in the back bedroom.

Shug was calling 'take your partners'? He could always charm the old dears out of their seats with his cheeky smile. Soon geriatric joints were creaking up on to the floor. A wee wifie in a purple and silver handknitted top came up to Murdo, her scent long since surrendered to the sweat and fags.

'Son, you play beautiful. Was tha' a Lonnie Donegan song?'

'No, hen, I wrote it mysel'.'

'Never! It's great that. Fair brill. You ought to go on *New Faces*.'

'Aye, it's fair brill, mither,' echoed Shug, taking her by the elbow and pushing her opposite a short-sighted old man in a moth-eaten kilt. Murdo played a nice loud opening chord. He hoped the sound of the accordion would carry over the water and make all the other punters realise what they were missing, so they'd book up for Saturday. He could do with the dough. With a bit of luck, he'd tire this lot of old buggers out by midnight and be back home by quarter past. Then Rena would hopefully have the beef links stew on the stove, some clean knickers in her handbag, and it would be a case of safe in her arms till seven o'clock. He hadn't had sex for days. Yeech! The eightsome reel quickened.

Edgware

Jester Dunne loved women too. He may have been eighty-two and suffered a stroke, but he could still pinch a nubile bottom with his bony fingers and wink at a pretty girl. Whether he had his teeth in or out, his wolf whistles were still audible at a hundred yards. Sadly for him, however, the world had moved on and in the politically correct atmosphere of The Willows, or 'the Willies' as he called it, this attention paid to the opposite sex was despised, denounced and, worse, ignored.

'Harry! You there? Where is the girl?'

Harriet found her father in his room, in his dressing gown, with the radio on too loud, and painting. Both were against The Willows' regulations, but Jester had always lived by breaking the rules. He had never cared what anyone thought — the secret of his success as an artist Harriet had long realised. Though not as a parent. He greeted her, vaguely, patting her on the arm as she bent to kiss him while waving his palette around in his other shaking hand. He was now using just three colours, still mixed with fierce abandon and spread thickly upon the board; he could not afford canvas. The stroke had cost him his sense of perspective, but the tremors in his hands gave the paint a new quirky energy.

119

Always a wild child skirting between the figurative and the conceptual, his paintings now were fierce shapes jutting into landscapes. They were neither pretty nor comfortable and were not admired by the staff, even after they had stopped lecturing him for not painting in the Activities Room.

'So, Harry. What news?'

She told him about the funeral, the plumed horses, the East End wide boys — edited highlights leaving out the wrenched up floorboards and the inheritance bloodbath. He seemed to enjoy it all. Then she produced the usual illicit acrylic paint. Out of devilment Harriet would often bring him a tube of cyclamen or fern green. He looked at the paints critically, grunted and stuffed them into his dressing-gown pocket.

'Won't you get into trouble again, for painting in here?'

'Why should I want to paint with that lot of clittering, clattering old biddies? All scraggy tits and no conversation, except the weather and how many bloody grandchildren they've got getting divorced. What I would give to get out of here! Bloody useless body, what's the point of me keeping alive with all this lot?'

This was said through a mouthful of chocolate cake, another visiting prerequisite. Some days Harriet felt she was getting male temperament from every angle: from Billy and Jamie as they stormed through adolescence, from Richard in a teenage strop about his money or lack of it, and from her father, Mr Charm. How selfish they all were!

She cleaned him up and switched off the radio and went down the hall to the tea machine. The Willows had its own particular smell of disinfectant and rubber. A large vase of artificial flowers on the hall table pretended to add perfume, but they were dusty and unconvincing. Odd sounds escaped from rooms off the long corridor: a shred of laughter, a tinkle of a glass, murmurs of voices and the slow tread of footsteps. A young nursing assistant came round the corner, her hair drawn back with an elastic band. 'Hello, Mrs Longbridge, your dad's been asking for you since breakfast. What a temper he's got!'

This observation was made without affection for Jester was the resident dog and had long been given a bad name. Although he was far outnumbered by female residents he was no good for dancing with at the tea dances and wouldn't join in the bingo, was hopeless at small talk, and so was regarded as a nuisance. Mediocrity was more comfortable than Jester's restless genius and the old ladies preferred to cherish the retired accountants and bank managers. His few remaining 'nasty nudes', painted in his heyday when he had the most beautiful women in Europe running after him, now hung unappreciated on the walls of his £650-a-week room rather than in the main hall where the other residents' paintings were mounted for the benefit of visiting relatives; there had been too many complaints.

When Harriet came back into the room carrying the plastic cups, Jester was studying her other piece of news. It was a photograph of the portrait. He had stuck it up on the side of the window. His arms were folded and his chin was jutting out, Jester's familiar contemplative pose when looking at paintings; for he did not simply look, he devoured them. Under this fierce examination the woman seemed to be looking back at him, daring him to find fault with her beauty.

'I'll decant this into your special mug, and I brought extra milk.' Harriet might have been talking to herself. The old man continued to stare.

His room looked out over the formal gardens where once traumatised, convalescent soldiers had been wheeled around. Now in the afternoon sun there were just a couple of old ladies on a bench, gossiping. The woman framed in the window looked incongruous as if she, like Jester, would hitch a ride to the bright lights given half a chance. Even in a photograph, the colours of the hills and water behind her looked rich and inviting compared to the tame south-east scenery behind the picture.

In the distance, Harriet could hear the white noise from the Edgware Road as the Saturday afternoon traffic ground its way in and out of North London. 'Father, what do you think of it? I had it cleaned. This is the painting Mary Ellen left me. The artist's Scottish apparently, Forbes Houston. There were various notes hand-written on the canvas which the framers found when they took the back away.'

Jester continued to stare at the painting. So Harriet read from her notebook. ''This portrait is of Lady Isabella Fairlie, wife of Sir Gifford Fairlie; painted at the age of twenty-three at Castle Wemyss, the property of Lord Inverclyde.' I don't even know how to pronounce it. I wonder if that's where that china comes from? Anyway, it goes on to say, 'The lady was known to break hearts and wreak havoc in the lives of the men who knew her best.' Then it gives the date it was painted, 1872. I need to look up Forbes Houston, but he was obviously a fine painter. Look at the yacht behind her, and the cloth of her dress. Richard has been offered a fortune for her by one of his clients, but I'm keeping her. It was probably the nicest thing Mary Ellen had in her flat.'

'I should think you would keep it! Why let that snake oil salesman get his hands on any more of your pictures?'

'Oh, give the man a break, Dad. I only sold a few to buy us a house. The tax people took some but I've still got most of Marcus' stuff, though quite a few are away on loan.'

'Blah, blah. So, do you think Marcus would have liked her?'

Harriet was not used to her father asking her opinion and for a moment couldn't answer. Marcus, dealer extraordinary, who had made her father famous throughout the forties, fifties and sixties, had been such an arch-squirreller away of beautiful paintings, surely he would have loved this *femme fatale*? He would certainly have loved her flamboyance.

'Yes, I'm sure he would. I don't think this painting is a question of liking — you either adore or despise it. Richard calls it chocolate boxy.'

Jester shrugged, and his gesture conveyed just what he thought of Richard. How wearing it is, loving a man your parent despises. How much energy it uses up.

A bell went in the distance. 'Supper bell,

Dad, I'd better go.'

The old man turned and looked her. He seemed to be really looking at her, from the top of her head to her neat blue shoes. 'Ah, Harry, if you had been a real woman like her, you would have been worth painting when you were young.'

There was silence between them then. Why could he still do it to her so easily? Why after all these years did his relationship with her have to be so toxic? And she never failed to react with a whine. Why? How pathetic. Stop being such a bully, she wanted to say. But instead, as usual, out came her voice like a plea. 'Why was I never worth painting, Dad?' Hit me, go on. Into her mind came Tuscan hills and French villages with dusty squares, her own gypsy childhood as a small girl following him round the world as he bedded and painted rich women. Forever sent out with small coins for Oranginas to while away hours in streetside cafés while her father was otherwise occupied.

Over his shoulder, the woman looked down at her, the ice violet eyes smiling a challenge. Why had she, Harriet, always known she was not worth the cost of the paint? Why were some women so adored by men while the rest were just meant to cope with their egos? The injustice of it was like salt in her mouth.

Jester had turned away and started pushing her tubes of paint into a large biscuit tin.

There was a knock on the door and the nursing assistant she had seen earlier popped her head round. 'Time for tea, Mr Dunne. Naughty! You've been painting again. You *must* use the Activities Room. Anyway, aren't you lucky to have had a visitor?'

'She's just going.'

Why did she bother? Dismissed, Harriet picked up the photograph, kissed him goodbye quickly on the forehead and left the room. 'She's just going.' The visitor Jester had really been grateful for was the woman in the painting. For he loved beautiful women, while she was always plain Harry. She suddenly knew with complete certainty that Isabella Fairlie must have broken the hearts of just as many women too. Ignored, unfeted, unappreciated women did not inspire such adoration from their men. Judging by the care he had taken, Houston had obviously been as smitten by Isabella's beauty as all the other men. So what could Harriet learn from her, even if she was the wrong side of thirty-five?

★ ★ ★

Georgiana was good as her word and whipped up a little Sunday night supper party for Richard and Harriet in double quick time with a highly spiced variety of guests. Being Georgiana whose perfectionism was, as any psychotherapist will tell you, a clear sign of low self-esteem, a typed resumé of the guests arrived on Saturday morning. This was her own innovation because, as she said, 'It cuts out all the phatic communion about weather.' (She had once read a book on socio-linguistics for a bet.)

''*Charles Kirby is vice-president of Inter-Agum Plc and is a specialist in marketing syndicated loans. He lives in Wandsworth* (poor him) *and shares a rough shoot in Oxfordshire.'* God, he sounds boring! Probably up to his eyeballs in debt and wondering where the telephone-number salary he was promised went to.'

Sunday evening. Richard was in the bath reading aloud the fruits of Georgiana's social endeavours to Harriet, who was getting ready in the bedroom. The bath was very large and squat and stood on clawed legs in the middle of the yellow stippled bathroom. Yet large as it was, it was insufficient to accommodate Richard's feet which stuck out over the top with a yellow rubber duck perched precari-ously on his toes as if about to slalom into the bubbles. Splashes accompanied each well-honed Longbridge put-down.

'Well, if our host bores on about topping out ceremonies and City plague pits once more, I'll poison him. They may be rich, but don't these overpaid surveyors *know* how boring they are? Now besides the divine Charles we have '*Venetia Leblanc, top PR for the Huitton range.*' Ring-a-ding! '*Whose hobby is collecting ceramics and lives in Fulham.*' As they all do. Now, she'll obviously be thirty-something, on the look out for a banker with a Porsche, only instead will be besieged by penniless beautiful young fogies from the auction houses, who all know their Wedgwood. Are she and Charles an item already? one wonders. Or is Georgiana, matchmaker from hell, doing her stuff?'

'Won't it be fun finding out!'

'Indubitably. Now, who else have we? Hooray, your old friend Laura's coming! We haven't seen her for . . . what is it now? Years and years. Which is absurd.'

'Oh, yes, isn't it?'

'I like Laura! She's fun. Now Laura is described as, '*Laura Marchant — star of television and screen. Currently starring in* All About Bette *at the Fortune Theatre in the West End. She is to work later this year with Anthony Hopkins on a new film about the Profumo affair.*' Do we really need another one? Still, she's come a long way since you

128

both left Brackenbury Village.'

'You would say that, wouldn't you?'

'Very droll. Now who's showing their age? I don't understand why you have it in for Laura these days, you used to be such good friends.'

'I'm not going into that now, Richard. Hurry up.'

'I love it when you do your Snow Queen act. Well, kiss and make up. Life is too boring to do without people like Laura. Now, last but not least, '*Jonathan Harbour, features editor of* King's Quarterly *Magazine.*' Who apparently, according to Georgiana who wouldn't know loft living if she fell through a skylight, '*lives in a loft-style apartment near Tower Bridge. Collects 1950s retro chic.*' How predictable. Is he Georgiana's walker do you think? A nice, glossy gent for her to maul at the pudding stage. The usual crowd of ghastly people!

'Now, Harriet, my darling, how do you think the divine G will have described us? Would we be '*gilded couple whose parties, when they could afford to have them, made history and column inches*'? Or will it be '*my down-on-their-luck next-door neighbours, Richard Longbridge, picture dealer extraordi- naire, who alas has not inherited the millions he was expecting from Mummy but has the* good fortune *to be married to the beautiful Harriet Gosse Longbridge, widow of Sampson House star Tom Gosse and now supporter-in-chief of her impecunious husband, son and stepson. Formerly Laura's landlady, former language school supremo, and now thinking about how she can keep her darling husband in the style to which he thinks he should bloody well be accustomed'?'*

'Richard, shut *up!*'

'Why are we going? I can still barely believe that your neighbours actually followed us here. It's a conspiracy.'

'Stop moaning and hurry up! We're late already.'

'Go on, loofah my back, there's a darling girl. Fancy a quick one?'

'On your bike, Longbridge. Here's your towel.' Harriet threw it from a wary distance. He had been known to pull her into the bath fully clothed. 'Come on, Richard! *Out!*'

★   ★   ★

Georgiana was on top form. She could have lit up a small industrial town with her nervous energy and the dinner fizzed as dinners only can when one huge dominant ego which doesn't have to work for a living is

130

intent on forcing together people who do not know each other, face yet another week slaving in London, and would much prefer a steak and an early night.

'Darlings!' Georgiana cried as Harriet and Richard entered the room, as if she had not seen them for months. 'Darlings!' cried Laura with equal fervour, who really had not seen them for years. Both cries made the other guests, who had clearly been waiting for some time, look at them as if they were a pair of strays brought in from the rain. As greetings go, Georgiana, frustrated superstar of the local amateur dramatics, did not pitch hers quite right. Whereas Laura's 'Darlings!', the product of far too many years playing Noël Coward in the provinces for fourpence-halfpenny, was right on cue for maximum drama. She embraced Harriet with every appearance of joy. She hadn't seen her for so long! Life was such fun at the moment. She had been in L.A. for months and now was back slumming it in the West End. Ho, hum!

Of course. Hence the reason this party was happening on a Sunday. Arranged for Laura all along, Sunday being her only night off. Slow thinking, Gosse. And you an actor's widow. Harriet smiled and said life had been busy for her too. Then Richard, now grinning from ear to ear, pulled Laura into the corner.

For the rest of the evening their flirtatious laughter punctuated the conversation, much to Georgiana's annoyance who, seated nearest the kitchen, was furthest away from the merriment and nearest silent Charles and cool, careerist, inadequate-making Venetia.

To fill the silence, Georgiana declared that all the food was from Bunny Halifax recipes and that she was starting a course at the Bunny Cooks school in Wandsworth in June. People dutifully exclaimed how lucky she was, and what super food — baked goat's cheese with mulberries followed by smoked duck with orange coulis! Conversation juddered along. Strangely, the fact that everyone had been given a resumé neutered the usual opening lines. For Georgiana had held back on the important details: how often they had been married, which school their children went to, their politics/newspaper/car/salary. The small dining room was airless, in spite of the French door being open on to Georgiana's fashionably potted little London garden. Harriet felt suddenly dog tired, as if she couldn't be bothered to smile anymore.

The features editor from *King's Quarterly* was a plump, sad-looking man in his fifties, dressed twenty years too young. He had almost certainly been invited to be impressed with the efforts of Georgiana's interior designer and consequently was keeping his head down, literally not looking at the walls while steadily rolling small pieces of his bread roll in circular movements up and down the damask table cloth. To be polite, Harriet told him about the picture she had just inherited and cleaned. Richard's and Laura's laughter at the other end of the table seemed to give her the first permission she had had since Mary Ellen's death to discuss the picture with anyone apart from Jester. She did not want a row with her husband, but she really did not want to sell it. Almost furtively, she took the photograph of Isabella out of her handbag.

It became a game. Robert was badgered into going upstairs to find his wife's encyclopaedia of stately homes, while Venetia, Charles and Jonathan each decided to think of the most outrageous way such girls could break hearts in 1872. Had she been married off to Sir Gifford Fairlie to repay a gambling debt? As a Scot, did she most resemble a) Kirsty Wark, b) Annie Lennox, or c) Lorraine Kelly? Or Stanley Baxter on a good day?

They decided that her purple eyes either meant some rare vitamin deficiency or that the artist had run out of blue paint. Finally Georgiana, flushed with triumph, found Castle Wemyss on the map, by the sea just outside Glasgow. The seat of the Lords

Inverclyde. They peered at the map. Near Glasgow. Yuck! Cold and wet. Still, Lady Isabella Fairlie rescued the dinner party until eleven-fifteen, when normally one could decently start talking about breakfast meetings. But still the wine flowed and from sheer exhaustion no one moved. Richard and Laura, having found their second wind, continued to monopolise each other.

'Have you ever written anything, Harriet?' Jonathan Harbour asked. She was now sufficiently squiffy to note with fascination that the little veins running down his nose were as red as the wine.

'Only business reports.'

'Why not have a go and find out who this woman was? Write me 1,500 words and see if you can find some juicy stuff. Scottish history is hot at the moment with *Braveheart* coming out in the summer. Anyway I need something for my grouse-shooting issue in August.'

'How would I go about that from here?'

'Don't. Write me an outline, we can agree the angle, and then go up there and have a dig. I gather the Mitchell Library in Glasgow is rather good.'

'There, Harriet. And you were wondering what to do with your life now you've no business to run! You know, *I've* always wanted to write,' said Georgiana, who had always known she had a novel in her but was far too canny to try and extract it.

At that moment Richard was throwing back his head and roaring with laughter, while Laura was lighting up another cigarette. Harriet suddenly felt as if the grooves of the record of her life were stuck and the same people were driving her round and round at will.

'Yes, please,' she said. She knew she sounded like a little girl of about six and three-quarters, accepting a boiled sweetie, but there you go. Any port in a storm.

5

Largs

Mad Izzy was a woman of mystery. This was not because she was not well known. In fact, having been born and brought up in Largs, there was not much locals did *not* know about Izzy Finlay. It was just a mystery to everyone how, as she had been a widow for years and old Alec had not exactly left her flush, she always managed to have so much free money to spend; enough to buy young Murdo the lease on his shop, for instance. And why she always insisted on wearing long, floaty dresses instead of sensible tweeds like the rest of the civilised world, plus big, fancy hats even on ordinary weekdays, which were pinned on to her head with vast terrorist hat pins.

She also favoured huge carpet bags out of which would come assorted bargains she had picked up from skips and jumble sales. These bags, which were usually bright red or purple, were, even in these cynical times, still a wonder to the local schoolchildren. But back in the seventies, when Murdo was a child, the bags were regarded as pure *Mary Poppins*. As Julie Andrews had managed to produce a standing lamp out of hers, naturally Murdo and his friends expected Mad Izzy to conjure up at the very least a camel or a light aircraft. In the West Coast winds, her flowing dresses would stream behind her, making it appear as if she were flying into view, and secretly Murdo had always thought his granny was a witch. Though such a relative was embarrassing when adolescence hit, it was good having her on your side. Many a time her ire had scared the shite out of his enemies.

Mad Izzy had always been on his side. He recognised that this was not just because he was her only grandchild, but also because she so loved the company of young people. As long as he could remember, she had been an agony aunt and primary source of contraceptive advice for local girls. He had been used to dropping in at her house after school while his parents were out at work to find a crowd of young women in the kitchen, alternately moping or celebrating over a plate of shortbread. Women were therefore never a mystery to Murdo. He had heard their talk since childhood, together with the stern lectures Mad Izzy would dispense along with her sweet tea. He had seen her, too, surrounded by young people of an evening in

McGuffey's Bar, knocking back the gin and lemon while drawing on untipped cigarettes and putting the world to rights. He had once heard malicious gossip at the bus stop that that mad old Mrs Finlay's knitting needles weren't only used for woolly jumpers. This, when he had reported it back, had made Mad Izzy almost hit five feet with rage before muttering darkly about the curse of Finlay.

In short, by the age of eleven, there was no part of the female condition Murdo had not only heard about in detail but understood too. This early upbringing had the effect of allowing him really to like women and to enjoy their company. Which made him rather unusual among his peers for the average West Coast Scottish male, as a general rule, prefers to socialise separately from the female of the species.

'So!'

On this particular morning the sun was streaming into Mad Izzy's small kitchen where she sat shelling peas, slitting them open ruthlessly with the thumbnail she kept 'specially long for the purpose while seagulls wheeled and whined across the back drying green, as if adding dramatic emphasis to her indignation.

'So!'

She may have been eighty-six but Mad Izzy

still retained the ability to make such a very small word very threatening indeed. But Murdo was determined to brazen it out; for God's sake, he was a big boy now.

'Yep, Granny. We've done it. Rena said yes and we're engaged.'

'So. That was *after* the *ceilidh*, when you were too tired to put up a fight, I suppose?'

'Och, Granny, give it a 'bye. I thought you'd be pleased? You're always wanting me to settle down. Though with the shop, I'm so settled at the moment it's driving me mental. No, I'm not complaining, I'm very grateful. But Rena — she's good for me. She's full of ideas. She's planning to do corporate catering, she says, and . . . '

As usual he didn't get to finish the sentence for Mad Izzy, pursing her lips, was stomping around the room with her back to him, looking for another bowl for the peas. Though tiny, in her own domain she still seemed enormous to Murdo who somehow was always transformed back to a spotty twelve-year-old in her presence. He wanted to please her, he always had, which was why he was taking this. As he always had. From the other side of the hall the sounds of canned audience laughter was followed by applause. His mother, pale and sleepy after working a night shift, was getting her fix of daytime television before sloping off to bed. She had barely registered the news of his engagement, merely smiled wearily before once more turning up the volume. She would not be worth talking to until she had wakened at about five o'clock this afternoon and had had her first drink.

'I only wonder what that Rena'll be like if you go into politics.'

'Oh, Granny, be realistic. We won, sure. It's great we're making headway. But it's only the local ward. Labour still have control, the bastards.'

'Well, they have at the moment. But listen, that will change. I'm no' talking about local politics, son. I'm thinking big. We need young men like you in the Party to go out there and talk to people, win them round. The Parliament in Edinburgh will come first, but then one day the Scots will stop being such a bunch of fearties and realise they need the English like a bad dream. It'll happen. I've seen it.'

'You've seen the future in those stewed tea leaves of yours? Gran, it's too early in the morning.'

'I'm no' arguing, son. You just wait. Anyway, you've done it now and got engaged. So as long as she makes you happy, I'm no' arguing the noo. Now, give your granny a wee kiss and let's go out and you can buy me a coffee. There's a horse I quite fancy in the 2.15 at Epsom.'

'But that's an *English* race course, Granny. Dear me, consorting with the auld enemy now, are you?'

'See me, mister, I'm no provincial. I'd bet in Kentucky if it was worth my while.'

Would he always be feeding her the straightlines?

'OK, Granny, which one is it this time?'

'Crackpot,' Mad Izzy said promptly, wiping her small, wrinkled hands and pressing an enormous violet and orange hat on to her head. 'Like you son. Crackpot. Fourteen to one. Out of All Passion Spent. Just like your ma. Anyway, I need to get your engagement present somehow.'

Murdo handed her the five hat pins needed to anchor this creation against the fierce winds outside, then lifted her off the floor until her face was level with his and kissed her gently on the cheek.

'Right, well, let's get up the bookie's. But, Gran, face it — I'm not going to be giving Alex Salmond sleepless nights. I've got too many songs in my head I want to write. I'm not cut out for politics full-time. I'll just settle for being a foot soldier in our so-called glorious struggle for Independence, all right?'

141

'Och, well, I suppose so. And you're not all bad, I suppose.' She kissed him fiercely back. 'But you're not all good either. In fact, you're a lazy wee shite, so y'are. Just be happy.'

'I am happy, or I will be. Don't you worry yourself. Anyway, tell me, is Crackpot going to win? Have you seen him romping home in yon shiny crystal ball of yours?'

''Scuse me, son, I don't need any wee bit of cheapie glass to see into the future.'

She was pursing her lips again, still frowning. Murdo wondered why and hastily told himself it was just because the television was on so loud.

Glasgow

Everyone in the Mitchell Library was sniffing. It was all done in a strange contrapuntal rhythm. Sniff! went a man with a beard. Sniff, sniff, went a pale-looking girl, obviously a student in need of a large steak and to hell with BSE. Sniffsniffsniff. A middle-aged man with vast amounts of A3-size paper was having a field day with his family tree. Bits of paper and old books were spread out all over the table. He was clearly a person of some lineage, judging by the self-satisfaction in his sniffs.

What did the sniffing rhythm remind her of? *The Magic Flute*! Into her mind, covered with feathers and confusion, came Papageno and Papagena. Pa! Pa! Pa-pa-ge-na. Sniff-sniff-sniff-sniff. Harriet felt like getting up and plonking a wadge of handkerchiefs under their noses. But she forced herself to concentrate, kicking Mozart out her mind and into the bookcases behind her.

Harriet had forgotten how much she loved research. She had not been in a library since she started the business, researching different sectors and the vocabulary each needed; she had an instinct for books, had almost always been able to smell her way through them like a tracker dog.

The photograph of Isabella Fairlie looked up at her from the desk. She looked pale though still interesting in the silent library, egging Harriet on with her smile. After two hours sitting here, she had found out that Sir Gifford Fairlie was a landowner and business-man who had lived in Fairlie Mount, an estate near the village of Fairlie outside Largs. He had owned mills and bakeries, and a small fleet of 'puffers' delivering the mail from Glasgow to the Western Isles and the highlands. Harriet could imagine him, a stern Victorian with a pocket watch and a large grandfather clock chiming behind him. Time

143

cost money. His first wife had died in 1866 and two years later he had married again, Isabella née Piper, a local farmer's daughter, when she must have been just nineteen. A pretty trophy wife for a rich man and a good catch for a farmer's daughter. Money for youth and beauty, the oldest trade in the book. Looking at the lace on her dress and the large diamonds on her fingers and at her throat, Harriet decided that the farmer's daughter must have turned out to be high-maintenance indeed for the ageing Sir Gifford, who had been sixty at the time of their wedding. Had she exhausted him? Had he driven her mad with his fussy ways? Had they been happy? How could anyone say whether any marriage was happy? It was like looking at a tapestry, seeing nothing but knots and tiny stitches crawling over one another. You had to stand back to see the true picture.

The artist Forbes Houston had been easy to track down. He had been born in 1840 and brought up in Paisley, the son of a hat manufacturer. He had studied in the Hague and Paris, was a contemporary of William McTaggart, the leading Scottish Colourist, and had lived near Isabella and her husband. Both Houston and McTaggart specialised in broad brush strokes, though Houston's bold use of colour was said to have much

144

influenced the popular society painter Sir John Lavery. In European terms, Houston was an also-ran; he had not travelled widely enough to make the right connections. But Harriet could find real genius in his work, that same cheeky exuberance as in the portrait of Isabella. She found an old book of his paintings. A small girl in a red hat; two sisters gazing with a distinctly un-Victorian lack of sentimentality at a small dog, looking as if they wanted to get a good price for it. There was a worldliness about the eyes of his subjects which was quite shocking; they refused to play pretty pictures. She even came across a small self-portrait of a dark swarthy man with a high forehead and thick curly hair. By 1872, he must have been a sophisticated thirty-one-year-old. No wonder Isabella looked as if she was enjoying herself away from her elderly husband.

'The Inverclyde Collection,' whispered an assistant, piling huge scrapbooks on to the table in front of Harriet. Perhaps these would suggest why the artist had painted Isabella in the Inverclydes' home rather than her own? The scrapbooks had been bound in leather and made of paper so thick it was almost cardboard. The pages creaked as she turned them over, adorned with receipts and newspaper cuttings and menus and invitations, some of which were chronicled by Charlotte, the third Lady Inverclyde, who must have had a lot of time on her hands.

The Collection went on and on. Menus of grand dinners, newspaper cuttings detailing family largesse and successes at regattas all along the West Coast, charitable teas for Missionaries and poor children. The family name was Burns. Originally, old George Burns had run sailing ships delivering the mail between Glasgow and Liverpool in the 1820s. Very Onedin Line. Then, in the 1830s, he had gone into steamships, delivering the mail between Glasgow, Belfast and Liverpool. A good business with nice juicy Government contracts. In 1840 he had founded a consortium to put up £270,000 to launch the Cunard Line with Samuel Cunard, delivering the transatlantic mails. George Burns became chairman, quickly buying out the rest of the consortium. He bought the Castle Wemyss Estate in 1860 and retired there, leaving his son John Burns, later the first Lord Inverclyde, to take over from him.

By the 1870s Glasgow was fast becoming the second city of the empire, a fine, self-confident mercantile city putting up flaunt-it buildings like the Mitchell. Glaswegian businessmen had the flair to back their judgement, a potent combination of thrift and Samuel Smiles' dictum of self-help through education. Shipping the mails must have meant gaining control of the flow of business information, just like the Internet today; fortunes could be made if you were in at the beginning. Judging from these articles the Burns were ruthless in their battle for market share in the lucrative mail business. They had approached the Government and offered to carry the mails for nothing, seeing off all the competition.

Harriet found a picture of Castle Wemyss Estate. The Castle itself was a huge Gothic house, with towers and picture windows looking out on to sloping lawns. She could just make out the pier in the portrait, too, beyond which the Burns' pleasure yachts must have been moored. How grand it must have seemed to Isabella, up from the farm. In one scrapbook an article from *Scottish Field* written in 1914 in rather breathless reverential tones, described how the building was of red sandstone and stood on a cliff above the Firth of Clyde opposite Arran. How all the woodwork on the walls was enamelled white to give a sense of space and air, while the reception rooms were situated on the first floor to give wide panoramic views of the Clyde. Isabella in her chair had obviously been painted there; she had not been on the ground-floor level, judging by the view from the window behind her.

What fun, playing croquet there and eating cucumber sandwiches, strawberries and cream — the epitome of Victorian luxury living! Harriet closed her eyes and imagined the huge beds of rhododendrons sloping down to the sea, with the regulation walled kitchen garden to one side.

There was so much more to read. After leaving Glasgow University, John Burns had set up his own walking and networking club which he called the Gaiter Club, a dining club for cronies who liked to walk the Munros in the fashionable gaiters of the day. Club motto: 'There shall be no upright speaking', either alluding to the fact that there could be no ego trips, or possibly banning boring after-dinner speeches.

She nearly missed it — there were so many menus of heavy six-course dinners — but suddenly the hairs on the back of her neck began to tingle like a cat's: A Gaiter Club dinner menu, more splendidly engraved than usual. John Burns, Sir Gifford and old George Burns were guests on this Club night at Maclean's Hotel, Glasgow on 26 January 1870. The menu was *saumon with sauce concombre, comprote de pigeonneau, filet de boeuf, jambon de Brunswicke,* polished off by *tarte de rhubarbe* and *glâce d'orange.* Gifford Fairlie was there too. And the guest of honour was another member: the writer Anthony Trollope!

No wonder the menu had been pasted in so carefully. The creator of *The Barchester Chronicles* had been a Gaiter, one of John Burns' networking chums! What a mine of material Trollope must have gained from these men with their tales of business ruin and success.

The librarian did not take long to track down Trollope's collected letters. On 18 December 1869 he wrote to a friend from his country home in Waltham Cross: 'I purpose being in Glasgow on the 25 January — Tuesday — at some hour, viz as soon as I can get there from Hull; I have engaged myself to go to George Burns on the Wednesday and shall stay there Wednesday and Thursday . . . '

The dinner was on the Wednesday night, the day after his arrival. So had Isabella as the local beauty been invited over to Castle Wemyss Estate the next day to entertain the famous author? It would have been worth being a fly on the wall to hear them.

Two and two began to make five. Dimly, memories of Harriet's long-forgotten English lessons at school surfaced. Hadn't Anthony Trollope worked for the Post Office in Ireland? She remembered how impressed the class had been when the teacher had said he wrote 10,000 words a week while holding down a full-time job. And something else. Why had he arranged to stay with George Burns, even though it was John and not his father who had set up the club for his chums? At the time, Anthony Trollope was fifty-five, a retired civil servant, whereas John Burns was comparatively young at forty-one. Hardly of the same generation. John had already moved into Castle Wemyss and taken over shipping the mails, while old George, then seventy-five, was retired and living on the estate in Wemyss House. So it looked likely that Trollope was originally George's friend not John's — a friendship dating from his civil servant days when he had worked in the Post Office and negotiated mail contracts? The Burns had shipped the Irish mails for years before Samuel Cunard had showed up. The author and the retired shipowner would have had much in common to chat about over their brandy and cigars.

A Mary Ellen phrase darted into Harriet's mind: 'Something's failing t'sniff test, bejeesus!' and she sat back in her chair, smiling. Life was suddenly a party again.

Hackney

What was she doing behind the canvas? There was a scratching sound and a curse, then more scratching. A shaft of sunlight was scything down from the skylight, hitting him in a positive swathe of dusty air, its harsh rays showing up all the muck in the airless studio. The grind of traffic and the unmistakable stagnant odour of the canal mixed with acrylic paint disorientated Richard until he felt he was suspended in some smelly, noisy limbo. Scratch, scratch. Still he could hear Katya's charcoal or, worse, a palette knife working the canvas. Richard felt nervous but sat there posed with one arm on his hip, showing off his Dior watch and his malachite and gold cufflinks which flashed in the sunlight. He hoped the light would not show up his wrinkles.

Was it vanity or newly discovered paternal instinct which had drawn him here on a Wednesday afternoon when he should have been preparing for the following week's trip to Rome? The whole weekend had been a write-off, with the boys back home from school demanding money and trips to go-kart tracks where he'd nearly done his back in. Yet here he was trying to please another child, wearing the prescribed green suit and purple tie, and feeling like death. He'd thought she would be pleased to see him, but the girl had just nodded when he had shown up at the filthy ex-factory studios where she worked. He suspected the chair he was sitting on would leave nasty marks on his trousers.

Richard tried to keep looking at the fruit of his loins without a shudder. He took in the five studs in her ears and the tongue stud with wonderment and the sudden painful realisation that he was at last starting to get old. It was like that sad moment when you first look at a pair of open-toed sandals in a shoe shop window and find yourself thinking how comfy they look! He stretched up, trying to look handsome and virile.

'Stop wriggling, Rich!' Katya's voice was sharp. 'Now go on, what was she like then?'

'Well, luscious,' he replied, still puzzled to think that the voluptuous Amanda had produced such a skinny stick insect. Black eye shadow ringed Katya's panda eyes but the effect was hardly cuddly, more spidery. Richard sighed. This was obviously a very bad idea indeed.

'So, how did you and Mum meet?'

'Through friends. I'd always wanted to be an artist, and would hang around studios, when I wasn't working for my dad and putting in time at art college. Soon found out

I didn't have what it takes. But your mother was everyone's favourite model. Beautiful, lively and . . . '

'Did modelling turn her on?'

'Of course.'

Katya didn't answer. He could not even begin to fathom her relationship with her mother. Didn't want to. Amanda had always been trouble. Richard suddenly saw again that white skin, heard her fierce, cruel laughter. She had been famous for her practical jokes and he had played along. Now he could barely see Katya over the huge canvas. Was Amanda's giving birth to this skinny, feisty, angry girl her best practical joke ever, and at his expense? A love child he couldn't love, yet who seemed determined not to be ignored. There was a coldness and lack of involvement about Katya which was difficult to take. His charm singularly failed to work on her. Oh, why the hell was he doing this?

Richard had turned up punctually at three o'clock, having managed to induce a cab to bring him into the wilds of Hackney, a foreign land of pale children with runny noses, where even the heads of the flowers in the council park, he noticed, had their heads cut off, either by the east wind or the local vandals. He thought he had been rather brave in dismissing the cab. He had visited Flowers East Gallery in London Fields then walked down Mare Street to Katya's studio, in the expectation that he would be mugged at any moment. What struck him most strongly, however, was the feeling that somehow the contemporary art scene was moving further and further away from him into unfamiliar territory. It seemed to need flashing lights and interactive parts these days whereas he only knew about selling pretty pictures to hang on people's walls.

'So where do you meet *your* men?'

'Parties. Around.'

'Anyone special at the moment?'

'No, I do not have 'anyone special'. You sound like my mum. You'll be asking if I have a 'nice young man' soon!'

'OK.' Richard privately thanked the Lord he did not have to worry about her coming back late. 'Mind you get my mouth right, that's the key to getting a good likeness. So what do you do when you're not going out with friends?'

'Work. I'm doing more conceptual stuff now. And I work for my mum sometimes if she's got an event on, or veg out and watch telly. Soaps, mostly. *EastEnders, Brookside, Sampson House* on cable.'

'Did you know Harriet's first husband was in that?'

'Yes, she said.'

After which, nothing. It was like trying to talk to a cash machine, except the cash machine was slightly more animated.

The rediscovery of Katya had been all Harriet's doing. She had insisted that the girl should be free to get to know them and had actually taken her out to lunch, making every effort to be kind and interested. Obviously it was all water off a duck's back. He suspected that this wooing of Katya was designed to give Harriet more power over him. Wrong-footed, he had had to go along with it. But he hadn't realised until recently how much Katya had seen of his mother. Behind his back. Then of course she had turned up to the old girl's funeral — difficult and not a little painful. And worst of all this thin frowning Nemesis had more talent in her little finger than he had ever had. It was plain to see in the work lying around the studio, blazingly dangerous and exciting. How very complicated it all was.

Second marriages were difficult; even more so than first marriages if that were possible. Harriet had been furious with him for not telling her about the girl and, oddly, even more angry that he had never told Anne. Why? As if either of them had told him all the nitty-gritty about themselves. What was so wrong about mystery? Second marriages brought so much baggage with them. Laura, the other night, had gone on and on about Harriet's hubby Tom, while Billy had obviously adored his father. But Richard couldn't compete because the guy was dead. Strangely, Harriet never discussed him. Or her old business. She could cut parts out of her life without visible regret, whereas he still bled everyday for his lost gallery and his father.

They ticked so differently. Take money. She saw piggy banks while he saw cashflow. She saw assets, he saw sales. Mercer had rung again asking if she would sell him the picture but of course Richard had to say she was now writing about it for *KQ* and was up in darkest Glasgow. Mercer had sounded thoroughly pissed off to hear it.

Was this why he was subjecting himself to this sitting, to gain a picture of himself to get under Harriet's skin? Don't get mad, get painted. Yet he missed her. Without her the house was empty, dusty and dark. He was just no good on his own.

'Oi, Rich! Put your chin up. Is it true you used to give girls your card with one number wrong, and call yourself Rich O' Riley?'

'Did your mum tell you that?'

'Among other things.'

The door opened and a tall, very thin

156

young man stepped inside the room. He had a thick mane of hair and a starfish tattooed on one cheek.

'Felix!'

To Richard's astonishment this cold thin girl began to go pink. A miracle. Did she bat those panda eyelids? Almost. Certainly there was a gushing sound as she spoke.

'Hiya, Katch. You coming to Ute's housewarming, then?'

It might have been an invitation to the Ritz for Katya went white and then red. It was fascinating.

'Sure. See you there.'

For this generation, these words were clearly an exclamation of impassioned commitment. Richard studied them. They were a new species to him. The boy shrugged and looked at him.

'Who's this?'

'Rich Longbridge. My bio dad.'

'Cool.' Felix half nodded and walked out.

'Your *bio* dad! What's that, for God's sake?'

'Biological father. Well, you are. But then, most of my friend's parents are divorced and never see their fathers. So you're not alone.'

'So that's all right then, is it?' He and his fellow men were just so much sperm with chequebook attached. She hadn't asked to be born so perhaps he deserved the label, but it made him feel very small.

His mobile rang and Laura's voice came bouncing into the dusty air. 'Richard darling, it was so great to see you after all this time. I don't want to lose touch. H and I have some ground to make up, I know, but I want to make amends so I've a couple of comps for my show tonight. Any chance you're free? We could dine at the Caprice afterwards — my treat. Bury the hatchet.'

'Laura, how lovely. There's no hatchet, I'm sure it's ancient history. Sadly, though, Harriet's not here. She's in Glasgow.'

'What on earth for?'

'Researching her picture for that magazine bod we met on Sunday. You know what she's like — everything has to be done yesterday.'

'Well, I think H should have a media career and replace that old nun on the telly. Tell us what to think about art. I never know. Are you abroad too?'

'Nearly. Hackney.'

'Good God! Why?'

'Don't ask.'

'Well, I shan't. So are *you* game? Go on, bring a friend and we can eat out. Better than moping at home and heating up a tin of beans.'

'I'm rather more competent than that, Laura sweetie.'

'OK. But do come.'

'All right. See you there. Break a leg. 'Bye.'

'You're smiling,' Katya said accusingly.

'Sorry, ma'am, I'll try not to in future. Would you like to come to the theatre with me to see Laura Marchant?'

'That old slapper from *Sampson House*. Is she still alive?'

'Less of the old, please.'

'What's she in then?'

'A one-woman show.'

'Who about?

'Is that grammatical? Bette Davis.'

'Who's Bette Davis?'

'That's it! Had enough. Time's up.'

Richard stood up, stretching his stiff legs and looking out at the oozing green slime of the canal. He did not ask to see Katya's work, he had had enough staring into the black abyss of the generation gap for one afternoon. If he started praying very hard to the Good Lord, He might bless a bio dad with a miracle taxi heading in the direction of civilisation.

Glasgow

With a flash of plastic Harriet was out of the Mitchell Library and into a hire car, a very neat, very white Renault 19. It was exhilarating after the constraint of the last few months to feel like a jack-in-the-box who had escaped with the spring, with no notion of where to go or how long she would spend when she got there. Would Richard notice? Would he care?

Glasgow is a city built for fast drivers. It celebrates the car and its roads whoop past high newspaper offices and quayside warehouses. Glasgow, City of Culture, miles better, positive PR land. Soon she was up above the city, roaring over the Clyde with the sunroof open and the wind whipping up her hair. The radio blared as loud as she could bear for in such circumstances you need savage music, the louder the better. Blondie singing *Call Me*. Harriet had a glimpse of her younger self jumping up into the air, dancing with Tom. A seventies babe. Life had changed since the days when she had envied Debbie Harry her cheekbones. Another Harry with a complicated life.

'*Call me!*' As Harriet belted out the chorus, more or less in tune, she switched her mobile off. No, she didn't want Richard calling on her, thank you very much. He would be busy anyway, arranging his Rome trip, buying young art at hopefully low prices. His Italian was respectable now, she'd done a good job there.

'*Buongiorno, Signorina. Come sta?* 'Ere that all right then, 'Arriet?' She couldn't help smiling. '*Sono bellissimo, simpaticissimo e molto intelligentissimo.* How about that then, 'Arriet? Always liked those *issimos*!' What fun she had had giving Richard tele-lessons Italian! He was a natural. She hadn't even known it was Richard, of course. He'd just put on his old dad's cockney accent and fooled her into believing he was ace PR man Roger Descartes-Jones, keen as mustard to learn Italian at six in the morning over the telephone. With lots of excuses why they could never meet up face to face to plan the sessions. To think that a man so used to women falling over in their rush to get into his bed, had sat every day doing his Italian homework. What an irresistible compliment! How seriously he had taken his grammar exercises, faxing work through each evening to her poky office in the Portobello Road, little jokes squiggled in the margin. *Bravo!* Oh, the allure of courtship without sight. How expertly Pyramus had flirted with his Thisbe in Beginners' Italian. She'd never had a chance. Tumbled for it like soft spaghetti!

Vrroooom! It is hard to convey to the Scots themselves just how exciting Scotland can seem to a Londoner. Londoners tend to buy the Johnson line that if you are tired of

London you are tired of life. So, long past their sell-by date, they continue the capital treadmill, running so fast that the tiredness never catches up with them. Until they hit Scotland. Something in the air and the wind there seems to make them stop running and look about them. Then the matchsticks holding up their eyelids snap and their eyes, taking in unaccustomed heights and distance and fierce vivid colours, stay wide open all of their own accord. Then the bone weariness suddenly hits and they see that there is more to life beyond the M25 circle, beyond Harrods, the Tate and the West End; that in other parts of the country people are leading perfectly satisfactory lives without the crippling stress. It is like being given a brand-new map. Harriet, driving now like an Italian superstud, wheeled in and out of the traffic. Before long she was in open country with white cows and white cottages, with the shire fields sliding by. She should have got out years ago, she realised.

Finally, she descended a hill and the Firth of Clyde punched her between the eyes. Largs lay below, the brilliant paintbox blues and greens of sea and grass more like some optimistic poster put out by a desperate tourist board than the real colours of a real town.

She parked in the centre and walked along the road by the station. In front of her lay the sea and seagulls wheeling round a ferry. There were amusement arcades and shops selling knitted bonnets. The wind came out of the sun. Its freezing freshness took her breath away. Commuters poured out of the station from the early-evening train and schoolchildren clustered outside shops swapping coloured sweets. She wandered down the road along the seafront, taking in the green islands on the other side of the Firth, and saw the Tourist Board, the ice cream shops, the restaurants, tea rooms and amusement arcades stretching along the coast road into the distance; it was like being back in the sixties, a real British seaside town. She felt almost a child again. A ferryboat with passengers leaning out of it was making its way towards the quay above which seagulls wheeled hopefully. What had Isabella made of all this?

A girl with a blonde ponytail was washing a teashop window with a mop on a long pole, while groups of women, obviously having had their fill of tea and cakes, were standing outside pulling on their gloves. 'Cheery bye the noo!' they were saying. 'Cheery bye the noo.' Foreign country.

'Excuse me.' Harriet's voice, such a

163

perfectly normal sort of voice in London, suddenly came out sounding like Joan Collins in *Dynasty.* So terribly Noël Coward. 'Excuse me — could you tell me how to get to Wemyss Bay?'

The women stopped talking and looked at her kindly. Harriet repeated her request, wondering if they had understood. This time she seemed to sound more like Deborah Kerr in *The King and I.* Then one of the ladies took her arm. She was very old but upright, dressed in bright colours like a small bird. The red hat and yellow knitted scarf looked eccentric with the Raybans she wore against the fierce late-afternoon sun.

'Just you go along there for about five miles and you come into Wemyss Bay. Are you going for the ferry?'

'Is there still a ferry?'

'To Rothesay.'

'Actually I'm looking for Castle Wemyss, although I'm not sure if it's open today — I haven't checked.'

'You go on past the ferry, hen, up the hill and the Castle grounds are just on the left.'

'Thank you.' This time her voice was pure Julie Andrews. Harriet had the curious impression that the old woman was wanting to listen to her talk. To hear her vowel sounds cracking glass all over the pavement. It was a curious feeling. She was looking at her from behind the dark glasses intently and seemed about to say something, her head cocked to one side like an inquisitive canary. Then suddenly she turned her back and made off in the opposite direction.

★ ★ ★

Rush-hour commuter traffic swooped past Harriet for several miles as she followed the twisting coast road. On her left, the Firth of Clyde bordered by islands slipped past, the sun's early redness lapping the edges of the woodland on the opposite hills. At the small town of Wemyss Bay, she saw the ferry which took tourists over to Rothesay. Several recent passengers were crossing the road, laughing and joking, large ice creams in their hands. Then came a lodge house leading down to a private road, but she carried on up the hill and the Clyde disappeared. There was a stone wall, obviously belonging to the estate; she kept expecting to see a sign, perhaps from the National Trust, for the entrance. It would almost certainly have closed for the day, but it was worth checking out before finding a hotel for the night.

Then she found she had somehow passed it by so she doubled back and came across an opening where iron gates must once have been. 'Private Property' the notice said, yet unkempt rhododrendron bushes and the empty space where the gates must have been lent an air of neglect which encouraged her to walk in. She remembered being told as a student that there was no law of trespass in Scotland. Could this really be the Castle Wemyss Estate? At any minute she expected an irate landlord with a couple of rottweilers to come round the corner, but still she went on.

The ground was muddy and the vegetation thick. It was hard to tell where the path had once been. What had happened to the estate barely a century after the good and great had come to call? On and on she went, not noticing the mud on her trousers and the pieces of twig in her hair, for in her mind's eye she could hear the swish of Isabella's dress, after dinner perhaps, joining the gentlemen for a walk with their cigars. Then she rounded the bend and suddenly there it was, Castle Wemyss, framed by the Firth of Clyde.

It was a monster pile of rubble. Perhaps as high as several double decker buses and extending for several hundred feet. So much for the National Trust! Harriet stood there for several moments, trying to equate the house she had seen in the photographs with this scene of devastation. It wasn't even a ruin. She picked up a glazed tile which must have been from a fireplace, painted in Delft blue with just part of a sailing ship showing. She put it in her pocket and then was filled with anger. Unwisely she began to climb the pile. She knew any self-respecting surveyor like Robert would say, 'Far better leave it to the experts, old thing,' but still she scrabbled up the pile of rubble, suddenly furious that the background to Isabella's portrait was obscured.

Finally she stood on the top. Had Isabella been queen of the castle here as Harriet's London friends had suggested? Down below she could see more trees and to her left the remains of what must have been a Victorian kitchen garden, built to produce the family's fruit and vegetable in a micro climate. In front of her lay the Clyde. A yacht was sailing past, catching the evening wind. The sun, still huge although it was early evening, made her blink. What a waste. Yet the pragmatic side of her brain was starting to say that from the point of view of the magazine, a pile of old sandstone in a wilderness hardly made for eye-catching pictures.

Then she remembered the photographs of the lawn leading down to that magnificent sandstone pier. In one of the many pieces of hagiography in the county magazines it had said that John Burns and his friends had spent more of the summer on board his yacht than on shore. Lord Shaftesbury had called it 'his old Scotch home'. Hell! Harriet scrambled down the rubble and headed for where once the lawns had run down to the water. Now wild grasses towering five or six feet high grew in boggy water. She slipped and slithered, tripping over broken masonry and twisted roots. She knew that a farmer's daughter like Isabella would have hitched up her skirts and told her to pull herself together, but Harriet felt locked in the dream she had so carefully nurtured over the past few days. She could almost hear Isabella and Mary Ellen cackling behind her, sitting up on their cloud laughing at her disappointment. Her castle in the air.

She struggled on until finally she broke through the grass and saw before her the pier, now neglected and uneven but still with the same flagstones and the tall rusty pole to which small boats would once have been tethered. A man was sitting there. At first she had taken him for a rock, it was hard to tell through the grass. Then he moved and she saw that he was wearing a black leather jacket and had a fishing rod in his hand. Damn!

Now she felt both fearful and at an enormous disadvantage. Did he own this land? What could she say to him? Perhaps he was just a tourist like herself? Or a rapist? Now he had seen her and had stood up. A giant! Oh, God. Could she jump in and swim away? Hardly in these tight trousers. Resolutely she stepped forward.

'You lost, hen?' His voice was Scottish and young and did not sound thrilled to have the fish disturbed.

'No. I beg your pardon. I was looking for the Castle, you see. I didn't realise that it would be like this. In ruins. Are you one of the Burns family? I'm sorry if I'm trespassing but there was no gate.' Harriet's voice gushed out. She sounded like the Queen delivering a more than usually apologetic speech on Christmas Day.

'The Burns family? Are you joking? Which guide book have you been reading?'

He was smiling at her and Harriet wondered how she could get away quickly and back to her car. 'Ah, I see. It doesn't matter. I'm sorry to disturb you.'

'The Burns family died out years ago. This place has been sold for development. You English?'

'Yes. From London.'

'Hard luck!'

Was he joking? Didn't he like London? Incredible!

'You see, I rather hoped — well, I'm doing a bit of research for a magazine article.'

Wearily Harriet turned to leave. What a waste of time it had been, coming up here. Trollope connections or not, it was just depressing. Richard could sell the bloody painting. Her own fixation with it had probably only been because she had sold her business and was bored. Pathetic.

'Murdo Wilson,' the man suddenly announced, laying down his rod and coming towards her, holding out his hand. She automatically shook it and opened her mouth to say 'Harriet Gosse', only to find herself staring into his eyes. Violet eyes, smiling at her. Real violet this time, not out of a paintbox.

'How do you do?' said Harriet, sounding like Eliza Dolittle at the races in all her Cecil Beaton splendour. 'How do you do?'

6

London

The coach parties were in for Laura Marchant. All down Drury Lane the buses had decanted their perfumed, giggling occupants in good time for the performance and now the drivers were standing out in the evening sunshine, having a smoke. Of course they might have preferred *Cats* at the New London Theatre, but Laura Marchant at the tiny Fortune was a good night out. *All About Bette* gave La Marchant the chance to act shamelessly in a bewildering variety of gorgeous costumes. 'A mesmerising performance which will have you drunk on glamour!' — *Evening Standard*. It was doing good business and was almost sold out for the run.

Richard slipped into the stalls just as the curtain rose, near enough to see Laura in glorious technicolour. Tonight she was on top form. Her timing made the house rock and huge waves of sympathy rolled towards her. Her noisy gay following seemed to be concentrated at the back of the stalls.

171

When does an actress become a star? What is the mental adjustment that a good jobbing performer makes to earn the oofle dust? After years of tatting around doing small parts and out-of-town runs, Laura had now sprinkled herself with it in bucketloads. Her six years in *Sampson House* as the man-eating Davina, her part in *Auctioneer*, and several brilliantly witty chat show appearances on Channel 4 which had had the cynical post-modern young audience howling, had all helped her find the magic formula for national stardom; leaving Harriet, former landlady and best friend, far behind.

Tonight, Laura was Bette in scenes from *Of Human Bondage*, living by her wits; Bette in *The Maltese Falcon*; Bette in *Whatever Happened to Baby Jane?* Bette's battle with the studios, Bette's battle with her daughter. In the final act, the speech from *All About Eve* had the hairs rising on the back of Richard's neck and the theatre fell quiet. It was as if Laura was playing the audience like a zither, tossing it aside or lovingly wooing it into complete submission. At the end, there was loud applause and well-bred calls for 'More!' There would have been a standing ovation, had the English not been so very inhibited about such things. Laura, hard to recognise under the wigs, smiled and for a

172

second Richard could see her relief before greed and her enjoyment of the applause took over. Three curtain calls then she was off stage right.

As the lights rose there was a hurried powdering and blowing of noses and quick sweeps of lipsticks out of handbags as Middle England prepared to catch its coaches. Superlatives streamed past him as he stood outside in the fine evening watching the audience pile out. Next to the theatre was one of London's only two Church of Scotland kirks, dark and locked up now. It made him suddenly remember that Harriet was up there and, judging by her message, would be staying for some days. At the Ben Doran Hotel, Largs. Whoever Ben Doran was. Sounded like a nice Jewish boy.

In her dressing room Laura was in high-octane heaven. Her dresser was fighting with armfuls of forties flounces and wigs and Laura had already cracked open the champagne. 'Darling, you were marvellous!' Richard knew how a back stage Johnny should behave.

'I hope you're going to buy me a steak, Richard darling. I'm ravenous.'

'But of course.' He knew his lines. So much for her treating him.

After dinner they wandered down to the

American Bar at the Savoy. Laura had stopped gushing and Richard found it strange to be alone with her; he realised that it was the first time he had been out for dinner with a woman since he had been married. Harriet's spirit seemed to hover pleasantly but did not intrude.

'So love is the disease and marriage is the cure, is that it?' Laura suddenly said.

'What do you mean?'

'Five-year itch. Harriet going buggering off to darkest Scotland and you coming to see me like a wet weekend. I suppose you were in Hackney visiting that daughter of yours? Oh, yes, Georgiana told me all about the little love child. No secrets from her, you know. Now don't look like that! Lots of people have children knocking about. I had one adopted when I was eighteen — he might even have kids himself now. Horrible thought. Don't beat yourself up, Richard darling.'

'I'm not.'

'Well, you're looking positively haggard these days.'

'That obvious is it? Well, things are difficult. Business is tough. The new VAT changes are hell. And Eastern Europe is becoming a nightmare with the Mafia taking over. A French dealer was shot in Moscow last month.'

'Yes, I read about it.'

'Then there's been all the hooh-hah with my mother's estate, a Grade A mess. And Harriet doesn't see things as I do. She's so firm and crystal clear about everything. Her life is run on such straight lines. No wavering. No ducking or diving to sell a few pictures and help me out.'

'That's our H, straight as a die.'

'Exactly. Particularly about money.'

'Yes, money is very important for Harriet. What's hers is hers. But you see how much easier it is for duckers and divers like me and you to survive? Tom dies, apparently of a heart attack, and Harriet goes into mourning and does without sex for five years. As you probably know. Then I eventually tell her that he died while he was with me, and yes, we had been having an affair. You probably knew that, too. Anyway, then she rushes over and proposes marriage to you. After the wedding I was sacked, presumably because you'd filled the vacancy of confidant.'

'I didn't know — about you and Tom.'

'Didn't you? She *does* play her cards close. Well, I never realised she hadn't even suspected so in the end I told her, to make a clean breast of it. More fool me. But that's Harriet. It comes from being Jester's daughter. Try making sense of the world with a bonking bastard like that for a father, trailing round after him over two continents for most of your youth. She has to have fixed points, however destructive they are. Have you ever noticed how those paintings of hers are hung in straight rows, one after the other, like a sentence with a full stop at the end? Portraits — like that one she was going on about the other night — well, they're perfect, because the person in them can't change or let her down. They just hang there, fixed in paint.

'Harriet self-destructs almost all her relationships — with her father, with me, with other friends — because she won't risk messiness. Most people *are* messy. That's why she can't forgive me, because it would mean admitting that untidiness exists. Sorry, I don't want to sound disloyal. I wish I could make it right with her, but I can't. It didn't mean anything, that fling with Tom. It could have been anyone.'

'What was he like?'

'A lad. Big hands, big ideas, big bullshitter. He could make us laugh on the set but he needed Harriet to organise him like a mummy. And, like all little boys, he needed to be naughty once in a while. See what he could get away with. Poor Tom. But that's why she is as she is. Beautiful, inflexible, morally above reproach in all things — and infuriating, not because she hasn't been tested, but because she has and unlike the rest of us, has come through with flying colours.'

'I've never discussed Harriet with anyone before. I've never thought of her like that.'

'I'm still very fond of her. But I failed the test and so I can't compete. I've had to let her go. There's more to life than certainties. Take you, for instance. Just because you don't have the money you thought or the business you thought, doesn't mean to say there aren't thousands more new opportunities just out there, waiting. You need to start thinking like an actor. Put yourself about a bit and the phone will ring.'

'I'm forty-six, I doubt it.'

'Well, you're pretty gorgeous for forty-six. Go on, buy us a gin and stop sounding like a male menopausal Margo Channing. Luv!'

She made him laugh. Muscles in his face he had almost forgotten how to use began to ache. By the time they left the Savoy, Richard felt as if he had grown at least five or six inches and lost half a stone; he was almost walking like a rich man again.

Largs

Harriet was sitting cross-legged on the bed in the hotel room which the chambermaid had bullied into submission while she was down at breakfast pigging out on prunes and crispy bacon. Outside, the weather was crystal clear. The sun brought out the green hues of the hills opposite on the Isle of Bute. Photocopies and notebooks were strewn all over the bed. It was time to take an inventory of what she had learned.

She'd already spent a day on the Isabella trail, at Largs Museum and at the local newspaper offices, then down at Fairlie. Gifford Fairlie, Bt had married Isabella Piper of Cock Law Farm outside Fairlie in August 1868. The ceremony had taken place at the new Episcopal church on the Wemyss Estate. She was his second wife. In those days, Harriet supposed, if you were a rich and successful widower, you would not be called a dirty old man for marrying a girl young enough to be a granddaughter. Men had it all their own way then. Had they rowed over the time he spent away with his cronies at the Gaiter Club or walking the Munros, while she had been stuck at home getting on with her embroidery? Or had she been pleased to see the back of him?

They lived in Fairlie Mount, which Sir Gifford had bought with the profits from his milling business. He had received his knighthood in 1858 for services to Glasgow's civic life, wheeling and dealing on the council and endowing libraries and the Young Men's Christian Association, and had obviously decided it was appropriate to buy a house in a namesake village. What fun for Isabella swanning around as Lady Fairlie! Gifford had acquired a small racing yacht called the *Isabella* after his wife and his name featured each summer in the many Largs regattas. Then, in 1878, he suffered what the local paper called 'business reverses' when competition from American wheat began to bite and the City of Glasgow Bank failed. The Royal Bank of Scotland stepped in to help out the creditors and account holders, but shareholders like Gifford who had big holdings must have been hung out to dry. One night in September he drowned in the Firth of Clyde in a great storm which sunk dozens of ships and boats, causing many deaths. The *Isabella* hit the rocks too that night and so the widow was left alone at twenty-nine with a small daughter, facing all the insecurities of being poor and pretty. Like Harriet herself had once been.

After this date she could find nothing more

on Isabella. It was as if she had ceased to exist, her name disappearing from reports of Largs society. John Burns had gone on to become Lord Inverclyde, ever more rich, successful and respectable. While Isabella must have been that dangerous animal, a beautiful, single woman of few means. Society was suspicious of such mavericks.

At Fairlie, nothing seemed to remain of her either. Fairlie Mount itself was not even a pile of rubble. The land had long been used for private housing, and there remained only one wall at the back of a garden centre which had once formed part of the kitchen garden. The transitory nature of property suddenly hit home to Harriet; all the current newspaper stories about John Major and interest rates seemed suddenly irrelevant, for houses currently being paid for so expensively through mortgages each month, could so easily metamorphose into farmland or high-rise blocks in a few generations, given a Depression and a couple of wars.

She then reread her photocopy of an article in *The World*, dated 23 October 1889. In its time it must have served the same sort of readers as *King's Quarterly*. She had been lucky finding this in the Mitchell for John Burns' eldest daughter Caroline had made critical annotations in the margin.

Mr John Burns At Castle Wemyss

Castle Wemyss, with its covered turrets, crowstepped gables, high-pitched roofs, flamboyant windows and heavy battlements, is thrown into bold relief by clumps of Austrian firs, sturdy larches and clumps of rhododendrons . . . it is an undisputed fact that the view from Mr John Burns' drawing room extends over no fewer than six counties and stretches from Kilcreggan to the Cumbraes . . .

Next to this Caroline Burns had written, 'John Burns . . . later added a hideous wing which spoiled the appearance of the house.' She had obviously had no time for hagiography. Had she known Isabella?

Anthony Trollope was supposed to have sketched Castle Wemyss as Portray Castle in The Eustace Diamonds, and it was here that he thought out and wrote a great portion of Barchester Towers *. . . Your host [John Burns] forgets all about the cares of business at Liverpool and Glasgow and laughs as heartily as he did when the uproarious merriment of Norman Macleod, Anthony Trollope and J.B. at a Highland tavern provoked an imputation of* *inebriety, although they had partaken of nothing stronger than tea and herrings.*

Opposite this: 'The butter's spread too thick!' Caroline must have written this for her sister-in-law Lady Inverclyde, who had put together some of the Collection, showing a nicely cynical sense of humour. But whatever her criticism and corrections elsewhere on the article, she had not disputed that Castle Wemyss was the model for Portray Castle in *The Eustace Diamonds*. The chronology fitted. Trollope was already writing the book when he had attended the Gaiter dinner in 1870. He had talked about 'castle building' in his autobiography when discussing how he thought out his stories. Hardly surprising when he must have visited one so often. But how ironic too that *Barchester Towers*, that most English of novels, had been thought out there.

Harriet had now read right through his autobiography and had trawled the book-shops and local libraries. It struck her as interesting that Trollope had never mentioned his Scottish friends in his autobiography. But what ex-civil servant would want to highlight his junkets with those who had become super-rich in the postal business! His long list of earnings also struck Harriet as iffy, as they would anyone who had run a profitable small business. Earnings from every book were detailed in the autobiography, totalling £68,959 17s 5d. A huge fortune then. Top-earning books were *Can You Forgive Her?* at £3,525 and *He Knew He Was Right* at £3,200. Even *The Eustace Diamonds* had come in well at £2,500. But at the bottom there was an intriguing entry: Sundries, £7,800. Over 11% of his total income completely unaccounted for, unexplained. More than ten times his income when he had been a Surveyor for the Post Office in Ireland. Sundries? For doing what? What a convenient catch-all term! Richard liked words like that at the end of his accounts. Like his father, old George Longbridge. Whereas Harriet had always detailed for the taxman every penny of her income and outgoings, to the point of driving her accountant mad. She needed clarity to feel secure. On the other hand, clarity was what ambitious duckers and divers really hated. Say no more, squire. A bit of this, a bit of that. So where had Trollope derived his sundries?

He had resigned from the Post Office on 7 September 1867, yet in her hand lay a photocopy of another Gaiter dinner invitation complete with members list including the name Anthony Trollope dated 12 November 1866. So he had been one of Burn's happy band of mates. Was that the reason why he had been overlooked for promotion and instead resigned without taking his pension? To relinquish both salary and pension seemed a very extreme action for someone as money-minded as Trollope. The autobiography had detailed his dealings with moneylenders as a young man and his terrible insecurity about money so it didn't seem to make sense for him to walk away from financial advantage — unless he'd been pushed into it. On the quiet. 'Don't want any fuss, old boy,' his bosses might have said in their mahogany-panelled offices. Reputation had its value too, after all. No one could say she was not getting some good stuff for her article!

The Gaiters had obviously been an important grouping. How many had admired Isabella's glamour? She must have made every A list party. Exhilarating stuff for a girl off the farm. It was beginning to come together.

And yet the mighty Burns family died out in the 1950s and now their splendid castle was reduced to a pile of rubble. Families were either in ascendancy or in decline. 'Clogs to clogs in three generations' was the old saying.

Harriet thought of old George Longbridge with his ducking and his diving all over the East End, grubbing out a fortune with his Romany luck, and of Mary Ellen who'd decided that in the end it had not been worth hanging on to, her son almost scrubbed off the balance sheet. With divorce and remarriage nowadays, life was even more messy. All you could do was cling on to assets like a crab.

Harriet left the hotel and walked along the coast road into the town. The east wind made her eyes stream and she took in big gulps of salty air. All of it was foreign to her. The buns in the bakers were different; the colours of the buildings were different. The charity shops too were not the shiny London designer variety but had itch-inducing window displays full of woolly bobble hats and rayon dresses and baskets of sheepskin gloves. But on the plus side there was a sense of space. The eye could range for miles here. Almost everywhere in London it was caught up short by buildings and street furniture. John Burns had been able to see six counties from his first-floor drawing room; no wonder the all-conquering Isabella had wanted her portrait painted there.

The young man Harriet had met the previous day had suggested she should visit his shop. Murdo — a good Scottish name. Eventually Harriet found The KOOC in the square opposite the Tourist Board. Copper jugs were strung across the entrance, with huge baskets of old books and magazines and knick-knacks pushed outside. It was as if the shop had simply burst its buttons and spewed its contents out into the square for relief. 'Short for knocked off old crap,' he had told her, laughing at the joke. To her London eyes, it looked more thrown out than knocked off. Murdo. Like a Lachlan or a Gregor, striding through the heather in a kilt after eating his bowl of porridge oats. Nothing like a bit of racial stereotyping.

He was inside, up a ladder, hanging iron buckets and assorted horse brasses on a frame by the window. Two students were mooching around the paperbacks, and in the middle, sitting on the table drinking coffee and swinging her legs, was the old lady from whom Harriet had asked directions. She was dressed head to foot in bright purple with a large amber necklace and two improbable peacock feathers in her hat which curled around her head to her neck. She had a beaky nose, and every so often dipped a hand into a bag of cakes which lay on old copies of the *National Geographic*, beside her.

'Good morning.'

Again Harriet's voice metamorphosed into cut crystal. The young man and the old woman looked at her. Incredibly, they had the same intense, unnerving violet stare which had followed her around the drawing room at home for weeks.

'You found it then?' The old lady was smiling at her mischievously.

'Castle Wemyss, yes. Though it was not as I'd expected.'

'Gran, she thought it would be owned by the National Trust!' Murdo and the old woman laughed.

'How do you do? I'm Harriet Longbridge. As I told your grandson, I'm doing a bit of research.'

'That's nice.'

The old woman did not introduce herself but continued to drink her coffee. Unsure what to say next, Harriet looked around the shop and remarked on a couple of the prints.

'English, are you?' said the old woman eventually.

'Yes, from London. Mrs . . . ?'

'We get a lot of visitors in the summer up from London. In the winter it's nice and quiet.' The old lady sipped more coffee and stared at Harriet. She clearly preferred the winter.

It was the eyes. These people had to be

related to her quarry, unless the colour was a local genetic characteristic. Harriet took a deep breath. 'I'm researching into a girl called Isabella Fairlie who lived here towards the end of the last century.'

'That's nice,' the old woman commented again.

The phone rang and Murdo came down off the ladder. He was rather beautiful, Harriet thought, in a big, slightly brutal way. To him she was probably just another snotty English tourist. On the table by the phone she noticed piles of electoral leaflets for the Scottish National Party, then dimly remembered that Scotland had just had local elections.

'Did he get in, the SNP candidate?' she said to the old woman, to be polite.

'Aye. In our ward.'

'Oh. Good,' said Harriet. The old woman continued to sip and stare. She had obviously never been told it was rude to stare. Or perhaps she had.

'Look, excuse me,' Harriet tried again. 'You see, you have her eyes — Isabella Fairlie's, I mean. She lived over a hundred years ago but I just I wondered if you might be descended from her — related in some way?'

'Why do you want to know anyway?'

'Well, you see, I inherited a picture. Look.'

Harriet took out the photograph and

unfolded it on the table.

Murdo was now laughing on the phone, talking about *ceilidhs* and boats and tides. He took money from the students at the same time and slung it into the till, slamming it shut by kicking it with one foot, before taking the phone out into the front entrance. The old woman picked up the photo and stared as if she could eat it.

Intuitively Harriet knew she had got her. Years of selling had taught her the value of silence. Give her time, thinking time. Then the old woman just plonked the picture down.

'Meet me in McGuffey's tomorrow at seven. That do you?'

Her accent was so strong Harriet nearly missed the sentence which was flung at her as the old woman slid down off the table.

'Thank you,' said Harriet, sounding like a nice girl from the Home Counties who had just been to such a jolly tea party. 'I'm sorry, I don't know your name . . . ' But the old woman had already ducked underneath Murdo's arm and was out of the shop, walking quickly across the square.

Odd. Harriet decided to wait for Murdo to finish his call.

Looking round, she could see this was exactly the sort of shop Richard loathed.

Dust everywhere, the cheap, the nasty and the intriguing all mixed up together, in clashing periods and styles. She turned the pages of a book of fashion plates, priced at £15. The Victorian ladies looked pale and uninteresting compared to the passion of Isabella. That old woman *obviously* knew who she was! How old was she anyway? Eighty perhaps or older, hard to tell because she still moved so quickly. If she was related, how reassuring that genes were carried through the centuries, imperfections and advantages sneaking out in baby after baby. Harriet fancied that she could see even now just a hint of Isabella's magic in the way Murdo was laughing down the phone. How old was he? Twenty-five, twenty-six? A little older than Katya, but without the hard shell of indifference.

Harriet started walking around the shop. Scottish history and culture were big sections, there were six copies of *Whisky Galore* and dozens of books on the Clearances. Eventually, she came back to the piles of Scottish National Party leaflets. She picked one up and read it: *An Independent Scotland in Europe.* 'Last year we secured 33% of the vote in the European elections, returning two of Scotland's eight MPs.' There was a stridency and determination there which appealed to her, reminding her of student days in Edinburgh when she had first discovered the minefield fact that she was English not British. Things had obviously moved on since then. You could tell from all the St Andrew's flags fluttering around the town. How foreign to someone more used to the louche delights of the reigning navy blue regime of Kensington & Chelsea. Richard had found plenty of new clients at the Tories' last Christmas Fair, charming his way through the blue-rinsed Tory hens like a hussar, with Georgiana as cheerleader. It was probably the only thing he and Jester, who was somewhere on the right of Galtieri, had ever agreed on. Mary Ellen on the other hand had kept the red flag flying almost single-handed in her mansion block. Harriet found herself almost missing her mother-in-law these days.

'Excuse me, missus!'

A short young man with a lot of red bushy hair and the most extraordinary Brezhnev eyebrows she had ever seen had come in and was grabbing the leaflets.

'Waste not, want not, eh?'

'I beg your pardon?'

'Shug, mate, are coming out the night?' Murdo had broken off his conversation and was covering the phone with his hand.

'Aye,' said the young man, Shug.

What a funny name, thought Harriet. Sounds like a carpet. No, that's shag pile. The thought in connection with gorgeous Murdo made her smile.

'Found anything interesting, hen?'

He had come off the phone and was piling up more of the leaflets into Shug's arms.

'Well, I'm just re-acquainting myself with the joys of the Scottish National Party. I was a student in Edinburgh in the eighties.'

'Ah. Then you went south again. How could you leave us?'

'I know, how could I?'

'So, just what are these whingeing Scots up to, you're thinking?'

'No, not at all. I wish the English could rediscover some of your national pride.'

'You do all right. Anyway Scotland will be independent one day and the English will just have to get used to it.'

'But could you really afford to go independent? Ian Lang has just said there'd be an eight billion pound deficit?'

'What a big wean he is! With North Sea oil, we'd be the eighth richest country in the world on our own. Anyway when Labour gets in they won't be able to sell us down the river like last time. They're committed to a referendum on devolution and that'll be just the beginning.'

What do you say to all that, as a nice English girl? 'How interesting, and isn't the weather wonderful!' Just like the Queen Mother?

'Och, Murdo, give the lassie a break. The election's over. We've packed up the soap box.' Shug had come back from his car for another load of leaflets.

Scotland without England, what an unfamiliar idea. Though Murdo's glorious eyes would convert anyone to Independence.

'Your grandmother said you did well in the local elections?'

'Aye, we won. Increased our vote too.'

'Oh, good.'

Just when does a generation gap open up? You're bowling along year after year feeling twenty-five inside — twenty-one on a good day. Then you go back to a place you once visited as a student, look in a shop window, and suddenly see a grown-up woman in a well-tailored jacket and a Bruton Street hair cut. Harriet now remembered visiting Largs en route for a camping holiday in Arran with a crowd of friends in a van. She had worn a blue beret and vamp lipstick and they had eaten ice cream in a tea shop. She remembered the photographs taken on that holiday. How young she had looked then, free and full of hope. Murdo would have been at primary school at the time. Horrible thought.

'I'm meeting your granny tonight at McGuffey's Bar, can you tell me where it is?'

'Just along by the station.' Shug had come back in for the final load of leaflets. 'Just you watch her, though. Mad Izzy drinks brandy by the bucket.'

'Why do you call her Mad Izzy, Shug? Do you mind if I call you Shug?'

'She's always been called that because she's mad. And Izzy short for Isabella.'

Yes! Harriet could have hugged him.

'Anyway, you watch out because she eats English tourists like salt and vinegar crisps,' Murdo warned.

'Ah, well, one way of getting rid of the Oppressors!'

The two young men laughed and the little shop seemed to shake in sympathy. It was rather fun finding a sympathetic audience, Harriet decided.

Whitechapel

THE REAL MEANING OF MONEY — WORK BY FIVE PROMISING YOUNG LONDON ARTISTS. THE NATIONAL BANK PLC IS PROUD TO SPONSOR THIS UNIQUE EVENT.

Wicked to see artists mixing with business-men! Katya could tell by the polite, uneasy wonderment of the grey suits that they could not see the point of these works. They still had to sleep at night after all. The two groups were as different as sheep and goats, or lions and camels. Both insecure as hell about money. Both with their own high moral ground to gaze down from. As good as a play. Katya knew that one day she would be more than a promising young artist. She would collect. It was just a matter of finding the right niche. She would make art pay. For money was as important to her as these overpaid sleek bastards. You just had to visualise it and the freedom it would buy you.

A five-inch-thick metal chain wound round the gallery space as if imprisoning the politely cheerless throng who had come up from their City offices to the Whitechapel Gallery. Attached to the chain every eighteen inches was a money box with a key in the lock. Blown up on screens were actuarial tables showing just how debt could accumulate. The pattern of the numbers had a beauty all its own. A deadly science where a person could owe £500 and at 20% compound interest could end up owing thousands. Some of the more cheerless banker types were standing glass in hand checking the figures; anything was better than having to interact with the artists who wandered round hoovering up the free drink.

Katya's own installation was causing ructions. She'd adapted an old slide projector. Visitors could touch a button and bank statements and loan arrangements and other financial details would appear on a large screen. People were laughing for here were cashcard payments to the off-licence, to the Caprice restaurant, to a well-known Welbeck Street massage parlour, a four-figure direct hit for the mortgage, and so on and on. A fascinating glimpse of others' financial stew. She had found the actual statements outside the back entrance of the bank's Piccadilly branch. There had been poorly tied bin bags waiting for the dustmen. The bags were too full and slit, the wind threatening to decant them into the street. Hundreds of customer records were potentially on view, confidential details of overdrafts and loan arrangements. Had banks never heard of shredders? She had taken them home and had inked out the logo and the names, though through the bank's own carelessness she now had details of hundreds of customers' financial details. Some very well-known customers indeed. How careless of an MP actually to put through cashcard payments to a massage parlour. She could have cleared her overdraft by selling this to the Sunday tabloids.

Every sixth button press showed up a card which explained how the statements had been found. Then the smiles would suddenly fade. The execs would never know whether these statements had come from their bank or not, though by the worried looks she knew they probably did. A little joke on her sponsors. Katya had explained her ideas to Harriet at the funeral. She was cool. She'd told the girl that her idea was showing what Italians called *'il cullo'* of banking, the arsehole. Customers went into the marble-floored front of the bank, bursting with solidity, integrity and trust, and then their personal details and records, for want of the cost of a shredder, were excreted into cheap plastic bin bags for Westminster Council to clear up. A perfect metaphor. Whereas money itself was pure energy, flowing through buildings and lives for good or ill. Katya took a sip of champagne. This was bloody good.

The bankers' wives had been let out for the evening on good behaviour. They toyed with their champagne flutes, laughing prettily like little corporate dolls. Their nails gleamed in the gallery lights, their clothes were stylish, expensive but discreet, not rocking the hierarchy. Katya could even tell which wife belonged to which husband; in the corporate pecking order, no superior's wife could be outshone by a junior's spouse. And they were all spouses, solid rocks on their fingers, no messy liaisons here. Katya christened them the Whining Wendys, for they were just the type who would wait until their overworked providers were on the second drink of the evening before starting: 'Darling, *when* d'you think we could buy . . . ' She'd heard them at work this evening, whining for an extension, a second foreign holiday, a new car. Get him in a good mood with the free champagne. Though of course it was anything but free. The men here were paying for it with their life's blood, poor bastards.

'Lighten up, Katch, get a life!' Felix Rosen, another of the promising young artists, had come over to her. He was dressed unexpectedly in a Paul Smith suit and wore a black patch over one eye. Conjunctivitis, he said, but it gave him a convenient air of glamour.

'You're a bit bitter and twisted about money, aren't you?'

'I'm not.'

'Oh, please, bin bags and bank statements — how morbid!'

'Piss off!'

He bent nearer to her and Katya could smell him. It was dizzying. What was his magic? Money probably, Hampstead Garden Suburb moolah, which was why his show had been based on the power of the City and had been the most popular with the sponsors. Both his parents were literary agents; his mum had been in earlier. Instead of being embarrassed by her, Felix had paraded her around to meet the bank's top brass. The diamonds on her fingers had been so large she had barely been able to lift her hand to say 'how do you do?' Interesting to see the effect that jewels could have on people who worshipped money. That flicker of eyes over those rings before the smile was painted on to the face. Katya thought of her pearls now, safely stuck under her mattress in her flat. She had been offered £4,000 for them but she damn' well knew they would cost £25,000 if she had wanted to buy them in the shop. What a mark-up! What a con.

Then she saw her mother enter the gallery. The Whining Wendy who didn't have a man to whine to. Amanda was obviously looking for her. Katya could imagine how many tastefully printed business cards nestled in that Prada handbag. Amanda had been to the hairdresser and her make-up had been carefully applied so that she looked quite starry in a way. Katya could almost see what those old guys had found to paint in her.

Then she saw Richard come in. In work mode. Oh, God. She could tell by the way he greeted the bank's chairman with such easy familiarity. But he looked a bit fragile compared to how she had first seen him. Of course he was not now as rich as he'd thought he'd be which must affect his standing with this lot. How could she convey that fragility in his portrait? Something about the skin . . .

How interesting to watch them, for neither Amanda nor Richard knew the other was there. The two people who'd created her were circulating professionally at either side of the room like repelling stars. Amanda had reached the kitchen table where one million pieces of paper had been arranged in piles with a photocopied £50 note on the top. You have to visualise money to make it, the card explained. Katya had spent too many nights sitting down with a pair of scissors cutting up old envelopes.

Felix was looking at her. 'Why don't you take that disgusting stud out of your tongue? Who wants to shag a girl with metal in her mouth? Even mercury fillings make me puke.'

'What's wrong with my stud?' she snapped back at him.

'It's dangerous and it's costing you, because you're not fitting the corporate bill. If you want to make money, you have to play the right games. Don't rock the boat.'

'Like you with your eye patch and suit, I suppose?'

'Sure. I've just picked up twenty-five grands' worth of commissions this evening.'

'What! For installations?'

'Please, get real. No, I've nicked your idea, sweetie. Portraits. Get established and it's £80K a time with the big corporate boys. Think of a number and double it. It won't take me long. But I don't mind starting with these poor old bitches. They need the attention.'

Katya wished he would pay *her* some attention. She could just imagine what the portrait sessions would end with. But twenty-five grand!

'How's your big, broke bio dad's piccy coming along? Do you know he's over there? I read all about his mummy. Dear, dear. What a shock for both of you. Better get painting.' Then Felix was off like a sniffer dog on a successful trail.

Simultaneously, Richard and Amanda saw her from different parts of the room and came towards her. Katya shone a bright smile at them both. It was as if they formed a triangle, with herself as the sharp point.

'Hello, Mum. Hello, Rich.'

'Richard!' Amanda literally jumped and spat out the word like a cat, loud enough for one or two of the executives to stare uneasily.

'Amanda darling, you look so jolly. How super to see you. Hasn't our girl done well?'

Richard kissed her with practised ease, though Amanda's body was still tense with shock.

'*Our* girl?'

'Yes. Anyway, if it's any comfort, I am commonly known as her bio dad. You should be proud of her.'

'Don't be absurd. Of course I am.'

Neither sounded as if they were proud of her. They were squaring up to each other. Katya suddenly realised then that she was merely an extension of their own egos. Perhaps you had to be grown up before you really knew your parents' agenda. No, Felix had the right idea. The only way to insulate yourself was to make so much money nothing could ever touch you again. Like a crab, Katya side-stepped away. Amanda and Richard did not notice. Too busy giving each other press releases on their lives.

Why had she been brought up not knowing her father? What sour battles had gone on over her baby head? Only money seemed to make sense. Positive energy. Katya put down her glass and went over to the kitchen table.

To keep the piles of paper intact, she had stretched cling film tightly over the top and wound it underneath the table and right down the legs. With just one fingernail she could puncture it and crawl inside that cocoon of wealth. She could visualise just how warm a place with all that money could be. No one would ever be able to touch her again.

7

Largs

Harriet had done her stuff on the phone with the Scottish Registry of Births, Marriages and Deaths. Isabella's death certificate would soon appear. She had also mooched around the old cemetery at Fairlie and found Sir Gifford's gravestone complete with weeping angels. He was 'the greatly loved husband of Isabella'. Had he been greatly loved? Who knew? Of her there had been no sign.

Harriet had told the hotel that she would be staying a few more nights. It made sense to have a little holiday and some space to think. Was she a phoney? Probably. But this research was a perfectly golden excuse to take a break with Billy at school; Jester rarely missed her and Mary Ellen was now a memory; she had left behind all the mess for solicitors and other fee-munching professionals to sort out. Now the Ayrshire wind and sharp sea smells of fish and seaweed made her feel alive and in holiday mood, wanting to eat ice creams and kick off her shoes and feel the sand between her toes.

The moment she opened the door of McGuffey's Bar, the smoke and the smell of stale beer hit Harriet in the face like a cosh. A group of men stood by the bar watching a football match, groans and cheers punctuating the action on the field. Teenagers were playing a whining fruit machine; a few morose older married couples were staring into pallid fish suppers, making small talk. At the rear a large group of women were knocking back the sherry and roaring with laughter. Crisp packets were already piled up on the table and the young barman was trying to pass drinks from his tray while the women threatened to pinch his bottom. The tray wobbled. There was a small stage in front of which was a small dance floor, partially covered by Formica-topped tables and chairs.

Mad Izzy was sitting there with a Guinness, a packet of untipped cigarettes and the racing pages for company. She had a cigarette drooping from her mouth and was wearing a purple coat which seemed too big for her, and a red beret which gave her the look of a more than usually desperate member of the French Resistance.

'Good evening, Mrs Finlay. Can I get you anything?' Harriet's voice was drowned out by loud male cheers at a goal scored and Mad Izzy looked up and gestured to her full glass.

So Harriet fought her way back to the crowded bar, waited to be served, and in a voice which seemed to sound like Mary Poppins flirting with Dick Van Dyke asked for a pint of Guinness and a glass of white wine. The men smiled at her indulgently before returning to debate just why Kilmarnock were playing crap.

Mad Izzy neatly arranged her full pints next to one another. 'I don't know if I should talk to you, really. Not if you're going to dig up dirt on the family. But it would be fun to see the old girl in print. She'd have liked that.'

Harriet began to assure her that digging dirt was not the idea, but Mad Izzy began to cough and it was several minutes before she got her breath back. Harriet was strangely shocked that the divine Isabella should be referred to as an old girl.

Izzy had obviously worked for the Spanish Inquisition in a previous existence for it was not long before Harriet was telling her about her own life and not Isabella at all. She told her about Billy, Jamie, Richard, Jester, and life in London, but as usual the moment she said she had once been married to Tom Gosse, long-lost heart throb of *Sampson House*, Mad Izzy's attitude changed. It always did and Harriet always dreaded it.

People always asked the same question: 'What was he like?' How could you ever tell anyone what anyone else was 'like'? Even when you were married to them and had a child? 'Oh, he was such a lovely man. He died of a heart attack in the process of fucking my best friend,' was the one answer she had yet to give.

For once Mad Izzy did not ask questions; she seemed instead to take her more seriously. Harriet took out the photograph of the portrait out of her handbag and Izzy looked at it. 'That was my granny,' she said as if she had been looking at a holiday snap. 'I haven't seen this since 1946.'

Like most family histories it had a bit of everything: sex, money and missed opportunities, for the real Isabella had only been human after all. Sir Gifford had apparently been a decent old stick but had rowed with John Burns over mail shipping routes and made bad decisions during the 1870s, which had meant that poor old Isabella had not been happily swanning about in society for some months before her husband drowned in the Clyde. She had been left with one daughter, Eugenie, Mad Izzy's mother, who had been sent off to live with Gifford's sister. Very strict and very proper with maids who changed uniforms in the afternoon and where every possible economy was made with Presbyterian fortitude.

Isabella had somehow managed to salvage an income from the wreckage; Gifford had apparently had money settled on her in a small trust in the good times and she had quietly salted away possessions which she could sell at her parents' farm, so with her child off her hands she headed for the bright lights of Glasgow, renting rooms off Sauchiehall street. An art school was nearby and Isabella had taken classes there. But the need to remarry must have been pressing, so she had married a dentist in his fifties by whom she had two children and then, less than a year after his death, she'd had an illegitimate child. No one knew who the father was. What followed was a rapid descent down the class ladder. The money went and finally Isabella had married a railway worker from Govan, producing another child. After he had died, she had returned to live off Eugenie and her Minister husband. Her own brother who had taken on the family farm had died and she had nowhere else to go to. And so Isabella moved into the Manse, stretching her daughter's Christian charity almost to breaking point and scandalising the Largs neighbourhood with her tales of Glasgow, high and low. What a life! She had known Charles Rennie

Mackintosh when he had been starting out, and the celebrated not-proven murderess Madeleine Smith. She spent her last days telling stories, drinking brandy, and being a constant source of frustration to her respectable relations.

'What happened to the other children?' Harriet asked.

'One went to India, two went to Australia and the girl married in Glasgow. They didn't get on. Isabella wasn't much of a mother — she seemed to shed children like a chameleon. She and my mother were never close. Well, my mother had grown up hardly seeing her. She would say Gran could charm the birds out of the trees, forever bribing the small boys of the neighbourhood to go out and buy her brandy.'

By now the pub was full and the football was over. Small groups of men seemed to be in post-match analysis and groups of young people were taking up every table. Harriet moved closer to the old woman. 'What happened to your mother — Eugenie?'

'Died in 1947. My mother and my father, the Minister, found Isabella a trial. They would read the Bible at breakfast. I was brought up on the good book morning, noon and night. My father would thunder from his pulpit, scaring us all to buggery. But Isabella

209

would have none of it. She said God helped those who helped themselves and on most days when she was well, she'd be out, buying and selling old stuff. Murdo has taken after her. And me too in my way. She loved jewellery most and would always be going to Glasgow with a piece to flog at the West End jewellers. They used to say she could sniff out good pieces like a pig after truffles. I'd get to hear her stories of the Burns family and meeting London aristocrats up for the yachting. The treasure hunts and the balls. She said everyone in Largs who mattered dropped her after Gifford's death, her family were only small tenant farmers after all. But she was never bitter. It was always the next opportunity with her. She was fun. I was ten when she died. She was seventy, her heart just gave out. My mother wrapped up the picture in a cloth and stuck it under the bed. She never ever spoke of Gran, even though there were pieces of hers all over the house.'

It was a curiously depressing tale, Harriet thought, but typical too.

'But why did you ever sell the painting?'

'Money,' said Mad Izzy, as if it was obvious. 'I loved that picture. I loved my gran too, but my father died in 1939 and we had to leave the Manse. We went to live in a small cottage in Kilbirnie and I got a job as a telephonist in Glasgow, travelling up and down by train. But things were tight. My mother needed a nurse often, and medicines, and they cost a lot of money then. During the war we took in evacuees from Glasgow but they usually left us with fleas and often nicked the silver, if we hadn't sold it already. My ma hoped I would marry well, but it didn't happen. I was too rackety, I suppose, too fond of my own way. One day, just after the war, I came back from work to find she had given it to the local auctioneers. I was furious, went round to see them and begged them to give it me back but the young man there said it had been sold that day to a London dealer before the sale. I was gutted and told him for five minutes what I thought of him.'

Izzy smiled and took a big gulp of Guinness. 'He was young Alec Finlay. His pa had worked on the railways but he was keen to better himself so he married me. I was well on the shelf at the time — thirty-seven. He was twenty-five. People were a wee bit shocked. Toy boys had no been invented then! Then Maggie, that's my daughter, came along and we were happy. He made me laugh!'

Izzy's smoky laughter crackled around the pub and made others turn and smile. It had obviously been a love match.

'You must come tomorrow morning, hen,

I've a tin of papers you can go through. Just promise me you won't write anything bad about her? Isabella was a gutsy girl with funny coloured eyes like me, who loved life and men and looked good in a picture.'

'What happened to the artist? I know he died in 1906, but I wonder whether she carried on knowing him?'

'Don't know. Though the Houstons are a big family round here. Oh, look! My Murdo's about to strut his stuff. Isn't he grand? See that wee blonde lassie? That's his Rena. Just got engaged, God help him.'

Something jolted in Harriet's mind and she felt uneasy. Isabella was not exactly material for a glossy magazine like *Kings Quarterly*. Who would want to know about a girl who went off the rails with a Govan railway worker, for God's sake? Its readership was nothing if not aspirational. Give up, Gosse. Dig some more into Trollope's dodgy dealings instead, then go back to London and get a proper job. Did she even want to keep the picture now? That mixture of respectability and infamy, that racketing about on the very rim of social acceptance, was what she had known too nearly all her life. Far too near the knuckle.

Murdo was obviously hugely popular. His tall figure seemed to fill the whole of the stage; he was assured and seemed used to the calls for 'Mur-do!' 'You can do it son!' 'Give us a song, Murdy boy!' Mad Izzy seemed to Harriet to expand with pride. She sat up straighter, stopped fiddling with her drinks and cigarettes, eyes fixed on the stage. Then he was away, off the leash with *Green Door*. Men as well as women were almost dancing in their seats and clapping to the rhythm. Whoops of joy as the old pub rocked. He was a natural performer with a great voice. Harriet could not take her eyes off him.

Rena was sitting on the edge of the stage, swinging her legs. She was one of life's natural molls: blonde curls, sweet grin and a long, slim body. Murdo was now flashing his eyes at his granny. Mad Izzy laughed and clapped. 'Go it, son!'

The song ended with a crash, but before the audience had stopped clapping Murdo had picked up his acoustic guitar and was into a lilting celtic ballad about getting dumped. He sang with great feeling, though Harriet could hardly believe that anyone would ever dump such a gorgeous male, especially one with such a successfully Italian sob in his voice. Sex on a stick.

'There's a look in your eyes
That makes me feel uneasy.

213

Something is hurtin' you, deep down
  inside
Has the feelin' gone?
I still see a reason
To wait for the season
of its return

For Love has no pattern
to grasp or pin down.
Aye there for the takin'
next time around.

Don't walk away and leave me here
  with only heartache,
Come back and let me know you'll
  stay.
Please stop and think about the love I
  still believe in,
Don't turn your back on me this way!'

The crowd erupted. 'We'll never leave you, Murdoooo!' 'Nae fear a' that!' 'Pin me down any time! Any place. Mine or yours!' 'Over here, darlin'!' 'Just say the word! I'm all yours, wi' knobs on!'

Murdo carried on strumming his guitar, ignoring the catcalls and lust behind the women's eyes. Harriet looked around the room, fascinated. You could cut the sexual tension by the slice. What a pro! He obviously knew his market.

And he was off again with another ballad. An instant hit with the older women who obviously knew the song.

> 'Should a tear fall on your pillow, I will
>   dry your eyes.
> A cloud burst on a summer's day, I will
>   clear the skies.
> When you're sick, I'll hold your hand,
> When you're poor, I'll pay demands,
> I will always understand.
> 'Cos that's what life's about.'

'That'll be the day he pays demands for anyone,' chuckled Mad Izzy. 'Shh!' hissed a woman on the next table.

> 'When this world has made you weary,
> I will make the tea.
> Take yi' to the pictures
> If there's one to see.
> When your smile has lost its trace,
> I'll put it back upon your face
> Wi' perfume and some pretty lace.
> 'Cos that's what life's about . . . '

The women swayed as he went into an instrumental break, looking straight at Rena. He had obviously written the song for her. Murdo smiled around the room. Every

215

woman there was now clearly yearning for him. Harriet included, rather to her surprise. Eyes flashing pure violet sex appeal, he was loving every minute of it. 'That's right, son. You've got us well sussed!' an old woman called out. A pair of lacy knickers landed on the stage.

Murdo caught them, wiped his forehead and put them into his shirt pocket. 'Come and get them later, hen!' Laughter. The applause was deafening.

'He's very talented,' Harriet said to Mad Izzy, who was half out of her seat with joy.

'Aye. You come and see me tomorrow. Nelson Street, fifty-three. Anyone'll tell you. Ten o'clock. Look, now! Here are my friends!'

It was a dismissal. Harriet pushed her way out of the pub and out into the cold street. In the distance the lights strung along the sea front were waving in the wind, while the street lights on the other side of the Firth winked. She made her way back to the hotel and checked her mobile. Richard had left a message from the airport.

'Missing you, Harriet. Hope you're enjoying yourself and digging up juicy stories. Mercer was being such pain about the picture, in the end I gave him your number. Doesn't take no for an answer. Which is why he is worth a billion, I suppose. Wish me luck with the Latins. Love you.'

Did he? God knew.

ITALY

Richard took a deep breath and held it for as long as he could while counting how many dusty red cottages he could see from the *autostrada*. He'd got to eight before he let out the breath in a great gust right across the front seat of the car. The chauffeur quickly glanced in his mirror. He could have had a cartoon bubble coming out of his head. *'Pazzi! Sono tutti pazzi gli inglesi.'* The English are all mad. Particularly, as Richard thought to himself, if they are half Irish. Not a hope then, Leprechauns fighting lions for your soul.

Thank God he was out of the UK! Three days of good food and wine and playing the big shot picture dealer lay before him, not a buff envelope nor a snotty bank manager nor a hand-wringing accountant nor a bastard lawyer in sight. How cultured the Francoboni family were. What good, loyal customers; they had stuck with him all these years, passing on his name to friends and getting him out of tight financial holes more than once. What a

217

magnificent disregard for taxes and rules and administrative details. How rich and civilised. Bliss! What is it about Italy which connects you to your soul and lets it soar?

Richard looked out of the window. The fields were flat at this point, full of maize or something firm and profitable. In the distance, hills layered with vines glimmered purple and inviting. Soon they would be leaving the *autostrada* and heading deep into Chiantishire. '*Benvenuto*, Riccardo,' he said to himself. There can surely be few things more civilised than the morning flight to Rome to be met by a uniformed chauffeur before being whisked to a *palazzo grande* in the middle of vineyards and family splendour. Please God he'd remembered his calculator. One nought wrong and he could find him offering to sell pictures for millions too much or too little. Done it before. A red Lamborghini smashed past. Vrooom! Richard felt a stab of pain as he remembered his own red souped-up gorgeous girl. How he had loved her! When the man from the garage had arrived to drive her away, it was as if part of his body had been amputated. 'We'll get what we can, Mr L, but we're in a recession. Prepare to take a hit.' He had looked after her as she had headed down the road to Knightsbridge, realising that the self-righteous, snotty little man inside was carting away his youth. Harriet had told him to pull himself together, it was only a car. Only a car! It had hurt far more than losing the house.

All the women in his life seemed to be dancing in his brain, demanding his attention. He had expected Amanda to be at Katya's show, in fact had been almost curious to see what she looked like after so much time. He had once seen her come out of Fenwick's and had almost called out, but something had stopped him. He had been married to Anne at the time and did not need any more complications. But why had Amanda been so hostile? So childish in spite of that make-up and power dressing. He'd never said anything against her, she had obviously done well for herself, but it was as if she resented his very existence.

And Harriet — she might as well be in Australia as Scotland. Did she ever have her mobile switched on? In the end he'd rung up her hotel and been told she had gone to McGuffey's Bar. Didn't sound like Harriet's sort of place at all. He could hardly see her downing Guinness and singing round the piano. She had always been so prim and proper in an unconsciously sexy way. Possibly why, after so many years of too many stimulants and too much casual sex, he had found her so attractive.

Then Katya, who seemed to have barged into his life when he wasn't looking as Mary Ellen's onstage replacement. In one way this was better, a ready-made daughter in place of the mother from hell. She had talent too. But she never tried to look pretty. Her make-up was either black or purple lines, usually smudged. And she didn't know how to smile, or please, or tease or flirt. As if the muscles in her face had not been properly trained. Perhaps her generation didn't need men anymore.

'So, Rich, I want to know — exactly what happened? I want to know how on earth you and Amanda got it together to have me.'

He could hear her voice. That faint and fashionable estuary twang in spite of all those years at private school. He'd spent yesterday afternoon in her hot little studio, having another sitting. Katya as usual was fighting the canvas with her palette knife. She must use up tubes of paint. No wonder she was always complaining about her overdraft. His arm was aching from the hand on hip pose she had insisted on and it was then he had decided to tell her the truth. She was such a cold little sausage there didn't seem any point in holding back.

January 1971. He and Amanda had been twenty-two. He remembered that month really well. There had been a terrible disaster during a football match at Ibrox in Scotland, the IRA were bombing and the postal workers had gone on strike for a 19% pay increase. Everyone was on strike or discontented. And, in bizarre counterpoint to the country going down the tubes, top of the charts was Clive Dunne singing *Granddad*, and George Harrison *My Sweet Lord*-ing it. But if you were young, rich and in Soho with money to burn, the sixties were still swinging. The Stones reigned supreme with Marc Bolan as Crown Prince. Richard and Amanda had been in the same set. Mostly art school people, or hangers-on around the Wardour Street music industry. Richard had been a bit different from the others. Pushed on to a boarding school conveyor belt, he had been carried into a history degree at Oxford. He had partied for Britain, the hottest member of the hottest crowd, and had done as little work as possible, scraping a third. Mary Ellen of course had made a point of turning up in the most enormously politically incorrect fur coats at every opportunity. There had almost been a riot at his graduation when she had appeared in leopardskin. Then he had come back to London to do a foundation year before art school.

After just one term he had had the first glimmerings that he did not have the talent he'd thought he had. And this had made him party all the harder. His dad had been generous, buying him a little red Morgan, giving him a large allowance and inviting his gang back to the club for drinks. Everyone either had titles in their family, or trust funds, or real dosh from big business. Amanda's daddy had been a stockbroker with a big pile near Haywards Heath. He had died when she was a child and she had been sent to boarding school young. Her real speaking voice was just like the Queen's, though of course everyone tried to talk just like Tommy Steele. George had revelled in all these posh connections and had readily picked up the tab. This had bought Richard popularity but not talent.

Everyone had been feeling rather flat post-Christmas until Amanda had suggested having a Bring A Creep Nite. Their friends all jumped at it. The idea was to find the creepiest, most ungroovy person you could find and bring them along to a party. They had to be really adenoidal, boring brainiacs into obscure hobbies with really bad breath. Two of the group offered to hold it at their flat in Chelsea, near the World's End, because they had conveniently deaf people living beneath as well as a really big drawing room where one could roll up the carpet and dance. A prize of the next Stones album, to be paid for by the rest of the group, would be given to the person who had brought along the creepiest creep, who danced in the most embarrassing way. The rule was, if the creep asked you why you had invited them, you were to be honest and tell them. Otherwise you were to keep stumm.

Richard had trouble finding a real creep because he only knew beautiful people. In the end the day before the party he had asked a woman in his dad's back office. She was in her early-thirties, hugely fat with spots. Her name was Maureen and she would always wear ghastly nylon dresses even on a hot day and ridiculous strappy shoes. She lived with her mother in Greenford and kept tropical fish. In fact, she looked rather like a fish, a prize guppy perhaps for her mouth was always hanging open. She had always smiled at him when he came in to get his money, but when he had asked her to the party, he'd thought she was going to faint. She went red then white then blue and finally gasped, 'Thanks ever so much.' He had managed to keep a straight face as he had promised to pick her up in darkest Greenford in his little car. As he left she had been opening the window to let in air, and the other women's exclamations and chatter had followed him down the stairs.

Then the big night arrived. What a lot of creeps they had amassed! Curiously, even after all this time, he could still remember them. A little weed from Essex into birds' eggs; a long gangly ticket inspector on British Rail who talked about nothing but the unions and working conditions; a bespectacled housewife called Sandra from godforsaken Shepherd's Bush who wore a bunny fur which was three sizes too big for her and refused to take it off however hot the room became. Maureen had been a triumph of creepiness. She had obviously spent a fortune on make-up at Woolworths and wore a bright red rayon dress which made her look like a double decker bus. She also stank of cheap perfume and as the evening progressed her eye liner melted, giving her the look of a ghoul at a Halloween party. She kept on asking for Babycham. Richard had had to run down to the off-licence and risk the mirth of the other Chelsea-ites queuing up for vodka. He had bought three dozen little bottles with Bambi on the front. How embarrassed he had been!

It was Amanda who actually won first prize. No contest. God alone knew where she had picked up old Colin! Everyone just gathered round in awe because he was *so* gruesome he was a collector's item, a prize nerd. Stick thin, white, with a huge Adam's apple which bobbed up and down like a buoy. People kept plying him with cider (the only thing he would drink) just to see him knock his head back and his Adam's apple going boing, boing, up and down. It was fascinating. He wore a brown suit with a blue knitted tie and said he had just started work for the Water Board. His hobby was walking along canals, looking at barges. He could reel off all their names and kept showing everyone a stupid book about the Grand Union Canal, which barge was where and who owned what. He had a lisp and a stammer, imagine! Plus BO *and* bad breath. A cornucopia of creepiness!

Just the thought of Colin made Richard smile as the car swept through a small deserted village. *L'ora di pranzo.* The tobacconist was shutting up his shop for lunch while a hundred pans of pasta would be bubbling away in houses all along the street.

It's funny that when one can't remember a name or what day of the week it is most of the time, one can remember parties and events from years ago, so clearly they might be on film. Katya had made no comment as he'd described the party. Just continued to stare at him then look at her canvas. Stare, silence, then more scratching.

'What happened then?' she'd said finally.

'Well, I seem to remember Amanda had to submit to a snog and I did the decent thing and put my hand down Maureen's dress, just to let her feel appreciated. No, don't look at me like that. That's what you did then. Usually to *I Can't Get No Satisfaction*. Then I treated everyone to my Tom Jones impression. *What's New Pussy Cat?* Anyway then we discovered that Maureen and Colin both lived in Greenford, apparently only a road apart, and so we shoved them into a taxi. What a relief! That was about at one o'clock in the morning. I suppose, looking back, it was obvious we were all bloody pleased with ourselves. Just as the cab was pulling away, Colin stuck his head out and asked Amanda why she had invited him. So because we had all agreed the rules, she told him. Just gave it to him straight. No mucking about. He stuck his head back in and the taxi went off. I never saw Maureen after that. She left the following week to go and work for Brentford Nylons. Rather appropriate, I always thought, given the amount she used to wear!'

'You were a pair of bastards.'

'No, not really, just young. He *did* ask. And we gave them a nice time. Anyway then Amanda and I went back to the party, got pissed and one thing led to another. She was very beautiful, your mother, that's why all the big boys in Soho wanted to paint her. By the time she realised she was pregnant, it was too late for an abortion. In those days it was still very *Alfie* — you know, gin and knitting needles and old women in the back streets, so Amanda had you at Queen Charlotte's. I think she was pleased. I would have married her actually, but Old George, my dad, had big plans for me, thought I could do better than a dead stockbroker's daughter, wanted me to marry a Lady with a family pile attached. So he went round with a cheque book and bought her off. I was forbidden to see her.

'Of course, that made me want to see her even more and I went over to her digs. She was living in West Kensington, it was very cheap in those days, but her flat mate told me she had taken you to work. She was a model and I gather you were brought up among the paint pots in Bacon's studio. She didn't want to see me. Still, you survived.'

'And you forgot me.'

'No, that's not fair. It was just . . . you see, I never saw you, and I thought it was probably better that way. I thought Amanda would marry and you would have a proper father. Anyway time went on, I married, had Jamie, and I did wonder about you. My accountant organised the school fees. And then suddenly fifteen years had passed and you came into the gallery. Very Queen's Gate. Anyway you've done all right. You've got more talent than I have.'

'How much did he pay? Old George?'

'Oh, I don't know. A fair amount, I would have thought. I think he even offered to buy Amanda a house but she refused. Still, he did his bit.'

'Got you off the hook.'

He had looked at her pinched little face. She was scratching away with such fierce concentration, painting his portrait. 'Not really.'

'*Eccoci, Signore!*' The chauffeur had pulled aside the glass partition and turned towards him. They were now on a road fringed with olive trees, the early-afternoon sun filtering through, leaving a pattern of light and shade on the road in front. In the distance was the yellow stucco of Palazzo Francoboni. Richard could see a figure looking out from an upstairs window, holding a cup and saucer in his hand. That would be Guido. Richard sat up suddenly and straightened his tie. Eyes and teeth, old boy. Eyes and teeth. What had Laura said the other day about learning to think like an actor?

They complimented him on his Italian, they always did. He had once told them how Harriet had taught him over the phone *lezioni telefoniche*, without knowing of his true identity, and Giovanna sighed and said, '*L'amore*,' in that satisfying way Italians always did. Now, alas, he struggled to recall vocabulary but quickly rediscovered the Italian shrug, the small idioms and, after a few drinks, the capacity to tell jokes.

A bit of cheap sympathy perhaps but he told them that his mother had died, forgetting the absurd importance Italians attach to '*mamma*' — they were not of course sent off to boarding school at eight — which again led Giovanna into flurries of protective cooings and billings as she called for the manservant to fetch the best champagne. Richard supposed he could drink to his mother through gritted teeth. Method acting.

Of course, along with all this, it was important not to forget that Italians are the most splendidly cynical and businesslike race, who would sell their granny for fourpence, but that was what he really liked about them.

Rather that any day than the ridiculously sentimental Germans.

Giovanna was small and dark and in her fifties with one of those huge Italian mouths which, coated in bright red lipstick, resembled a large red pepperoni. She wore beautiful shoes. Richard always noticed her shoes, which seemed to be made of leather which looked like melted butter. She also had an emerald on her finger as big as a small boy's prize marble. Guido, on the other hand, reminded him of the prince Julie Christie went off with in *Darling*. Tall, soldierly, deliciously cold and civilised. Probably kept a mistress, but no one would ever know. His family had lived in San Gerardo for eighteen generations, producing a cardinal or two and a gaggle of *deputati* — MPs. Now his eldest son Marcello was a lawyer in Rome while his younger son Stefano, who was supposed to be working in the family business, lolled about the estate looking boyish and useless, Richard thought, spending most of his time on the mobile phone. This was until he realised that he had been just the same at that age, about the time he had fathered Katya in fact, and speedily revised his opinion. The boy must have hidden potential.

They drank *aperitivi* on the loggia overlooking the valley where the vines continued for miles. Terracotta roofs were dotted all over the landscape but there were no towns. The sun beat down, but here on the terrace the air was cool and perfumed. Then came lunch, course after course of pasta and meat and *fagioli* and beef tomato salad. Fine wines flowed and Richard could feel his waistline giving in gracefully. What the hell! Guido sat in a magnificent carved chair at the head of the table while Giovanna charmed their guest at the other end. Stefano smirked prettily and wanted to know if he had met Emma Thompson while in London. Sadly not, Richard replied.

'Why did you not bring your wife?' asked Giovanna. Harriet had never met them, though she had always accompanied him on buying trips when they were first married. He explained she had gone up to Scotland to research a picture. He tried to remember what Scotland was in Italian. '*La Scozia,*' Stefano supplied. Richard explained that his father-in-law had been an artist who had lived in Italy for many years, and so his wife was fluent. But they had lost interest. If Harriet was not before them, flesh and blood, they could not imagine her; for them she did not exist. Richard then remembered the Italian expression '*Sa com'è*' — you know how it is. And he knew how it was. It had begun to seem she did not exist for him either.

Afterwards they would look at the paintings. Guido, of course, was far too civilised to say how he had come by them. Were they family paintings? Richard asked in the vague way that one did when not wanting to pry. Some, and others were in exchange for debt. Guido did not elaborate. 'Sa com'è?' He had the insouciance which came from owning land, and having money and vines and a well-connected wife and no intention of paying any more tax than the average rural primary school teacher. Once only some years before Richard had seen the real Guido talking on the mobile, spitting venomously that if someone did not pay up he'd break their legs. 'Cornuto!' The worst thing any Italian male could say to another. Cuckold!

After lunch he led the way. The paintings, however they had come to be there, had been hung for Richard's inspection. What a haul! 'I can't sell these — they're Renaissance. You'd never be allowed to take them out of the country. The Belle Arti brigade would be down on you like a ton of bricks!'

'I don't want them. Where can I sell them? And I don't wish just to hand them over to decorate the public office of some useless southerner.' Guido sounded like a spoilt child. Richard had to think quickly. Think, Longbridge. What's best for you? He had to screw as much as he could out of Guido this time. He needed the money badly. Playing for time, he asked for the works to be brought down one by one and taken out into the light. They were all from the Renaissance period. First an Orazio Vecellio Madonna and Child. The Madonna was a nice little peasant girl, the sort he had seen running all over the streets as they had passed through innumerable villages on the way from the airport. The chubby baby was magnificently painted. The painting would possibly be worth £30K. Then an Andrea Schiavone Adoration of the Shepherds, approximately £25K. Then a Baccio Bandinelli, not very good condition, Daniel in the Lion's Den, black chalk, brown ink. But still worth £15K to the right buyer. There was possibly a Livio Agresti, very exciting, and an Antonio Molinari showing the Sacrifice of Isaac. They were all marvellous paintings. Inspirational. My God, it must have been some debt. Now for the hard part.

'Look, Guido, you can't get these out of the country, you know, not unless you put them in the removal van of some friendly travelling diplomat.'

'My cousins, they are diplomats.'

'Do they ever travel to New York or Geneva?'

'I could arrange it.'

'Good. No VAT on pictures sold in either place. But you'd have to get them out of the country.'

Richard was soon tapping away on his personal organiser, which made him feel a bit like a pensions salesman, but no matter. He selected four clients in the US and Switzerland and was soon making calls. He calculated he could make a 10% introduction fee from both buyer and seller on the deal. Not as good as a profit share, perhaps, but much less hassle in the circumstance. There must be £400Ks' worth of canvas, which would mean £80K for him. He might even be able to go a bit higher. Nice work, Riccardo.

Guido went out on to the loggia while he made the calls. Richard could see a slice of green hill and pines in the distance wreathed in the curving smoke of his cigarette. He made contact with the offices of the chosen ones, who would kill for such art on their walls and the hint of danger it would bring.

'But why do you want to sell them?' he called to Guido who was outside on the loggia smoking a cigarette.

'They are not my style, which is for modern. Like Mario Schifano, or Tancredi.'

'How big is your collection now?'

'I have four Tancredi and three Schifano. But Tancredi, he is expensive.' Richard remembered he had sold Guido an abstract piece of Tancredi's he had got from old Elsa Minetti. The artist had given it to her. He had given her £500 and sold it to Guido for — what was it? — £40K. Still Tancredis were holding their own in the sale rooms so he could not complain.

'If you're interested, I have a client keen to sell a Schifano. She must pay school fees, she is a widow. I could perhaps get it for you for around a million and a half.' Selling, Richard tended to calculate at 3,000 lira to the pound. Buying 2,000. It made life more comfortable.

'Send me a photograph. And, remember, do not insult my intelligence, Richard. We all have to live, but . . . '

Guido left the 'but' delicately falling into the air, but Richard got the message. Too much cream off the top and he would be a legless '*cornuto*' too. Risky, but he would have to sail as close to the wind as he could. What wouldn't he give to see Guido and Matt Mercer crossing swords!

Soon all the arrangements were made. Guido would get the pictures Stateside and thence to Switzerland and on arrival Richard would '*sistemare tutto*', a marvellous phrase which meant something much more exacting than the translation of 'sorting everything out'. They would deal through the escrow account in Monaco, as they usually did. The sun was setting into that late-afternoon mellow warmth and this time Giovanna had ordered iced lemon tea in the drawing room where a magnificent Julian Schnabel leered. The Italian eternally worshipped the new and young and modern. Perhaps their history weighed too heavily on their backs.

Then Richard was being kissed on both cheeks by the fragrant Giovanna and packed off to Rome. What a shame he could not stay, she would exclaim. She did this every time, but there never was any suggestion that he would be invited. He was only the hired help after all, however fussed over. Guido shook his hand and they parted. As the car moved down the hill, Richard glanced back and noticed that she had already walked inside and Guido was already back on his mobile phone. Alarm bells rang in his mind. They were not usually quite so quick to move indoors, but then, he did not really know them. Even now he knew them not one iota better than he had done when they had first met. Which was why the relationship worked so well, of course. He didn't need to know his clients too well. Only their desires.

Relax, Richard old son. You did well. Now for *bella* Roma and the latest crop of young artists who might want to dazzle London. He leant back, closed his eyes and let the sun warm his face. *Coraggio!*

8

Largs

'So that's how we met. Of course I said to him later, 'Darling, how could you do that with the boa constrictor?' but there you go. Tom was wonderful!'

Laura was in full flood. She had dyed her hair golden and was looking really rather good for such an early hour, 9.15 a.m., which for Laura counted as the middle of the night. But the *Jenna Grace Breakfast Show* was probably as good a reason as any for getting up before 10 a.m. That or an audition for Spielberg. Laura wasn't proud. Harriet found she could look at her former friend quite dispassionately. The betrayal was ancient history and the hurt more or less plastered over. It takes two to tango, and as an actor Tom had certainly known how to strut his Latin lover stuff when it suited him. Wow! That she could think like this was progress. Must be the fresh Largs air blowing through the window.

Then she realised that Mad Izzy was

watching her. 'You don't like her, do you, hen?'

'Oh, I do. Yes. What makes you think that, Mrs Finlay?'

'Och, your lip's curling, hen. Watch out, or it might get stuck like that!' Harriet smiled and laughed and sat down again at the kitchen table. The small TV perched on top of the fridge could be ignored if one looked down.

'So there is life after *Sampson House*!' Jenna Grace was saying. Harriet couldn't help but look up. Laura's Cheshire Cat smile seemed to reach beyond the sides of the small TV and encompass the small kitchen of Mad Izzy's flat.

'Oh, darling, yes. I *loved* it. We were one big happy family. All the actors' families grew *terribly* close. It always happens on long runs in the theatre, you know. But then people leave, the show closes, and one simply must move on. I've been having fun learning to drive around L.A. Doing a couple of films which are opening here later in the year, and of course now I'm back with my one-woman show — *All About Bette* at the Fortune Theatre in London's West End. The theatre *earths* me and it *really* is enormous *fun!* The audiences have been fan*tas*tic. Theatre, you know, is *so* special.' Laura smiled confidentially, as if telling a big secret.

'Do you still see the cast of *Sampson House*?' The Jenna woman was like a mastiff with half a lamb, refusing to let go.

'Oh, well, occasionally if we do publicity stuff for the cable channel. And of course the early episodes are being bought up on cable in the States. They're a great crowd — Melissa, David, sweet Fenella — but they're all busy, busy, busy. Except, of course, dear, darling Tom Gosse whom we all miss so much!'

'May I turn it off?' Harriet said to Mad Izzy, who was sitting at the kitchen table drinking black coffee from the most enormous mug Harriet had ever seen. It might as well have been a coffee bucket.

'You go ahead, hen. I always thought those two with their rumpty-tumpty were too good for acting.'

'I beg your pardon?'

'That Laura and your husband. No, don't look like that. You're rummaging around in *my* family. A woman always knows. I always knew when my Alec was playing away from home. Men are hopeless. They think they're so clever, but they're not. Can't hide it. Unlike us.' She laughed with all the ease of fifty years' too much brandy and cigarettes.

Harriet was silent. She'd never guessed Tom had been playing away from home. Too busy trying to keep that home going for Billy. But she did not intend for Mad Izzy to draw her out. She had an article to write. Or not. Depending on what the biscuit tin revealed. At the moment it did not look promising. All over the kitchen table the contents of Mad Izzy's rusty old Carrs of Carlisle biscuit tin were spread out for inspection. How had it survived being put up for sale in Murdo's shop? Old ration books were mixed up with faded letters, speckled photographs of unknown people and the other detritus of the past. Harriet thought of her own blue archive files of memorabilia which one day would go to Billy, assuming he even bothered to go through it before chucking it on to a skip.

Here was an old ferry timetable to Rothesay, price 3d; a crumpled leaflet announcing the annual concert of the young Men's Christian Association; a performance of *The Voysey Inheritance* by the Largs & Fairlie District Amateur Dramatic Society. There was a sepia photograph of Eugenie in the Manse garden with her husband, a stern-looking man who looked as if he never experienced a drop of fun in his life. Another photo showed him standing with five very similar women, presumably his sisters, who looked like tall poppies grouped together. Stern, as if they had swallowed the Old

Testament whole as a test of their digestion. Being so respectable in a society without a safety net must have been hard work on a Minister's stipend. Eugenie, with her Mary of Teck curls across her forehead, did not look a bundle of laughs either. How had Mad Izzy kept sane? Presumably she hadn't, hence her name!

Another photograph had obviously been taken in a studio with a carefully artificial background of stuffed birds and silk flowers. An old lady sat ramrod straight, smiling at the camera. Her fixed and quizzical stare was certainly telling the man to get a move on. Isabella in her sixties, living with her daughter and son-in-law who must have constantly been at her to toe the line, for the money had gone, and the men and the reputation. Harriet looked from the picture to another old lady who was ladling yet more sugar into her huge coffee cup, and smiled at her. Izzy smiled back, violet eyes full of mischief.

'Aye, that's Granny. My mother paid for it on her sixty-fifth birthday. One final stab at respectability.'

'When did you last look through all this?'

'It's been years. I've always felt better letting sleeping dogs lie. Too much of the past is bad for you. Says me, talking to you! When Murdo started his shop he came by wanting me to flog him the ration books, but I told him I wanted to keep them. What a boy that is! He does make me laugh, him and that Shug with his tin whistle. You know they play all over the West? Down at Dumfries they were last week. Circuits they call it, same as electricity. Not a care in the world, those two. Though that'll change when Rena cracks the whip.'

Yes, Murdo was gorgeous, but too lazy to survive Rena's ministrations for long. Harriet had seen them walking down the street, the little blonde girl wrapped round him like Tom's famous boa constrictor in *Sampson House*. Harriet could even see Murdo in her mind's eye, in a couple of years' time, domesticated in a long grey men's M & S cardie, sitting reading old comics in The KOOC with twins perched up in baby bouncers on the counter. A sorry picture. No, she preferred him untamed, moody and hating the English.

'Do you mind if I read these letters?'

'Aye. Och, with my eyesight it's hopeless. My mother wrote like a spider. She was a quiet woman, like a kettle with all the warmth trying to whistle out of her, but it had been bunged up. My father was a kindly man but older and his sisters ruled her with an iron rod. None of them ever married so they were always streaming around the Manse, eating up the parish with their good works.'

'Poor Eugenie!' said Harriet, thinking of how difficult it had been trying to share a kitchen with Laura even when they were bosom buddies.

Mad Izzy stood up, creaking like the kitchen table. 'Aye, Isabella coming back was like a cat among a flock of birds. Feathers and shite everywhere! Now, I'm going next door to see my neighbour, that's Mrs McInery, to see if she wants any messages. I'll be back in a minute, hen, OK? Maggie, my daughter, will be back soon off her shift. That's Murdo's mother.'

Harriet smiled and carried on looking at the letters. It was easier anyway without the old lady's eagle stare. Tomorrow night she would be back in W11, with money once more at the centre of her life, and Richard would be back from Rome. Master of the house, opening a bottle of expensive wine in spite of all the nasty letters from the bank which would be lying unopened on the hall table. Then the usual swinging from the chandeliers. Did he 'play away from home' to use Mad Izzy's expression? As with Tom, she preferred not to know. There had to be some mystery. But if he was Tigger, she was rapidly turning into Eeyore.

The letters were mainly short notes, either from Eugenie to Izzy or her husband, mainly of lists and arrangements, or from her husband, the strict Reverend Wishart, to her. There were invitations to summer sales of work and, more interestingly, a crumpled cutting from May 1925 from the *Largs & Millport Weekly News* showing some gathering on the lawns of Castle Wemyss, with the Reverend and Mrs Wishart standing stiffly next to Lord Inverclyde. John Burns' son? Grandson? Eugenie did not look amused. Possibly because the Inverclydes had been Episcopalians!

Next, a large bulging envelope sealed with red sealing wax; Harriet did not know whether to open it without Izzy's express permission, but given the old woman's offhand attitude, what the heck? She split the seal and letters spilled out on to the table.

Eureka! They had been written by Isabella. Some had been sent from Glasgow to Gifford Fairlie's sister, asking for money. The writing sloped and had obviously been tossed off in a hurry, but there was much humour in them. One had a description of going to Glasgow to the 'barras'. 'I bought a most sweet little violet vase. J said it looked as if it could contain whisky just as well, with a drop of good hill water. I told him it was going to be sold for good profit!' Who was J? Would it have been 'done' in those days for a middle-class woman to go haggling in a Glasgow street market?

The kitchen door suddenly opened and a middle-aged woman in a white nurse's uniform came in. Her face was gaunt and tired and her hair, which must have been blue-black once, was streaked with grey and pulled into a bun. She had the transparent, fragile look of someone who worked at night. She seemed unconcerned to see a stranger sitting in her kitchen.

'Oh, how do you do? I'm Harriet Longbridge. I assume you must be Maggie, Murdo's mother? Your mother's gone to see a neighbour.' Harriet stood up and offered her hand. The woman took it but her handshake was limp and wet, like an eel.

'Aye.'

The beginnings of a smile glimmered over her mouth, which looked as if several hours ago it had started out with lipstick and the best of intentions, then faded. Just then the front door opened. 'Margaret — you home, hen?'

'Aye, Ma. I'm just in the door.'

It was odd seeing the two of them together, Mad Izzy so small and pert and Maggie big and plump and curvaceous. She must have been a very attractive girl once for she had the same round, pretty face and eyes as Isabella, though in her case the purple was so dark as to be almost black. With the streaked grey hair she had a rather dramatic appearance now, like a coot prematurely aged after too much nest building.

'You up from London?'

'Yes. Just for a few days. I'm going back tomorrow, actually.'

'I lived in London once.'

'Did you? Did you enjoy it? I imagine it must have been nice coming back to all this fresh air!'

Silence.

'Er — do you know anything about Isabella? What would she be? Your great-grandmother?' Harriet decided to risk further conversation as Izzy bustled to get her daughter some food. 'No, not Maggie, I never talked to her about it much. This lady is doing an article for a magazine, Maggie, about the portrait of my granny. Her pa-in-law bought it at an auction up in London.'

'That's nice,' Maggie said, staring rather absent-mindedly out of the window.

This was a characteristic which was pure Ayrshire, Harriet had discovered. 'My son is marrying Madonna!' or 'My daughter has won £6 million in the National Lottery!' and the answer would be the same. 'That's nice. How's your mum?' It took a little getting used to after Londoners' over-the-top exclamations.

'Er, yes, I'd better get on so you can have your kitchen table back.'

But Izzy was already slicing up white bread and making tea to put on a tray. Maggie left and reappeared in an off-pink dressing gown. She said that she did the early shift at an old people's home in the town. There was a curiously childlike quality about her, and Harriet found it odd that her elderly mother should still be fussing over her. Not that she knew anything about having a mother.

'Does Murdo have brothers and sisters?' she finally asked to be polite, wondering if Izzy had noticed that she had broken the seal round the letters, but Maggie merely shook her head and sipped her tea and carried on looking vaguely down into the back green where the wind was whistling round the washing on the line. Mad Izzy was mouthing something behind her daughter's back, like Les Dawson. Obviously babies were a sore point.

Soon Maggie had her boiled egg with soldiers ready on a tray and Izzy was taking it through to the sitting room where already daytime TV was blaring loudly. Harriet took her coffee through and was struck by the curious mixture of furniture in the room. A very beautiful satinwood bracket clock stood on a Victorian rosewood writing table. There was also a walnut high-back chair with an embroidered silk panel, but these pieces were mixed in with mass-produced repro. There were also good pictures on the walls amongst the dross. Harriet's practised eye automatically took in some oils, landscapes mostly, one or two quite good. They overpowered the small sitting room where, oblivious, Maggie sat engrossed in a talk show about incest. As she went back to the kitchen Harriet remembered how Isabella, like Mad Izzy and Murdo, had loved buying and selling. All part of her gypsy charm. Hadn't Izzy said she had originally hidden some of old Gifford's assets down on the family farm?

My dear Isabella,

I am looking forward to our meeting immensely. I have instructed Mrs McAllen to cancel all patients until two in the afternoon until after our luncheon. I trust the cold gammon will be fresh at MacLean's Hotel.

I remain your obedient servant,
MFW

The letter was dated 9 May 1884, the address Niddrie Square, Glasgow. That must have been the dentist! Poor Isabella, just cold gammon to look forward to. The writing was parsimonious, the paper cut and crossed and recrossed in order to avoid waste. But by the grace of God, if her own language business had failed and Marcus had not left her all those pictures, she too might have been satisfied with a gammon-loving dentist, God forbid! The 1880s must have been difficult times for a single woman. And hard to accept. Isabella could well have imagined that Gifford would have been just the start of marital riches.

Something had been written in pencil on the letter. Harriet took it over to the kitchen window to see it better in the light. 'Pickled in brine!' Isabella had obviously kept the letter and her sense of humour. Who was pickled? The dentist, the gammon or the marriage? All three probably. Still, she hadn't had long to wait. What did Mad Izzy call it? Popping your clogs. Well, he'd duly popped his. The mystery was there must have been some money, so why did she have to marry a railway worker the next time round? Had the lover of the illegitimate child taken the money and run? Mysteries.

The next husband had obviously not been

250

able to write for the marriage certificate was also in the package, recording the union of Isabella Watts and one Alexander Geddes of Elder Street, Govan. The bridegroom had simply put a cross where his signature should have been while Isabella's signature was so small as to be invisible, as if she had been trying to deny this was happening. Pinned next to it was an old photograph of a small back cottage, it did not say where it was, with a late-thirty-something Isabella surrounded by children. Long pinny. Hair scraped back in a bun. Sore-looking hands. She was not smiling, just looking at the camera. The sparkle had gone.

Harriet wondered who Isabella's picture reminded her of, and then remembered a diary picture in *Tatler* of herself and Richard at some Sotheby's pre-auction party. Richard had been standing next to the Italian Ambassador's wife, his head thrown back in laughter, while Harriet had been caught staring straight at the camera. It had been taken on the evening of the day Katya had arrived on their doorstep at Notting Hill announcing herself as Richard's little mystery. 'Hiya! I'm Rich's daughter.' That was when Harriet had finally realised that she did not really know her husband after all. She had forced herself to be terribly nice and liberal and reasonable. And, as a reward, had never seen Richard look so insecure. But you would not know from the picture. Her stare, as fixed as Isabella's, said that youth was slipping away and the men you loved did not tell the truth.

Harriet went through the other letters quickly. Isabella had really been unwise. Without the advantage of the Pill she had had a fifth baby, poor girl. But it was the picture of that small cottage and the grimy washing hanging outside that made Harriet finally decided that enough was enough. Let her go. Concentrate on Trollope and the Burns instead if she was going to do an article at all. Isabella was a non-starter. She would ring *KQ* and tell Jonathan Harbour that Isabella's life just was not aspirational enough. Too much like real life for readers grimly clinging to partners and property in W8, SW7 and assorted Wiltshire villages. Isabella's life was every middle-class woman's worst nightmare. Apart from anything else, Isabella, Govan railway worker's missus, would hardly do the value of Harriet's picture any good. Oh, God! Now she was starting to think like Richard.

Suddenly impatient to be out of Mad Izzy's overfurnished flat, Harriet began to stuff the letters back into the envelope. Then applause from the TV show next door momentarily distracted her. A thick folded piece of paper looked to be of much better quality than the rest, though brown and old. More applause came from the next room as she unfolded the letter.

It was dated 30 January 1870, Castle Wemyss.

My dear Isabella,

How kind of you to entertain us to luncheon on such an inhospitable day. What rain! I am surprised you did not report that the Clyde had grown two feet higher in consequence. Your energy and charm as a hostess remain unsurpassed in all of Scotland. George Burns was also in splendid form, was he not, regaling us of his exploits as a horticulturist? What a good evening we also had at the Gaiters. John Burns was mightily amusing and I have engaged myself to stay at Castle W later in the year. Gifford also entertained us all with his tales of your recent efforts at croquet in the great hall. It seems a very good notion to me, given the weather you enjoy on this wild West Coast. You will beat us all come the summer, if of course the season decides to favour us all with a visit this year. Yes, indeed, we all enjoyed ourselves hugely and, it must be said, the meringue à l'italienne was pronounced too light and fluffy for the heavy company.

This morning, I am hard at work on a tale in which you feature. In some way. For my Lady Eustace is both sweet and expressive, though full of cunning and could easily be on the stage if she had to earn her bread. And of course she does so love diamonds, like yourself. Her little eyes quite sparkle when she sees them. Her eyes however remain untouched by that magnificient violet hue. This touch would frighten the publishers and possibly dear Gifford too! She lacks all your many good qualities, my dear Isabella, but your beauty and spirit inspire me as I write of her.

My wife is flaunting about with those buttons you gave her.

Most sincerely yours,
Anthony Trollope

'Are you all right, hen?' Mad Izzy's voice called out from the sitting room.

'He slept with my sister on our wedding day, the bastard!' the voice of some suitably worked up interviewee on the talk show was yelling, while the audience hissed and booed.

'Yes, thanks, Mrs Finlay,' Harriet croaked. She held the letter in her hands. She was trembling. Her instincts had been right after all. Isabella *had* been somebody special. In spite of all her mistakes, she had inspired Trollope to write one of his most successful novels. *The Eustace Diamonds*. (Earnings £2,500, no less!) What had Harriet's old English teacher once called her? 'The poor man's Becky Sharpe'. And that had been right. Isabella had in the end been just that, Govan's Becky Sharpe. Trollope must have sensed that capacity for self-destruction in her energy and wilfulness. After all, he was a middle-aged man living a very settled life, he had to get his ideas for his books from somewhere. All writers constantly fished about for ideas, just like painters, and God help her, she knew about them. But this letter had been written by the civil servant Trollope, keeping his nose clean, tugging the forelock so that he could keep in with his Ayrshire set. Portray Castle had been modelled on Castle Wemyss, Caroline Burns had not contradicted this, so was that why Isabella had had her portrait painted there, dripping in diamonds, rather than in her own home? But why had the fact she had been the model for the character never come out in any books? Harriet had now read four biographies of Trollope and the Burns were merely a footnote, with Isabella's name nowhere. Perhaps it had just remained an in-joke amongst a rich group of friends. Friends who had a business relationship to hide, maybe?

She had to go and buy a copy of the novel. What a find! Still she held the letter in her hand, desperately thinking what she should do with it. Instantly her mobile phone began to ring, like Big Brother, and she nearly leapt three feet into the air.

'Mrs Longbridge, Matt Mercer here. Your husband gave me your number. Look, I understand you're in Scotland but I wonder if we might meet when you're back?'

'Mr Mercer, the painting's not for sale, I'm sorry.' Her voice trembled, like a six-year-old's who has just been found with her hand in the cookie jar.

'Yes, I realise that, but I would be grateful if we could talk. I'm in town this Friday. I was wondering if we might meet. At my house, Wilton Place?'

'I suppose so.' Why should she go to him? Presumably when you were worth a billion normal rules did not apply. People would always be summoned to him. The man's voice sounded persuasive. He was obviously someone who was used to getting his own way.

'Five o'clock? I'll look forward to it.'

So, Matt Mercer, near the top of the *Sunday Times* Rich List year after year, making you feel sorry for all the minnows who were only worth £25m, now wanted to see her. All right, H, you can handle that.

'You OK, hen?' Mad Izzy was looking at her hawkishly from the doorway.

'I'm fine. Thank you so much, Mrs Finlay. It is kind of you to let me do this. There's one letter I would like to photocopy, if I may? It could be important for the article. May I leave my stuff here and pop out to the post office?'

'Aye, I suppose. Isabella liked the men — found another one?' Mad Izzy's raunchy laughter followed her down the stairs. Isabella and hairy old Trollope, surely not? Yuck!

In the post office, waiting for the photocopier to be free, a non-stop video informed Harriet of the benefits of stairlifts, pet insurance and tin openers for the elderly. The queue of elderly men and women, flapping their pension books, seemed unimpressed and shuffled forward making small talk, before diving energetically to the counter as soon as a bell pinged, just in case anyone else got in first. Harriet reread the letter. What had Isabella made of the great writer Trollope putting her in a novel? *Sweet and expressive, though mischievous.* Heady stuff. Or would she just have shrugged it off like Katya? Maybe to her the great Trollope was just some boring old fart who was friendly with her old man? What an article it was going to make now! But was Harriet qualified to write it? Should she not be hot footing it to the Trollope Society who would know their man in every detail.

Then she remembered Jester saying how ignorance of a person was a very good basis on which to start a portrait. For you looked at the face unfettered by prior knowledge. All those eminent biographies of Trollope had always started with the premise that he was straight as a die, when given the financial disasters in his family and his lack of progress in the Civil Service until quite late in life, short cuts would in fact have been only too tempting. His was a well-known portrait which now needed a fresh pair of eyes.

'You in a dwammy, Harriet?' Coming out, she nearly collided with a large pair of feet, and, looking up, saw Murdo. He was standing in overalls in the doorway of the next-door shop, while the young man he always called Shug was painting along the inside sill, grinning at her.

'Murdo, hello. I've just come from your grandmother's. What on earth's a dwammy?'

'A confused dream. Aye, she said you'd be rooting through the biscuit tin. Found anything good? A nice juicy will?'

'No, alas. Some goodies, but not a will.'

'Shame.'

'Is this your new shop? Is The KOOC moving?'

'Naw. This is the beginning of the Wilson property empire. I bought it at auction up in Glasgow the other month, for five grand. Now me and Shug are doing it up for a charity shop.'

'Not another one! What will your fellow traders think about that?'

'Not a lot. But then they pay the full market rent. I'll have a wife to keep, so it has to be good news.'

'Yes, Mrs Finlay said. Congratulations.'

He was smiling down at her, probably as he would look at a little old lady who was about to buy a knitting pattern. Harriet suddenly felt a hundred years old and rising. God, he was handsome! If she were Rena and twenty-one, she'd be wound round him like a lasso. Then she saw he was laughing.

'No, Murdo, I cannot, simply cannot, call her Mad Izzy! I don't know why she puts up with it.'

''Cos she's *mad*, that's why! Listen, me and Shug are doing a *ceilidh* the night. At McGuffey's. Want to come?

The second invitation from a businessman in half an hour. Things must be looking up.

'But I haven't got a partner . . . '

'Och, come on, Harriet, hen! Chill out.'

'Well, it's years since I've been to a *ceilidh*. I don't know if I'd remember the steps. But what the hell? It's my last night. I'm going home tomorrow. Yes, please.'

'Look, even if you've two left feet, we're used to teaching the English how to be civilised.'

'How kind!'

From inside the shop she could hear Murdo's voice singing the song from the previous night in the pub, the one which had made Mad Izzy's eyes light up like a young girl's. 'That's you! Have you recorded your songs?'

'Aye. Made a new demo tape last month. Shug says he'll stuff it in the paint if I play it once more.'

'You coming, Murdo, or what? They do-gooders will be wanting in with their boxes at five!' Shug banged on the glass, his knuckles leaving smears.

'Aye. OK, I'm coming. Want a copy?' Murdo proudly produced a cassette from the top pocket of his overalls, white fingerprints over the sticker: *Murdo Wilson: Songs From Largs' Modest Living Legend.*

'Yes, please,' said Harriet again, deciding that she was in a dwammy and that his smile could sell Heaven to devils. No wonder poor old Trollope hadn't stood a chance with Great-great-granny!

Chelsea Barracks, Kings Road

'Canapés, anyone? That's the vegetarian choice on the left.' Katya was circulating, holding out her tray to tempt middle-aged men expertly wooing their clients. She might as well have been invisible. They just stretched out and took the whirls of smoked salmon and caviar and wolfed them down, never taking their eyes off the prey. It was very instructive and the beginnings of a picture came into Katya's mind. The Deal. A full-length group portrait, herself pictured as the weary young waitress while the eyes of the podgy middle-aged men remained fixed, elsewhere as on a Holy Grail. You could even do it like a faux-Chagall, with someone flying over their heads waving a cheque. How these men loved having client bashes in a barracks, as if some of the army Action Man magic might rub off and give them back a bit of their lost youth and vigour. How boring business was. All they ever talked about were margins and bottom lines. Hardly any women here, only a couple of French clients to vary the diet, but she could tell by the way they turned their mouths down that the food stank as much as the forced jollity.

In the distance, she could see her mother jerking her thumb fiercely over to another group of canapé-less men at the far corner. Amanda the control freak was dressed in tasteful black with discreet gold earrings and dark red lipstick, but she might as well have been a carrion crow sitting in the corner, thought Katya. There was nothing soft about her attitude to her daughter; if anything she was more pleasant to the other girls. Katya was also under strict instructions not to smile and show her tongue stud. 'What would people think!' 'That you can't get the staff nowadays?' she had replied. 'Oh, yes, we can, sweetie, don't you worry. There are dozens of little South African girls and Australians and students in debt who would give their eye teeth to be working for me.'

Amanda had just become a partner in the business and so was even more certain of her power over others. Katya thought of her overdraft and smiled with her mouth closely shut. 'Would you like a canapé?' Oops, the tongue had slipped out. A man with a paunch and a bad Roman haircut looked at her, fascinated. 'Does it hurt?' 'No, sir. Smoked salmon or roast beef? The vegetarian choice is on the left.'

The real meaning of money was power. Like Amanda had over her now. For Katya's generation, it also meant you could never, ever get out of debt. She'd never even looked at the personal finance pages in newspapers. None of her friends did. It was all irrelevant crap when you had no chance for years of ever owning a home of your own let alone a PEP, whatever they were. One thing she did know, though, she wasn't ever going to lose her home. If she ever got one. Unlike Richard Dickbrain. What would he have done without Harriet? Yet he never seemed particularly grateful to her.

She could feel the sweat about to trickle down her face. The whole capital was on fire this summer, the Underground reduced to a long stream of sweat. Up here, in this overcrowded drill hall, it was no better. Why didn't Amanda get a soldier to open the windows?

As she continued to circulate another picture swam into her mind, Richard's portrait, emerging like a fish to the surface of a pond. The big masculine features were strong but still too young — she'd have to age him, the plonker! Still, there was plenty of time. A week before it had to be submitted. Then the big bash in July when they announced the winner. It had been one hell of a rush, but hopefully she'd get something for it. It was good, she knew it. First prize? I wish. The noughts in her overdraft seemed to stretch impossibly long.

Her tray was still half full. Why did anyone go in for this corporate hospitality anyway? It didn't fool anyone. 'All part of the marketing mix these days. One has to give added value,' she could hear her mother saying brightly to some poor sod over the phone. What was a marketing mix? Felix would know. He had put his work on to the Internet to gain more commissions. Was it like a cake mix? You added food and wine to the marketing, which meant you could whip up your clients to make them buy more. It made about as much sense.

'That man over there at the end says he'd like some vegetarian.' A girl called Susan from New South Wales came up to her, swerving her tray right over Katya's head. She saw the man. Oh, joy, he was standing at an open window! Wishing she was a figure from Chagall who could just take off and fly over the heads of all these chomping, swilling businessmen, Katya made straight for the window. Keeping her mouth shut, of course.

Largs

She liked jewels. She liked admiration. She liked the power of being arrogant to those around her . . . There were some who said that she was almost snake-like in her rapid bendings and the almost too easy gestures of her body: for she was much given to action and to the expression of her thought by the motion of her limbs . . . They were long large eyes — but very dangerous. To those who knew how to read a face, there was danger plainly written in them . . . Lizzie's eyes were not tender — neither were they true. But they were surmounted by the most wonderfully pencilled eyebrows that ever nature unassisted planted on a woman's face.

Trollope's own portrait of Lady Eustace. My God, thought Harriet, he was sailing a bit near the wind. But how delicious to be portrayed as a dynamic baddie rather than one of the usual prim angelic heroines the Victorians went in for.

The seagulls could have been bashing themselves against the hotel window, the clouds scudding across the bay at a ridiculously breakneck speed, Harriet would not have noticed. She lay on her stomach on the big double bed, reading. Outside in the corridor a phone rang and footsteps carried on past the door down to the entrance hall. There were German voices but Harriet barely heard, for she was back in the 1870s. Isabella had come alive and was young and lovely, laughing with triumph.

How fiercely her alter ego, the tempestuous Lizzie Eustace, clung on to her diamonds come hell or Mr Camperdown, the Eustace family lawyer. The worthy Frank Greystock was manipulated mercilessly by her as he fought to keep his better feelings for Lucy Morris — one of Trollope's more boring, gutless heroines. Other characters vented their disapproval of the gutsy little widow who so flaunted her beauty and property: the ghastly Lady Linthingow who was said to cheat at cards; the sententious Lord Fawn whose lengthy courtship of the undeserving Lizzie seemed to occupy most of the book, and then creepy Mr Emilius with his thick black hair and uncertain past.

As Harriet read, it was the continual theme of the importance of wealth being retained in the family which was hammered home. She thought of Isabella who had carefully filched Gifford's furniture to hide on her brother's farm before the bailiffs arrived. She had also been dripping in diamonds in the portrait.

What had happened to them? Lizzie's exploits and her desperate manoeuvrings to avoid giving back the family diamonds to the lawyer were foolish but understandable given a society where it was dangerous to yield an inch. Her energy made the book zing.

Concentration had always been Harriet's chief asset. It had helped her get her business off the ground, for she could read fast and thoroughly, absorbing information in filing cabinets in her brain. The mobile rang, but without taking her eye off the page she bent down and switched it off. Dusk came and the early-evening lights from Millport began to twinkle across the bay. Then the sun disappeared. Still she read on.

Finally, she took a deep breath and put the book down. She looked at the clock. Half-past nine. It had taken her nine hours. Apple cores lay all over the bed and two empty packets of biscuits scrunched beneath her. Her eyes ached from the poor overhead light. Poor old Lizzie Eustace was in the end forced to marry Mr Emilius at the Episcopal Church in Ayr to avoid comment. He had demanded all her property as a husband could, so she would never have been independent again, poor girl. '*After a certain fashion he will, perhaps, be tender to her ... The writer of the present story may, however, declare that the future fate of this lady shall not be left altogether in obscurity,'* Trollope had written, followed by the all powerful Duke of Omnium pronouncing that she did not have '*a good time before her*'. The readers were therefore left in no doubt that poor Lizzie was damned indeed. A tidy downbeat ending, redolent of Trollope's Civil Service mind, which left the requirements of property law satisfied but a sour taste in the mouth. An unpalatable tale for any woman who had married for the second time with less than 100% success.

Harriet could suddenly see why Isabella had screwed up so badly after Gifford's death. As Trollope, seeing that Gifford was so much older than her and likely to die first, had known that she would. Too much nervous energy there, not enough knowledge of the world. Fact, of course, had been sadder and more squalid than the fiction; for while Lizzie had been left rich with Portray Castle, alias Castle Wemyss, poor Isabella had been left in precarious circumstances just as the economy started bubbling, fuelled by the spoils of the Empire. And she would have had too much spirit and independence to have knuckled down and been the poor relation; too much pride and faith in the effect she could have on men. She would also have been used to a man handling the money.

> *'She had learned to draw cheques, but she had no other correct notion as to business. She knew nothing as to spending money, saving it or investing it. Though she was clever, sharp and greedy, she had no idea what money would do.'*

A classic woman's financial education. Learning how to consume, not to control. So Trollope had met this energetic young woman on the make and had portrayed her in Portray Castle as a widow. In the end, Lizzie had settled for Mr Emilius, described in that anti-Semitic way as a 'bohemian Jew', a bigamist fraud with a wife in Prague. Of course, the human spirit being infinitely more complicated than a mere character in a novel, Isabella had been a survivor, buying and selling furniture and mooching round the barras. She had tried settling for a respectable dentist but, widowed a second time, had lost the plot; an ill-judged affair and a bit of Govan rough finished her off. Much more poignant than Trollope's tale.

But marriage for women who were no longer young *had* to be made, for better not worse. Suddenly, Harriet knew she had to hang on to every picture she had, as well as the Notting Hill house. She would not bail Richard out this time, whatever he tried on when she got back. She must remain mistress of her own fate. Otherwise she would hit her fifties like Isabella or sad Maggie, who somewhere along the line had given in to despair.

That was why the Victorians fought so frantically for the maintenance of assets within family. They knew that once families went into decline there was no safety net, only the poorhouse. Nowadays credit cards were juggled for years and bankruptcy carried less stigma, but Harriet admired Victorian financial caution. It was more grown-up.

Trollope started writing *The Eustace Diamonds* on 4 December 1869, finishing on 25 August 1870. He had resigned from the Post Office two years earlier and was then an established writer although he had not had a successful book for some time.

The novel was published in *The Fortnightly Review* in instalments the following year, and well received by the critics, who compared Lizzie to Becky Sharp. 'Mr Trollope is himself again,' wrote the *Saturday Review*, while Disraeli congratulated Trollope on his 'new adventuress'. His trips to Scotland had been very worthwhile.

Harriet went back through the books she had collected, piecing her notes together all over the bed. Trollope had kept stumm about Isabella, probably out of gallantry, for while his inspiration for his character would have been a source for private fun between friends, Lizzie Eustace was hardly an angel and out of context would not have reflected well on Isabella. But surely another reason was to avoid shining a spotlight on his Scottish friendships? She would have to go back earlier in his life to complete the jigsaw.

Trollope had first visited Ireland in 1841 as a surveyor's clerk for the Post Office. He had arrived under a cloud of suspicion over the theft of a £3 Irish note which had been wrongly sent in a newspaper through the post and which he had been put in charge of. The money had disappeared but Trollope had apparently wriggled out of disciplinary action by applying for the Irish job. For a while, his superiors refused to reimburse his travel expenses, in lieu of the missing money, but in the end had backed down, probably to avoid a fuss, just relieved to have got him out of the London office. But £3 then, even Irish pounds, must have been worth a bit. It showed a side of Trollope predisposed towards short cuts. Mary Ellen would have been unsurprised that his career had prospered from then on. She always said Ireland was the perfect place for a bit of private enterprise.

George Burns had been developing profitable mail services between Glasgow, Liverpool, Belfast, Londonderry and Larne for eleven years before this, an established player in a small country and so undoubtedly in regular contact with Trollope. In 1854, he was finally appointed Surveyor for the Northern District of Ireland. In January 1855 he began writing the first chunk of *Barchester Towers*, apparently working in railway carriages on a home-made tablet. This location was suitably anonymous and also meant that the manuscript had to be copied by his wife Rose. The biographers lament this period from which few letters or papers survive, yet here was a man who was meticulous over detailing his expenses and noting Post Office journeys. What had he not recorded? At this point Trollope was an unsuccessful writer, still to make any real money and desperate to get to the top. If that article in *The World* was right, written after his death and detailing long-standing family history even the cynical Caroline Burns did not dispute, then instead of the railway carriage, he could have been quietly scribbling away at Castle Wemyss on the early chapters of his second successful book, unperturbed by the weather. A senior civil servant, desperately insecure about money, in the lair of ruthless mega-rich businessmen! Was this why his wife had copied the manuscript, because he had used Castle Wemyss embossed paper? Like the Sherlock Holmes story, it was the dog that did not bark. What was left unsaid in Trollope records? Unaccounted for in the Sundries column of his life?

If Harriet had learned one thing from running a business, it was that businessmen never rated artists for they have nothing to bring to the party. The Burns seemed typical in their love of yachts and the outdoors. But Trollope had inside information and, as Surveyor, decision-making power. Two years on he was telling a Select Committee on Postal Arrangements: 'I have local knowledge over the whole of Ireland.' How true. Plus he had been distrusted by his bosses as a troublemaker but as a star negotiator was sent on postal missions to America, Egypt, Gibraltar, Malta and the West Indies, some even after his resignation. How very useful. What contacts and whispers of contracts had he brought down to the castle on Firth of Clyde? Where he could come and go quietly by boat, exciting no interest at all. No wonder he described his day-dreaming about his characters as 'castle building'.

Harriet had a lot to think about now. Feeling stiff and cold, she ran her bath, pouring in bubble bath and watching the foam rising up the tub. Had society changed at all since Trollope's day? Not one iota. *The Eustace Diamonds* centred on the retention of wealth and property and Trollope knew the consequences when both were lost. As a young man, a £12 debt with a tailor had ballooned with compound interest into £200, more than a year's salary, leading to a money lender hovering behind his chair at the office. It was this emphasis on money management and mismanagement which gave his books their contemporary kick and collected such a fan club of Establishment admirers. Perhaps she ought to buy Richard *The Way We Live Now* and stick it on his pillow with a two-page summary.

Now Matt Mercer was a real Trollope character. Who wants to be a billionaire! She would be visiting him tomorrow and would now picture him through Trollope's eyes. She had seen him before at various events Richard had taken her to. Midas Mercer. You couldn't help noticing the way people would hover round him and his wife, as if they breathed special air. She knew Lindsey Mercer, too, who had been a client at the school for two years, efficiently fitting in Advanced French during early-morning phone calls while jetting around between homes and helping the needy. Harriet had last seen them at the Christmas Fair at the Royal Society of Obstetricians at Regent's Park. Georgiana had come with them, giggly on champagne and spending hundreds on designer children's clothes. There had been more titles per square inch than Ladies Day at Ascot, but when Matt and his wife had appeared, the crowds had parted. 'Have you seen that woman's diamond ring!' Georgiana had blurted out before a fit of hiccups.

At that moment, standing with a glass of champagne in her hand, Harriet had finally realised just where Richard stood in the scheme of things. How Trollope would have enjoyed describing her realisation, expert that he was at showing the onion layers of society. You thought yourself carefully ensconced in one layer only to find that there were other layers far more entrenched, monied, fêted and successful. Enough to bring tears to your eyes. Poor Isabella must have found that out. How she must have missed 'the power of being arrogant to those around her' in her grubby railwayman's cottage. It is painful suddenly to realise you are seller not a buyer. Poor Isabella. And now poor Richard too.

9

London W11

*Pay Off All You Owe Right Now — And
Have More Money In Your Pocket Every
Month!*
*What if you could borrow right now at our
cheapest interest rate ever and receive a
superb FREE Colour Television? With
Solitaire Trust you CAN! Complete a
secured loan with us before 1 August 1995
and you can . . .*

The operative word was 'secured'. The other
little sentence was underlined in blue at the
bottom of the paper. **Your Home Is At Risk
If You Do Not Keep Repayments On A
Mortgage Or Other Loan Secured On It.**
A bit bloody late for that. He wouldn't
know what 'security' was if it ran him over.
Richard scrunched up this latest bit of
junkmail and threw it overarm into the bin at
the other end of the room. Howzat! He'd be
pulling out his hair if he could afford to lose
any more.
The next envelope came from Central

England Water Plc. Oh, God, another bill! But no, an invitation to the awards ceremony on 11 July of the annual portrait competition at the Old Brewery, Chiswell Street, EC1. Ring-a-ding! Couldn't wait. What a fool he now felt for having volunteered himself to be captured on canvas. Katya had been on the phone just after he arrived back from Rome, assuring him the picture was 'brilliant', which of course, knowing the visual values of her generation, had really worried him. She said she'd been working for Amanda as a waitress to get her overdraft down. Perhaps he ought to offer his own services as wine waiter, cash in hand? Presumably her corporate customers were the same boring old farts who used to come in to his gallery once a year when their bonuses arrived, looking for a print. Until he had re-educated them into making really seriously expensive 'personal statements'. A fool and his bonus are soon parted. He had been so *good* then! If he could just get another break ... It made him furious to think who was flying high in the game now.

Richard tossed the invitation into his in-tray and rocked back on his chair. The morning was sunny and light was streaming in through the third-floor window of the little office. In the distance, he could see the roofs mounting the hill to Ladbroke Grove. He could even see the spire of St John's peeking through some regulation London plane trees. It would have been perfectly pleasant if there had not been a ton weight sitting on his shoulders. Debt. Ghosts of past excess flitted around the room. His mother's spirit was in all probability perched on the filing cabinet, knocking back some heavenly gin and enjoying his discomfiture.

The large desk was completely covered. Catalogues from salerooms were generously distributed in large piles, in between invoices not paid by clients and invoices not paid by Richard. His VAT book lay open, an enduring reproach to his inadequacies. Any minute now Vatman would parachute down into the fireplace like a sour-faced Father Christmas demanding gin, mince pies and Richard's balls *au gratin*. Piranha fish bank statements were loosely shoved inside archive files. The little letters DR on every page might as well have read RIP. There were also invitations to the Contemporary Art Fair at Olympia. Various dealers for Germany and France would be making eyes at him, trying to lure him on to their stands, but he knew in advance there would be no bargains. There were also piles of transparencies from hopeful artists, from Tirana to Timbuktu. Richard could not be bothered even to shake them out of the Jiffy bags and look at them. They would all want him to sell them for fortunes for a fourpenny cut. There were also invitations to parties at one or two American fairs. He no longer had the energy. Then there were the inevitable Access card statements and Visa card statements and Barclaycard statements and statements from lesser known credit companies who give you just a couple of extra inches of rope before stringing you up. Plus receipts and all the other detritus of civilised western living. Here Richard's private and personal lives met head on. The hellhole of self-employment.

It must have been the Romany in his soul which had consistently ignored good advice from assorted accountants, insisting he would always have something to sell. He'd trusted to his judgement and his luck, and nine times out of ten had been proved right. Of course he had done his best to be businesslike. He had brought in a book-keeper and a secretary who would come in every week to peer gloomily at the figures. In his gallery days it had been easier for his two worlds had been separated by St James' Park and he had managed to scrape by with much expensive paid help. But since he had downsized his business and his life, he seemed to have downsized his capacity to keep his two worlds separate. Until both coexisted uneasily here, tucked up under the eaves, in what must once have been a bedroom for a tweeny maid.

Perhaps the real problem was that his bank had given him not too much rope but a positive skein of excess, based on the good will and generous income of George and Mary Ellen. They had upped Richard's overdraft limit regularly over the years, and had positively blessed his offloading of the Cork Street lease, little knowing that it had been in the nick of time. Ditto the Lamborghini. Of course he had supplied pictures to most of the bank's board, as well as to some of their richest customers, and so had generally been thought a good risk. Each year, up his limit had been stretched with barely a nod and, so long as the pictures flowed in and out and he could show he had enough assets of his own, he had managed to scrape by, even when he no longer had a house to secure the overdraft upon. Selling house, gallery lease and car had not only avoided repossession but other messy court proceedings which would have demanded the full light of day be cast upon his finances. After which, expecting at any moment to be bailed out by his trust fund, he had pretty much continued as normal with a few gestures towards economy. Since 1993, he had bought only one Huntsman suit per year instead of three, and one pair of Lob shoes instead of four. What more could they ask of him? But the shock of his mother's perfidy had rocked him to the core. He would go into therapy if it didn't seem such bloody hard work. Frankly, Harriet had not been sympathetic. The worst thing about money worries is that they put you off sex.

He looked at his watch. Ten-thirty. The girl was due in soon to type his bits and pieces. Could the day get any worse?

Dear Richard,

You will remember some time ago I instructed you to sell my Maximilien Luce titled Au Bord de la Route. My price was £40,000 out of which we agreed your commission of 20%. You took possession of the painting on 20 March. I have a receipt in my possession. On our discussion on 14 April you said that the client who had bought it would take delivery at the end of the month. Since when I have heard nothing.

If the painting is unsold, I insist on its immediate restitution. If, however, the painting has been sold, I insist on receiving immediate payment or else I shall be forced

to institute legal proceedings.
Yours sincerely,
John Gruneberg

OK, so he *had* been a naughty boy, but frankly why couldn't Johnny G wait? Time was of the essence when you were self-employed. Cash flow ruled. It wasn't as if he had stolen it! He had just let it rest a while in his personal account to make the overdraft look less desperate. Of course he would have put it into his business account long before the VAT quarter ended. Trouble was, if Gruneberg started proceedings, the whole pack of cards would collapse.

Money was now more fiction than fact. How humiliating to be written to in such a peremptory fashion by such a little turd who had first come grovelling into his gallery thinking Van Dyke's first name was Dick. And who had bought him the Luce in the first place, at a bargain basement three grand? Slimy got-on pawnbroker who ate peas off his knife! Even his name was an invention. Just because he'd bought a repossessed pile in St George's Hill in '92, he thought he was a big shot. How dare he!

OK, the money should have gone into Richard's business account straight away, but no one knew what stress he'd been under.

Jamie's school fees were already late. He couldn't say anything more to Harriet. Oh, yes, she had made it quite clear that what was hers was hers, like the old song. She wouldn't even part with that bloody Scottish painting which should have been his anyway.

Where was he going to find £32K now? He was up against all his limits — and the Italian bills hadn't come in yet. The only game on the table at the moment was the Francoboni stash. Answers, please, on a postcard.

Richard prowled around the room before deciding he needed black coffee. He ran down the stairs and, as he did so, caught sight through the drawing-room door of the portrait Mercer wanted. There was a man who could write a cheque instantly, without even thinking about it. If Harriet had not literally been on her way back from Heathrow, Richard would have shoved it in a taxi and taken it over to Mercer's place in person and she could just have yelped. Everyone expected him to keep up a front, always beautifully dressed and looking the part. He'd have to start travelling around by bus soon. What the hell was he going to do? He'd run out of ideas.

The kitchen phone rang. Charles Kirby, vice-president of Inter-Agum Plc, one of the client friends Georgiana had filched over a quiche. 'Richard, glad to catch you in. Georgiana said you were on your own this week, with Harriet away. Are you coming to Olympia? There are one or two Spanish people I want to see. I would value your advice.'

'I was thinking of going tomorrow.'

'Well, come with me, there's a good man. I'll buy you lunch.'

It comes to a sad pass when one of London's former most eligible bachelors can be bought for the price of a few langustines.

'I'll meet you at the Information Desk, eleven-thirty,' he agreed.

Richard picked up the champagne stopper Harriet had bought in David Mellor's the previous month. He tossed it in the air and caught it. His champagne days were well and truly over. He had to *think*. What could he sell? The barrow boy in his soul came to the rescue. He finished his coffee and started in the drawing room. The *famille rose* dish — say £500. An oak side chair, English, round about 1867 — say £600. An Etruscan terracotta head of a boy, circa 4th century BC — say £800 on a good day. Clarice Cliff umbrella stand, nice one, possibly £2,500. What am I bid? Then the side tables could go along with the most valuable chaise-longue, two Edwardian busts and a rather fun seventeenth-century Chinese silk rug. He called the removers and a couple of chums in the auction game and soon another slice of his life was out of the house to be knocked down. At least he could show Harriet that he had tried. She might then after all be persuaded to part with that blowsy girl in the portrait. How much had Mercer offered? £20K. Ridiculous!

He looked out into Harriet's pretty landscaped garden. The sundial . . . Eighteenth-century, Italian. He had bought it for her on their honeymoon. £1,500? The chips were well and truly stacked against him, but when playing in life's casino, it is just a question of keeping one's nerve.

Largs

'Sometimes in life,
You must wake and look around you.
Sometimes in life,
You must see what you must see.
The game's not worth the candle,
It's time to turn the key.'

Murdo was in Nashville accepting the Country Music Award for Best Male Vocalist from Dolly Parton. She was dimpling up at

285

him from above the most famous breasts in the world. She just loved him! The stetson and big hair crowd were up on their feet cheering and in the wings, just about to join him on stage, was the even more gorgeous Shania Twain, set to duet one of the numbers from his triple platinum debut album. She was fantastic and so was his bank balance.

'And so I know I'm going back to Arizona
I know that's where my spirit wanders free
The desert sand that shimmers like the finest silver sea.
I know I'll find that peace of mind so absent all these years.'

Murdo was actually singing to three seagulls and a curious middle-aged woman who said she was from Worms, jah, and please could she haf a photograph? Murdo obliged. He was sitting outside the shop in the hot sunshine on a chair with bits of wicker sticking out at right angles. A large cup of coffee steamed by his foot. It was hard imagining Arizona when you were sitting in Largs with a view of the ferry and the Tourist Board and old Dougie cleaning the pub windows. Now for the eight-bar break, country boy.

> *'It's never easy*
> *To break the ties that bind you.*
> *The path can be tortuous to find,*
> *But nothing can keep me*
> *from reaching my journey's end,*
> *Only the sands of time.'*

Oh, yes, he knew all about breaking the ties that bound him. Big joke. He was the town's resident knot expert, bound hand and bloody foot. America glistened before him, the land of milk and honey. Independence or no Independence, he'd be there like a shot if he ever had the chance. Americans liked themselves. Whereas the Scots loved nursing their self-hatred. Just look at the bloody awful housing stock they spat up for each other all over the Central Belt.

'You have been to Arizona, yes?' the woman asked him. She looked like a geography teacher; they always had that same awful brand of curiosity. Murdo had to admit that he hadn't, but it was a good word to use, with four syllables. Heat in the sun most of the year. Seemed a good place to want to get back to. When the logic of this sank in, the woman smiled and thanked him.

As she had already bought some books and an old pewter tankard with 'Maybole 1946' inscribed on the front, having his picture taken was OK by him.

Thank God he and Shug were booked up for the next six months. There were some good clubs here in the West. Murdo stretched out his legs, closed his eyes and tried to imagine himself playing to packed stadiums right across America, never again turning out of bed for the Saturday morning jumble sales.

It was America for Murdo. South of the border held no allure. Murdo had never actually been to London. He'd thought about going down south, but look what it had done to his mum. Uppers and downers and roundabouters, until his dad keeled over from the stress of it all. As if London was some great wonderful Nirvana she could never get back to. Constant dribbling on about the high life. She'd only been down there three years, yet it had been everything to her. Largs could never live up to it. Pathetic. Well, he wasn't going to do that. Glasgow had everything London had. Except the English.

Rena always said those English were dead ignorant. See those game shows on the telly, couldn't answer the simplest question. What was it the other day? 'What is the capital of Finland?' The woman on the show, from

Blackburn or somewhere, had just looked like a rabbit in the headlights and said, 'Legoland.'

Harriet wasn't pig ignorant, of course. She'd have known. She'd probably been to Helsinki. He'd never met any English like her. She was what? Mid-thirties, late-thirties, really well-dressed. You couldn't say well-preserved because she was just herself. There was a fragility about her — as if, held up to the sun, she would be transparent.

He'd seen her come into McGuffey's straight away. Most of the English visitors marched in as if they owned the place, but she was obviously shy and just edged into the room. Even though her clothes shrieked Bond Street! He'd just finished a set so he bought her half a pint and she said she'd done a really good day's work and that Mad Izzy was a star. He liked her voice: posh, not grating, a real lady's voice. Like his gran, he kept wanting her to speak so he could listen. It was like listening to Joanna Lumley. She'd given him her card, told him to give her a ring if ever he came to London. She had just sold her business so she knew all about the grind of keeping your head above water. Even suggested he brought more of the shop out into the street, some bins of bargain books and more rugs and fabric draped about

289

— until he'd told her that with the Largs climate it would all float away if the school skivers didn't nick it first. She'd laughed. Really good teeth. He always noticed teeth. Shug had taken over onstage so Murdo danced a reel with her. She seemed to know the steps and when he whirled her round, she smiled at him. He felt he was holding hands with a china doll which would smash if he pulled her too hard, but she just laughed with him, hair flying out. Good fun watching Rena sulk.

Her husband sounded a right arrogant bastard. A picture dealer called Richard. He probably wore aftershave and red braces and had gold cufflinks with his initials on in squirly writing. Didn't like to think of Harriet married to such a scumbag. She deserved better. Anyway, she'd gone back this morning. *Arrivederci*, Murdo. Fiercely, he tried a riff that had come to him in the night. He had nearly got it right, when the postman came by with the second post.

'Och, Murdo, quit that thumping! The seagulls are having heart attacks. Are you coming to the meeting tomorrow night? We're having a speaker on land reform down from Glasgow.'

'Sounds like Comedy Night, Jim. You're never going to get those posh bastards giving

290

up their bloody land.'

'We've just got to make them! We're also going to decide who's going up to the Annual Conference.'

Man the barricades, the Largs SNP is coming! Murdo decided Spanish chords were in order and felt like a red-blooded revolutionary, until he saw he had been sent a gas bill. Bugger. See me, pal, I'm going back to Arizona!

Wilton Place, London SW1

'Good to see you, Mrs Longbridge. Come in. Or may I call you Harriet? Please, it's Matt. Don't go testing Lindsey on French verbs, will you? Don't think she's up to it today.'

Matt Mercer was being charming. Staff of various size and shapes took her coat, asked her if she would like iced tea, home-made lemonade, a glass of cold white wine, perhaps? She was shepherded up the stairs into the drawing room, a cream and pale blue exercise in expensive understatement. It belonged to a couple used to having everything under their direction. Even the family photographs were sensibly ranged in rows of silver frames. Teenagers on horse-back, graduation pictures, a wedding group, professionally taken portraits. A handsome couple. There was Lindsey Mercer meeting the Queen and Prince Philip. Matt Mercer greeting Mrs Thatcher, Chancellor Kohl, John Major, Nelson Mandela.

He stood in the doorway giving instructions that he was not to be disturbed and to take up Mrs Mercer's medicine. A phone rang in the distance, smoothly answered by some unseen underling.

Harriet went over to the picture windows. In the distance were ugly aerial and satellite dishes belonging to embassies of various suspect countries. If she looked to the left she could just see the orange trees on the roof terrace of Richard's old house. The new owners had added tall bay trees and ivy had been trained over the trellis walls.

Some homecoming she'd had, arriving back from the airport to find a note: 'Welcome back, darling H.' Where had Richard gone? His office had been the usual jumble and there had been no appointment in the diary. He had come back eventually after placing a bet for a horse running in the 2 o'clock at Epsom. A dead cert apparently. It had turned out to be dead meat, put down before the race result had even been announced. They had eaten a late lunch together in the garden, Murdo and Mad Izzy and Maggie now seeming like creatures from another planet. Harriet told him that she had found out some interesting stuff for the article, and that she was seeing Mercer later. She had been about to tell him all about Trollope and Lady Eustace but he had not been interested. Just whining on about how the bloody Romans wanted ridiculous amounts for their paintings and how he was going to get back his inheritance, raising his voice and giving the neighbourhood great gossip and entirely ruining her lunch. Harriet's patience eventually snapped. She had stood up and hissed at him to shut up! They could discuss it tomorrow. Then she had gone indoors to find most of the furniture in the sitting room was missing.

It had been his furniture, she had told herself, but yet again Richard's money problems were being stuck right under her nose. He had just stood there looking like a spoilt boy, about to stamp his foot. She told him to not be so pathetic and walked out, slamming the door behind her, slashing on her lipstick in the taxi. Happy homecoming. His and hers, money and cashflow. Was it the fresh, harsh West Coast air which had cleansed her brain and made everything seem sharp-focused and intolerable? He had run after the taxi, asking where she was going, and she'd remembered how he had once run after her barefoot right down Cork Street the first time she had visited his gallery. The difference now hurt. Where was she going? To see Mercer, she told him. 'Thank God you're seeing sense over that painting!' She just asked the driver to drive on.

'Don't worry, the lemonade you're having is the one with sugar. I'm a sour swine on a permanent diet. Here you are.' Matt Mercer was smiling at her. He was fifty, according to his dates in *Who's who*, but money, self-discipline and years of being a buyer had given him extended youth. Of course she had checked him out before when his wife had signed up for classes. Midas Mercer. Harriet always kept character notes scribbled in each client's file. Periodically, there would be articles about him in the business press which she had cut out for reference to avoid gaffes or in case the wife said anything which needed a suitable response. Information was the key to good business. She had rather hoped to get his company contract but it hadn't happened.

She remembered reading in some glossy that he had met Lindsey on the golf course at Turnberry in Ayrshire in the early-seventies. She had been a local girl caddying for one of the players. Their marriage had been a success. Four children, a Wilton Place house, a Georgian pile in Hertfordshire, an estate in Bermuda with private airstrip. Not a bad haul. Yet here he was, one of the richest men in the country, wanting something she owned. A buyer not a seller. How remarkable.

'Richard well? I saw him a couple of weeks ago.'

'Yes, thank you. He's just come back from Rome and will be spending most of the week at Olympia. Sniffing out the talent!' She smiled at him, not entirely successfully. Let him think any sourness in her expression was thanks to the lemonade. 'I see you still have the Jackson Pollock?'

'Yes, Richard's a good boy when he puts his mind to it. That was a great buy.'

'Yes,' she agreed. Got it in one. Richard Longbridge, boy wonder. 'I have been admiring your family photographs.'

'Yes, my brood, now in the process of marrying penniless public-school educated soldiers all earning fourpence. They are, however, fast cultivating expensive tastes and are constantly on the phone suggesting that pa-in-law buys them a home counties rectory.' He pulled a wry face which made her laugh. Then he pounced.

'Now this picture my wife would like to buy . . . '

'Oh, your wife, not you?'

'Yes, Lindsey. You told me it was not for sale, Richard too. I appreciate that. I understand you got on well with Mary Ellen and she left it to you. My wife knew her through their committee work for the Heart and Stroke Society. Both lost fathers to heart attacks, I understand. I remember the day Lindsey first came back from your mother-in-law's flat in Fitzroy Square. She was really excited. Anyway, speak to her yourself. You'll understand the situation better then.' He waited while Harriet finished her lemonade then led her upstairs.

Lindsey Mercer was lying in bed propped up on cushions. The room was large and once again a vision of cream luxury. The late-afternoon sun filled the room, but even that could not lend the allure of life to Lindsey Mercer's face. She had always been dressed in Chanel and Yves St Laurent when Harriet had seen her popping in and out of the school. Now, tucked up in bed, pale and fragile, she suddenly struck Harriet as a real West Coaster. Small, dark, still pretty; the archetypal wee wifie, however sparkly the rings on her fingers.

'Mrs Mercer, good evening. How nice to see you again.'

'I'd greet you in French, Mrs Gosse . . . no, Longbridge I should say, I'm sorry. My head is full of cotton wool. The drugs steal away the vocabulary. And, please, let's make it Lindsey and Harriet. Have you given her something to drink, Matt? It's so hot today.'

Harriet was uncertain where to sit, until Matt Mercer gestured to a chair. 'I'm leaving you two now. I'll come back in half an hour. She tires easily, you see, mustn't overdo it.' He bent down to kiss his wife. Then Harriet understood. She knew that white look, had seen it on her own mother's face. Long ago.

Lindsey Mercer smiled at her uncertainly, pleating and repleating the satin counterpane with ringed fingers. 'The doctors tell me I've got six months. Some days I feel like surprising them, others I think they're being over-optimistic. It's a question of attitude. Bowel cancer. It came as a bit of a shock. A nice, quick heart attack I would at least have been boned up on. You tend to learn by osmosis, doing committee work.'

'I'm very sorry, Lindsey.'

'You know, the problem is not actually facing death. It's leaving your children

297

behind, not knowing how their stories will turn out. If you've done a good job. Not knowing what sort of people *their* children will be. That's the real pain. And it makes me very keen to understand the past. While there's still time.'

Just saying this seemed to exhaust her. 'Matt tells me you have been to Largs?'

'Yes. I got back this morning.'

'Did you visit Nardini's?'

'I had lunch there one day.'

'Their ice creams are part of my memories of childhood. Going there after playing the puggies down on the front. The knicker-bocker glories with all those wee umbrellas they put on the top. My granny used to tell me that when old man Nardini opened the restaurant in the 1920s, it was a revelation to the locals. They'd never seen those long ice-cream spoons before. Used to try and nick them when the waiter wasn't looking!'

The way she said 'my granny' in just the way Mad Izzy had described Isabella . . . Big breath. Come on, Harriet.

'Look, Lindsey, are you related to Isabella Fairlie, the woman in the picture?'

'In a way. You see, Harriet, she had a child by my great-grandfather — Forbes Houston. She was married and they had an affair while he was painting her portrait. Your portrait.

298

Two years ago Matt bought me some new software for tracing family so I've become quite a genealogical freak in between stays in hospital. I'd always known quite a lot but I began to piece it all together then. Made myself start by going through the letters my father had left. Forbes Houston was from Fairlie. I was brought up down the coast, Troon actually, but my family originally came from all round Largs. I'd always known about him, and when I grew older I really liked his work.

'Once I married, of course, I had the means to buy up every piece I could find, from all over the world. They're mostly on the stairs, Matt'll show you. But I could hardly believe it when I was having tea in Mary Ellen's drawing room. I remarked what a lovely picture it was — the woman's face nearly knocked me out of my chair. I asked who had painted it and Mary Ellen said Forbes someone. Then I knew. It had his typical use of colour though he usually stuck to marine scenes and landscapes. I knew who the woman was, too. I couldn't believe my eyes. I begged Mary Ellen to consider selling, but she said her husband had bought it for her and she wouldn't. I even thought of having it copied, but it would have seemed a travesty.' Lindsey's voice trailed away.

'Were you sitting in the yellow chair next to the fireplace when you first saw it?'

'Yes. Mary Ellen said that was her posh visitor's chair. The picture just hit me. It was so vivid! You know, I never connected her new daughter-in-law with Harriet Gosse from the language school. It was only when she said your first husband had been an actor that I made the connection. I'm sorry I missed her funeral. I bet it was a party.'

Harriet thought of Richard that day, doling out the Bollinger like a madman. 'You could say that.'

'You see, in the letters he said he'd painted her at a rich friend's house just outside Largs. I don't know if the husband ever knew. About the child.'

'She was a girl, Eugenie,' Harriet interrupted. She was thinking very fast now. So had Gifford Fairlie wrongly suspected it was John Burns' child when his wife had chosen to sit in Castle Wemyss? Hence the row with Burns? Fellow Gaiters weren't supposed to cheat on each other.

Harriet took out the photograph of the portrait and laid it on the bed. Lindsey Mercer picked it up and stared at it intently. Then looked up. There was pleading in her eyes and so Harriet explained it all very carefully. It took quite a long time. A childhood spent in bars listening to storytellers weaving tales of Mafia magic and betrayal had taught her how to spin bare facts into gold and by the time she had finished the sun was turning the room to apricot and shadowing the woman's face.

'So, family I didn't know about, living in Largs! I wish I could meet Mad Izzy and Murdo. You make them come alive. To think those strange purple eyes have carried on down the generations! Is Murdo good-looking?'

'Very!' Harriet smiled, remembering him whirling her around at the *ceilidh* the night after she'd finished her research.

'Imagine wicked Lizzie Eustace being modelled on her! I read it at school. Poor old Forbes would have been putty in her hands. I'll get my secretary to sort out the papers for you to see. I think it must have been a passionate affair for them both. Nice that they had a child.'

'Well, a bit inconvenient, but you can see it was the real thing from the painting.'

'Yes. How dangerous and exciting, being painted by your secret lover! And he was good, wasn't he, Harriet?'

'Of course he was, Lindsey. And look.' Then she took out of her handbag the letter Trollope had written. Now hers.

After photocopying it she had run back to the flat, writing out a cheque as she had waited for Mad Izzy to come to the door. It was a dealer's trick Richard had taught her. Harriet made it out for £2,000. Mad Izzy's eye had narrowed to purple slits when she had seen it, but she had taken the cheque in her clawed hands. Inside, Harriet had heard the sound of Maggie howling. A keening, moaning sound. There was obviously something unbalanced there. You never knew what went on in others' lives. But money alone never made people happy. Not even £16 billion under Matt Mercer's management in a bull market could save this poor woman now leaning back exhausted on her pillows.

'Lindsey, I don't want to sell the painting. I love it. It is probably the best thing that came out of my knowing Mary Ellen. But what if I were to loan it to you? For as long as you want. It could hang here on this wall opposite the window. The light would bring out the colour of Isabella's eyes. I could come and show you all the material I've gathered. We could pool our researches.'

Somehow Harriet's voice was pleading, coming out all wrong. 'Though Richard, I know, would like me to sell it.'

'He's a dealer, my dear, everything has its price to him. He's always been the super salesman, of himself as well as his paintings. And how few of us managed to resist him!'

The wryness in her tone made Harriet look up. Lindsey Mercer was looking back at her with infinite understanding. Richard, you bastard! Harriet thought. It was like a replay, of Laura.

'When?'

'Don't worry, a long time ago. Long before you met. Matt was away for long periods and I had children to get through years of unending exams so I stayed at home, nose to the grindstone, visiting the galleries and auction rooms for light relief. Marriage isn't all Nardini knickerbocker glories, as you know. Thank you, Harriet, I accept your kind offer.'

Matt Mercer was at the end of the bed. They hadn't heard him come in.

'Darling, Harriet has very kindly agreed to let me have the picture on loan. Until . . . well, until I'm not around to look at it. Isn't that kind?'

'That's an intelligent compromise. Thank you, Harriet. My people will sort it out with your lawyer tomorrow morning. Obviously we'll cover the insurance. I'll send someone round to collect it when it's convenient.'

She shook hands with the sick woman. It was a weak handshake now and Harriet hoped she had not stayed too long. 'Take care, Lindsey. I will come again soon, if I may?'

'I would like that, Harriet. God bless you.'

Matt Mercer took her downstairs, pointing out the Houston pictures which ran from floor to ceiling. It seemed strange to be seeing scenes of the Firth of Clyde, great crashing waves and brooding skies, in the gentler environs of richer-than-rich Belgravia. Could Forbes Houston ever have imagined his great-great-granddaughter living like this?

In the hall they shook hands. 'Goodbye, Harriet. She hasn't got long. Less even than she thinks.'

'I'm very sorry.'

'Yes, it's tough. For the kids too. Though they have all got their own lives.' Only then did a flicker of feeling come into the man's tanned mask.

'Goodbye, my people will be in touch tomorrow. How much will you take?'

'What for?'

'For the loan. As I said, we'll pick up the tab for the insurance, of course.'

'Nothing. I wouldn't take a penny.'

'That's absurd! I prefer to pay something.'

'Well, I prefer that you should not! I won't accept. Your wife needs to have the painting near her and it is my pleasure to lend it to her for as long as she wants.'

He looked at her coolly. 'Well, thank you for coming. I can't believe it — Richard Longbridge's wife not taking any money. And you once ran a business!'

She smiled up at him. 'Very successfully, I assure you. I sold the language school on a big multiple. Haven't you heard of the woman whose price is above rubies?'

'No, that's a myth. She never existed.'

'Wrong! You've just met her. Good evening.'

She walked down the steps and into the street. As she turned the corner, just out of the corner of her eye, she saw that he'd remained on the doorstep, looking after her.

Strong meat being in that house for an hour, with all that money and power and sickness. Harriet suddenly found she was too wound up to go home and face Richard, having to give a blow by blow account of what had been said and justify, endlessly, why she had not taken any money. She stood for a moment watching the rush hour crunching past Knightsbridge Corner. Then made a decision and hurried down into the Underground.

★ ★ ★

You could hear a pin drop. Laura sat leaning against the proscenium arch slowly smoking a cigarette. She was wrapped head to toe in a fur coat, the audience mesmerised. Smoke drifted across the lights. She took her time. This was the big speech. When Margo Channing sits in the taxi in the dark, knowing Eve would be going on stage in her part. Magnificent in defeat. Give it all you're worth, girl. Milk it, Laura baby, milk it. Margo was the best role Bette ever had. It's a funny business, a woman's career. Yes, Laura herself knew all about careers and ladders and treading on others. Not for her the ignominy of ending up some dated unknown in *Spotlight*, or one of those names in the long, sad lists printed in *The Stage* each month, of lapsed Equity members who've given up all dreams of stardom and torn up the Union Card they once would have sold their bodies for. As she spoke the words, one part of her brain was taking note of the audience. White hair brigade. It was the best part of the show, when she was really close to the audience out on the apron stage; part of them, breathing in the cheap scent. At this moment, Laura was Bette and Margo rolled into one. Only better!

Then, suddenly, she saw Banquo's ghost. That familiar hairline. Harriet! Middle of the stalls. Laura had felt all evening there would be someone she knew in the audience. It was an infallible instinct. She always knew. The night Trevor Nunn had come along she had known, even before he had been spotted by the stage manager. Something about the chemistry with the audience when there was a person out there who knew you. It was only in these last moments of the show, speaking these lines, that she could see them. On stage, the lights blinded her and the audience was just a pride of invisible lions to be tamed. But out here, where she could give the lines some welly, the audience became real to her. Take it easy, Laura, don't rush. Harriet would understand the lines where Margo finally realises that without a man in her bed, even the most formidable career woman is not a real woman at all. No one better.

Her own situation gave the lines bile. Single. Forty-six. Late for making babies. Her only baby would be — what? Twenty-seven, twenty-eight now, with a wife and mortgage, even a baby of his own. He was the big thing she had dropped so that she could move up the ladder faster, God forgive her. As for men, none of them lasted.

When she'd finished Laura stood quite still, her eyes fixed on Harriet who had a son and a handsome husband and a beautiful home and everything in her designer garden super-duper. She blew a long stream of smoke into the stalls and stood daring all of them, Bette-style, not to adore her. There was silence, then the applause ripped through the tiny theatre as Middle England remembered why, after all, they had stuck by their boring, selfish husbands. Laura felt the applause like silk. She looked full at Harriet who was clapping too, unsmiling. Her face, beautiful and distinct even in that sea of faces, seemed to Laura to represent one word: retribution. Suddenly she saw the face of Tom above hers, contorted, not from the climax of lovemaking but through his heart giving out in the effort. Then, superimposed as in a film, there was Harriet's face on the evening when Laura had told her of their *affaire*. Before she had rushed off through the London traffic and proposed to Richard. Little fool! Out of the frying pan . . .

Backstage, it took a while to remove the make-up and the wigs and come down off the cloud the show always put her on, making her, according to the *Daily Mail*, 'a rare star who brings all the glamour of old Hollywood flashing like fireworks into 1990s Theatre-land'.

Don't believe your own publicity, Laura old pet, she said to herself, pouring a glass of wine from the wine box which stood ready on the table. All about the tiny star dressing room lay the usual Laura detritus of dirty handkerchiefs, photographs, telemessages, red roses, cards, exotic flowers from Chelsea florists and half-eaten food. God, she needed this wine. Would this be a three-drink evening or a four?

'Don't I get a drink?'

She turned, startled. Harriet was being ushered into the room. The dresser left to take the costumes back to wardrobe. It was the first time they had been alone in a room together for years.

'I hope you're not going to say, 'Darling, you were marvellous'?' Even to her own ears Laura sounded nervous.

'Of course not. That would mean you were crap. Which you weren't. I haven't forgotten all Tom's little rules.'

The name, spoken out loud, scampered around the room, a silent terrier.

'No, Laura, you were good. Bette would approve, I'm sure. That last scene gave me goosebumps.'

'Thank you. It was good of you to come. Richard was here, did he say?'

'Yes. He was raving about the show. I was in town so I thought I would see if I could get a ticket.'

'Look, Harriet . . . ' Laura began.

'Forget it, Laura. I've just come from a woman only four years older than you who's dying. And, you know what, she had a fling with Richard. And I don't even feel jealous. None of them is worth it. Richard's crazy about you, and that's all right too. You're a star and so is he, in his way.'

'Harriet, we haven't . . . if that's what you're thinking. Richard and me. Not even I could be such a putz.'

'It wouldn't matter even if you had. You make him laugh. I don't seem able to anymore. Mary Ellen and the money was the last straw.'

'Yes. She always was an arch bitch, wasn't she?'

'Good material there for a part.'

They smiled at each other. It was a broken friendship, irreparable, but forgiveness is still a good thing to have on the balance sheet, Laura thought. Harriet had been a special friend, and you don't make many new ones at forty-six, however good your reviews in the *Daily Mail*.

10

The bedroom had been designed by one of Harriet's more outré friends on the theme of peacock tails. Shades of green and turquoise blue had been used in the upholstery, walls, bed linen and hand-woven rugs. She would have been just as happy rushing out to Laura Ashley for a few rolls of floral sprig, but three years before, Richard, still nursing his pride after losing his Belgravia home and dismissing the little stucco house she had bought as a bit of a dump, had insisted on the best. For even though the property market had recovered in the mid-nineties, until Notting Hill was so fashionable it ached, for Richard it could never, ever be Belgravia.

Back in those first years of married life, she had thought his choice of motif rather suitable. But now, on this warm June morning with the sun streaming in, Richard was looking bedraggled in the peacock stakes, while Harriet, a brown and mousy peahen, lay in bed, nursing a cup of tea and watching him stomp about looking for cufflinks, watch and handkerchief. She felt an overpowering need to cocoon herself in cotton wool.

Couldn't wait for him to leave.

'So when are you meeting Charles?'

'Eleven-thirty. But I want to see a couple of the Spanish lot before that. I should also hear today if the Francoboni stuff has arrived in New York.'

'Great.'

'Yes, but it will just scratch the surface.'

Harriet found the remote control among the duvet and turned on the breakfast-time news; a weather girl was announcing dry and sunny conditions in London and the south-east. She looked up to the top of the picture to see what the weather was like in Largs. That bumpy bit on the map south-west of Glasgow. Wind and rain with some sunny periods. Would Mad Izzy get her washing out? Would Murdo be flogging more stock outside the shop as she had suggested? Would the *ceilidh* boat trip be cancelled if there were 'increasing winds on the West Coast'? How extraordinary, seen from this London eyrie, that those distant strangers should have so thoroughly got under her skin.

Before her, the household peacock was now sporting a pink and purple tie, silk, hand-dyed. He checked his reflection in the long dressing-room mirror, turning to one side then the other, tummy tucked in, ruffling his hair to make it look more abundant, smiling at himself to show those famous Longbridge dimples. She remembered a wonderful verb in Italian: *pavoneggiarsi*. From *pavone*, peacock. Literally, to peacock yourself. Strut your stuff. The perfect verb for Richard. *Io mi pavoneggio* — I peacock myself, *tu ti pavoneggi* — you peacock yourself, *il si pavoneggia* — he's at it, *ella si pavoneggia* — so is she. *Noi ci pavoneggiamo*, we peacock ourselves — that was Richard and Charles, swanking round Olympia Contemporary Art Fair checking out the talent, in every sense. *Voi vi pavoneggiate* — you (plural) peacock yourselves, ditto. *Loro si pavoneggiano.* They peacock themselves. Every time.

'What on earth is the matter with you, H? Your lips are moving.'

'I am declining a verb.'

'Painful! Well, I'm off. Sorry about yesterday. We'll go over everything when I get back. But do think again about selling old Matt that portrait while the going's good. Victorian art can't hold its own forever. Anyway, it hardly goes with the rest of your collection, does it?'

'No, Richard, I told you last night, I'll loan it to them. I'll sell one of the Freuds if it will just get you off my back. The one with the girl on the table, with the oranges.'

'No. Not that one.

'Why not?'

'I like it.'

'Or the one with the same girl in the bath.'

'None of the ones with the girl.'

'Why not? You want me to flog Mercer the portrait of Isabella which I've just learned so much about and, if you'd only bother to listen to what I have discovered, will have soared in value once my article is published. Whereas you won't let me get rid of any of the ones I've never much liked. And, unlike Isabella, we don't even know who the woman is.'

'I do.'

'So what's so special about her?'

'I made babies with her. That's what!'

'What do you mean? 'You made babies with her'? How primitive. Were you and she in some Christmas Sunday school, messing about the crib with the *papier-mâché*?'

'Very droll. No, she's Katya's mother, Amanda Holland. When she was young and completely beautiful. Never anyone to touch her.'

'I see.'

'Yes. Happy memories. That's why I don't want you to sell those in particular. I couldn't believe it when I realised old Marcus had collected them over the years.'

'Right, well, thank you so much for telling me. *Finally*. Katya never mentioned it. And what a luscious, willing creature her mother looks too. Have a nice day!'

'I love it when you're jealous.' He kissed her briefly, smiled at her, and grabbing his briefcase, shut the door. Harriet lay back and closed her eyes. Thank God I didn't have a child by this man! she thought. Thank God. Thank God. Thank God. That woman had been draped all over the house for the last five years and still she hadn't twigged. Tears started at the very edge of her eyes and for a moment she held her breath, waiting for the slamming of the front door and the quick steps going down the road to Holland Park tube. She did not need to get out of bed to know exactly how Richard would be peacocking down the road: the set shoulders, the big smile, the glamour, the mask all brilliantly set in place. *Si pavoneggia!*

She flicked channels, intending to get out of bed and try and make something of her day, but there was Matt Mercer on the Channel 6 breakfast business news, discussing personal equity plans and the strengths of the markets. Most of this went over Harriet's head. She went to an adviser twice a year and trusted that her money was in the right funds, but still she listened, fascinated, looking at the man she had seen kissing his dying wife only the night before. 'Investors need to be sure that the fund management team with whom they place their money has good researchers and analysts who can spot the winners on the rise. Increasingly the direct link between company and investor is being taken over by middle men, like me, who invest for them. So there has to be real confidence and trust. The financial services sector must guard against arrogance and complacency and never forget that this is not *our* money but our *investors'* money.'

The discussion then continued about bond equity ratios and other gobbledegook, but she could tell it was a cool performance. Probably there would be some PR minder in the background smiling with relief at the excellent impression his client was making. The interview ended and she switched off, lying back to think. Richard with Lindsay Mercer. Richard with Katya's mother sprawled all over the bloody hall. What was she supposed to think about that? She never knew what was coming next.

In her hand was the annual invitation to Speech Day Richard had flung over to remind her to ring the school and say they would be going. Billy and Jamie were visible in a picture on her dressing table. They had their arms round each other's shoulders, grinning and covered in mud, just finishing a school orienteering course. Stepbrothers. They were what really mattered. Family. This was just a rough patch. Work through it, girl, you've done it before. Richard will simmer down. Some time.

She showered, changed and was soon at her desk. She rang the school who were delighted that Mr and Mrs Longbridge would be attending, the secretary gushed. But then, even after five years, she and Richard were still the resident school love match. 'Your husband always makes such a *party* of Speech Day. We will miss him *so* much when Jamie leaves!' Excuse me, Harriet thought. What about Billy and me, are we invisible? But then that was Nature's way. Everyone always looked at the peacock, didn't they?

She spread her files on the kitchen table and set to work on the article. Back to the future!

When Anthony Trollope had written *The Eustace Diamonds* he needed money. He had resigned his Post Office salary and pension two years before, taking on the editorship of *St Paul's* magazine which had bombed. He had then stood as a parliamentary candidate for Beverley, losing the election and more money. His sons were another drain, one requiring money for a partnership and another for an Australian sheep farm. His two previous books had not sold well.

But by then he had so much front to keep up; rich friends, expensive tastes and habits. His wife Rose too was noted for her fashionable clothes (no charity shops for her!). He badly needed to play the superstar and to play for time. So wasn't his solution ingenious! Taking a leaf from Thackeray's book, enter a bad, beautiful, feisty heroine, Becky Sharpe with Scottish castle attached and a penchant for flaunting jewels. Though diamonds had turned out to be a boy's best friend in this case.

In one of Lindsey Mercer's stash of letters, Isabella had explained to Forbes Houston that it was John Burns' wife who had persuaded Isabella to have her portrait painted at Castle Wemyss. As if she would have needed much persuading!

Morning bled into afternoon and still she worked on. Isabella was weaving her magic and Harriet was back in Largs, happy once more.

* * *

The Contemporary Art Fair at Olympia was one vast, glorious stage for dealers and

318

Richard loved it. Showed he was still alive and kicking. He had had a stand here for years, pouring wine of varying degrees of bubbliness down everyone's throat, but now a sadder and a wiser man, to quote what's-it, that poet chap with the cocaine habit, today he merely visited everyone else's. Drank their champagne, got their hopes up for once. No, today he had a good strategy. He would wander around looking with patrician interest at the spoils in front of him. Be seen, show he was still on the planet and check out the prices. Then, if anything interested him, he would make a quiet call or two after the show had finished and the dealers had lost hope and got real on the prices. He still had one or two clients with walls needing to be sorted out.

There they all were, the Cork Street crew, clinging on by their fingernails while the new boys from the East End looked avant-garde and exhausted. The Germans were trying to look exciting, never a good idea, and the Italians efficient. Even worse. Everything was so expensive. But then, you needed ten thousand to cover the stand and all your expenses. London was out of recession and everything once again was booming and costing the earth. You couldn't get a parking space even on a Sunday, let alone a table in a decent restaurant. Everyone knew the price of everything and then multiplied by five if they were selling. All this activity on the back of City profits. Could it last? What would happen if all that lovely invisible wealth ever dried up?

Richard greeted one or two friends from the old days and met with cheery insouciance all questions as to his well-being. Mary Ellen might as well have put a posthumous ad in the *Times* Arts section for no man in history surely ever received as many condolences about their bloody mother as Richard Patrick Longbridge, Esq. Who had blabbed? It was as if news of his less than great expectations had seeped through the brickwork of some London office like a noxious gas and floated down Cork Street and up Bruton Street and Bond Street, swirling in and around every smart crevice in Mayfair before heading down Park Lane and Belgravia to acquaint all his former neighbours before splitting in two for America and Europe. 'Poor old Longbridge.' He could just hear them all, and gritted his teeth. It was very hard to bear.

What a dodo Harriet was not to flog that picture! Matt Mercer was a rich man with a fancy. If Trollope had used the girl for a character in a book, then ask for £40K and run! Anyway it had been his parents' picture, not hers! He remembered George bringing it home when he had been back from University one vacation. 'Give us a bit of class, eh, Dick? Nice big bazoomas, ain't she! Prime Scotch beef. Always go for women with a bit of meat, boy, something to grab hold of.' Richard smiled at the memory. His father had been all right. In every respect. How he would have loathed skinny Anne and ethereal Harriet. He would also have understood the need to flog that picture.

Why the high moral ground anyway? It wasn't as if Harriet's pa was any holier than thou. Jester was just an old gypsy dauber; he'd flog a drawing on the back of a beer mat for a blow job. Couldn't blame him, Richard wasn't getting much of it either at the moment. Harriet was probably going to do something really stupid like sell the most valuable of her pictures for fourpence and then sulk for months.

Richard's mobile rang. Francoboni. *Il maestro!*

'Richard, how are you? A pleasant trip to Roma, I hope. Listen, we have decided not to sell. My son, the advocate, he is getting married. His *fidanzata*, she would like the pictures for their villa. Her father is buying it so I too must give to them. You understand. *Sa com'è?*'

'I quite understand. Of course. How marvellous. Do please give the family my many congratulations. *Auguri a tutti*! Keep in touch, I'm probably coming to Milan in September.'

'I don't know, Richard, *Ciao*.'

'I don't know, Richard. *Ciao*.' Christ! He'd been too greedy and the bastard had tumbled to it. He'd just lost one of his best customers. No young couple would want all that Renaissance religious crap on the wall. Not unless Francoboni Junior was marrying an ex-nun. No, there was another deal somewhere, Richard could smell it. Some *Mafioso* fence had undercut him and Guido had decided to deal elsewhere. Now what the hell was he going to do?

'Richard!' On cue his lunch date appeared from behind a stand twenty yards away, wearing a flowered waistcoat and looking to Richard's eyes like a prize prat. 'How are you? I saw you muttering conspiratorially into the mobile and thought, That boy has a deal afoot! Come and meet one of my fellow directors. I've told him you would advise him on some French stuff he's got his eye on over there. He's just bought a new holiday place in the Bahamas.'

Richard slapped a smile on to his face with such force he almost yelped at the pain. He stood up and shook hands. 'Charles, I'd love to meet him. I've just been on the phone to Italy sorting things out for this vineyard owner. Italians never do anything by halves, do they? Now let's have some fun.' God, just listen to yourself, what an old tart you are, he thought. He managed to walk more or less in a straight line across the floor. No one would have known from his smile or his ready laugh that now *la bella Roma* really was bloody well burning in every conceivable direction. But that's the problem with old peacocks, they never know when to give up.

Edgware

The Willies was in full bloom. Recently, there had been a spate of elderly residents who had met their Maker, leading to small groups of tightly smiling, desperate relatives being shown round. Harriet had long suspected that the cold-eyed couple who ran the business knew that if there were enough flowers around, the visitors would not notice how depressing the place was, or how expensive. A few bright residents studied with the University of the Third Age, while one old lady out of sheer bloody mindedness was doing a degree with the Open University; but most preferred to sink into crosswords and reminiscence. Harriet had offered to move Jester into sheltered housing instead now he had made such good progress recovering from his stroke but he was firm about wanting to stay and finally she had realised that he needed a system to buck. He enjoyed pushing the rules and adding wrinkles to the faces of the staff who, after a morning sorting out Mr Dunne, would ask themselves whether the NHS working conditions were actually all that bad!

'Oi, Harry! Call this a green?' The familiar voice followed her down the corridor as she went to make his pot of tea. Her palette never measured up. She always offered to run him down to the art shop, but no, he preferred to complain. It distressed him how bad his latest paintings were. Some days he would snarl like a wounded animal, others he would silently attack the canvas in frail revenge. It was not going to be an easy winding down to eternity. Jester would never give in gracefully. Like so many of his generation, he was unthinkingly selfish, accustomed to women waiting on him like little maids all in a row.

They had tea. The window was open and they could see the other residents perambulating slowly to and fro over the lawn in the afternoon sun. Harriet told him about her research and her work. How she had loaned the picture to Matt Mercer's wife because she was ill, and that she had pieced together the woman's life. 'You know, Dad, the one in the portrait.' But the old man only half listened. He sat with a chocolate muffin in one shaking hand, crumbs all round his mouth, while the other hand clawed at his new tube of paint. He had not let it go in spite of the fact it was the wrong shade.

Every visit had to be thought through and completed with good grace and gritted teeth when affection and patience gave out. So there were the paints, the chocolate cake and the regulation letter from Billy. Jester usually pulled out a £20 note for his only grandson for Harriet to send on. Her father's money affairs had long ceased to intrigue her. He was always stony broke until some dramatic head-turning gesture was required, such as when he had bought her and Tom their little house in Hammersmith. For cash. In his way, he was not unlike Richard. There was always something to sell.

He complained he had nothing to listen to. That the regional accents of the Radio 4 presenters got on his nerves; Classic FM was irritating because the presenters did not know how to pronounce the names of the composers. 'They say 'bark' like the bloody stuff on a tree.' Harriet laid Murdo's demo tape on the table.

'What's this? There's paint on it. White. Never use white.'

'No, he was painting his shop.' Harriet smiled at the memory of Murdo in overalls, Shug banging at the window sill, shouting about 'they do-gooders'. The imprint of Murdo's white thumb lay on the title. *Murdo Wilson: Songs From Largs' Modest Living Legend.*

'Dad, it's sung and composed by the great-great-grandson of the woman in the picture! He's a musician, lives in Largs and plays country music. Try it, you might like it.' She placed it in the cassette recorder. Jester merely grunted. Then Murdo's voice sang out into the bedroom. Rena. Never had the name Catherine sounded so alluring.

'Cathe-e-rena,
Tell me have you seen her?
The beauty of Athena.
The girl who changed my life . . .
Oh, we got talkin'
Then we went a walkin'
It was really shockin'
How hard in love I fell.'

It was a gentle country number. His low voice hit Harriet like a wave, reminding her of Largs' sharp wind, the fierce colours of the sea and the hills. She felt almost . . . what? Homesick? Absurd. How can you be homesick for a place you've only spent a few days in? Yet his voice signalled escape in a way nothing else did. Lucky Rena, having a song written about her. Lucky Isabella, being painted by her lover and inspiring a top writer like Trollope to use her as his dangerous heroine. What Harriet herself would give to inspire men like that!

Earlier that morning, the immaculate men from Harrod's had arrived to remove the picture. She had taken a last look at Isabella and had said goodbye. 'Reason not the need.' Then Isabella had been wrapped up and gently carted away. No one had been able to understand why she would not take any money. It discomfited the lawyers as much as it infuriated Richard. But Harriet knew Lindsey would understand. As she had been about to leave the house, Matt Mercer's secretary had rung to fix up lunch at San Lorenzo's. Obviously payment still had to be made, even if it was in fine food.

Jester had stopped fiddling with his paints and now sat listening.

'But she had to go back,
On the railroad track.
To the hills of Cincinatti.
So I'm waitin' alone,
by the telephone,
For a long-distance call
from my one and only,
Rena.
Tell me have you seen her . . . '

Lucky Rena. It didn't matter what happened to a relationship once it was fixed in art. It didn't matter if domesticity or debt killed the love, for the passion was there, captured for all time, at its height. In fact, Lindsey's letters had shown that for Forbes Houston, the affair with Isabella had been just a fling. He had married a rich chandler's daughter the year after the painting, the very year Eugenie was born, and had naturally been more interested in keeping his new wife happy.

But even though Govan and the brandy bottle had beckoned, Isabella had been luckier than most women. Her beauty and high spirits had been captured for all time in paint and in words. That was real magic. The pure alchemy of eternal youth. Get used to the wrinkles, Harriet, she told herself. Not even your old dad wants to paint you!

There was a pause in the tape and then came a ballad which made her suddenly want to weep.

'*You are always by my side*
There is nowhere I can hide.
In my mind I feel a strength,
I never knew before.
I can climb a mountain top,
See the world and never drop
To the darkness down below,
Your love will keep me in its glow.

Safe in your arms,
You are the heart of me,
The part of me
That's sets my spirit free . . . '

'What do you think, Dad?'
'Well, it's better than Andy Lloyd Williams anyway.'
As she rose to leave, he almost smiled, his twisted mouth trembled, though as usual he never thanked her for coming. She left him squeezing out the paint on to his palette, listening to Murdo's voice. The music, turned up extra loud for Jester to hear, accompanied her as she walked down the corridor and back to real life. *Safe In Your Arms*. Inexpressibly comforting.

The next days passed in a blur for Harriet. She took over the big kitchen table with her notebooks and research and pounded away on her old office computer which had been stuck in one corner. She liked the kitchen for it had always seemed to her to be the heart of the house. Meals, when they were eaten, were taken more or less in silence for Richard, having promised to explain exactly what his financial problems were, had gone into prize ostrich mode. Strangers started coming to the house to be taken upstairs to the office, and Richard was never in when the recorded delivery letters came, delivered by the once smiling postman who now was clearly smelling barrel loads of rats.

Then more pieces of furniture began to disappear. Nothing of hers was taken, but still there was a sense of unravelling. So Harriet buried herself in the 1870s, and allowed the pure joy of research to blot out the present. Soon Isabella, Forbes Houston, Gifford Fairlie, the Burns family and Anthony Trollope occupied all her thoughts, becoming more real than the husband she half lived with or the people who knocked at the door or phantom friends who rang up to ask, 'Harriet, where the hell have you been!'

'*From the Muse of Anthony Trollope to Govan railway worker's moll, Isabella Fairlie was beautiful, self-destructive and impossible. Inheriting her portrait, Harriet Gosse Longbridge tells the incredible story of the woman who was the real Lizzie Eustace of Trollope's hit novel* The Eustace Diamonds *and reveals the cover-up of Trollope's secret life* . . .

She spent hours trying to work out how journalists wrote this sort of thing. It seemed to be a case of listening to the staccato rhythm of the prose, being economical with words. A challenge for someone who had spent most of her adult life writing reports which began: 'Mr Bloggs has made satisfactory progress with Intermediate French. He has mastered the subjunctive, the major tenses and has acquired a vocabulary of 500 words for business and private use . . . ' What the hell had she taken on?

Isabella was the star of the piece, but she had also to show there had been a conspiracy of silence between Trollope and the Burns family.

In the late 1840s/ early 1850s the mail service to Ireland was becoming a cut-throat business. George Burns had been fighting off his rival the Earl of Eglinton's Ardrossan line by approaching Trollope's old London boss and offering to carry the mails from

Greenock to Belfast for nothing. 'Burns, you are a fool!' he had apparently exclaimed. Far from it. In the summer of 1854 Trollope was writing *The Warden* when he heard he had been promoted to Surveyor for the Northern District of Ireland. Yet he apparently put off his summer holiday to Germany and Italy for a one-week trip to Oban and Stirling. Why Scotland? The temptation to 'pop in' to show his rich Scottish contacts on the Clyde that he had become a somebody at last must have been strong.

On 8 October 1854 he sent the manuscript of *The Warden* to Longman's, the publishers. On 9 October he was officially appointed. Surveyor. Normally once he finished one book he started another, and yet it was a mystery undecided by all the experts where and when he actually wrote *Barchester Towers*. The railway carriages tale struck Harriet as too pat and convenient. It could not be the reason why he wrote *Barchester Towers* improbably faster than *The Warden*. Also, in his biography, George Burns was described as never forgetting a detail of date or place. Yet the fact that one of the most popular novels of the period had been written in his home was never mentioned. It only slipped out in print during an interview with John Burns in *The World*, seven years after

Trollope's death, when the Burns were all-powerful and liked the literary cachet.

'*It was there that he (Trollope) thought out and wrote a great portion of Barchester Towers.*' It didn't exactly sound as if he had stayed for a mere night's bed and breakfast, did it? No, he needed space to write before taking up the big job. And what a very useful, kindly act it had been for the Burns who were hardly known for their artistic tastes. There had been very little memorabilia about the arts in the Inverclyde Collection, rich Philistines that they were, into yachting and tennis. Even by the corrupt standards of the Civil Service of the time, Trollope would have been sailing near the wind if this had got out. There might have been more than just hospitality involved. Something to add to those Sundries perhaps?

Trollope's attitude to his finances seemed to mirror Richard's. Both men craved money to prop up their self-esteem, their status in the world, put up a front of success. Money helped them feel in control. Both were desperate when confronted with a shortage. Now deprived of his inheritance, Richard was getting rid of his furniture like a man possessed, just as Trollope had downsized his grand Essex house only a couple of years after resigning from the Post Office.

Once again it struck Harriet as out of character that he would ever willingly have resigned. He had been trying to make it as a writer for years and had managed to juggle both lives successfully, so why give up when in another eight years he would have drawn his pension? He must have known that his work could easily go out of fashion. And although he had been overlooked for the post of Assistant Secretary, he had been offered other promotion and had also been given considerable time off for hunting each winter so he was hardly unindulged. For a public sector institutional animal like Trollope, used to harbouring his literary career under the umbrella of a safe salary, to give up all that security for freewheeling self-employment seemed extraordinarily out of character. He had not left before when younger and fitter, so why then? Unless there had been rumours circulating about just how much in bed he had been with the Burns. Or other business-men of their ilk. In negotiating international contracts he was hardly a backroom boy.

No, there had to have been a conspiracy of silence. In George Burns' biography Trollope is mentioned only as a friend of his son's, quite incidentally in a tale about how they had once enjoyed tea and herrings walking in the Highlands — at a period comfortably after Trollope's resignation. And in Trollope's autobiography there was no reference to the Burns family at all.

Harriet went on to the Internet. Trollope sites were abundant with top names from the Prime Minister up praising him to the skies. But the Burns, with all their might and splendour, merited not one site. Anywhere. Businessmen, no matter how rich, never enjoyed immortality, Harriet thought. Only artists, saints and the occasional king or queen achieved that.

How to put it all in! She sweated blood in the effort. At first she overwrote, then cut back. So it went on until steam came out of her WP.

'What are you going to wear?' Harriet jumped. Richard had come in and was standing waiting for the kettle to boil. He seemed unimpressed by the books and papers which by now were strewn over the table, the floor and the sideboard.

'What am I going to wear? When?'

'Speech day, H. Come on, darling! Tomorrow. We're showing up, united front for the boys. Scene of my boyhood triumphs. Stiff upper lip. Boy on the burning deck stuff and all that.'

'No, I hadn't forgotten. I've no idea, though. I imagine I'll wear what I wore last year, and hope everyone will have forgotten. I'm not in the mood to be a fashion plate.'

'Oh, don't be like that. I know I've been uncommunicative, but let's have a nice day out. Dress up! I promise once I've got things a bit clearer, we can have a nice Harriet-style in-depth chat. By the way, Katya said we can invite a couple of guests to that portrait awards 'do'. Apparently she's in with a chance. Down to the last three, unbelievably. Wouldn't let me see it before it went off, of course, wretched girl, but she said I'd like it. So I've invited Laura, OK? Kiss and make up time, I would have thought. You didn't tell me you saw her show.'

'Yes, she was very good.'

'A cracker. I think she's hitting the big time now.'

'I hope so. I'm glad you've invited her.'

'Good. See you when I see you. Happy writing.' He blew her a kiss and took his coffee upstairs. He had not, she noticed, offered her one.

The piece could probably be finished off tonight and faxed over to the magazine. She hoped they liked it but it almost no longer mattered if anyone else was interested, it had become a personal quest. Never very logical things to let into your life at the best of times. She looked at the

336

clock: eleven-thirty. She'd be meeting Matt Mercer in just over an hour. More to the point, what was she going to wear for him?

In the end, her sense of the ridiculous overcame her scruples. She dug out the pink Jean Muir, reacquired from the Hammersmith Save The Children Fund shop. Dry-cleaned, it was now hanging in her wardrobe ready for another joust. What a good joke! Everything else required changing shoes or handbags anyway, and Harriet could not be bothered. It was too hot. London was doing its best to suffocate its population and she had no energy except for the most basic of decisions. She stuck on some lipstick, brushed her hair, and grabbing her bag, rushed down Elgin Crescent to catch the bus to Knightsbridge Corner.

It was only when it was hurling down Kensington Church Street in a mad few yards of zero traffic that she saw Richard coming out of an antique shop with a tall, handsome man who might have been an Arab or Italian. Richard was smiling, nodding, shaking hands. They made an eye-catching pair. Harriet could see the other women in the bus, mainly middle-aged with shopping baskets prepared for Barker's, ogling them approvingly. Hard not to. She sighed and looked down, hoping Richard would not see her as the bus passed by.

* * *

It was cool inside the restaurant. Matt Mercer rose when she arrived and shook hands, and there was flurry of linen table napkins, water and bread rolls. Harriet saw a couple of former City pupils from her school lunching in one corner, perhaps plotting a divorce or a take-over, while a member of the Royal Family picked at a salad on the next table. The atmosphere was calm and unhurried, rather like Matt Mercer himself, who wore a well-cut black suit, white shirt and grey tie. No peacock silks for him. Harriet bent down ostensibly to put her handbag under her seat to catch a glimpse of the man's socks, always a give-away according to Richard, who himself went for bright yellow silk on principle; not this man, his socks were black silk, as well-regulated and inscrutable as his portfolio. He was being utterly charming, but then, as Harriet thought, you would be charming if you had £16 billion worth of other people's dosh to play with. Look at the effect a few decent pictures had had on Richard in his time. Somehow, the fact that she was wearing a fourth-hand dress made her feel terribly relaxed. On some important level, nothing mattered now.

She asked after Lindsey, told him how the article was progressing and of her trip to Scotland and the results of her research. She expected him to be bored, they could hardly talk about the Dow for more than a nano-second before her ignorance was exposed, but the story of George and John Burns and how they had started the Cunard Shipping Line obviously intrigued him. It was relaxing talking to a rich man you weren't trying to flog something to; someone who so obviously had the whole world and its markets taped.

Finally, Matt Mercer leaned back in his chair and looked at her appraisingly. 'You sound as if you are at a crossroads now your boy is growing up and the business has been sold. What next? More journalism?'

'I'm not sure.'

'Well, I find myself at a crossroads too. My life is going to change very much, very soon. I am prepared for it as much as one can be, but I find myself wondering what sort of difference I can make. A sense of mortality, I suppose. Do you ever feel that? I need to begin. I'm fifty. Time to start putting something back.'

Before long Harriet, who of course knew

everything there was to know about charities, especially if they flogged old clothes in empty high street shops, was telling him that he should form a charitable trust which would make grants to individuals and other charities, within his own favoured criteria. That there should be a board of trustees and a director. Which was when he said she was quite right and offered her the director's job, on a salary in line with her business expertise for, say, three days a week, plus an office near home, that sort of thing. Lindsey would love the idea, he told her. And so Harriet, thinking that an excuse to get away from Richard would be rather good said yes, please, rather as she had said yes, please to the *zabaglione*. Giving money away which didn't happen to be hers rather appealed. She was tired of donating to the Save the Richard Longbridge Fund. Sick children and animals would be a pleasant change.

They walked back to Wilton Place. The nurse said Mrs Mercer was sleeping, but Matt asked Harriet to come upstairs just for a moment to see where the picture had been hung.

She might have known Isabella would never do anything by halves. Today she was mounting guard from the wall facing the door, alongside the bed. Not where Harriet would have put her at all, but the light from the window made that smile and the violet eyes and flashing diamonds almost bounce off the walls. Here was passion personified; the moist pink and cream tones of the skin were more alive than the crêpe-paper face which lay so still facing the picture, barely making an impression on the pillow. Underneath Isabella, a forest of medicines stood on a small table. Harriet now knew that she had done the right thing. It's hard to help the rich but her strange journey had been worth it for she sensed an unexpected sisterhood between the three of them — Isabella, Lindsey, Harriet — which somehow reached out across time, money, culture and generation. Suddenly, Lindsey Mercer turned, opened her eyes and looked at her husband and Harriet as they stood in the doorway. Just for a second, she smiled.

★ ★ ★

Harriet dutifully acquired a new hat in Harvey Nichols on the way home and the next day played the demanding role of Mrs Richard Longbridge. It was not, thankfully, much of a speaking part, for she had finally finished the article at midnight, reread it first thing in the morning, made a few last

341

changes and had faxed it off to *King's Quarterly* with a short covering letter. It had been like giving birth and, as after any birth, she had no intention of doing anything like it again for a very long time, if ever.

No, today it was Richard's turn to be centre stage; old boy supremo of St Anthony's, he was going to show all the others that he was still a star. Harriet could tell by the way he drove down in the car that this was going to be an Oscar-winning performance.

'What I thought we'd do, Harriet, is sit down tomorrow. I've been working terribly hard, paid off a couple of the credit cards, seen the bank, tried to have a sensible conversation with the accountant and instructed my solicitor to sue Mary Ellen's trustees — or at least rattle their cage so that they may offer some kind of reparation. The point, you see, was that the old girl wasn't ever destitute, it was just sloppiness on their part rendering up the dosh as and when she said. OK? Then, if you can see your way to selling just one of the pictures . . . perhaps the Freud the Tate has. Offer it to them anyway. You wouldn't miss it, would you? They'll soon have lots of Lottery money sloshing around. Well, that would bring in half a million at least, even after tax, and really clear the decks. I've got to restructure, you see, and it's been difficult to do that while I've been so angry.'

It all added up. But how did she know that there was not some other sum lurking in the background in which two and two made thirty-five and three-quarters? Forget Trollope. She was married to the most handsome of Micawbers who, like Dickens' character, was equally infuriating. But did Harriet have the sticking power of Mrs M? 'I never will desert Mr Longbridge.' She'd married him, made the vows. And yet in the end he drained her blood as well as her bank account, however much of a fight she put up. It was a virtuoso act of seduction without a curtain call to tell you the show had finished. Yet he was still her husband and she still loved him. But at what cost?

Suddenly as white and exhausted as poor Lindsey Mercer, Harriet lay back, closed her eyes and did not open them for the rest of the journey.

They were greeted in the Great Hall by Billy, who in the last month had become even more of a beanpole, albeit a white, spotty, charming beanpole, who was just confident enough to greet his mother with a large hug, as long as she didn't hug back. Jamie was another beanpole, even taller but not quite as spotty nor quite as charming either for he hated his father's guts; it was all part of life's rich battlefield and nothing was going to change there. But he managed to pat her on the shoulder and say, 'Hi, Harriet', in that unwilling embarrassed way boys do when their best friend's mother has had the bad taste to marry their father.

The school, most of it built in the seventeenth century, was en fête, awash with streamers. Show time! Bums had to be put on seats next term and, as with most boarding schools, the fees of just nine boys were the difference between profit and unsustainable loss, so parents were there to be wooed for siblings however young and networked ruthlessly for cousins and colleagues' children. The boys' mothers vied to outdo each other in style, and bonhomie was apparently exuded by the sun, as A level results were discussed and the cricket first eleven praised. Under a tree the fifth-form band played Cole Porter. Strawberries and cream were served in the marquee down by the lake, a blessed relief after the interminable speeches. Speech Day as usual. But some parts of the landscape had changed; couples had split up and found new partners, sometimes fellow parents, so one had to be quick on one's feet to remember who was with whom. Harriet and Richard skilfully picked their way through the minefield, smiling side by side. Some of their London friends were also there, but the ones who had been briefed by Georgiana were too pitying for Richard's taste and after his second helping of strawberries he left Harriet to find the Head Master. He had succeeded in flogging off almost all the school's pictures, which had kept the fees reasonable and the building more or less still standing, but there was one small Whistler lurking in the library. The commission on the sale could be knocked off against Jamie's fees.

This was England at its best, the England the rest of the world admired and paid for until it really wasn't very English at all, more a parody of a previous age. Harriet suddenly wondered what Murdo would make of it. She greeted a few of the parents, earnestly discussed Billy's A level choices, and then, as her son was helping organise the prize giving, she walked up the slope towards the school; the band was playing *I've Got You Under My Skin*, small boys scurrying about like ants with chairs following instructions. She remembered the sleepless nights she had had over making the fees in the first few years, even Jester had helped out when the business nearly tottered in its third year through late payers, but she had somehow managed. Billy had needed more male company than an old granddad in a home and a cat. She had worked fifteen hours a day then to get the business off the ground and pay the bills, for Tom had left her nothing but fame and reporters knocking on the doors hoping to do yet another piece on the 'sexy young widow of dead soap star stud', until she had turned thirty and they had mercifully lost interest.

She turned back and saw the several hundred guests shifting in small groups by the lake which now shimmered in the heat. The marquee and the table cloths of the long tables glared whiter than white in the sun. Parents and teachers stood in small groups, plotting, planning and competing, but at one side there was a larger group clustered round a tall man. She didn't see who he was, for his head was thrown back, but the glorious peacock laugh which had pitched her soul into heaven years before, came floating on the still hot air towards her. Just one word came back to her from a thousand language lessons when clients' time was up.

Basta!

★ ★ ★

There was a ringing in his brain. It might have been the fault of the seedy character who was demanding something from him, only he was speaking a funny language full of glottal stops. He kept saying to the man that if he did not speak English, French or Italian, how was he supposed to know what he was talking about? But still the character persisted and so did the ringing. Until Richard woke up and realised that it was daylight and the ringing was coming from downstairs. Why didn't H get it, she was the morning person around here? The ringing went on and on. Muttering, he got up, shuffled into some slippers, grabbed his robe and went downstairs to the front door. He blinked in the harsh morning sunlight as the postman silently handed him a recorded delivery letter to sign for. He signed automatically, then he saw the logo on the envelope. Gruneberg Associates. Oh, God! Here we go.

Where the fuck was Harriet?

'Harriet!'

He stumbled down into the kitchen to find those godawful papers of hers he'd been tripping over for days had now disappeared. A fax came through on *King's Quarterly* writing paper, hailing Harriet as a star. That would be the day. He made real coffee, double blackness. Then, still calling her name, went around the house until he found the note on the pillow. She could have thought of somewhere more original to pin it, shown a bit more style. But that was good old Harriet, always predictable.

11

From the window of the aeroplane Harriet could see the West Coast spread below her, green and empty to Londoners' eyes, the fine chisellings of its landscape challenging the eye into the distance. She hadn't been able to get out of London fast enough.

Richard had drunk so much champagne, she had driven back from St Anthony's. As usual when he had drunk too much, he had been alternately affectionate and aggressive. She had barely listened to him for the traffic had been heavy, with one or two drivers trying to die young. She had also been thinking about which picture to sell or wondering whether, now the time had come for some tough love, to let him go bust and sort himself out. She was driving up the overpass into Chiswick, greeted by the familiar glass stumps of the office buildings to either side, when a sudden wave of weariness engulfed her, so powerful she had to move down into second gear and crawl. It was like being a widow again, having to make big decisions when all she wanted to do was sleep.

She had woken early at 5 a.m. and though her mind was still tired, her legs had forced her to get up, her hands had dressed her and packed a case, her voice had whispered for a cab to Heathrow where she had found a seat on the seven o'clock Glasgow flight full of businessmen rustling their *Financial Times*. Getting away had to be a good idea. Richard would probably run amok and flog everything she owned, but that would almost make things more simple. She practically hated those pictures of Marcus' now, for she had finally realised — a bit slow on the uptake here — that they represented possibly the only good reason why Richard had married her in the first place. Saleable assets while waiting for Mummy to keel over.

No. Money, or the assets which represented it, merely made life unbearable if you were living with a human money pit. What she needed now was a new recipe for living. First find your hire car, briskly drive for forty-five minutes in a south-westerly direction and wake up your life.

Largs hit her with the charm of the familiar. The schools had broken up for the holidays in Scotland and now small children with their grannies were trailing in and out of the sweetie shops even though it was just after nine o'clock in the morning. She parked her

350

car behind the station and walked through the centre. It was going to be hot. Scotland was enjoying a summer of almost Mediterranean heat and there was now the same expectancy as the morning sun bounced off the buildings and trees that you might find in any self-respecting holiday spot. Welcome to Largs Adriatico. She shut her eyes and imagined the buzz of the *motorinos*. 'Eh, Jimmy, mind yersel! I'll get yer up the road,' was now translated into the cheery, laddish shouts of a thousand Italian boys in the seaside towns she had drifted through as a young girl. '*Eh, Giuseppe, dovè vai? Vieni con me! Pren'amo un cappuccio.*' She would not think of Richard speaking to her in the Italian she had taught him. No, she would not.

Harriet looked into a few estate agents' windows. The prices by London standards were a dream; she saw herself and Billy in a small house filled with their friends, spending the summer eating ice creams at Nardini's and messing about in boats. She went to a florist and asked for a bouquet to be made up, with only violet, blue and purple flowers. Armed with this, she walked down Nelson Street. Mad Izzy opened the door to her. She had obviously been cleaning for she carried a feather duster and wore a large red bandanna which made her look like an inquisitive cockatoo. As usual she exuded the energy of a fifty-year-old.

'You back? Your cheque didn't bounce anyway. Man in Glasgow reckoned you were spot on with your money for that letter. They flowers for me? Terrible prices they charge, that shop.'

'May I come in, Mrs Finlay?' Harriet began. 'I'm back, as you see, for a second flying visit. I have a letter for you from a distant relative of yours that I've found. And I did say you could see my article. The thing is, you will find some of it may come as a shock.'

Again the miracle occurred in which her perfectly ordinary London voice was transformed into a debutante's cut-crystal vowels, honed at the finest Swiss finishing school.

Mad Izzy took the flowers awkwardly. 'Aye, come in. Maggie's just gone off to her work. I'm having a clean up, so take as you find. Milk no sugar, isn't it?'

'Yes, please,' said Miss Sunningdale 1955.

Harriet sat in the small overfurnished sitting room taking in the ornaments, now newly dusted, which crowded the window sill. It was only if you looked closely that you could tell they were actually rather fine porcelain figurines, valuable and in mint condition. The nylon curtains and swirly carpets belied the quality that was there in the room. She noted the good pieces of furniture which would set many a dealer in Kensington Church Street drooling, mixed up with fifties tat. A monstrous hostess trolley took up almost a quarter of the room. A large black cat sat on it, bad-tempered-looking even in sleep.

Mad Izzy came back with a plastic tray on which stood two mugs of tea and some chocolate biscuits. Her attitude wasn't unfriendly, just wary and ready to bristle like a porcupine. Clearly delving into the family history had exposed nerves which had not been danced on for decades.

She put on thick reading glasses and read through Harriet's article slowly, her mouth moving. When she finished, she put it down and sat for a few moments in silence. 'My God, I never knew half of this. Can't imagine why Granny never said about that Trollope man. If I was put in a book, I'd be yelling it out at my Bingo, good style. And I'm Forbes Houston's granddaughter! God Almighty.'

'I hope it hasn't come as too much of a shock?'

'Well, you're not writing for ordinary folk, I can see that. I suppose I should ask for more proof. But I know that it is right. It explains my mother's attitude to the portrait . . . I think Gran only told her who her real father was just before she died. You see, she'd lived her whole life believing she was a baronet's daughter as well as the Minister's wife. That really gave you status in those days. No wonder the portrait went under the bed afterwards.'

'I think you've been very brave helping me, Mrs Finlay. Thank you.'

'Och, well, it's better the truth comes out, I suppose. But it's going to be difficult when the magazine comes out round here. You see, hen, love children weren't exactly something to shout about from the rooftops. Well, not in those days. Now girls screech and drop weans at sixteen to get a nice wee flat from the Council, but it must have come as a terrible shock to my ma. She knew some of the Houstons, even said to me once what a cold, stuck-up lot they were. Forbes Houston left a bit of money, you see. He'd bought houses with every penny he earned and rented them out all over north Ayrshire. Murdo comes by it honestly, I now see, with that wee shop he's just let out. The older lot of Houstons probably knew about her all along and were terrified she'd make a claim. Property and money . . . they bring out the worst in families.'

'They certainly do, Mrs Finlay. Believe me,

I know. And about love children too. My husband has a daughter. I only found out about her after I married him. Though she's talented and means no harm, it was a shock. It was part of his life I knew nothing of.'

'Aye. Funny, it's the parents who are often rather pleased with themselves, as if they've been clever. But for us, the rest of the family, when we find out we have to chuck out that wee jigsaw puzzle we thought made up our life. It hurts. See me, I'm not Sir Gifford Fairlie's granddaughter, but then, I've always had an eye for colour and paintings. I'm still taking it in, but I suppose it's better to be descended from a really good painter, than a penniless baronet who drowned hisself!'

'My father's a painter, so I can vouch for it being interesting, if uncomfortable!'

Harriet then gave her Lindsey Mercer's letter. News that she was a distant cousin of the wife of one of the richest men in the UK was greeted in true Ayrshire style.

'That's nice. Nice house, has she?'

How to describe Wilton Place, SW1 to Nelson Street, Largs? 'Yes, a very nice house. The thing is, she's dying. Cancer. She's very frail and they've brought her back from hospital. Nothing else they can do. I've lent her the portrait of Isabella to look at, from her bed. She's lent me the letters from

Isabella to Forbes which I quote in the article. I've copied them for you. She asked me to. Too much secrecy, she said.'

'Aye, that's my proof. My poor mother was a Houston. No wonder old Gifford never wanted anything to do with her as a small child. Seen and not heard, she was. His sister treated her like dirt after Isabella left. When my ma took her in, it must have been hard. Still, this Lindsey sounds nice. Though the Houston money brought her more, obviously. Otherwise she'd have been out on the Council golf course like Murdo, not at that posh Turnberry when his nibs showed up looking for a wife.'

'I don't really know. I've taken the liberty of telling her about you and Murdo. She was brought up in Troon and always knew there was another family but found it too difficult to know where to start looking, after so many years. Now it's really important to her.'

'An elephant's graveyard, that's Scotland. They always come back when they're dying, ex-pat Scots. Can't keep away. You see them wandering all over the old cemetery looking for relatives they last saw when they buggered off as teenagers.'

'I don't think it was like that in Lindsey's case. She came back here to see her mother until she died.'

'Aye, well. You know what they say: 'A daughter's a daughter all your life. A son's a son until he gets a wife.' Isabella's buried here, did you know? With my parents. I kept meaning to get a posh gravestone but never managed. It's just a plain slab. She must give my dad uneasy nights. What a trial Gran was to him! All that brandy she'd knock back and him never touching a drop. Though she never drank in the Manse. Well, not so he could see!'

'Could I visit her grave?'

'Aye, the wee man will look it up in his book. You just go up the hill.' Mad Izzy sipped her tea. 'You can take some of these to lay on, for a bit of colour. I'll write to that Mrs Mercer, but I'm still taking it in. It's a wee bit of a shock. Old Isabella — she's still pulling out the rabbits from the hat even after all these years. My ma always said you never knew what she'd get up to next! And they call *me* Mad Izzy!'

She suddenly laughed, picked up the flowers and gave a good long sniff at their perfume. The sunlight filtering through the net curtains brought out their pure colours which matched her eyes, as Harriet had known they would.

★   ★   ★

How many babies people had then, and how many had died. Names with barely a life attached, aged three or four or five, were crammed on to headstones. Brothers and sisters were remembered on barely visible mossed over gravestones. The sun beat down as Harriet stood where the keeper had pointed: Isabella Geddes, 1849–1919. 'Much loved'. Eugenie Isabella Wishart, 1872–1947. 'Her soul rests in eternity'. That's more like it. Reverend John Wishart, 1865–1939. 'A doughty fighter for the Lord'. Was that an example of Mad Izzy's irony? But for his disapproval of his mother-in-law, he had never inspired men with such God-given gifts as she had, nor been as loved.

Harriet took a photograph, then sat down on a nearby bench to scribble an extra paragraph which she could hand write and fax down to the magazine. She looked down the hill at the town. She may not be a real writer, but she had found new material no one else had pieced together and understood. That Trollope had had a questionable Scottish hinterland, and that a young Ayrshire farmer's daughter had drunk life to the lees. Isabella may not have hung on to her money, she had been as bad as Richard in her own way, but she had lived with spirit and had both inspired great art and given birth, achievements for any woman.

Harriet closed her eyes and let the sun drench her face. Since Isabella's lifetime, men may have landed on the moon and the Internet promised to be as revolutionary as the mail service on which the Burns built their fortune, but human nature did not change. In this deserted graveyard, she felt real peace, a stranger curiously at home. As Matt Mercer said, this was crossroads time.

'I wish you could tell me what to do, Isabella,' she said aloud.

★ ★ ★

It was after midday when Harriet finally walked back into the town centre. The heat had decided to give them a run for their money and the streets were full of young, light-skinned Scots roasting nicely, downing Irn Bru and ice cream and wrapping their woolly cardigans round their middles. Glasgow trippers who could wangle a half day out of the office were pouring off the train. A notice board outside a bakery announced optimistically: 'Meat pie and chips, £1.85'. The very thought of mutton, chips and pastry made her want to heave and Harriet decided to get out of Largs and buy herself a picnic. She headed for a delicatessen which offered

French sticks and *charcûterie*, where she bought far more than she needed but she damn' well deserved some comfort eating — and drinking — and then headed out along the coast road to Castle Wemyss, hoping it would be deserted.

When she arrived there was no sign of life. No cars, not even Murdo's blue jaloppy. She parked and made her way through the long grass. This time she skirted round the mournful remains of the Castle, though she picked up a piece of cobalt blue tile lying on the grass, for luck. It was obviously from a fireplace, perhaps the one in the corner of Isabella's portrait. She needed to be all alone to think and dangle her feet in the cool water and watch the yachts and have a private nosh and a small swig of white wine from the bottle in her bag — virtuously screw-topped as she was driving. She was tired of dieting and doing the right thing. From now on, she was on Harriet Time with just her *Evening Standard* for company.

Then she noticed the small rowing boat moored to the pier. Damn! She rounded the corner and saw Murdo scribbling in a book. Typical. No doubt writing his latest SNP newsletter about John Major and the bastard Westminster government when all she wanted in the world was some peace from other people. Men in particular. She'd noticed his shop was shut as she'd driven past the Gallowgate. All day closing, naturally to avoid serving any tourists. This time he did not have fishing for an excuse, but his guitar was lying next to him. Great. Today he was the singing revolutionary.

She turned and began to tiptoe away. 'Harriet!' His voice boomed across the wilderness grounds. 'Great! You've come back! Don't go! Have you come up from London?'

'Er, yes. Hello, Murdo. I wanted to see your grandmother and tell her a bit about my research. She'll tell you.'

'Great. Sit down. This is just too perfect to waste. Today is probably all the summer Largs'll get and you've been lucky enough to catch it. I've got a piece we can share.'

'A piece of what?'

'A piece! Sandwich. 'Luncheon', don't you know?' His Bertie Wooster accent was absurd.

'Oh. Well, I've got a piece as well, but I did actually just come for peace. As in quiet. Not wishing to be rude but . . . '

'Well, you'll get more peace here than anywhere else with all those bloody tourists everywhere. Just look!'

He waved his hand and Harriet did look: at the small white sails of the yachts skimming off in the distance, the green hills on the opposite coastline, the blue-green of the Clyde. There was not another soul or another sound for miles.

It is the great curse of the English not to wish to appear rude so she joined him on the pier, setting out her plastic bag of cheese, ham and wine.

'You've got a flaming banquet there! Now, do you want to hear my new song?'

She was a captive audience. Or captured?

'Well, not if it's political. I don't want to be got at for being English, I'm not in the mood to feel guilty. I'm having enough problems with my half-Irish husband, OK?'

'You can't help it. Anyway, Alex Salmond would tell me my lyrics were off message. He's into power big time. No, this is a new song. When I hear a phrase I like, I build a song round it. There was this guy talking on the radio. 'I've been happier almost any time than now,' he said, and stuck in my mind. So I thought, Bugger the tourists, and locked up.'

'I've been happier almost any time than now,' Harriet repeated. Funny grammar. She tried translating that into Italian. Then gave up. Too tired. Have a slug of wine, Gosse. The Generation X-ers are so different from us knackered post-babyboomers. They are so totally self-centred it's quite admirable.

Murdo picked up the guitar and strummed a few chords, while Harriet concentrated on removing her shoes and dangling her feet in the icy water. She could feel the black blocks of stress on her shoulders beginning to melt.

'When that lady goes,
It's never easy
In the afterglow
Of a mad affair
I can safely say,
I've been happier
Almost any time than now.'

He might have been writing it for her. She had never felt such a loser on so many fronts.

'Love plays a waiting game
To keep you in its thrall.
You spend your life looking out for her,
Waiting for that call.
But when love comes it often leaves you
    when you're least aware.
You look around,
There's no one there,
There's nothing left to share.

'When that lady goes . . .'

Thrall, that was a good word. That's what she had been kept in: Richard's glamorous, impossibly romantic thrall. Murdo's voice was low and unpolished, but it had power and a sincerity which suddenly brought the most un-English tears into her eyes. Bugger! The song wasn't what she'd expected from Murdo, more sophisticated, more Jacques Brel. How it summed her up. The tears were about to lose the battle and start rolling down her cheeks so she began hacking at the French bread which was now a blur, and whacking ham and cheese inside. She poured wine into a plastic cup and sat on the pier's edge, swinging her legs, remembering a childhood of solitary picnics on hot Mediterranean hillsides.

Murdo changed key and tempo, causing an inexplicable tingling on the back of Harriet's neck. Give us a break, Murdo, she thought. You're twenty-seven, engaged to a blonde supercook with the biggest tits this side of Glasgow. You don't need to know how the rest of us feel.

'*Now she's gone, I haven't got the heart for it.*
With love gone, I want no more a part of it.

I've been there so many times and
    fouled it up.
It's true, I know. I'll never love again!

When that lady goes, it's never easy
In the afterglow of a mad affair
I can safely say,
I've been happier almost any time than
    now.'

That was it, once more into the chorus with feeling, and Harriet turned her back on him and abandoned herself to tears.

'You OK, Harriet?'

He had finally let her off for good behaviour. Silently, she handed him the bottle of wine.

'Yes, I'm OK. Nothing a bit of Largs sunlight won't cure.'

'Bugger skin cancer, eh?'

'Yes. Bugger everything. Where's your piece, then?'

He produced two bits of stale bread hiding a slice of cold bacon.

'Well, if you don't mind supping with the auld enemy, I think you'd be better off with some mortadella.'

'What's that? That two-tone ham stuff?'

'Yes, from your classy new deli.'

'What's in your paper?'

'Oh, the usual. Sleaze. Just another back-to-my-place scandal for John Major. At least it's not money in brown envelopes. Funnily enough, Major's a big Anthony Trollope fan, and thanks to your gran I've found out *he* was on the take. So, nothing changes.'

'Well, that's money for you. People behave like shite when there's money involved. Big Al down the folk club still seethes 'cos Jimmy Kennedy talked his granddad into selling him the copyright to *Harbour Lights* back in the thirties. All that Hawaiian guitar stuff The Platters put into their cover made everyone think the harbour was somewhere like Honolulu, but actually it's jist dear old Ayr. If I ever make it, I'll be on to the lawyers and accountants before you can say Sheena Easton.'

No flies on him, Harriet thought. Unlike Richard.

After lunch, she lay down looking out at the water while Murdo sang some more. She told him she'd lent her old dad the tape, how they had listened to his song about Rena, and how miffed she'd felt. There was his great-great-granny, made a heroine by Anthony Trollope and painted for posterity, while no one had ever made up so much as a limerick about her.

'Well, you'd hardly blame them.'

'Charming. Why?'

'You try rhyming with Harriet.'

'I know. It's an awful name.'

'It's not. A bit prim perhaps, but quite pretty. But hell to rhyme. Let's think now . . .'

Murdo strummed a few chords before loudly launching into the tune of the old T-Rex number *Deborah*, his voice carrying over the water.

'*Oh, Harr-iet,*
On the shore with a carry-out.
Seems that she's been up tae London,
Whar the streets jist gi'ye bunions.
Oh! Oh! Oh! Harri — et!'

'See, hellish.'

Harriet lay back on the flagstones, laughing. She couldn't stop. Her lungs ached. How good it felt to laugh.

'Ow!' Murdo clapped the side of his neck. 'Bloody midges! I'm going in. Sea water puts them off. Coming?'

Before she fully understood, he had put down his guitar and run off into the rhododendron bushes. Then she heard a splash and a shout.

'It's cold! Pure dead brilliant! Come in.'

He must be joking, Harriet thought. The water must be freezing and dirty. She caught a glimpse of bare male bottom as he turned over and dived into the water. Help!

Still, she watched him, sipping her white wine. She tried splashing fizzy water over her face; she'd have to find some shade soon. Midges buzzed round her head, in her hair. She could see Murdo had already swum further out. The water looked cool and green enough to tempt anyone, let alone a slightly squiffy thirty-seven-year-old mother of two (counting Jamie), or three, (counting Richard). It would be OK. Gingerly, feeling rather ridiculous, she quickly stripped off in the bushes and, cautiously checking he was two hundred yards at least away, slipped into the water. The coldness made her cry out until, kicking her legs through the weed into the clear depths, bliss hit. Followed by an overwhelming sense of freedom. This is life! Notting Hill, eat your heart out. She was alive after all! Who'd have thought it?

Suddenly there he was. He must have swum many yards underwater, obviously a well-honed Largs seduction technique. Oh God, oh God, oh God. His body was powerful and muscular, beautifully made and young. Like Richard's must have been before he had developed that thickness and the vulnerability of the older male's torso. Murdo just trod water looking at her. No. He was no Greek god. Just prime Celtic beefcake. Could have been a new *Braveheart* warrior, judging by the stills she'd seen in the newspapers. All he needed was a blue and white flag painted on his face and Mel Gibson would be reduced to a comic turn. Never taking his eyes off her, he slowly swam up close. No wonder the Romans never got past square one with this lot, Harriet thought. Let's hope he's not thinking about Butcher bloody Cumberland!

He was not. Nor Culloden either it seemed. He looked at her in wonder, as if studying a picture. She felt horribly white in the green waters, though they were thankfully brackish enough to hide all stretch marks. He was so close now she could see the wild flecks in those violet eyes. Then he kissed her. How exciting to discover there was still enough electricity in the world to make you go weak at the knees. She knew this was foolish, had warned Billy repeatedly about such situations. But who wanted to be sensible? He carried her back to the bank. Then Harriet, forgetting her stretch marks or, perish the thought, cellulite either, gave herself up to the raunchiest, noisiest, most un-English love-making. She came, loudly enough to scare all the wildlife on the island opposite, but then it had been a very long time. You try having a multiple orgasm with Georgiana sleeping the other side of the party-wall.

She felt giddy, silly and triumphant like those easy English girls Italians joke about as they arrive, white and hopeful, off flights from Luton airport. She had always been too uptight to join them, disapproving of her father's lazy conquests. But now, how she loved the muscular shoulders and the gentle power of this younger man. Big like Richard, but with nothing to prove.

Afterwards they lay naked, crushing the long grass. Then she pulled on his shirt, deciding to quit while she was behind. Or before he was. Together they watched the yachts which still sailed by. With binoculars trained, if the skippers had a spark of spirit.

'Well, you've done it now.' She was laughing into Murdo's black hair.

'I have?'

'Making love to the auld enemy, you traitor! Bonking an Englishwoman, and one from London too. Shame on you!' Her Rab C. Nesbitt voice made him wince. She laughed gently, tugging his hair, tickling behind his ears.

'Well, you wee stoater, do you want to know a secret?'

'I'm not sure, Murdo. Do I like secrets? I've found out rather a few lately.'

'If you're interested — and don't mention this around the Largs SNP office, will you? — actually I'm half English myself.'

Harriet sat up and looked at him. 'You're not! Your father was from Largs. Mad Izzy told me.'

'Aye, he was. But when my ma came back from London she was already in the club. Some bastard who'd buggered off. Which is why I've always hated the English. Even more than most. Nothing personal. She never seemed to get over it, or want any more children. Endlessly greetin', making my father's life hellish, unless she was on the ran-dan with her friends. Or on new pills, which only seemed to work for five minutes. Gran was the only thing to keep us sane.'

'Did she ever tell you anything about him?'

'Och, she was at Queen Charlotte's, nursing. A wee Mary, you know, nineteen, naive. Very pretty. The sixties may have been swinging then down south, but it didn't reach Largs till the late-seventies. My mother was doing her training and was swept off her feet. Met him in a club in West Kensington when she was out with the girls. He was rich, big car, fancy clothes, tall, dark and handsome. Usual story. His family were from the East

End, in business, ducking and diving. He spent a little of it on her. She'd never had any before so of course she was smitten. Probably only dipped her a few times, but it was enough.'

'I see. Charming expression.'

'Then he disappeared, good style. Bastard!'

'Did she not try to find him?'

'Aye, but she really was a mug. He always did the phoning. He'd given her his card but the telephone number on it was wrong. No such number. He was into pictures and took her to Sotheby's and galleries. Very sophisticated, well dressed. But when she found out, it was too late for the knitting needles and so she came back home to my gran who fixed her up with wee Eric at the draper's. He was a nice man. I only found out the truth when I was fifteen, after he'd died. A shock that. My real dad's name was Dick, as in dickhead, I suppose, Bridge. As in over the River bloody Kwai.'

It may have been the wine but there was a spinning feeling in Harriet's head. There was a curious sense of tragic inevitability about what he had just told her which, had it been delivered to a packed house at the National, would have seemed entirely satisfactory. She discovered she couldn't breathe.

'Where did he live?'

372

'West End. He was rolling in dough. Said he was part Romany. Took Ma to the Colony Club. She even met Tommy Steele one night, and Sean Connery. Poor Mum! Bastard didn't want to pay that bill. She never got over it. Dick Bridge: super rich, super shite.'

The screams in Harriet's brain were now so loud she almost expected every seagull for twenty miles to shoot into the air. She was gasping for breath.

'You coming again, hen? What a stayer!'

Harriet tried, but could not speak. She leapt up and pulled on her clothes. She could not look at him. She grabbed her shoes and handbag and ran away as fast as she could. She didn't feel the sharp stones beneath her feet until she came to the pile of rubble where there were enough to make her swear. She could hear Murdo shouting, but too many years evading local lads in unfamiliar city streets had taught her how to run away, and fast, even though twenty years of London living had slowed her down. She could hear the distant crack of branches and sticks but didn't stop. Somehow she got the key into the ignition and, doing the messiest three-point turn since her third driving test, roared down the hill.

Luckily, there was no policeman to nab her for drink driving. Somehow she got back to the hotel she had left just a few days before and booked a room. She lay sobbing on the bed and then threw up in the sink any evidence of the liquid lunch which had made her feel so alive and loved just half an hour before.

★　★　★

The weather broke about eight o'clock. Rain lashed down in true West Coast-style, uninterrupted. Harriet did not even notice. She walked along the front with its swaying lights, ignoring the whining sounds from the amusement arcade and the twang of the fruit machines and walked down to the Gallowgate. The shop was in darkness, but above she could see light. She could hear Murdo playing the guitar.

She rang the doorbell several times. There was the sound of footsteps and then he opened the door. He stood there looking at her.

'Look, I'm sorry to disturb you.' She might have been a nice home counties lady collecting for Christian Aid. 'You see, Murdo, I think I know who your father is. Certainly you could do a DNA test to find out. If you want to know?' Disbelieving, he looked at her as she wiped her face, tears and rain indistinguishable. 'I'm married to him.' She smiled up at him uncertainly. What a mess. Perfidious Albion indeed.

12

Hackney

It was her birthday. Twenty-four. A round number, two times twelve, four times six. Almost a quarter of a century. Katya stood looking at herself in the long studio mirror. Holding her breath, admiring the cheek bones and the high forehead, as a painter will. She wore the pearls under her black T-shirt for luck. They felt cold against her bare skin. She was OK. But twenty-four was getting serious. Time to take charge.

Bulging black bin bags stood all about her in a Stonehenge circle, already half-filled with paper, cardboard, old apple cores, empty wine bottles, all manner of gunk, along with some embarrassingly poor work. She put on some old Julie London. The voice filled the studio with black, Manhattan velvet. *Cry Me A River.* As black as the lonely Saturday night outside. Now she was going to sort out her life, starting with this hellhole. All artists had to reinvent themselves constantly, the status quo sucked.

Katya had always hated her birthday. Her

mother always got drunk and then abusive, and Richard always forgot it. Friends' presents were just consolation prizes. No, when you were a love child, birthdays had to be worked through.

Methodically she twisted any tops she could find on to tubes of paints, and washed out dirty stuck-together brushes, cleaned her palette and chucked out rusty old knives. She was going to change. She was rewriting the script. Then she thought of the awards ceremony, now just days away. A public judging, with a critique delivered on each of the finalists' work by her old principal. Her entry had only just scraped in under the wire before the closing date and there had been a binge of late nights and constant work before hand. What a risk! The idea of Richard, Harriet and Amanda together under one roof with all those corporate types standing around judging her work was terrifying, unless of course you were intent on change.

Katya then attacked a huge pile of sketches of Richard stacked in a corner which represented hours of work. The big handsome figure was lying sideways and upside down, but he was still hard to ignore; the same good-looking face which had once starred in the *Standard* diary, though the glamour was just beginning to go to seed and the hardness of disappointment and worry remained even when he was smiling. Poor bio dad. Katya looked at her work. Pride in that knock-out portrait filled her. She really had got him! He was flawed, hopeless, exciting. Infuriating, when not dazzling her with his knowledge of painters and paintings.

Yet somehow painting his portrait had transferred power from him to her. In just a few weeks he had become weaker, while she was no longer the little puppy dog, desperate for affection and acceptance. Anger and sorrow had been mixed into the paint and layered on to the canvas and now *she* owned *him*. She knew her father's every hair, wrinkle and expression so intimately she wasn't sure if she wanted to know him much better.

Under the table were sketches of her mother, drawn on the hoof as Katya had observed her leaving for work. Power suit, power briefcase, power house. Amanda had managed to change. Just one lucky break and she'd metamorphosed from overweight drunk ex-artists' muse into Corporate Lady waving her mobile phone like a wand.

Suddenly there were footsteps on the bare floorboards outside, coming along the corridor of the deserted building. They stopped. Nervously Katya grabbed the window pole for protection. The door opened and Felix

Rosen stood there with a bottle of champagne in his hand.

'Hello, Katch.'

'Felix! How did you get in?'

'Got a key from Becca.' He came into the room and began looking round at the bin bags. He was wearing a herringbone tweed jacket and jeans and a purple scarf, and exuded the usual Rosen brand of wry amusement. Katya just stood there clutching the pole, feeling a fool. The bottle was Pol Roger. Cool! He circled the room, pulling a face when he saw the sketches of Amanda, the artist in him taking in the curves of her body which once had inspired others.

'You giving up your studio then?' he said finally.

'No. It's my birthday. I'm having a clearout.'

'Happy birthday. So how old?'

'Twenty-four.'

'Oooh! Ancient. Getting on a bit. Where's the portrait then? Of your old dad? The sketches look good. Poor old sod. Where's the magnum opus?'

'In a safe place.'

'Sure.' He smiled at her. Julie London was now on to Cole Porter. *Always True To You In My Fashion.*

'Didn't know you were into easy listening.

I'm into Andy Williams myself.'

She didn't know if he was joking, but as he came towards her she thought that Jewish men were incredibly sexy. The most worldly, devilish, purposeful eyes on the planet.

As a lover he was gentle and persistent and she was probably just too bloody grateful. So by the time Julie London was hitting the Gershwin with *Please Do It Again* Katya was naked and sitting on his face. Mary Ellen's pearls gleamed expensively on her pert small breasts. That would show him! Mr £25K Commission. Happy birthday to me, she thought, just a millisecond before she came. Bloody hell!

It was only after she had stopped screaming that she noticed he had not removed any of his clothes, not even his scarf. How incredibly erotic, fucking a man in a herringbone tweed jacket. It smelt of sex. Probably hers. Then he was whisking everything off to steam train into her body. The pearls were between her teeth and he was grinning at his own taut hard body in the mirror. *Love For Sale*, sang Julie. Name your price, big boy, thought Katya, nearly choking.

It was only afterwards, when he'd left, that she realised he had taken the bottle of champagne away. He'd been looking for Philippa, the rich Norfolk farmer's daughter, he'd said. But Katya had been on hand instead. A first, she felt as used as a bit of old canvas then thought instead she had had a bloody good birthday present. A love child couldn't be too proud. On cue Julie London began a new number. *Why Don't You Do Right?* Well, perhaps he had.

Katya dressed and made some tea with plenty of sugar. She wished he had stayed. The newspaper lay on the table. She picked it up. Kingston had just been voted top for quality of life in a Guinness survey; the Lebanese hostage John Macarthy and his girlfriend Jill Morrell had split up; London was baking in temperatures of eighty degrees and the railway drivers, not coincidentally, were taking strike action. Then came the knockout punch in the diary pages. Felix pictured standing at a party, glass in hand, between the usually reclusive Charles Saatchi and a blonde girl. His fiancée. '*A rising star in contemporary art circles, move over Damien Hirst.*' The art community's new Persephone, dividing his year between conceptual art and portraits. Already knee-deep in commissions from both sides of the Pond, charging £80K a face. Madonna had just commissioned a full-length portrait. The fianceé was the sort of blonde tabloids love: slim, cool, daddy an energetic billionaire. Wealth and power oozed out of her eyes. And Felix's too. He had now joined the rich-are-different club. The ego had landed. From now on he would live in Chester Square and the Hamptons and send his children to Eton. Not bad for a pushy boy from Hampstead Garden Suburb. Katya knew she had more talent than him, a bigger range, but now after a monumental piece of social mountaineering done on the quiet, while the rest of the Hoxton crowd were busy nursing their wrath and espresso, he was up there breathing different air. Tonight he'd just been having his little bit of fun. It could have been her, or that Philippa or anyone.

'*There'll be some changes made,*' came the throaty growl from the CD player. Yes. The differences between them lay only in the level of their self-esteem. His was Canary Wharf high, while Katya's lurked somewhere at the bottom of the deepest bit of the Northern Line. It had nothing to do with talent; they both knew he was mediocre. Nursing her mug of tea, Katya looked at herself once again in the long mirror. Her skin was still pink from Felix's hard kisses. Her short, spiky hair was filled with dust and stood on end, as if she had been electrocuted. Her face was pale and bony, her shoulders defensive, clothes cheap and dirty. Only the pearls spoke of that rich-are-different life. Which was a start. Outside the hum of Hackney's traffic seeped through the skylight and surrounded her in the airless studio. Katya smiled with conviction as a girl does after an evening of unexpected great sex. It was all going to be OK. Good material to work with.

★ ★ ★

Harriet was looking closely in the dressing-room mirror, attempting to put on some eye pencil in a clean sweep, but her hand trembled and the pencil blotched. Pale blue eyes, on the point of tears, so different from the violet fire in different faces which had so recently burned into hers. Just who is your 'auld enemy', Harriet?

What the hell was she to do now? The blue eyes looked back at her, weak and pleading. Did she love him? Of course. Had she done wrong? Yes. Could she give him any more benefit of the doubt? Probably. So what was she going to do now? Pass.

★ ★ ★

'*Evening Standard! Evening Standard!*' The voice of the newspaper seller followed Richard as he entered Kensington Gardens. In the hot, still, choking London heat it sounded like 'Heathen Strangled'. On his left, stood the aunt heap, Kensington Palace, gracious and cool, apart from the tourist swarm whose rapidly reddening flesh disgusted him. These tourists wore flip-flops and slummocked along eating ice cream, reading guide books as they licked. London office staff, chancing their arm on a late lunch break, lay basting in the sun, their peeled off office stockings beside them like snakeskins. Still, Richard walked on, his shoulders hunched, carrying his heavy leather briefcase. He would never have time off again.

He kept to the path, his feet too tired to cope with the grass, however yellow and short cut. In the briefcase lay the ashes of his life; the accounts, the books, the statements, the reconciliations, the final reckoning. His accountant had looked at them like a bad Indian meal. Said he was also an insolvency practitioner. Luckily, it would save time as Gruneberg had petitioned for bankruptcy. 'Well, at least it's for a decent amount, old boy. Did you know you can be made bankrupt for as little as £750 quid?' Richard had not. He merely sat in the airless office behind Barker's, listening but not listening, as if the real essential soul of Richard Patrick Longbridge was sitting on a cloud high above Kensington, having a

383

pleasant out-of-body experience.

The figures numbed him. His business overdraft was now £160,000; in fact it was more than that; that was the limit which he had exceeded a month ago, hence the reason the bank had got nasty. His personal overdraft was £40,000, which had been kept down by keeping the Gruneberg picture sale money for a while, hoping against hope something would turn up. It had not. The VAT had had to be paid the week before last. It had not been, for he'd had nothing to pay it with. Tax was also due at the end of the month. He also had debts of £15,000 on three credit cards. Itemised, the noughts rolled around the page which the accountant had pushed over to him. His turnover had been £108,000 gross in the previous tax year. Did he have the tax saved? No. What had he earned this year to 1 July? £25,000. He was still owed around £8,000 of that. The man's sympathy was scant. Thick reserves of disdain and contempt lay barely a millimetre beneath the professional surface.

Now to tell Harriet. She'd no doubt be sitting at home waiting with that stupid smile on her face she'd worn since coming back from Scotland. She'd alternated being girly and giggly and energetic with being very serious, and had arranged so many days out and meetings with the saintly Matt Mercer and his wife, to discuss this absurd little job he'd offered her, she had managed to spend less than an hour a day in her husband's company. She had even spent two days down in Wiltshire near the school, to have a last weekend exeat with Billy and Jamie before school broke up. Richard had not been invited. He had not asked to come.

The injustice of it all burned in Richard's soul so strongly he could feel the sides of his mouth curling at the edges, like a piece of paper about to catch light. It was so unfair. He would be left with nothing. Nothing.

Of course, he'd always had bits and pieces tucked away for a rainy day. He had taken two days making an inventory of it all before this morning's meeting. But what was left now only added up to £10,000 maximum at today's prices. He had even included the little mandolin musical box his father had once taken in part-payment for a debt. As a young boy he had loved the tinkling sound the box made and the finesse of the mechanism, which played four tunes, as well as the beauty of the aged rosewood veneer. It was one of the few objects that brought back happy memories of his teenage years and was insured for £16,000, which had impressed the bank when he had asked them to extend the business overdraft. Now even this would have to go.

It would be better, the accountant had said, if some way could be found to organise an Individual Voluntary Arrangement with his creditors. This would enable him to keep on working while paying them something. Gruneberg had perhaps been hasty or vengeful in going the 'B Route', as he called it. But the bottom line had been clear to Richard, even before he had taken his leave of the man and had started the harsh data processing as he walked through the park. He was a busted flush. Out of the game. And as for the musical box, who was he kidding in today's market? Even if the mechanism was rare and almost unique for Messrs Golay-Leresche of Geneva, it would fetch £3K at auction if he was lucky. So all his assets would be knocked down for peanuts, because the market had hardly come out of the doldrums long enough to gather steam. Unfair. Unfair. The word screamed in his head and his briefcase brushed against the bare legs of a girl who crossed his path with a dog. Richard failed to look up or apologise. He was an Irish peasant who owed rent, heading back for the potato fields, wet with sweat and despair.

★ ★ ★

Harriet was waiting in the drawing room. She was wearing a white suit and looked cool and well made up and in control, which irritated him. She had poured lemon juice into tall Italian glasses and the French windows were open on to the black wrought-iron balustrade which looked out over the garden. There was precious little in the room now, except paintings. The effect was a hollow minimalism.

Richard went upstairs and washed his face, changed his shirt and came downstairs. He smiled at her, accepted his glass and, after taking a big breath, quietly and reasonably told her the upshot of what had happened. He expected her to say, I told you so. She had warned him last year of the effects of the coming Self Assessment, that he would have to start putting by his tax much more efficiently. She had also told him that he had to cut back his business activities to those which paid upfront. He had done neither. Because of course he'd always counted on Mummy leaving him the loot. All that had changed. Now he finally knew, Chekhov-style, he would never get to Moscow. There would never, ever be any money. But still he kept his voice level. What a pro.

He was doing rather well, sounding terribly grown up and contrite, outlining his debts, until he reached the bit about the Gruneberg petition and the consequences. Still Harriet listened. She seemed politely distant, as if it really hadn't a great deal to do with her. Then, against his will, the leprechaun in Richard's soul began to smoulder.

'So what does bankruptcy mean? In practice.' She might have been asking how the new toaster worked.

'What does bankruptcy mean? Well, if you like, I can type out a nice, neat list of bullet points.' He knew she hated him being sarcastic. 'It means, sweetheart, that I cannot carry on trading or employing anyone. I cannot easily have either a bank or building society account, nor hold some varieties of public office. But the great news is that I may keep essential items for my family and my work. Most of which, I seem to remember, you own anyway.'

'Stop it, Richard. What is the total amount you owe?'

'Two hundred thousand. With invisible debt two fifty.'

'But why on earth did the bank give you such huge limits? They must have known you didn't have a house to sell. How did you guarantee it?'

'Amanda guaranteed it.'

'Don't be absurd.'

'I'm not. That big beauty over there is worth £800K, you and I both know that. OK so it's yours, but the bank wasn't to know that. I had to get the limits up. I told them you'd given it to me and produced a valuation. Don't look at me like that! No, the real hit is the cash from the sale of the Gruneberg picture I had to put into my personal account to tide me over. But as I had a letter from Matt Mercer offering me £20,000 for that blessed Scottish portrait, I thought it would be only days before I could get the personal overdraft down and start working on the business account.'

Harriet seemed to take ages to speak.

'But that's my picture . . . '

'Well, *he* didn't know that. Anyway, I thought that as it had originally been *my* mother's picture, it could be sold to help the cashflow. As in 'for better or worse, richer or poorer'. Remember that? I didn't expect you to hang on to it and use it to launch your new career as a hotshot writer and suck up to the Mercers.'

Richard could feel his voice rising, anger pushing it upwards however hard he fought.

'The picture's only worth £2K and he's offering you ten times that. And it's a drop in the ocean given that my share of this house would by now be worth £500K — £300K *more* that you gave me for it. So I didn't feel it was unreasonable that my own mother's picture could be sold to pay a short-term debt.'

'And that was your opinion, was it?' Harriet's voice cut through crisply. 'Easy come, easy go. What's yours is mine, so let's throw it all down the bottomless black hole.'

'Oh, yes. Harriet, my darling. That was my opinion. And my opinion also is that you have all the pictures on these walls, the share portfolio you put together from selling the business, the house, which will soon be worth nearly a million quid, and the portrait on which you have had an incredible offer from a guilty millionaire trying to please his dying wife. If I have to go out now and sell my last few remaining assets at auction, they'll fetch knockdown prices which may be enough to get me slightly out of the shit, but only temporarily. Basically I will be left with nothing. Nothing! Bankrupt. Not even able to work and with my reputation gone!'

'Then so be it.'

He could not believe that soft, ethereal Harriet was now this hard woman, sitting so still and upright, not giving an inch.

'But it's so unfair!'

'Money and assets are too hard to come by, Richard. I spent my whole childhood living off other people's plates and fag ends while you were swanning about Carnaby Street with your friends. May I also remind you that we've already been through this merry dance once before. You lost the Belgravia house, the Lamborghini and the Cork Street gallery. Remember? I sold my own house when I married you. There was no mortgage on it but I gave it up. Willingly.'

'But it was in darkest Hammersmith, for God's sake!'

'Exactly. Darkest Hammersmith. Entirely affordable and wholly owned. As opposed to a Belgravia stucco money pit you could not afford. You are a financial black hole. It doesn't matter how much you have, there will never be enough. I read Nigel Dempster's column every day and I can anticipate before they happen the stories of people's bankruptcies. You can just see the pattern. Like Sir Hugh Fraser, who inherited millions and left fourpence-halfpenny. You are one of a breed.'

'Don't preach to me, Harriet. You were nothing . . . '

Suddenly she was standing up, fists clenched, a granite expression on her face. 'Nothing, was I? When you married me. Was that what you were going to say?'

'Well, in those days you were hardly an 'it' girl, love.'

'How like Laura you sound! Am I surprised? No, not really. You both have similar habits and ideas about enjoying yourselves at other people's expense. Neither of you ever stops to count the cost of the harm you cause, or the money you squander! You had a business that was going under but hundreds of inches in the gossip columns. So that was all right. You poured champagne down other people's throats and called it cashflow. And that was apparently all right too. I *warned* you that you were running up invisible debt. I *begged* you to sort yourself out. More fool me, I assumed you had. But while Mummy was around to bail you out, you wouldn't change because you didn't need to. The only reason I had a successful business was because expenses were kept to a minimum.'

'Not all of us can think like cheap Korean immigrants, cutting out coupons, squeezing the ends of bloody tooth-paste tubes.'

'No, but you're going to have to start now, aren't you? Welcome to bloody Korea, *love*! That portrait of Isabella Fairlie is *my* painting, not yours. So is that large Freud of the wonderful Amanda. I bought your share of this house for £200,000. Which, may I remind you, you were bloody glad to get your hands on at the time. These paintings are *my* paintings though, as you may or may not remember, I sold four, depleting Billy's inheritance, to keep you on an even keel and to buy a house with a fashionable enough address so that you could live in the manner to which you thought you were entitled.'

'Oh, yes. It's *Billy's* inheritance, isn't it? I've read your will, you ungrateful bitch!'

Suddenly the leprechaun was uppermost and Richard was screaming. Harriet quickly crossed over to shut the French windows. He felt like a big black bull about to charge. He'd never felt closer to hitting a woman in his life. But even in his rage, he knew the balance of power had shifted. She was not afraid. A different Harriet had arrived.

'How many more secrets have you got tucked away? Nice little offshore funds? Going to Jersey for a couple of days to see your bankers, with Matt Mercer to hold your hand?'

'Secrets? Don't make me laugh. Who had a daughter who just turned up out of the blue, five minutes after we were married? How many more bastards of yours are there out there walking around? Wouldn't you like to know? No, get this straight. I'm not the junior partner anymore. And you are no longer one of Nigel Dempster's golden boys. How curious I missed the pattern with you. You can stay here married to me *if* you bloody well get yourself sorted out. And get real!'

She was looking at him, teeth gritted, fists clenched. Hard as nails. Richard lunged forward, knocking the lemon juice on to the carpet. Neither of them noticed. The phone rang, both ignored it. The ringing continued. 'Yes! Who is it?' he finally snapped.

'Richard, Jester Dunne. Is Harry there?'

'It's your father,' he snarled, but Harriet was already walking upstairs.

'Tell him I'll ring back.'

'She'll ring back.'

Jester's tones were firm and triumphant down the phone.

'Tell her that Mrs Cohen's son who's a producer in films, you know, heard the tape Harry lent me. Her friend's. He heard it out in the corridor. I usually have it on too loud. Now he wants to get in touch with that modest murderer man, who sang on it.'

'I'll tell her. She'll get back to you.'

Richard slammed the phone and stood looking up the stairs at all those bloody pictures. His rage had gone and now tears began to prick the back of his eyes. He was breathing heavily and in pain; he could barely see. Only Amanda's wild body, sprawling across the wall in another time and place, could comfort him.

Harriet had a friend who was a modest murderer? All he bloody needed.

13

Harriet was putting on lipstick. She curved the brush right round her mouth. She had chosen red this evening. The shade was called Berry Rage. Seemed appropriate. She had chosen a peacock blue Donna Karan slip dress, which always made her look thin. Not difficult, for guilt, sex and naked fury had helped her lose six pounds in the last week. She stood away from the mirror, smoothing the material over her body. Her cheek bones seemed to jut out; she had lost weight from her face. How odd. There was a crash downstairs and the sound of Richard swearing. Another Edinburgh crystal glass bit the dust. He'd been drinking since six o'clock, and picking at the prawns which were still defrosting in the fridge, in spite of all her warnings.

In the days since the row, it was as if a pall of fog had descended on the little stucco house. While the hot July sun burned down upon the rest of Notting Hill, fog enveloped their house and kept Harriet and Richard separate and numb, wrapped in their own private thoughts. Richard bought a calculator.

He spent hours writing down long figures, slurping water and whisky as he did so. His language became coarser, his face red and blotchy. It was as if they were in some fog-bound waiting room on some deserted northern station, but waiting for what? For Richard to discover whether he would be heading for bankruptcy or merely the restrained hell of an Individual Voluntary Agreement, where your creditors had you by the balls in private? And Harriet? For she knew not what. In four days her beloved Billy would be home and then she would be able to think. All her limbs would be back in place. For a child at boarding school is nothing but refined amputation at the best of times, however great its benefits.

Tomorrow was their wedding anniversary. Five years. Harriet stood looking out of the window. She didn't see the evening crowds heading from their offices to Julie's Bar, she saw herself in Chelsea, surrounded by flowers and Richard's friends, none of whom she had ever met before, and Billy and Jamie tying balloons to the bridal car.

Then she came back to the present and saw a tall dark figure walking down the road. His clothes looked cheap and odd in these surroundings. A lost tourist perhaps, trying to find the Tube.

'H, I'm off out to get more gin. We leave at seven, OK?'

'Yes, and I'm driving. Katya says it starts at eight.'

The door slammed and she saw Richard walking away to the off licence. Looking down, she could see that his hair was thinning more visibly at the back and his blazer looked too tight. He passed the stranger, then suddenly she saw the man was Murdo. Next to Richard, the resemblance was uncanny. She'd been right. It had been something in the set of the shoulders and the hair and jaw. Why had she never really noticed when she had first met him? How had she allowed age and class and culture to get in the way of the blindingly obvious? Then the fog which had been swirling in her brain lifted just an instant in the split-second memory of their unexpected passion, only to descend again in double thickness round her brain. Oh, God, he was here! What on earth was she to say to him?

He was standing on the doorstep, looking huge and uneasy and out of place.

'Hello, Harriet.'

'Hello, Murdo. This is a surprise.'

'Aye, well I didn't know if I'd find you in. London's huge, isn't it!'

He stood shifting his feet like a small boy

before a schoolmarm. He explained that he was staying in Kilburn, with a mate who did the folk club scene who had come down to try his luck.

'Hit stardom in a Kilburn bedsit. But great news — I'm actually signed up with this film company. Working Plans. They want *Safe In Your Arms* for a new film. Just think, because your old pa had it blaring all over the Old Folks joint, I'm getting money, big time, enough to close the bloody shop for the winter and travel. Me and Shug might get to Arizona yet. And Nashville. Want to come?'

She smiled at him and went and fetched some lemon juice which he obviously found too sour; then she remembered he took three sugars in his tea. He was neither familiar nor cold. Just accepting. He looked around him, trying to take in the house and its now underfurnished elegance.

'Where's all your ornaments?'

'We don't have any. Or much furniture either. We've sold most of it lately.'

'Gran sends you her best. She's looking forward to that magazine coming out. August, is it? She actually liked your article once she'd got over the shock of being a Houston. She's quite pleased. Old Gifford always sounded like a boring old fart according to her mum, she says. Bloody hell, what a turn up! All

Largs will be blathering when that hits the news stands. In fact, she's grateful because she was always artistic. One of the women at her kirk is a Houston and they're always taking their bar suppers on a Friday. They're second or third cousins now.'

'I'm glad. I really like your grandmother, Murdo. She's an original. Like you.'

'Well, I don't know. But it got me thinking . . . you know, about facing up to myself. Not being scared of the truth. You've made me think about the English differently, too. I'm not letting you lot off the hook, you know, but I had to come and see you as I was down here already. See what I could find out.'

It was a real act of will not to march up to him and put her arms round his neck, feel his skin, smell his hair.

'Actually, Murdo, I wish you'd rung. I haven't said anything to my husband yet. He doesn't know. About us, of course, but about anything else, either. Are you sure you want to do this? The thing is, this isn't a great day. We're going out tonight. Richard's daughter's painted his portrait and we're going to see it unveiled — it's in a competition. I think it would be better if you come back.'

'Harriet, don't worry! I'm a big boy, I'll take my chance. But I need to know. And as for what happened with us . . . these things happen. Don't worry. I'm discreet, me. Blame it on the midges.'

'And the wine.'

'Aye. And the wine.'

They laughed. She didn't want him to leave. The front door slammed and Richard came in. He looked at Murdo suspiciously.

Show time.

'Darling, this is Murdo Wilson whose grandmother helped me in Largs on the article I went to write. You know, about the picture. Now he's down here having just sold one of his songs to a film company. Isn't that nice?'

With Murdo standing near her, her voice, even in this London setting, sounded like that of a frightfully nice Ealing comedy gel. Richard stood and looked at him for a moment. Then they shook hands and again the resemblance between the two men almost took her breath away. Same height, same hair, same jawline, same bloody mindedness, same swagger, same charisma. Two peacocks for the price of one.

'The thing is,' Harriet began, 'Murdo was telling me about his mother. Now, how do I put this?'

'It's OK, Harriet,' he cut in. 'See, your wife thought you and I may be related. That

. . . well, let's get to it good style. That you're my dad.'

Richard looked at Harriet. There was no love in his glance. 'Did she? She seems to think I've fathered half London, bless her. But I doubt that very much. You're not unlike me, but where are you from? West of Scotland somewhere? Well, not guilty. I've only been to a do at Inverary five years ago. I usually restrict my Scottish visits to Edinburgh.' Richard's voice had suddenly gone from Cork Street blah to pure Buckingham Palace marble.

'Well, that's it, you see. My pa was a Londoner. My mother Maggie met him in London in 1967. Maggie Finlay her name was, she was a nurse at Queen Charlotte's Hospital. She met the man at a club in West Kensington. They went out a few times. She wasn't very up on life, you know. Must have got blootered one night . . . '

Richard looked at Harriet, for a translation. 'He means tiddly,' she said quickly. 'She was very young. Girls didn't drink then as they do now.'

'Well, anyway . . . ' Murdo was now looking hard at a rather special Chinese silk carpet Harriet had bought in Sotheby's one wet Wednesday afternoon ' . . . when she found out she was in the club, she had his card but found the number on it didn't exist. She tried to find him but it turned out the telephone was one number wrong. And there was no Dick Bridge listed where he'd said he lived.'

Harriet found herself almost enjoying the spectacle of Richard turning from insouciant upper-crust London male into hunted beast. The promiscuity of his youth (she preferred not to think of his middle age) had always disconcerted her. Now he was looking at this powerful, fit, younger man with the eyes of a drowning man. Genetic Nemesis.

'Why turn up now? You look rather too big to need Child Support. What does your mother say about you coming sniffing around?'

'Don't be absurd, Richard,' Harriet snapped. 'Murdo is a businessman. He has a shop and rents out others and he's down here, as he told you, because he has just sold one of his original songs to a film company.'

'A man of many parts then. Positively Renaissance.' The sneer was evident. It made Harriet want to hit him. No wonder they can't stand the English, she thought.

'He just wants to know who his father is. Hardly an unreasonable request. Anyway having cards printed with false names and one digit of the telephone number wrong was a charming little stock-in-trade of your misspent youth, was it not? One of your many delightful oat-sewing methods, I rather thought. Take A Creep Nites being another. And, in case it has escaped you, you are incredibly alike.'

She dug the knife in and wiggled it about a bit. Then glanced at Murdo who did not seem at all perturbed. As if she and Richard were two quaint actors straight out of a Noël Coward drawing-room comedy. End of Act One, *Hay Fever*. 'He is your father!' Cue faint.

'Christ, I don't have to listen to this!' Richard lacked Coward's finesse.

'Look, I don't want to make trouble but it was just that Harriet said she thought you might be. We look alike, but it doesn't necessarily mean anything. Well, here's the card. I got it off my mum, she knew I was coming down. Wants to know as much as me. It's no fun, not adding up.'

Murdo took out his wallet. His big hands fumbled and he handed Richard the crumpled, faded business card. He took it with obvious disgust. Harriet was too far away to see it instantly but noticed the trembling of Richard's hand. There was a tentativeness about his grasp. He had also gone white.

'Come on, Richard, it's not the end of the world. I know I was shocked when Katya turned up, but we all make mistakes.' She found she could not look at Murdo. She couldn't bear it. He was no mistake. Best lover she had ever had, and he turned out to be her bloody stepson! Nice work, Harriet.

Richard cleared his throat and sat down. He wiped his face with his hand, over and over again, as if to change the mask. Murdo sat down too, on the edge of a seat, unsure whether this man opposite was going to hit him or run.

The silence seemed to last several minutes. The early-evening sun streamed through the window. Harriet looked around, as if to see the bare unfurnished room through Murdo's eyes. A noise made her look round. Richard was sitting hunched up, knees to his chest, his face contorted, just as the beginnings of tears were beginning to seep down his cheeks. But it was the mask-like howl of his silent mouth which left Harriet transfixed. He's going to have a stroke. Like her father.

'Father. Yes.' A sort of grunt echoed her thoughts.

'You're my father?' Murdo was just staring down at the distraught man. 'Look, for Harriet's sake, I won't ask why. I've dipped women and buggered off. It was all right while my dad was alive, but since he died, my ma, she's been brooding. It spoilt her life, you see. And she bloody well ruined my dad's, and mine nearly too. I didn't ask to be born.'

Richard was looking at Murdo as if he could not take his eyes off him. High-pitched voices came through the window from a crowd of girls heading to Julie's for an after-work drink. Inside, Richard seemed to be metamorphosing into a Kafka dung beetle, scrunched up and black. He seemed unable to speak.

When he did, his voice came out as if he had a pound of cornflakes trapped in his windpipe. 'Look, forgive me, I can't remember your name . . . George Bridge . . . his mother's name was Una Long and so he joined the two names. Dick Bridge was a name he used when he was doing deals on the dodgy side. He liked the name Dick, but actually he had several names. I always knew he played around. He actually admitted it when I grew up, but my mother always turned a blind eye. The cow knew which side her bread was buttered! He brought the picture back from Bonham's one day. Told me it reminded him of a girl he once knew. Prime Scottish beef.'

Oh, God. Poor Maggie! Poor cow. Why not? She must have been the spitting image of

Isabella at that age. He'd bought the picture to remind him of that little Scottish nurse he'd taken out and screwed, who'd probably made him feel young again! And all those years Mary Ellen had not known. Just as she herself had not known about Amanda's true identity in all those bloody pictures outside in the hall. The symmetry, the pattern of deceit, took Harriet's breath away. Bastards!

'So, Dick Bridge isn't you?'

'No, I'm sorry. This is my father's card. He had a share in the Bluebell just off the Talgarth Road. It was a pulling joint for him, he said. Kept it for the clients at the lower end of the scale. I'm sorry, I didn't mean anything . . . ' Richard's voice trailed away.

'Where is he?' Murdo asked.

'Died ten years ago, God rest his soul. He wasn't a bad man, just a ducker and a diver, up to every dodge. Arfur Daley in Jermyn Street kit. Great style he had, my dad. Very handsome. He showed me these cards. Used them to give the girls the run around. Told me to get some. So I did. Dick Bridge Junior, Rich O'Reilly.'

Murdo was just sitting looking down at the floor and Harriet was filled with shame and disgust. What a family! Amoral, selfish. How in God's name had she ever married into it? Again the sharp delight she had never given this man a child came back, stronger than a curse.

'So if your dad was my dad, that makes us half-brothers?'

There was silence as two and two made six hundred. Richard stared at the younger man.

'No!' Harriet started to yell, but she could see it was too late. Finally Richard had understood there was something in it for him; his desert island was no longer deserted. Soon, the brothers were embracing, hugging as if they feared each might escape the other. Exit stage right for Harriet, who now was needed no more.

It is such a wonderful thing discovering you are no longer an only child. It's like Christmas with no tax in January! Richard said this several times before opening champagne. Richard *si pavoneggia*! He grew at least three inches in height immediately and insisted Murdo should come along and meet the family. His daughter Katya was shortlisted for a portrait prize, he explained, and there was to be a champagne reception in the City. 'Persuade him to come, Harriet. I'll lend him a suit. We must show him something of London. Wasn't she clever to find you?'

So clever Harriet was soon driving along the Bayswater Road, while her husband and her lover sat in the back talking. Murdo looked glamour personified in Savile Row splendour with a hand-printed Italian tie. Another quirk of fate and he too could have been selling pictures from Cork Street. Harriet then realised just how very handsome Richard must have been. Before her time. How the brothers made each other laugh as she fought the rush-hour traffic up the Edgware Road! And when Richard discovered that Murdo's shop The KOOC was short for Knocked Off Old Crap, he roared with laughter, saying it was an apt description for his Cork Street gallery. What larks! thought Harriet wryly. What larks. She felt the beginnings of a migraine starting somewhere behind one ear. Murdo obviously thought Richard was rolling in it. And what was worse, so did Richard.

The migraine had built up nicely by the time she hit Pentonville Road, for by now Richard had taken possession of Maggie and Mad Izzy and Wee Shug and the SNP and was already arranging for Harriet and himself to come up for a holiday. (Paying with what? she thought.) Murdo stuck his Sony Walkman round Richard's ears for him to hear *Safe In Your Arms* which he pronounced 'absolutely marvellous, my dear bro.' Did he need a manager? By Old Street Station she could barely see and the two of them were going into business together. First prize in the lottery of life, one Richard. Second prize, two Richards. Oh, brother.

The Central England Water Plc Young Portrait Artist of the Year Award. They could see flags announcing the event fluttering from The Old Brewery. Murdo was silent now, ill at ease, but Richard took his arm and, as if they were about to sing *What a Swell Party This Is*, they entered the building arm in arm, leaving Harriet to lock up the car.

They were late. The room was already packed with City and Art World and the biggest and best of the company shareholders, institutional and individual. On a platform at one end of the room the three finalist portraits stood shrouded, waiting to be unveiled. Richard was in seventh heaven for the room was packed with clients, his and hers. Harriet's from the language school and Richard's from a thousand picture deals. They were a well-known couple in this company. People turned and greeted them as if pleased to see them, though Harriet knew it was more out of morbid curiosity for by now news of Richard's financial demise must be common knowledge. But with his gorgeous little brother in tow, he seemed to have contracted financial amnesia. The Scottish cavalry had arrived.

Katya was holding court in black. Not a facial stud in sight and gift-wrapped in the gull's egg pearls Mary Ellen had left her. Her hair was highlighted and the effect looked a million dollars. Across the room Harriet could see her being introduced to Murdo. She was obviously knocked out by his swaggering Scots glamour, kissing him on the cheek as if unable to believe her good luck. Harriet could feel tears at the back of her eyes; her head thumped. She no longer had the heart to join in the play. Was that Georgiana over there wrapped round Robert's boss? Why was Harriet not surprised? She had spread all over London like eczema.

Suddenly the crowd went quiet. Someone had entered: Laura Marchant in person, available for weddings, funerals and barmitzvahs, late entrances a speciality. She cut across the room towards Richard and Murdo, a skimming galleon in full sail through the parting waves of corporate London. Once again, there were the explanations and the delight and Laura was smiling and talking, Katya and Murdo a respectful audience. Harriet could see the way Laura was looking at Murdo out of the corner of her eye, while apparently looking at Richard. She knew only too well that dog with a steak look; she had looked at Tom like that before she had eaten him for breakfast. His official time of death had been 9.15. a.m. Once again, Harriet's man was to be gobbled up alive. Her body ached for Murdo's mouth and hands while her head throbbed in powerless anger. She could not compete with Laura; she had the superpower of the amoral. Now Laura moved between Richard and Murdo, her arms linked round them, two tasty morsels, looking from one to another as if deciding which would be most digestible while they smiled down at her, enraptured.

Richard then looked around for her. Harriet knew she would have to go over and join in. Play your part, Harriet. You should have just kept your big mouth shut and let Murdo paint castles in the air.

Slowly, head still throbbing, she made her way across the room. A waitress offered her white wine, but she took a glass of orange juice instead, and sipped it. She took in some of the well-known faces. TV cameras were discreetly mounted in the corner and City grey suits milled and plotted, all art for art's sake. Richard was now kissing a plump, exuberantly made-up woman whose frosty glance was melting; she could have been an older Laura, but as she stood next to Katya, Harriet could see this was Amanda, the dreaded Amanda whose body had flaunted itself all down Harriet's stairs, cheering her husband up all these years, unbeknownst to her. What a jolly little gathering. Murdo seemed pleased to be there. He was sipping his wine and looking around the room, wide-eyed as a kid in a Christmas grotto. He saw her across the room and waved at her to join them, his eyes tender and laughing. So Harriet did. They were without competition, the two best-looking men in the room.

Somehow, a fairy godmother magic had transformed Richard from broken and soon-to-be-bankrupt into an affectionate whirlwind glamour boy. He greeted her extravagantly, as if they had not seen each other for years. She shook hands with Amanda, said how talented Katya was, to be rewarded with an icy smile for her pains. Katya looked at her coolly, only smiling several seconds after the compliment. For the women were now all in competition for the men, Harriet realised. She was in the way.

A fork then tinkled against a glass and Katya was beckoned up on to the platform. The chatter subsided and the crowd turned to the stage, taking in the three young people on view. All were dressed in designer chic, as if daring the City slickers to price them down or write them off as a bad debt. Katya was the only girl and her pearls shimmered in the

412

lights, a challenge to every woman there.

An Arts Council bigshot welcomed the guests and introduced Sir Colin Webster, Chairman of Central England Water Plc, and his wife. The guests clapped obediently as a small man in an expensively tailored suit took the stage and, speaking without notes, explained why he had instituted the portrait competition. 'Portraits can tell us such a lot, not just about the people who are being painted but about our society. In looking at portraits we see ourselves.' His voice had a faint trace of Essex vowels but was confident, powerful and rich. 'Got £850K in shares when they privatised,' Richard whispered in Harriet's ear. 'Lucky bugger! They say his wife is a real Lady Macbeth, steered him up the ladder without letting his feet touch the rungs.'

Then the Principal of the City of London Art College, who had chaired the panel of judges, spoke at length on what they had been looking for. Perspective, depth, technique, interpretation; his words bounced off the Brewery's ceiling. The crowd shifted from foot to foot. Get on with it.

The runners up were called on stage. First was a young man called Gwent, for a picture of his small sister. Cameras flashed and the young man made a nervous speech before Sir

Colin's wife handed him his cheque for £5,000. Next, a tall sulky-looking youth called Felix Rosen, who looked less than delighted to walk off with his £5,000 cheque back to the well-heeled crowd he had brought with him. Katya looked after him with a wistfulness Harriet found sad. 'I think that's her boyfriend,' whispered Richard in her ear. Harriet doubted it. She knew that unrequited look. Then Sir Colin, in the market for a pound of flesh, drew Katya forward to the front of the stage.

'Milk it, sweetie,' Laura said. 'The audience always love it. Did I tell you, Richard darling, we're taking the show to Broadway?'

'Shh,' said a woman, turning round to glare before realising that the voice came from someone famous. The glare turned to a fawning smile.

'Let me tell you a story about this particular portrait,' Sir Colin began. 'Katya has painted her father, one of London's best-known picture dealers — Richard Longbridge. Now I owe Richard a lot, and indeed I owe a debt to Amanda Holland, Katya's mother too. I hope they will forgive me for telling you this. Before you were born, your father and mother, Katya, held a party with their Chelsea friends and Amanda invited me.' The audience tittered politely

414

with interest. Harriet smiled up at Richard and looked across at Amanda. They were smiling pleasantly. Public people on parade.

'Now, frankly I was rather flattered to be invited by the Chelsea set because I came from a very different background. At the time my chief interest was waterways.'

Knowing laughter echoed around the room 'Good God! It's nerdy Colin.' Richard's stage whisper came out too loud and Amanda hissed at him to be quiet.

Harriet was tired of telling Richard to shut up in public. She'd spent years trying to keep him out of trouble. Let Amanda do it now. Anyway it was her daughter who was standing on the stage, smiling broadly. Was this going to be another 'Richard Longbridge screwed up my life' story? It had that feel about it. London was full of them.

Sir Colin described the party while Harriet, sensitive to the subtlest put-downs after her own gypsy childhood, stood looking at her shoes, cheeks burning with shame. Sir Colin was putting the most positive gloss on the evening but there was an edge to his voice which only a skilled language teacher like herself would pick up. It must have been one of those Take A Creep Nites Richard had so often boasted of. Harriet's migraine took hold to the point of nausea but when she

415

looked up, she found Richard and Amanda looking at each other, grinning. They had obviously learned nothing.

'Get on with it, love. Leave them wanting more!' muttered Laura, and Richard and Amanda dissolved into giggles while Murdo, uncomprehending, joined in. The other guests looked at the ageing, giggling adolescents in the corner. Sir Colin then described with expansive boardroom confidence how he had been packed off to Greenford in a taxi by Katya's mum and dad.

'As these young people will find, the most wonderful results can come out of the unexpected. That night was the beginning of everything for me. I have achieved more than I ever thought possible, thanks to my lovely wife, Richard's guest, whom I met at that party back in January 1971. A proper little Cupid, your father, Katya. And I have always wanted to pay him back. Now I hear Richard's having problems of his own so I rather hope he will let me buy him a drink. But not perhaps this evening.'

Every head swivelled to look at Richard. Who could only stare at the well-dieted, beautifully dressed woman beside the speaker.

'God, it isn't — never! That's Nylon Maureen!'

They were his final intelligible words of the

evening. The veil was drawn back. Katya was now £25,000 richer. Though still pale, she was oozing as much glamour as her pearls as she stepped forward to acknowledge the applause.

Her portrait packed a punch. It stared back into the room aggressively, its eyes apparently taking in every person there, as a great portrait should. In your face, raw genius. For Richard sat there in his green suit, hand on hip, gazing at the packed room, at once challenging and weak. Then, as if getting the joke, the audience gasped and began to laugh. For the large glamorous man, the epitome of male charisma, wore a large pound sign over his face, curving up his forehead, down and round towards to his left ear.

'See that Richard Longbridge,' Murdo said too loudly, 'he's got more cash on his face than I've got in my pocket.'

The unexpected West Coast accent cut through the muted London gathering. Then came the laughter. Harriet heard someone call, 'Ask his mum!' 'Sir Colin could buy and sell him, the poor bastard!' Harriet, torn between fear and shame, could not take her eyes off the portrait. What a brilliant revenge for his casual fatherhood, dished up cold by two victims of Richard's cruel schoolboy humour, who had channelled their rage to make money and fight back.

She heard a gagging sound behind her. She couldn't look. Please God, no. He was throwing up the prawns! Everyone was looking. Another retch and Richard was now vomiting all down the back of a woman's dress. Her partner turned and glared. While Sir Colin was presenting Katya with her cheque and the grey suits at the back of the stage were clapping in corporate obedience, Katya was beaming like an assassin on pay-day. Harriet turned back to the stage. She heard the man behind her demanding Richard should leave; the wife whimpering in disgust for a Kleenex; Laura laughing and clapping Richard on the back; Amanda asking a waiter for some water; Murdo saying, 'Come on, big man, get a grip.'

Then came the sound of a scuffle and pushing as Richard fled. Harriet turned to follow and saw Matt Mercer, standing by the door. He looked at her, his face full of something she could not decipher. Then she realised it was concern. For her. Her aching head cleared a little at the sight of him, then Murdo was gently putting his arm around her and asking if she could take Richard home. But she knew he had gone. He was drunk, he had eaten a bad prawn, he was thoroughly discredited and he had his own set of car keys.

★ ★ ★

There were few cars at this point on the Embankment, which was just as well because Richard did not want them there. He changed gear with such ferocity, the noise made passers-by turn and gaze. He skirted past the Palace of Westminster and ploughed on. He could barely see, could not think. He felt shame and horror equally. Murdo and himself versus the rest of London. See you in the bankruptcy courts, bro. All he wanted in the world was to get home and curl up. Hide. That bitch daughter! What the fuck had she to complain about? Why stitch him up? What the fuck did she know about the real meaning of money? Stupid little cow. As for Sir Colin, still a creep and an arsehole, however much money he and that dog of a wife had got together.

The traffic grew heavier, which maddened him. Why a rush hour at nine o'clock at night, for God's sake! He switched lanes without signalling, causing hoots of indignation. *Fuck off!* On his left lay the lights of the South Bank, dainty rows of them strung across Lambeth Bridge, Vauxhall Bridge, Chelsea

Bridge, Albert Bridge. Then he passed the odd temple thing some Eastern religious group had stuck up in Battersea Park like a bandaged finger. How the fuck had they got planning permission for that? He couldn't stop looking at it. How bloody ridiculous! Then Richard hit Battersea Bridge. Literally.

★ ★ ★

Virginia Bottomley had had a rough year trying to close and rationalise London's hospitals. Next to Lady Porter and Mrs T, she was probably one of the capital's biggest wicked witches. Guy's and Bart's could bite the dust, however hard they fought, but everyone knew that St Thomas' Hospital, opposite the Palace of Westminster would be safe. The MPs needed their cottage hospital intact, well funded and on permanent standby.

Which was just as well for Richard, in the circumstances. When he finally opened one black eye to gaze out at the world, he met two white objects. They turned out to be his own legs, in traction and in plaster. He couldn't turn his head and when he tried to speak, barely a sound emerged into the room, which was small and all windows. His head, though he couldn't really feel it, seemed to have turned into cotton wool balls, the sort you buy to wipe babies' bottoms. Richard tried looking at the world for half a minute, then decided enough was enough and closed his eyes.

'I think he's coming round.' A voice which sounded vaguely familiar came out of the darkness then there was the sound of footsteps and a voice spoke. 'Richard, wake up now. Yes, I think he can hear us.'

He opened his eyes just a fraction and a plump, black nurse was taking his pulse and looking at him with professional concern. He felt comforted. That was what he needed right now. A mummy. Just, please, not his own.

'You've had a bad crash, Richard. Two broken legs, broken arm, concussion, multiple cuts, broken collar bone. You like to do a job properly, don't you?' He tried to speak and then once again gave up.

'I think he's trying to speak,' said the other familiar voice. He couldn't remember who it was he was married to, but it wasn't her.

A woman, curvy and immaculate in a red suit, was standing looking down at him. She was smiling and he noticed that her lipstick matched her suit exactly. There was nothing worse than when it didn't. He knew her. She was eating black cherries out of a paper bag.

There were also cherries in a big bowl at the end of his bed. It brought back memories of something safe and pleasant, a street market in the Soho direction. Berwick Street?

'Look, Richard, you old cretin, you rushed off in the car, sick all down you, and smashed into Battersea Bridge. You're up on every charge the police could think of — drink driving, dangerous driving. I suppose you could claim a sudden mid-life crisis in your defence. Don't know if it's been tried before. Luckily no one else was hurt. Harriet's car's a write-off. I imagine it was hers, wasn't it?'

Harriet. That was a name he knew, but this wasn't Harriet. Think.

'Amanda,' he said.

'Yes, it's me, Amanda. Fellow creep hunter. What a nasty trick to play on us! Now they're rich and successful while we roll on merrily into debt. They're still creeps, though. Harriet said she'd come in once she'd seen that brother of yours off on the train. Though the way she's looking at him, don't be surprised if she leaps on, too. There's been a train crash or something where he lives. Darkest Largs or somewhere. So it said on the lunchtime news. An early-morning commuter train crashed right into the high street, demolishing a wool shop. Anyway his grandmother's been injured.'

All double Dutch to Richard. Whose brother? Whose grandmother? His head finally cleared and he looked up at her. Then memories of the previous evening began to roll back in wave after wave. He was drowning. 'Help me, Amanda.'

'Of course I will, you old bastard. I'm a great sorter-out. Did Katya not tell you? I'm a walking block of post-it notes. And, God, you're one boy who needs sorting out. So you've no money? That's OK, I'm bloody good with creditors. I've got a nice house too and I always preferred you when you weren't being a cocksure sod. Katya won't be pleased, of course, but she can get over it. She's got twenty-five grand to keep her happy and we've given her lots of rage to work with.'

He didn't know what she was talking about, but she was here, with him, which was all that mattered. She was part of his youth and, though now plumper and lined, she was still a glamour puss. Big mouth, big tits. And she'd always been able to make him laugh. Richard closed his eyes, safe at last.

14

The sea outside the window was a deep, azure blue. All around her was white. White walls. White quilt. Heavily embroidered thick white cushions. White furniture. Everything was white these days; all her towels, all her bed linen. Whiter than white. She was reborn and never wanted bright peacock colours around her again. The white glare of the morning sun bleached the white around her still whiter, a daily act of renewal. This was exactly the effect she had wanted to achieve.

On the wall, framed, was the cover of *King's Quarterly* magazine from August 1995. Its cover screamed 'Exclusive!' in 32-point bold. '*From the Muse of Anthony Trollope to Govan train worker's moll, Isabella Fairlie was beautiful, self-destructive and impossible. Harriet Gosse Longbridge tells the incredible story of the woman who was the real Lizzie Eustace of Anthony Trollope's mega-hit The Eustace Diamonds and reveals Trollope's clandestine Scottish past, unexplained for 140 years.*' The cover picture showed the portrait of Isabella and a bearded Anthony Trollope. The piece had reportedly given Jonathan Harbour his first erection in six years.

It all seemed a very long time ago. Nowadays she blushed at such sensationalism, but that article had given her everything.

On the island, it was the women who impressed. Bermuda women were always dressed to kill. No down-at-heel shoes or overpriced clothes for them. She remembered the first time she had gone into a shop, asking for a simple cotton dress. 'Just something tidy,' she'd said to the assistant. 'No, mam, we don't do tidy. We stay on the bus way past Tidy, and we don't stop until we reach Drop Dead Gorgeous!' So Harriet had stayed on that bus and now only bought brand-new clothes which made her seriously gorgeous.

She sat up and rang the bell. The maid came in to take the tray away and brought in the morning post. UK mail! She turned it over. Charity benefits. An invitation to a Gallery. Cork Street. Nope. Been there, done that. A note from Katya hoping to stay on the way back from a month in the UK. She'd taken to New York like a sleek duck to water. Her portraits now had Forbes List chairmen fighting for them and she also had a Wall Street arbitrageur wanting to marry her, which added to her column inches every month in the *New York Times*. She was always at the right parties in those trademark Mary Ellen pearls: top British artist Katya Holland. The field was hers, after that Rosen man lost his fiancée to a software whizzkid.

Next a long letter from Billy which she would take her time over in the bath. It was scrawled over two pages. He was getting down to the final push to A levels. Then would come university and the rest of his life. What sort of grades will you get for his parenting, Harriet? Hopefully a pass.

Another UK invitation. A joint birthday bash at the Holland Park Orangery. Would they never learn? Pushing champagne down other people's throats still cost money, however tax deductible. But then Richard and Amanda were still rolling along, more merrily than ever now the mess of the divorce was over. Corporate hospitality was obviously Richard's métier, he had always been at his best at parties. The Freud pictures she had signed over had been worth every penny. Now Amanda's large breasts were, thank God, no longer part of her life. Her lawyer had praised her vision. 'Peace of mind, Mrs Longbridge, is all in your situation.' 'Gosse,' she had corrected him. 'No, Dunne. Harriet Dunne. I am Jester Dunne's daughter.'

All the rest of Marcus' paintings had been

put out on loan to national galleries, further clearing out the Augean stables.

They'd found Jester dead two days after the divorce came through. He must have been up all night trying to finish the painting for her birthday. He had been painting sitting down and his head had fallen forward against the canvas and stuck to the oils, which had dried in the overheated room. The doctor said he must have been dead since the early hours. When they had prised his head away, it had left an abstract swirl. It was she who had seen that it was a portrait of herself. The hands were marvellous, Jester at his very best, while the folds and texture of the pink dress were unsurpassed. But her face was unfinished, just a burnt sienna splodge made by her dead father's head.

She had decided not to be superstitious about it. For Billy's sake. He'd already been cut to ribbons by the divorce and Jester's death. It was the day after the funeral that she had finally realised she was not cut out to have her portrait done after all. She was no Isabella. No one would ever fix *her* in time and paint; she would keep on growing instead.

Harriet found the remote control panel and turned on CNN. Hot news was last night's Los Angeles premiere of *Old Money.*

Screaming crowds, flashbulbs popping, footage of Julia Roberts. Somewhere inside there would be Murdo and Laura, glamorous and networking; they preferred the States, perhaps it made them feel more of a couple. Laura had eaten him up as Harriet had known she would and Rena had apparently settled for an optician from Ayr. No one could fight Laura on the prowl. Harriet could just hear Rena's voice in Ayr High Street. 'Murdo's up for an Oscar for Best Original Song.' 'That's nice, Rena, how's your mum?' Disney had just signed him for their latest animation feature. What fun Laura would be having riding on his coat tails; did she realise he was the same age as the son she had given away?

Harriet had seen Murdo a month ago with David Letterman on *The Late Show* promoting the first album of his solo career. From that curious discovery by Mrs Cohen's son, he had, in just a year or so, been shoved along some conveyor belt all the way from Largs to L.A., where his talent had gone down a storm. His Celtic pop rock sound had hit the post-*Braveheart zeitgeist*. Scottish was sexy. He had grown his hair and looked dangerously glamorous. His SNP credentials had also been widely reported in the press, which had given him more *Braveheart* appeal plus a big chunk of Sean Connery's high moral ground. He and Laura were now favourites with Bill and Hillary at their White House parties.

Back in Largs, Mad Izzy still filled her life with bargains and storytelling at McGuffey's, though frailer and in a wheelchair since the train crash. She now kept scrapbooks with cuttings about 'her Murdo'. The *KQ* article had created a bit of a storm in the Trollope world, with scholars world-wide beating a path to her door. But judging from her last letter, Murdo rarely visited and certainly not with Laura; she had met her match with Mad Izzy who, impervious to the Marchant charm, could not stand her. At forty-seven, Laura was anyway too old now to have children and carry on Isabella's line.

There was a gentle knock at the door.

'Mrs Mercer, may I bring her in now?'

A uniformed nanny entered. Harriet found she could not quite wean herself off the morning feed, even though Bella was nearly a year old. This was their special time together while Matt was out on the golf course. She already had such beauty she made Matt go weak at the knees. His special daughter, he called her. Harriet's glorious gift to him.

'Lucky Midas!' the man from the *Wall Street Journal* had written in the latest profile. 'A beautiful second wife, a new baby daughter, and a billion rampant bull market winnings in the bank.' Harriet smiled at the child and drew her close to the breast. The baby began to gurgle expectantly, as if trying to tell some little story before nuzzling Harriet impatiently. Even now, she had a firecracker personality; dark, silky hair, pale skin and a temperament which could send a dish of baby goo spinning across the room. Harriet knew there was a real equality between them that no amount of baby talk could disguise. She did not have a clue what this little girl would do but it would be something world-dazzling, funded by her doting daddy's gold. Already, Harriet felt like a footnote in her love child's history.

The little girl, now fixed on to the breast, gazed up at her mother. Those clear violet eyes burned into Harriet's soul, as artful and passionate and mischievous as the violet eyes of the woman in the portrait which dominated the white room; her head half turned, smiling in flirtatious greeting, captured just on the point of laughter.

Isabella was back. Big time.

Author's Note

Anthony Trollope was a member of John Burns' walking and networking group, the so-called Gaiter Club in Glasgow, even while a professional civil servant. He began writing *The Eustace Diamonds* in December 1869 and the following month was guest of honour at a dinner given by the Gaiters, staying, as he disclosed in a private letter, on the Castle Wemyss estate with George Burns. An important point, because in George Burns' biography published shortly after his death Trollope is alluded to as primarily his son John Burns' friend. But it was a much deeper friendship stretching back across the generations.

Writing to John Burns on 12 July 1878, Trollope refers to this close relationship. 'Tell Lena [John Burns' niece] that as I have no stern parent to repress my feelings, I send her my love — which I think I may do to the daughter, seeing that I certainly love the father,' (i.e. John Burns' brother James Cleland Burns). I contend that such a familiarity would only have been appropriate if Trollope's primary relationship had been

431

with the father, old George Burns, and he had known both the Burns boys from a much younger age.

According to CP Snow, 'There weren't, and aren't any secrets about the routine of [Trollope's] life.' Yet is this true? Anthony Trollope never alluded to his close association with the Burns family in his autobiography. Few letters concerning the Burns family have survived. Why? The friendship spanned more than a quarter of a century, between men who were renowned for being meticulous about the details of their routine and business dealings, even by the exacting standards of the time.

From the mid-1820s George Burns shipped the mails to Ireland. In 1837 he founded the Cunard Steamship Company with Samuel Cunard to run the transatlantic mails — raising almost two-thirds of the funds via a consortium — which his son later ran. His business success bought him the magnificent Castle Wemyss estate at Wemyss Bay, outside Largs. Anthony Trollope was a career civil servant, who from 1841 lived in Ireland developing the Irish postal service with every opportunity to appreciate the great commercial interests at stake.

These are the bare bones. But I believe the truth is more complex. In his autobiography

Trollope describes his desperation at the time of leaving London for the Post Office in Ireland: 'I was at that time in dire trouble, having debts on my head ... and a full conviction that my life was taking me downwards to the lowest pits.' He had known years of poverty and insecurity and would have been ripe for wooing. As he achieved experience and promotion so his usefulness to others grew.

The mail service in Ireland offered huge business opportunities safely backed by Government contracts. A win-win situation for the ruthless George Burns who, as he describes in a letter quoted in his biography, offered to carry the mails between Glasgow and Belfast for nothing, an offer duly accepted in July 1849. This tactic successfully increased his market share while forcing competitors out of business. In Scotland we have seen similar buccaneering approaches adopted more recently, with the rise of Stagecoach.

Trollope must have felt the frustration of being a public sector employee witnessing and enabling others, often less intellectual than himself who were making millions from the flow of information, just as so many bright professionals today seethe at the millions being made in the dot com goldrush.

One should never underestimate the desperate importance of money and status in Trollope's psyche, emanating from his family's financial collapse as a child. This vulnerability pervaded both his work and his life and perhaps is one explanation for his enduring popularity in our own times when acquiring money, credit and lifestyle is a generational obsession.

While researching family history back in the early-eighties, my husband Alan Reid came across the interview with John Burns in *The World* magazine, published in 1889, which had been annotated in a delightfully waspish style by his eldest daughter Caroline for her future sister-in-law, Charlotte, the third Lady Inverclyde. We thought it interesting that Trollope 'thought out and wrote a great portion of *Barchester Towers*', such an English book, in such a thoroughly Scottish setting. But it was only when reading the 1996 revised Oxford World Classics edition of the novel and the expert introduction of UCL's Professor John Sutherland that we realised there was a real mystery surrounding exactly when and where he wrote the first portion of the book. Its writing was interrupted and Trollope then began *The New Zealander* following disappointing sales of his previous book *The Warden*. This was before he adopted his celebrated work calendars.

For the first time we began to understand why the Inverclyde connection was, so disappointingly, not mentioned in Trollope's autobiography even though the family's home Castle Wemyss had apparently inspired his rendition of Portray Castle in *The Eustace Diamonds* written in 1870, and he had later written *How The Mastiffs Went To Iceland*, a privately published account of a Burns jaunt. For our researches had now revealed that George Burns and his brother John, Church of Scotland Minister's sons turned general merchants had amassed their first fortune in Ireland from a standing start by delivering the mails between Glasgow, Liverpool and Ireland — obtaining six trading smacks in 1824 in lieu of a bad debt — only thirteen years later leveraging their stake to become part owners of the internationally celebrated Cunard Line, eventually taking control of one-third of the whole business in equal shares with Samuel Cunard and Liverpool ship owner David MacIver. The more we researched into Trollope's professional life in Ireland, the more we began to smell a cover-up. A conspiracy of silence at the very least.

We realised that George Burns' friendship

with Trollope went back several decades, that Trollope was George Burns' and not John Burns' friend, as officially put about. Also, why it was not known just where the first part of *Barchester Towers* had been written. George Burns did not actually purchase the Castle Wemyss estate until he retired in 1860, but was known to have leased substantial property on the West Coast. The land on which the Castle was built and the estate laid out already had a connection with Burns. It had been sold to the developer by Robert Wallace M.P for Greenock, who had been active in pressing for the introduction of the Penny Post in Parliament, debates which George Burns with such commercial interests at stake, had attended.

It seems to me that developer Charles Wilsone Brown's creation of Castle Weymiss and the massive Weymiss House on the headland had all the hallmarks of a Burns father/son commission. But perhaps the fact that the property was not yet George Burns' own primary residence was why Trollope could afford to visit. It was neutral ground, though sourced and paid for by Burns. For even by the sleazy standards of the time, knowledge that a senior official was writing a novel while staying at the home of a leading supplier would have seriously jeopardised

Trollope's recent advancement and Burns' bottom line. No wonder it behoved both men to keep their counsel indefinitely, not least in their later carefully handled life stories until John Burns put it in the public domain some years after Trollope's death, when the wealth and standing of the Burns was assured. But back in January 1855, as the struggling writer Anthony Trollope prepared to take up his powerful new post as Surveyor, it was most certainly not reflected literary kudos which would have made him an attractive house guest for the ruthlessly pragmatic Burns.

In his autobiography, Trollope describes his new 'system of writing' around this time which took place on a home-made board in railway carriages. How cleverly this description deflects awkward questions! If, as C.P. Snow asserts, the book has 'one of the most penetrating first chapters in all fiction' it would appear Trollope needed peace to effect such a piece of writing rather than a rackety, badly upholstered Victorian railway carriage. 'Castle building' was how Trollope later described his plotting and day-dreaming. The Burns, typical financiers and technocrats, were not noted for their literary interests, yet could easily have provided privacy and peace in luxurious surroundings on the Firth of Clyde. Professor Sutherland writes: 'The period 1853–5 is one of the darkest [i.e. of Trollope's life.] There survives . . . only seven letters for all three years (some of them incomplete and incorrectly dated'. Yet might this frustrating and unusual dearth of paperwork *not* be unplanned? Up to his promotion Trollope was getting nowhere in the Civil Service and had still to make any money from writing. Rapidly heading for forty and a mid-life crisis, short cuts to the top were a necessity for such an ambitious, insecure man. A key advantage of his job was that it was 'out of the office'.

Professor Sutherland notes in surprise that Trollope's description of Mrs Proudie's, the Bishop's wife, vulgar twelve gas-jet chandeliers in Chapter Ten of *Barchester Towers* is 'more appropriate to the gin palace than the episcopal palace'. This is perhaps explained when one realises that a nouveau riche businessman's gin palace on the Clyde was exactly where Trollope was holed up and getting his inspiration when he wrote the passage. Mrs Proudie's chandelier is notably similar to the extravagant, elderly specimen prominently featured in photographs of the over-furnished drawing room of Castle Wemyss in the At Home article in *Scottish Field* which appeared in March 1914.

While Trollope's friendship with the Burns

would have been known within certain circles, there is a further example in which he remained keen for the connection not to be made too public even years after his resignation from the Post Office. In June 1878 John Burns hosted a trip to Iceland for chums, Trollope included, in the 870 ton HMS *Mastiff* built for the Scottish/Irish postal service (presumably further drawing on Trollope's expertise) but fitted out first of all for a luxury spree — corporate hospitality Victorian-style. Trollope chronicled the trip for a privately published account entitled *How The Mastiffs Went To Iceland*, paid for by John Burns, as well as for the *Fortnightly Review*, both of which were illustrated by Mrs Jemima Blackburn, a fellow guest and friend of Millais and Ruskin. As Victoria Glendinning describes in her acclaimed biography, in Mrs Blackburn's own account of the expedition in *Good Words* magazine, Trollope was not mentioned, and all but one of the sketches of him as one of the group in her original fifty-six drawings were erased from the published accounts. Glendinning asks whether this was her idea or his. One could ask too was it shyness perhaps, for unlike Isabella, Trollope was certainly no oil painting? Or perhaps he was sensitive to pictures showing him enjoying this fat cat businessman's junket, preferring a position as professional in-house chronicler one removed? Remembering the role the ship was to have after the trip and within the context of his long-standing questionable friendship with George Burns, this erasure surely begs a more subtle explanation.

Alongside the article in *The World* Caroline Burns writes, 'Anthony Trollope did write *How the Mastiffs Went To Iceland*. I was much disgusted that no cheque resulted therefrom.' This perhaps provides another clue to the financial basis of the Burns' relationship with Trollope. At the time she would have been rather young for such financial cynicism? Had she suggested that old Trollope would be good at the job of writing up this junket to her father and expected some commission? As a young Victorian woman she would have had little financial independence of her own but had clearly inherited the Burns' intelligence and eye for the main chance. Were the cheques only going one way? Was this a further example of Sundries, as detailed in Trollope's well-spun autobiography?

'A kinder host I never knew, but seldom a sterner lord,' Trollope writes of John Burns. Again, there is a curious sense of Trollope as a social inferior, albeit a successful artist, gracing the rich man's table. How had Burns been Trollope's 'stern lord'? And just what added value had that lord exacted? Here is an example of Trollope prose used as an international PR and marketing tool. The Inverclyde Collection contains a letter from a senior official at the German Embassy thanking John Burns for sending the book to the Kaiser.

These relationships can now only be guessed at. Reputedly an honest man in spite of the little matter of the disappearing Irish £3 note detailed in R.H. Super's fascinating book, Anthony Trollope, professional public servant as well as useful friend of the super-rich, operated in a field in which he had huge knowledge and influence and I contend, only recorded what he wanted to record. Omissions could easily be missed in the haystack of his daily records. The high moral ground of integrity and honour which Trollope occupies in his autobiography has been accepted apparently unquestioningly by admiring biographers ever since. 'A man who takes public money without earning it is so odious that I can find no sympathy in my heart . . . nothing would annoy me more than to think I would ever be supposed to be among their number.' Reading this as a financial journalist rather than a Trollope scholar, methinks he protests too much. Trollope was a master of personal PR and spin, to use current jargon. Perhaps it is time for the experts to re-examine this end-of-year report more thoroughly, and question the financial side of his life more closely — not least the earnings under the Sundries as listed in his autobiography.

The Burns' world-class commercial success is long forgotten. By 1995, Castle Wemyss was reduced to a pile of rubble above the Clyde; the gardens where Trollope, and Lords Shaftesbury and Palmerston ate strawberries and cream lay neglected and overgrown, though they retained an indefinable magic, an overwhelming sense of vanished greatness. In 1996, Elmblock Homes began house development where Castle Wemyss once stood and a unique slice of Scottish business and English literary history was tragically allowed to disappear. Only Murdo's pier, now resorted at the end of a back garden, remains.

By contrast, world-wide, Anthony Trollope and his works have never been more popular. As it says on the dust jacket of Victoria Glendinning's biography, Trollope 'is today the best loved and most widely read of the great Victorian novelists . . . with a new high point of current interest in both the books and the man.' Despite this, editors and biographers have at best assumed that Lizzie Eustace's Ayrshire home Portray Castle in *The Eustace Diamonds*, was modelled on Inverary Castle, Argyllshire. Whereas, as my original research shows, Castle Wemyss, on the Ayrshire/Renfrewshire border, was the real inspiration. Lizzie Eustace delighted in riding out with the Ayrshire Hunt, as heavy, bearded Trollope doubtless did too.

Gifford Fairlie and the divine Isabella are, alas, fiction. Yet, however we may demur, all writers gain inspiration from those around them, so who knows what feisty Scottish beauty may have inspired Trollope as he created Lizzie Eustace, while staying on the Castle Wemyss estate in January 1870? My own character of Isabella is based upon Mary Wilson, a young gentlewoman born in 1869 and brought up to enjoy the high Victorian splendour of Castle Wemyss. Her life took a similar path to Isabella's. She is the great-great-grandmother of my daughter Ella, to whom this book is dedicated.

©Antonia Swinson,
East Lothian, Scotland, December 1999

We do hope that you have enjoyed reading this large print book.

Did you know that all of our titles are available for purchase?

We publish a wide range of high quality large print books including:
Romances, Mysteries, Classics
General Fiction
Non Fiction and Westerns

Special interest titles available in large print are:
The Little Oxford Dictionary
Music Book
Song Book
Hymn Book
Service Book

Also available from us courtesy of Oxford University Press:
Young Readers' Dictionary
(large print edition)
Young Readers' Thesaurus
(large print edition)

For further information or a free brochure, please contact us at:
Ulverscroft Large Print Books Ltd.,
The Green, Bradgate Road, Anstey,
Leicester, LE7 7FU, England.
Tel: **(00 44) 0116 236 4325**
Fax: **(00 44) 0116 234 0205**

STRANGER IN THE PLACE

Anne Doughty

Elizabeth Stewart, a Belfast student and only daughter of hardline Protestant parents, sets out on a study visit to the remote west coast of Ireland. Delighted as she is by the beauty of her new surroundings and the small community which welcomes her, she soon discovers she has more to learn than the details of the old country way of life. She comes to reappraise so much that is slighted and dismissed by her family — not least in regard to herself. But it is her relationship with a much older, Catholic man, Patrick Delargy, which compels her to decide what kind of life she really wants.

HOT POPPIES

Reggie Nadelson

A murder in New York's diamond district. A dead Chinese girl with a photograph in her pocket. A plastic bag of irradiated heroin in an empty apartment. A fire in a Chinatown sweatshop. The worst blizzard in New York's history. These events conspire to bring ex-cop Artie Cohen out of retirement and back into the obsessive world of murder and politics that nearly killed him. The terrifying plot uncoils first in New York — in Artie's own back yard — then in Hong Kong, where everything — and everyone — is for sale.